D0894318

MY
DARLING
GIRL

Also by Jennifer McMahon

The Children on the Hill

The Drowning Kind

The Invited

Burntown

The Night Sister

The Winter People

The One I Left Behind

Don't Breathe a Word

Dismantled

Island of Lost Girls

Promise Not to Tell

MY
DARLING
GIRL

Jennifer McMahon

SCOUT PRESS
New York   London   Toronto   Sydney   New Delhi

Scout Press
An Imprint of Simon & Schuster, Inc.
1230 Avenue of the Americas
New York, NY 10020

This book is a work of fiction. Any references to historical events, real people, or real places are used fictitiously. Other names, characters, places, and events are products of the author's imagination, and any resemblance to actual events or places or persons, living or dead, is entirely coincidental.

Copyright © 2023 by Jennifer McMahon

All rights reserved, including the right to reproduce this book or portions thereof in any form whatsoever. For information, address Scout Press Subsidiary Rights Department, 1230 Avenue of the Americas, New York, NY 10020.

First Scout Press hardcover edition October 2023

SCOUT PRESS and colophon are registered trademarks of Simon & Schuster, Inc.

For information about special discounts for bulk purchases, please contact Simon & Schuster Special Sales at 1-866-506-1949 or business@simonandschuster.com.

The Simon & Schuster Speakers Bureau can bring authors to your live event. For more information or to book an event, contact the Simon & Schuster Speakers Bureau at 1-866-248-3049 or visit our website at www.simonspeakers.com.

Interior design by Davina Mock-Maniscalco

Manufactured in the United States of America

10 9 8 7 6 5 4 3 2 1

Library of Congress Cataloging-in-Publication Data

Names: McMahon, Jennifer, author.
Title: My darling girl / Jennifer McMahon.
Description: First Scout Press hardcover edition. | New York : Scout Press, 2023. |
    Identifiers: LCCN 2023012573 | ISBN 9781668019061 (hardcover) |
    ISBN 9781668019078 (paperback) | ISBN 9781668019085 (ebook)
Subjects: LCGFT: Psychological fiction. | Domestic fiction. | Thrillers (Fiction) |
    Novels.
Classification: LCC PS3613.C584 D37 2023 | DDC 813/.6—dc23/eng/20230317
LC record available at https://lccn.loc.gov/2023012573

ISBN 978-1-6680-1906-1
ISBN 978-1-6680-1908-5 (ebook)

For every mother and daughter
who know just how complicated it can be

MY
DARLING
GIRL

Thirty-seven years ago

"ALI ALLIGATOR?" MY MOTHER whispered as she crept into my room, slipped under my heavy quilt, cuddled up next to me on my twin bed. I was eight years old, a big girl, too old for mommy snuggles, but still, when she pressed her body against mine, I sighed with contentment and tucked myself tight against her.

We fit perfectly together, she and I. So perfectly that I wasn't sure where I ended and she began.

"Are you asleep, my love?" she asked. "Or are you playing possum?"

I opened my eyes a tiny bit, enough to spy the numbers on the clock on my nightstand: 2:15.

My mother often worked late in her studio, sometimes stayed in there all night, painting. But every so often she'd take a break, come into my room, wake me up, so eager to show off her latest work that she couldn't wait until morning. Some nights she'd wake me up and ask if I wanted to bake cookies with her, or drive to the all-night convenience store for ice cream and root beer to make floats.

Now she ran her fingers through my hair, down my back, bumping them along the knobby bones of my spine; my mother's fingers, I knew without looking, were stained with paint. They smelled faintly of turpentine, like the rags in her studio—flammable, an accident waiting to happen.

She put her face up next to mine, cheek to cheek. "I know you're awake," she said, and then I smelled it, distinct from the faint turpentine scent. Her breath was thick with gin: a boozy evergreen scent that reminded me of a forest of Christmas trees.

Her fingers worked their way over the back of my nightgown, tracing shapes, making letters to spell out words. It was a game we played, she and I. A can-you-guess-what-I'm-spelling game.

I felt the familiar letters:

I-L-O-V-E-Y-O-U

I smiled, wriggled back closer to her.

"I do," she said, her words slurred in a way that made my stomach start to hurt. "You're my perfect girl. Too perfect for this world. Sometimes I think . . ." Her words were thick and strange. "I think I should have spared you. Drowned you at birth, maybe, not let you suffer the things that are to come," she cooed into my hair.

My heart pounded so loud and hard that I was sure she could feel it, ringing like an alarm bell.

She pulled me closer, squeezing all the air out of my chest.

I couldn't get away, even if I wanted to.

I imagined I really was drowning, being pulled under, holding my breath, lungs screaming for air.

I thought of the knife I had tucked under my pillow: it wasn't just any ordinary knife; it was a magic knife, because I'd cast a spell on it, charged it by the light of the full moon, purified it with salt water and birch smoke. I called my knife Descender, because any evil beings I conquered with it would descend back into the dark and shadowy place they'd come from.

I believed in magic then. I believed that everything had a spirit and energy that I could listen to and draw from, that rocks and plants could speak to me, that the geese flying overhead carried messages and were harbingers of things to come. And I believed that there was good and there was evil and they were curled up around each other, intertwined like thick vines. Sometimes it was hard to tell which was which.

I did other things to keep myself safe too. The ring of salt around my bed, the Bible Aunt Frances had given me for my sixth birthday tucked under my pillow beside the knife. It was a children's Bible with pictures.

Noah's ark was my favorite page: all those animals boarding the big boat, two by two. I'd stare at the illustration, worrying over it, sure the lions would eat the goats, the horses would trample the rabbits—and where were the smallest creatures, the millipedes and the worms? How would they be saved?

I held still, listening to my mother breathing.

In and out. In and out.

If I held still and played possum, she might just go away. Or pass out beside me, maybe.

In the morning, I'd tell myself it was just a dream. That I'd imagined her coming into my room, whispering these things. It wouldn't feel real anymore in the light of day when I was looking at her across the break-fast table. It would be impossible to believe this had happened when my mother, all lit up with morning light coming through the kitchen window, smiled and asked if I would like raspberry jam for my toast (which she'd kindly cut the crust off of, just the way I liked it), if my older brother, Ben, wanted extra peanut butter. If I dared ask her about her visit in the night, she'd call me a silly goose for making up stories. Then she might suggest some fun adventure for the day, like the time we took the train into the city just for chicken gyros, or the time we turned our living room into a circus and tried to get poor Lucky, our cat, to walk the tightrope.

But now I just concentrated on holding still, kept my eyes clamped shut.

I imagined I was dead. Buried deep underground, dirt in my mouth, roots tangled in my hair. I told myself that maybe my mother really did drown me when I was an infant. I imagined her sitting there on top of my grave, shoulders stooped under the weight of guilt and sorrow, talking down through six feet of earth to her dead baby girl in a rotten coffin.

"I should have saved you from all of this," my mother whispered. I felt a warm, salty tear drip onto my cheek.

She lifted the back of my pajama top.

Hold still, I told myself.

I'm dead, I'm dead, I'm dead.

"I have a secret," my mother said, voice soft, confessional. "Do you want to know?"

I felt something dig into my back, hard and sharp.

A fingernail?

A claw?

The tip of a blade?

I imagined it: something sharp and shiny about to be driven in at the soft place between my ribs, where it would be pushed all the way down to my heart and split it in two.

The pressure intensified, as did the stabbing pain. I felt her tracing a design: not a letter this time, but a circle, a spiral that went on and on, being etched right into my skin. Something with no beginning. No end.

I bit my lip to keep from crying out, and my eyes flew open.

"Mama, please," I whimpered.

Please stop. Please go away.

That's when I saw it: the shadow cast on the wall by my mother, backlit by the filtered moonlight coming in from the window.

Only this was not my mother.

Not anymore.

My scream seemed to fill the whole room, the whole house, the whole universe.

I reached under my pillow and grabbed the knife.

ONE

THE ANGEL WAS IN a thousand tiny shards.

It had slipped from my hand and shattered before I even realized what had happened.

"Damn it," I muttered.

I was precariously balanced at the very top of the stepladder in the corner of the living room, where I'd been trying to hang it up. The clear glass angel hovered there in the shadows every year at Christmastime, watching over us as we trimmed the tree, sipped eggnog, sat through sappy Christmas movies, then oohed and squealed as presents were opened on Christmas Day; a strange, emotionless observer, a passive spy.

The truth was, I kind of hated the angel. I thought she was ugly (her eyes were bulbous, insect-like) and more than a little bit creepy.

But I hadn't meant to smash her.

"Ali? Hon? You okay?" Mark called from upstairs.

"Fine," I chirped back, climbing down from the ladder and picking up the largest surviving piece: the angel's head. Her large pupilless eyes stared at me accusingly: *How could you do this to me?*

Christmas music played from the holiday classics music channel on the television—at the moment, it was a saccharine-sweet version of "Let It Snow! Let It Snow! Let It Snow!" Mark insisted on the music, saying it helped set the mood.

He wanted everything to be perfect when the girls got home from school: the boxes of ornaments out, the tree ready to decorate, the house smelling of gingerbread cookies, Christmas music playing. He'd even put a festive red Christmas ribbon on the poor dog.

This was the day Mark most looked forward to all year—Decorating Day. He even took December first off from work for it, as if it were an actual holiday. I bucked up and tried not to spoil it for him. Really, I did.

"Tradition," Mark said again and again, telling me how important it was for the girls, that we were creating memories that would last their lifetimes, traditions that would be passed down to their children and their children's children.

Moxie, our six-year-old black Lab, lay on her bed in the corner of the living room looking somewhat dejected in her big red bow. She had lifted her head at the sound of the angel crashing to the floor, then, seeing all was well, gave a sigh and settled back down.

"Let It Snow!" turned into "A Holly Jolly Christmas," and I couldn't help myself—I snatched up the remote and turned off the TV.

It was only the first of December. How was I possibly going to live through twenty-four more days of enforced jolliness without cracking? Twenty-four days of being called a grinch, of trying not to buckle under the spoken and unspoken pressure to not ruin Christmas for the girls by letting the cheerful façade slip.

That pressure wasn't just from my husband. My best friend, Penny, who lived right next door, was almost as bad. Though she and her wife, Louise, called themselves tree-hugging, earth-goddess-loving pagans, she was right up there with Mark with the holiday cheer. The two of them were thick as thieves this time of year. I loved them both, but I couldn't wait for our household's Yuletide spirit to wane. And, to add insult to injury, I received a nice royalty check twice a year from my most successful project as an artist: the children's book I'd done three years ago, *Moxie Saves Christmas*. It was a simple but cheerful story about a homeless black Lab—modeled after our own Moxie, of course—who showed a stressed-out, busy family the true meaning of Christmas. I'd illustrated it with my woodcuts, simple black-and-white prints I then hand-colored in places. The book, which I'd printed myself in a limited number for family and friends, took off. People shared it. Word got out. Orders poured in. I had more copies printed, and before I knew it, I was approached by a publisher who offered me more money than I would have believed possible—exponentially more than I'd ever made selling cards and prints at local shops and galleries. At the urging of my more successful artist friends, I found an agent and soon had a two-book contract: *Moxie Saves Christmas* and the follow-up I'd promised, *Moxie Saves Halloween*. And just like that, with one simple picture book that was only supposed to be a last-minute gift for family and friends, I was permanently linked to the holiday I couldn't stand.

Holidays in general had not been cause for celebration when I was growing up; they filled me with anxiety and dread, which had sunk their roots down deep. At least the second book under contract featured a holiday I did like. And our older daughter, Izzy, a fan of anything even remotely ghoulish, was excited by the Halloween book. At sixteen, my young goth wasn't especially easy to impress, so anything that brought us closer was something to celebrate. Now all I had to do was finish the project.

The *Boston Globe* had come to do a feature on me two years ago, taking lots of photos of me and Moxie in my studio and, of course, in front of the Christmas tree. Mark had gone all-out decorating before they'd arrived. I cringed when I read the article—the way the reporter had described our house as *a magical winter wonderland complete with dancing sugarplums, antique glass ornaments, and pine garlands filling the house with the scent of the forest.*

"You must love Christmas," the reporter had said.

And I had clenched my teeth and given a big smile. "Why, yes," I lied. "Yes, I do."

I'm a gifted liar.

Mark had started a goofy tradition of buying one special ornament each year that was supposed to symbolize our lives in some way. That first year, it was a graduation cap. Each year it was something new: baby's first Christmas when Izzy was born, a little house to celebrate when we bought the farmhouse, a stork when I was pregnant with Olivia, a black Lab the year we adopted Moxie. He was always on the lookout at craft fairs or when we went on vacation, always searching for new ornaments and trinkets to add to the ever-growing collection.

Now our entire attic was stuffed with boxes of them, and a corner of the basement as well. When Mark asked if we could store some of the bigger pieces in my studio, I'd put my foot down. The small barn out back wasn't only my printmaking studio—it was the one place that was mine and mine alone. Penny was one of the few people I let visit without permission. The house rule was that no one was allowed to come disturb me there when I was working. The barn was a chaotic jumble of tables, the antique printing press I used, all my tools, tubes of ink, and drawing supplies. The walls were covered with tacked-up sketches and prints. The barn was my refuge. No Christmas decorations allowed.

"What happened?" Mark asked now as he eyed the broken angel. His tone was slightly accusatory, as if I might have thrown the poor unsuspecting angel onto the floor and stomped on it. His gaze moved from the ornament's head in my hand to the shards scattered across the floor like bits of crushed ice.

He had not once fallen for the ruse of me being the Christmas Queen. He saw me for who I truly was and somehow loved me in spite of it.

"I was up on the ladder and it just slipped out of my hand." I gave him an apologetic shrug. "I'm sorry I'm such a klutz."

The angel had been from his childhood. When his parents died, Mark inherited all of their Christmas decorations (as if we really needed more), and he delighted in opening the boxes each year, regaling me and the girls with the story behind each one.

"That angel came from a trip my parents took to Germany," he reminded me, looking like he might actually cry, blinking his long brown lashes.

He was wearing his day-off uniform: Levi's and a flannel button-down—red and green, for Decorating Day. His face was a little flushed from his many trips up and down the stairs. He was nearly forty-five years old, and I'd known him since he was nineteen—over half our lives. Sometimes I still saw traces of that skinny, wide-eyed boy I'd met at a party freshman year at UVM who had books of poetry stuffed in his coat pockets.

"I'm sorry," I said again.

And I was. Sorry I'd destroyed a memory of his happy childhood. That I was ruining Christmas already.

My cell phone rang in the other room. It was plugged into the charger in the kitchen. "I'd better grab that," I said, relieved to have an excuse to walk away. I hurried to answer it. Probably Penny, calling to borrow something.

When I grabbed my phone and glanced down at the screen, I wished I hadn't run to answer it. Consoling Mark about the broken German angel was a thousand times better than this. I contemplated not picking up, but I knew he'd call back, so it was best to get it over with.

"Hi, Paul," I said, trying to sound as chipper as possible. "How are you?"

"Hi, Alison. I'm . . . okay." He didn't sound okay, though. He sounded tired. "And you? I hope you and Mark and the girls are well?"

Paul had been my mother's assistant for over fifteen years now, handling every aspect of her business and personal life. He arranged her travel, interviews, gallery and museum events, and all sales of her artwork. Paul even sent me and my brother cards on Christmas and our birthdays, signed *Love, Mom* in handwriting that was clearly not hers. He lived in the carriage house on her property in Woodstock and was always by her side, regardless of which city or exhibition.

She would be lost without him. And he, I knew, would be lost without her. In fact, he had been in a pretty bad way before she took him in. They'd first met at an AA meeting, where Paul, who'd come from nothing and sunk himself into heavy drinking at a young age, ended up after losing his hundredth contract job as a construction worker after one too many benders. I was concerned when my mother informed me she'd hired a complete stranger as a spare hand around her home and studio, but she laughed at my worries, said I didn't understand AA culture, the bond they shared.

She'd eventually helped Paul to get his GED and associate's degree, mentoring him with care to become her full-time assistant. I'd enjoyed watching his transformation over the years, from a guy in a ripped Carhartt jacket who wouldn't meet your eyes when you talked to him to a self-assured, worldly man who ran my mother's life and business and wore custom-tailored suits. He spoke of my mother like she was his hero, his savior. Her world had become his life.

"We're all fine," I said to Paul now, dreading whatever was coming next. From time to time, he called to extend an olive branch (something I was sure was entirely his doing and had not come directly from my mother), inviting me to a party or event, telling me my mother would be thrilled if I could attend. I never did these days; I always managed to come up with a perfectly reasonable excuse: sick kids, work deadlines, other obligations. "I wish I could," I'd say. "Please send Mother my regrets."

I used to go. Back when I let myself believe my mother might genuinely want me there. Back when I let myself hope that it might be possible for us to have a more normal mother-daughter relationship.

I remembered the last event of hers I'd attended—an opening at a gallery in New York about five years ago. Paul had insisted that I come, telling me it would "mean the world" to my mother if I did. So I'd bought a nice dress, new shoes, even had my hair cut. I took the train down to the city, and when I got to the gallery and caught my mother's eye, she'd looked mystified. "Alison? What on earth are you doing here?" she'd asked. I stammered out an explanation, that Paul had invited me. "I see," she'd said, angry eyes searching the room for him. "Well, you might as well help yourself to some wine." Then she'd scooted off to talk with a small group of sleek, sophisticated art appreciators who, within seconds, were all laughing at some charming thing she'd said.

I ended up sullenly drinking three glasses of wine while I watched her work her way through the crowd, seemingly doing all she could to keep as much distance as possible between us. I'd studied her paintings: an unsettling series of landscapes with anatomical parts tucked in here and there—a tree with lungs, a lake with a terrifying mouth and stomach, a mountain covered in eyes. I'd felt like an idiot, in my frumpy outfit that seemed so fancy when I'd gotten dressed at home in Vermont. Paul had made himself scarce and didn't reply to my furious texts. I slipped out of the gallery without saying good-bye to either of them.

"Alison, the reason I'm calling . . ." He paused. "It's your mother."

Well, obviously. Christ. What was he going to invite me to now? A cruise? A mother-daughter spa day in Saratoga?

"She's ill," he said.

My mother had never been sick a day in her life. My brother always said even viruses were frightened of her.

Ben had never even attempted to hide his resentment of our mother. He refused to forgive her for those things that had happened years and years ago. He even blamed her for our father's suicide.

As an adult, I had defended her to my brother. I reminded Ben that our mother's own trauma and alcoholism were behind that behavior— that raising two kids on her own after such a tragedy had been difficult. I believed she'd loved us in her own way and done her best.

"You should give her another chance," I told him. "She's changed. She's sober now."

Ben was quick to tell me I was a fool for forgiving her. That I needed to stop making excuses and see the truth: our mother was manipulative and cruel, and what she deserved was something closer to the nine circles of hell.

"Ill in what way?" I asked Paul now. I clicked back through the calendar in my brain, trying to remember when I'd last spoken with her. Texts were always easier for me—the last time I remembered actually speaking to her was back in July, when I got a little tipsy on my birthday and called, asked her if she even knew what day it was. And she'd laughed, said of course she did, then told me the story of her twenty-hour labor.

I blinked, phone pressed against my ear.

July.

Had it really been that long since we'd spoken?

"She has cancer," Paul said. There was a pause. "Pancreatic cancer."

The room seemed to sway. I lowered myself onto one of the stools at our breakfast bar. "That sounds bad," I said.

"It is," he said. "It's kind of a worst-case scenario, Alison. It's stage four. The doctors . . ." Paul's voice faded. "They say there aren't a lot of options at this point, other than keeping her comfortable. We've been to every specialist. The best of the best. They all agree—it's just spread too far for surgery or chemotherapy to make any difference."

In the other room, a singer warned, *He sees you when you're sleeping, he knows when you're awake. . . .*

"Did they say how long she has?" My voice came out wispy and meek.

Paul took in a breath, then exhaled. His voice was shaky. Was he crying? "Not long. A matter of weeks maybe. A month or two at the most. She's in bad shape, Alison."

I felt the walls closing in around me, the whole world pressing down, making me feel small and crushed.

"Where is she?"

"Columbia Presbyterian. I'm with her now."

I sucked in a long shaky breath, trying to get my head around all of this, to let it sink in.

I looked up, saw Mark there, holding a string of tangled Christmas lights, watching me. I must have looked bad, because he set down the lights and came toward me, concerned, mouthing: *What is it?*

The old steam radiator in the living room clunked and hissed. I glanced over at the refrigerator, covered in the bright, cheerful drawings Olivia had done, a photo of Olivia and Izzy holding hands and jumping off the dock at the lake last summer. The house smelled of balsam fir and the gingerbread cookies Mark had been baking. It felt warm and safe and like a place where nothing bad could touch me.

"She's asking for you, Alison," Paul said.

I closed my eyes. Just like that, I was five years old, holding her hand in mine as she walked me into kindergarten. I was crying, begging her not to leave me there, to please, please, please bring me back home.

She got down on her knees, there in the hallway in front of the kindergarten classroom. She looked me in the eye and said, "You won't be away from me. Not really. You'll be here at school, making friends and learning, and I'll be home painting, but really we'll be together. Do you know why, Ali Alligator?"

I'd shaken my head, tears dripping off my face onto my good first-day-of-school dress.

"Because we're connected, you and I," she'd said. "Close your eyes. Can't you feel it? There's an invisible thread going from me to you, so we'll never be without each other. Not really." She wiped the tears from my eyes. "So go on. No more crying. Be my brave trouper. And if you get sad, if you miss me, close your eyes and remember the thread. No one can break it. Not ever. Not even one of us. We're bound."

"WHAT IS IT?" Mark asked again in a whisper as he moved closer, put a hand on my back.

I clutched the phone to my ear, listened to Paul breathing, to the background hospital noises behind him.

"Tell her I'll be there as soon as I can," I promised.

I hung up and looked down at my hand. I was still holding the head of the broken angel, gripping it so tightly that the jagged glass on its neck had cut my palm. She stared back at me, her face sticky with my blood, her eyes taunting: *Got you back.*

TWO

I PAID A SMALL FORTUNE to catch the last direct flight of the day from Burlington to New York and landed at JFK a little after eight, then hailed a cab to Washington Heights with my overnight bag slung over my shoulder. The city made me feel panicked and tiny. The buildings were too tall. The streets and sidewalks too full of people and noise. There was a reason I lived in Vermont—the land of no billboards, in a town where everything shut down at six p.m. I needed to be in a place where I could hear myself think. I had enough overstimulation in my own mind; I didn't need it in my surroundings too.

I texted Paul when I arrived at the hospital, and he gave me directions to the unit my mother was in. I made my way along the polished corridor to the elevators and stepped on, inhaling the hospital smells—antiseptic, hospital food, and sorrow (if sorrow had a smell). I felt, as I always did in hospitals, as if I'd entered another world with its own rules, its own climate and air, sights and sounds. The elevator was crowded with people in scrubs and white coats, with visitors carrying flowers and food. I don't think of myself as being claustrophobic, but it was too much—the small space, all those bodies in it, the jolting movement of the elevator, the smell of stale coffee.

Paul was waiting for me in the hall when I got off the elevator, looking like he'd just stepped out of the pages of *GQ*—an even tan, freshly cut dark hair, khaki pants and a pale-blue button-down that looked like it had been custom-made. He didn't look like he'd aged a day. In fact, he never did. Perhaps he'd look thirty forever.

He even smelled amazing when I hugged him: like expensive after-shave, clean cotton, warm leather.

"How is she?" I asked.

He answered with a wordless sigh and a grim shake of the head.

"Paul," I said, hesitating but needing to ask the question, needing to know. "Did my mother really ask for me? Or was that actually you?"

I couldn't face the idea of walking in blind, seeing the surprise or dread or disappointment on my mother's face. I wasn't up for rejection. Not now. Not here.

"She asked for you. Several times." He looked a little pained by this, as if hurt by the realization that he alone wasn't enough for her.

I nodded. "It's just . . . well, you know, she and I . . ." I wasn't sure how to go on. My eyes pricked with tears, and I swiped them away.

"Alison," he said, taking my hand. He didn't seem to know what else to say.

I cleared my throat. "So there's nothing they can do? No treatment options?"

He shook his head. "You should talk to the nurses and her doctor, of course, but really, there's nothing. It's about keeping her comfortable at this point. Palliative care, they call it."

I took in a breath. Looked down the hall at a nurse rolling a cart into a room. Heard the mechanical beeps and hums, the low hush of voices, the ding of call bells going off. The overhead lights were too bright, too harsh, the floor too shiny and polished.

"They want to send her to hospice," Paul said.

I nodded like any of this made sense to me.

I was going to lose my mother. I'd spent years telling myself there would be time. That we could fix things somehow, that I could have the mother I'd always longed for. And now here we were, nearly out of time.

My chest felt tight. I forced myself to take a deep, slow breath.

"But the thing is," Paul said, "she's refusing to go. Says she doesn't want to die in a sterile, unfamiliar place surrounded by strangers."

"Can she go home? Receive care there? Aren't there private nurses or something?"

Money wasn't an issue. My mother had done just fine for herself financially. More than fine, actually.

Paul was silent for a minute. His eyes darted away from my face and fixed on the gleaming waxed floor. "That's an option, of course. But as I said, she doesn't want to die surrounded by strangers." There it was again: that hurt look, maybe even slightly bitter. Surely he didn't believe my mother viewed him as a stranger.

"Well, what is it she wants?"

There was a long pause. I heard more beeping, voices, a doctor being paged for a call on line two. Somewhere down the corridor, a patient moaned, low and ghostly.

"I think you should ask her," Paul said, looking down the hall rather than at me. "She's right down there"—he nodded—"room 412. I'm going to go down to the cafeteria and see if I can find a sandwich or something. Want me to bring you back anything? A coffee?"

"Coffee would be great," I told him. I'd had two cups of it on the plane and was already queasy and jittery, but the idea of hot coffee comforted me—something to help ground me. He turned and headed to the elevators. I watched him go, then walked along the hallway in slow motion, steeling myself, breathing in the hospital smells.

When I reached room 412 at last, I hovered in the doorway and peeked in, wondering what little drama I was about to step into and become a part of.

I hadn't seen my mother since Aunt Frances's funeral back in April. As I looked in at her now, it was as if she'd aged twenty years since that day only months ago. She was thin to the point of being skeletal, pale (not a trace of makeup), and even her hair looked sad and limp. She was wearing a faded hospital johnny and her body beneath it reminded me of a just-hatched baby bird; she looked that small and weak, that vulnerable.

I wanted to go to her, put my arms around her, shield her from whatever harm might come her way, from death itself. I wiped at my eyes, hating my own weakness and vulnerability, knowing my mother would never approve of such nonsense.

No more crying. Be my brave trouper.

I felt it then, the invisible thread that she'd once promised was there, keeping us linked together.

I SOMETIMES THOUGHT about Ben's theory that our mother had never wanted children. But she had been different once. When our father was still alive.

She was moody and reclusive at times, hiding out in her studio for hours at a time. But never cruel. Not until later, when the drinking started.

Once, Ben and I watched the old black-and-white movie *Dr. Jekyll and Mr. Hyde,* and from then on that's how I saw things with our mother. There was Good Mom, opening the bottle of gin, sipping at the potion until her whole self changed and she was transformed into Bad Mom. Mom who said she wished we'd never been born, Mom who pinched us, Mom who once twisted Ben's arm so badly she broke it.

The first time I met Bad Mom was right before my father died. I came home from school one afternoon in first grade, and my father was out at the store. My mother came lurching into the hallway, reeking of gin, looking perplexed and angry. Her hands were covered in red paint, which I thought at first was blood. Had she hurt herself? Or done something terrible?

"You," she said. "What are you doing here?" as if the bus didn't drop me off every day at the same time.

"I . . . I just got home from school."

"Who do you think you are?"

How was I supposed to answer? *Don't you know? I'm your Ali Alligator, remember?*

"No one," I said softly, confused.

She cackled and stumbled toward me, stabbing her index finger into the center of my chest and leaving a red paint mark on my thin T-shirt. "That's right," she said, swaying like a snake. "You're no one. Now get the fuck out."

She had never spoken to me that way before. I'd heard her snap at my father on occasion after too many drinks, but never me or Ben. And nothing close to this. Biting my cheeks to keep from crying, I turned, school backpack still on, and ran out to the end of the driveway, where I sat and waited until my father came home.

"What's wrong?" he asked when I threw myself at him, sobbing.

He rocked me in his arms and kissed the top of my head, his face buried there like he was breathing me in. "What's wrong, Moppet?" he said softly. "What happened?"

And I didn't know what to say, how to explain that the woman inside was not my mother. Not anymore.

I STOOD IN the doorway of room 412, looking in at my mother in her hospital bed.

She turned, sensing my presence, maybe feeling the tug on her end of the thread.

"You," she said, and I held my breath as I waited for her to ask me what I was doing there.

Who do you think you are?

No one.

But then her face twitched into a grin, her lips looking pale purple against her waxy skin. Her eyes, sunken in her small face, were rimmed with dark circles.

She looked so different than she had the last time I'd seen her, I wondered if it was really her at all.

"Yes, it's me," I said, stepping into the room, then moving slowly toward the bed.

"I wasn't sure you'd come," she said. Her pale-blue eyes stared up at me, studying me.

"Of course I came."

Was I supposed to hug her? Take her hand? Kiss her cheek?

I wasn't sure what was expected, so I just stood there awkwardly, holding my bag. The room smelled like antiseptic with something spoiled beneath it, like rotting fruit.

Her left arm was hooked up to an IV. She had wires running out of her gown to a monitor that displayed green and red squiggles and numbers.

"You had every reason not to," she said.

"Well, here I am," I said, almost defiantly.

"Your brother wouldn't have come." And I knew she was right about that too. That Ben lived on the other side of the country wasn't lost on me. He had come east to our wedding when Mark and I got married, but there was a reason he'd made his home in California. "Not that I would ever ask him to."

"Well, I'm not Ben," I said.

"Indeed you're not," she said, then asked, "Have you called him yet, to tell him the news? Ding-dong, the witch is almost dead?"

My throat tightened. "No," I said. "And when I do tell him, that's certainly not the way the conversation will go."

I'd thought about calling Ben but had decided to wait until I'd visited her, once I had more details.

She stared at me, narrowing her eyes. It was the way she used to look at me to see if I was lying. And she was always right. *I know you better than you know yourself,* she used to say.

"No, I suppose not," she said. "He might say something along those lines, but you never would. You've always been my good girl, my trouper, haven't you? Loyal to the end, no matter what."

I wasn't sure what to say, so I gave her a weak nod.

"I've never understood it, you know," she admitted.

"What?"

"Why you still talk to me at all."

"Because you're my mother. And I love you." The words felt strained. Rehearsed.

She only smiled, but it was a thin smile. An *I don't believe you* smile.

Our mother had done a lot of horrible things, things fueled by her alcoholism, but she was no monster. She wasn't going to win any mother-of-the-year awards by anyone's standards, but I believed she'd done her best. She was a brilliant artist who gave us drawing lessons, taught us to make lemon chiffon pie, danced with us in the kitchen, did silly scavenger hunts on our birthdays, took us on little adventures.

One time we even played hooky from school and she drove us five hours to Cape Cod for fried shrimp. It was during one of her good periods, no drinking, lots of art and adventures. As we drove, she described the little seafood shack she and her best friend, Bobbi, used to go to every summer when she was growing up. "The best fried shrimp on the whole planet," she'd promised. She worried it might not be there anymore, might have closed, but it was still there, exactly the way my mom remembered it. "It's like time stopped here," she said. "Like I just stepped up to the window with Bobbi, and we're kids again." She reached for my hand, although I wasn't sure whose hand she was reaching for: Bobbi's? Mine? It didn't matter to me; what mattered was how tightly she held on as we marched up and placed our order.

"Can I get you anything?" I asked now, forcing the words out through my tight throat. I saw the pitcher of water on her rolling table, the empty Styrofoam cup, which, for half an instant, became one of the cups we all drank from that day on the beach—as if time had bent back on itself and I was a little girl again. "Water? Juice? Anything?"

She shook her head, closed her eyes.

I wished Paul would hurry back, carrying coffee. This would be easier if he were here.

If anyone were here.

Mark had offered to come with me, but I'd insisted I was fine on my own. He'd taken me in his arms, done all the proper husbandly things after I told him the news. His arms around me had felt good—real and solid. I loved the way he smelled of tea-tree oil soap and the spicy after-shave he used.

I'd leaned into him, feeling numb, hollowed out inside. A woman on autopilot.

"I don't know what I'd do without you," I'd said.

Wasn't that what I was always saying?

Even back in college when we first started dating, I knew he was *the one* because of the way he grounded me, encouraged me to do something with my wild, flighty ideas despite my insecurities. He had pushed me to do my first show in the student gallery, and I'd landed a crucial internship with a well-known printmaker in Provincetown because Mark had encouraged me to drive up and meet the artist, show him how badly I wanted the job. Even the Moxie book would not have existed without Mark's cheerleading and encouragement. My husband believed in me, and that helped me to believe in myself.

This afternoon he'd helped me pack, booked me a flight, reminded me to bring my toothbrush, a book for the plane, a few granola bars, some Tylenol just in case. He'd asked several times if he should come along, but I insisted he should stay home and be with the girls, decorate the tree, keep things as normal as possible. He'd agreed, but promised to save the tree trimming and decorating until I got back from New York. When I told him that wasn't necessary, he'd insisted, said it was important to do it as a family. Tradition and all of that.

"Why are you here?" My mother's words brought me back to the present. Her eyes were open again, staring at me.

I felt dizzy, the room swimming slightly, the edges of things becoming fuzzy. She looked almost see-through. Like a woman made of glass, as breakable as the angel I'd dropped earlier.

I looked down at my bandaged hand, remembering how Mark had led me over to the kitchen sink to rinse my cut, then pressed a paper towel over it, saying, "You need to be more careful." How when he'd pulled the paper towel away, the bright-red bloodstain looked like a Rorschach blot—a moth. But a moth with a stinger. A wasp-moth, dangerous but beautiful.

I blinked at my mother, hearing Mark's voice. *Be more careful.*

Part of me wished I could backpedal, scramble out of the room, pretend I'd never gotten the call from Paul. But another part of me longed to be there, to make my mother see that I would do anything for her. To show her that I'd forgiven her for the terrors of my childhood.

I remembered all the times, when she was drunk and angry, that she'd called me a worthless girl. Maybe I was there to prove I wasn't so worthless.

If she acknowledged I was worthy, would that deep feeling of worthlessness inside me stop sucking everything up like a black hole? It was what any therapist worth their salt might say.

I took a breath. "Paul called me," I said, keeping things matter-of-fact, as my mother and I did these days. It was strange to always feel like I was making small talk with the woman who'd raised me.

"Yes, obviously. But you didn't *need* to come."

"Of course I did. You're sick. And Paul said you were asking for me."

She smiled at me. "I was scared, you know. That you wouldn't come."

Her honesty surprised and unsettled me. I'd never heard my mother admit to being frightened of anything.

I gazed down at her on the bed. She looked both very old and very young. I saw myself in her. I saw my daughters in her. I had my father's dark hair and eyes, but both my girls and I shared my mother's body type: tall and slim with narrow shoulders and an oval face with a pointed chin.

My mother's eyes teared up, and my chest clenched. There it was again, that urge to wrap her in my arms, to protect her.

She picked at the edge of her sheet, worrying the fabric between thin, gnarled fingers. "I know there's a lot of history between us, Alison."

My heart beat faster, and I swallowed the bitter lump I felt building in my throat. Why had she called me here?

She reached a hand over the railing of the hospital bed; I took it in my own. Her hand was frail and cold but gripped me back with a strength I wasn't expecting. With that one touch, I was a little girl again, being led off on an adventure with my mother—the grocery store, a museum, a trip to the playground. No matter where we went, my mother's hand around mine made me feel safe, like I was where I was meant to be.

We're connected, you and I.

"I have something to ask you," she said, gripping my hand even tighter. "Something I have no right to ask, but I'm going to ask it anyway. And I don't want an answer. Not right now. I just want you to promise you'll think about it. Can you do that, my darling girl?"

My mind spun. Was she going to ask for my forgiveness? For a favor? One last dying wish?

"Of course," I said, the words tumbling out. "Anything."

THREE

WHEN I WAS NINE years old, my mother played the cruelest trick on me. She often did things like this, telling me jarring lies just to get a reaction: that we'd lost the big gray house we lived in, the only home I'd known in my life, and were going to have to start living in her car; that she was sending Ben and me to live with old Aunt Frances, so I needed to go pack my bags; that she'd gotten rid of Lucky the cat—taken him out to the other side of the highway and dropped him off at a farmhouse there.

This time, she told me my brother was dead.

He'd gone to school and hadn't come home, which wasn't unusual. He often stayed overnight with friends—he did his best to be out of the house as much as possible. My mother and I had dinner. I went to my room to read until bedtime and she went to her studio.

She woke me up later that night to tell me she'd had a phone call and had terrible news. She sat on the edge of my bed and stroked my hair. She was turned away, her face in shadow. It was just before midnight. I could see the glow-in-the-dark hands of my windup alarm clock, hear it ticking like a mechanical heartbeat.

"There's been an accident," she said. "Your brother was riding home on his bike. A car swerved. The police said he was killed instantly."

I felt all the air go out of me, and I was unable to get any back in. Everything went out of focus.

And then I started to scream.

She turned toward me, watched me for a minute, smiling, then began to laugh. "I'm only fooling," she said. "Your good-for-nothing brother is alive and well at Ryan's house. They're probably eating Devil Dogs and watching porn right now."

"Why would you do that?" I asked, pushing the words out between sobs. "Why would you say something like that?"

She laughed. "I did it for your own good. To teach you a lesson."

"What lesson?"

"You need to be less gullible. You can't believe everything you hear, Alison."

I stared at her in complete disbelief. She'd said and done horrible things before, even told little lies to mess with me, but this was a whole new level.

I never told Ben what Mom had done. Even to this day, he didn't know.

I told Mark about it once, back when we were first dating, sharing a bottle of wine, confessing secrets. I think I was testing him, seeing how much I could share with him before I scared him off. Lucky for me, Mark didn't scare easily. This all happened before Mark met my mother. He already knew about the scars on my back. The names she had called me. But this story seemed to bother him more than any other.

"My God," he'd said. "Your mother was a monster. That is just sick. Who does that to a nine-year-old?"

When he finally did meet her he had been civil, and remained so, but over the years he'd never gone out of his way to develop a real relationship with her. He was very protective of the girls when they were around her too—rightfully so.

Now, as I told him about my mother's request, I watched my normally unflappable husband nearly fall off his chair.

"Here?" Mark sputtered. "She wants to come here? To stay with us?"

We were sitting at the breakfast bar, sipping tea as I did my debrief from the whirlwind trip to New York. It felt good to be home. When we had our 1893 farmhouse renovated, we'd kept as many of the original details as we could: the hardwood floors, the beautiful wooden banister (now hung with pine garland), the original doors and window trim and moldings. We'd replaced most of the other fixtures and systems and knocked down walls to open up the space.

My favorite part of the house had always been the kitchen, with its wide-plank pine floors, deep soapstone sink, and modern granite countertops. I breathed in its soothing atmosphere to regain some calm, hands around the cup of herbal tea Mark had made me.

I was exhausted. I'd stayed at the hospital until well past the end of visiting hours, tossed and turned in my hotel bed, then caught an early flight home. I nodded at Mark, looked around at the home and life I'd carefully built, full of real and solid things. But our old brick farmhouse now felt like a hastily built house of cardboard and cheap glue, a movie set ready to collapse around me.

My mother had never once come to visit us at the farmhouse in the nine years we'd lived here. She'd come to our apartment in Burlington well over a decade ago, when Izzy was a baby. She'd shown up unannounced, peered at little Isabelle for the first time, leaned close, pronounced her "an acceptable child" (which made Mark laugh out loud), then had a cup of coffee and made backhanded small talk—*what a quaint little apartment, it's nice that you've got the windows to make it feel bigger than it is, perhaps if you took down those dark blinds that would help too.* And then she was on her way.

Mark and I later referred to it as the "hit-and-run visit." When we saw her after that, infrequently over the years, we never went to each other's houses. When we visited her in Woodstock, she put us up in an inn, and vice versa. I was grateful to not have to return to my childhood home, to not have to watch my girls walk through the rooms where I'd suffered such unspeakable things back when I was their age. I was sure the walls of that old dark house held memories of every terrible thing that had happened there, that my daughters would feel it, the horror of my past pushing down on them, its own kind of haunting.

During our infrequent, brief visits from my mother, we went out to eat, toured maple sugar houses, explored galleries and shops. She never really spoke to the girls, only eyed them warily. She occasionally brought gifts for them, but they were all wrong—meant for children either much younger or older than they were. She gave Olivia a delicate blown-glass swan when she was only three; Izzy got a dollhouse when she was twelve and well over playing with dolls. It was as if she didn't understand children at all.

Mark frowned at me across the breakfast bar. "You're kidding, right?"

"I'm not."

"Oh my God." He rubbed his face.

"I know. It's crazy that she even asked. But she said Paul would set everything up: hospice care, nurses, whatever we need. I almost said no on the spot, but she insisted I wait to give her an answer until I'd thought it over and talked about it with you."

"And this all came straight from her? Not Paul?"

I nodded. "She said she wants a chance to try to mend our relationship. She doesn't want to die with things the way they are between us."

"And what did you say?"

"Not much. I was kind of shell-shocked."

"Wow. Understandable. As if you didn't have enough screwed-up mother issues already," he said.

"Thanks for the profound analysis, Dr. O'Conner," I said with a grim chuckle.

He smiled. His PhD was in literature, but I still got a kick out of calling him *doctor*.

Mark taught English at a private high school an hour away—a job he loved but for which he was vastly overqualified. He'd done a stint teaching at a prestigious New England college, but he'd hated the politics and found the students dull. The Farmstead School suited him. It was an alternative school for kids with behavioral issues who'd struggled academically. Somehow Mark found a way to get all of these kids to love writing. I loved watching him with his students, the way he came alive around them.

Mark reached over, rubbed my shoulder. "What do you want to do?"

"I honestly don't know," I told him. "Part of me wants to run scream-ing, and another part of me wants to believe that having her here would give us one last chance to make things right between us. And the truth is, she's got nowhere else to go." Ben certainly wasn't about to take her in.

Mark sighed. "She's got Paul."

"He's not family," I said. "He's someone she pays."

He opened his mouth to say something more, then seemed to change his mind.

"Isn't this what family does? Or is supposed to do, anyway?" I asked. "Take care of each other?" My husband had grown up in a big, loving Irish Catholic family from Connecticut; I looked to him to teach me how normal families ought to work. Our own marriage and family life was a beautiful but careful dance we did, with me following his lead.

"Yeah," Mark agreed. "It is. But your family situation is . . . unique."

"If by *unique* you mean my mother was incredibly fucked-up at times, then yeah," I agreed. I reached up over my shoulder and touched my back.

He knew what was hiding under my warm wool sweater: the tangled network of scars I kept carefully hidden, wearing T-shirts at the beach. My brother, Ben, had similar scars on his own back, likewise my mother's handiwork. Ben, like me, had kept his scars carefully concealed. We'd never discussed it. Maybe that was our way of surviving with her: to pretend everything was normal.

When I became pregnant with Izzy, I cried and cried, told Mark I was terrified to be a mother; it was almost as if I'd been waiting my whole life for my own craziness to come creeping in.

"That's not going to happen," Mark had promised. "You are not your mother."

I had nightmares about it, though. Dreams in which I went sneaking into my daughter's room to whisper terrible things to her, to cut designs into her back with the point of a blade. I'd wake up in a cold sweat, terrified.

Whenever the girls caught glimpses of my back—I'd worked hard to avoid revealing it to them—I told them I'd been in an accident as a child.

I'm a gifted liar.

Maybe it was the reality of those scars on my back, but I felt apprehension blooming inside me like a dark flower. "It's a terrible idea, isn't it? I should call my mother right now and say no."

Mark took in a deep breath and held it. Then he looked at me with such love, such understanding in those warm brown eyes that I felt my whole body relax. This man knew me better than anyone else.

"Ali, you've told me a lot of stories about your mother, some of them just plain horrific. But not all of them were, right? There were some happy memories too. Like the scavenger hunts? The silly riddles? The art lessons?"

"That was all before my father died, before—"

"I know. I'm just saying that the person you remember, the one who was good and kind and made you fall in love with art, she's still in there somewhere."

I wanted to argue, but he was right. Hadn't I seen a trace of her in that hospital room?

"I worry that if you say no, she might die without you two resolving your issues. You've been given this one final chance to process everything that happened between you, to make peace with it. I don't want you to have any regrets."

I looked at my sweet, always glass-half-full husband. Was it really possible? To make peace?

"This isn't one of your Hallmark movies, Mark. This woman isn't going to come breezing in and see the true meaning of family just in time for Christmas."

He laughed. "I know. But she's your mother, Ali. And it's her dying wish. She wants to make things right before she goes. Don't you think we should give her the chance to do that?"

"What about the girls?" I asked. "What will it be like for them to have a sick old woman they hardly know dying in their house? A woman who, let's face it, can be pretty frightening even in the best of health?"

• Mark thought a minute, stared down into his mug of tea. "It's true that the girls hardly know their grandmother. It would be a gift for them to spend this time with her. Think about it, Ali. My parents are gone. Your father died when you were young. Your mother is the only grandparent they have left. And I think having her here will not only let them get to know her, but teach them an important lesson about forgiveness. That this is what we do with the people we love—we take care of them no matter what."

"No matter what," I repeated, my voice sounding far away, like it was coming from someone else.

Mark took my hand. "We can make this work," he said. "We've got the guest room downstairs—it needs a little tidying, but it'll be perfect."

I nodded. "And we'll have help," I added. "You know how Paul is—he'll have the place turned into a top-notch hospice suite in a couple of days."

Mark looked at me for a long time, then smiled. There was worry there, but it was a smile nonetheless. "It's your decision, of course." He squeezed my hand. "I'm with you no matter what."

I lifted his hand, kissed it. "Forever and ever?" I asked.

"Forever and ever," he said, repeating the wedding vows he'd written himself, and the Emily Dickinson quote he'd used, "'Unable are the loved to die, for love is immortality.'"

I knew how lucky I was to be married to a man who would follow me anywhere, hold my hand and smile reassuringly, quoting poetry, as we stepped into a pit of vipers.

"Okay," I said, giving him a tight hug. "Let's do it."

He hugged me back extra hard. "I really think this is the right decision. It'll be difficult, but I think it's what we're meant to do. And we'll all grow from it. You most of all. Just promise me one thing," he said.

"Anything."

"No matter how crazy and hard things get, you'll talk to me. We're a team. If it's too much, you need to tell me. No secrets."

"No secrets," I said, my fingers crossed behind his back as if I were a little girl—my mother's girl, making promises I knew I couldn't keep because they were already broken.

FOUR

THE FRONT DOOR BANGED open, followed by the sound of arguing. The girls were home.

Moxie ran to greet them, tail wagging, nosing at them, but they were too caught up in their fight to pay much attention to her.

"The mice are *not* stupid!" Olivia said as she threw down her pink kitty backpack on the bench by the front door. She gave Moxie a halfhearted pat on the head, then peeled off her winter coat and hung it on the coatrack in the entryway.

"I never said that," Izzy retorted, tossing her own heavy backpack next to her sister's as she clomped into the dining room in her black Doc Martens. Moxie and Olivia followed her.

"Did too! You said they were babyish and dumb and who would want to be one? That's what you just said!" Her voice was high-pitched and squeaky—her *I'm about to cry* voice.

"I was only saying the rats are better."

"Only level fours can be rats," Olivia reminded her, sounding beaten, desperate.

"The rat dance is better. And they get to fight in the battle. The mice just sit around watching."

Izzy had played a rat in *The Nutcracker* once. The local dance studio did a Vermont-themed interpretation each winter, including a Maple Sugar Fairy, dairy cows, lumberjacks—and rats as well as mice. That was before Izzy had quit ballet for good, despite her teacher saying she was one of the strongest dancers in her class, that she showed real promise.

She still had the body of a dancer—tall and lithe, flexible and strong. She was a coiled spring ready to pounce with a strength and energy that often surprised anyone around her. Olivia, on the other hand, seemed to have inherited her father's two left feet. Despite three ballet classes a week (her choice because she loved it so much), she still fell over while doing the simplest pliés and relevés. She had a hard time keeping track of the positions. Most of the other kids who'd been in her class, kids she'd started with, had moved up to level two. She was still in level one. Her teacher swore she'd get better, that grace was something that could be learned and Olivia just needed to "come into her own body."

"But I—" Olivia began.

"That's enough, girls," I said.

"Mommy's home!" Olivia ran toward me and took a flying leap. I caught her in my arms and hugged her tight, burying my nose in her hair. She smelled like apple shampoo and the winter air outside.

Mark set a plate of cookies on the heavy maple dining room table. An antique wrought-iron chandelier hung above the table, the little candle-shaped bulbs emitting a warm glow.

"Gingerbread cookies!" Olivia squealed, turning her attention away from me. "Is today going to be Decorating Day?"

Mark nodded. "Just like I promised. I said as soon as your mom got home, and here she is." I gave a little bow, and Olivia giggled.

"Are we doing the tree and the cookies?" Olivia asked.

"Absolutely, little mouse," I told her.

"Oh, joy," Izzy said, rolling her eyes, which were rimmed with heavy black eyeliner.

I bit my lip to keep from smiling at my older daughter.

Her whole outfit was black: leggings, boots, a long tunic-style sweater.

"Where's the icing?" Olivia asked. "And do we have those little hot cinnamon candies? The ones that are good for buttons and eyes?"

"Of course," I said.

"We'll decorate the cookies in a bit," Mark said. "First it's family meeting time."

"Oh, perfect. How did we get so lucky? Christmas decorating *and* a family meeting in one day?" Izzy said in the most sarcastic voice she could manage. She looked at her watch. "As long as we're done by four thirty. I'm hanging out with Theo."

I shook my head. "Not today, Iz."

Izzy scowled and crossed her arms over her chest. "You're kidding, right?"

I could feel the tightness in my shoulders and neck getting worse. "It's a family day," I said.

"That's such bullshit," Izzy snapped.

"Isabelle," Mark reprimanded. "Language." He flashed a look at Olivia.

"It's okay," Olivia said. "Izzy says *shit* and *bullshit* all the time."

"Olivia!" Mark said. He glared at our older daughter. "Now do you get the no-swearing rule? Just listen to your sister!"

Izzy ignored him, locking eyes with me. "If I was still with Noah, you'd let me see him. You'd have probably invited him to come and decorate the tree and eat with us."

I shook my head. "This is not about who you're dating. It's about it being just family today and tonight."

"Theo *is* family," Izzy snarled. "She just doesn't meet your picture-perfect Christmas family vision."

"Come on, Izzy," I said. "You know—"

"What I know is that it's the truth. *Moxie Saves Christmas* doesn't have even one queer person in it, does it? It's all moms and dads with sweet little rosy-cheeked kids."

"You're being unreasonable," I said.

"And you're being homophobic!"

"Really?" I said, scrubbing a hand over my face. My eyes burned from exhaustion. "Let's not go there, Izzy." She knew that wasn't true. She was just trying to pick a fight.

"What's homophobic?" Olivia asked.

I blew out a loud breath, trying to take a few seconds to get myself together. Now was not the time to go head-to-head with my stubborn sixteen-year-old daughter.

Izzy was so much like me at that age. She was fierce and strong-willed, and lately she seemed to think the whole world was against her—I remembered the feeling well. Still, it hurt to feel her pulling away. I'd once been her best friend and ally; now I was just part of the system she hated and was rebelling against. It seemed that lately I couldn't do anything right in her eyes. She hadn't even acknowledged that I'd just been away overnight. I didn't expect a flying leap into my arms like her sister had done, but a *How was your trip?* or even a *Hi, Mom* would've been nice.

And it hadn't escaped me that neither of them had asked how their grandmother was.

"That has nothing to do with it!" Mark said, exasperated by Izzy's accusation. He was excellent at working with the kids at his school, but Izzy knew exactly how to push his buttons. Sometimes it seemed like a game she was playing, trying to see how quickly she could get her patient, mild-mannered father to lose it.

Olivia reached for a cookie, and Mark swatted her hand away, snapping, "Not until they're decorated." Izzy had gotten to him.

Olivia looked like she might cry. I grabbed a cookie, a gingerbread mouse, and handed it to her. "A mouse for my mouse," I said with a smile.

Mark opened his mouth, but I flashed him a look; he snapped it closed and nodded at me.

"Sorry, Liv," he said.

"Do I still get to go to ballet today?" Olivia asked worriedly. "Even though it's a special family day? We're rehearsing the night scene after the party. When Clara goes to sleep and the mice and rats come out."

"Of course," I said. "It's at six. We'll have our family meeting, decorate, feed you an early dinner, and get you over to the studio in plenty of time."

"Moxie should be at the meeting," Olivia said, reaching down and petting Moxie, letting her lick the crumbs off her hand. "She's part of the family."

"Absolutely," I agreed.

"I'm going to my room," Izzy announced, stepping into the entryway to grab her backpack.

"Izzy, wait, please," I said. "Let's just sit and talk. It's important."

"Me seeing Theo is important too," Izzy said.

"I know," I told her. "Maybe Theo can come over in a little bit and help decorate? She can stay for dinner and cookies and eggnog."

"Fa-la-la-la," Izzy said.

I flashed her an *I'm trying my best here* look.

She stared at me, her brown eyes so like my own it was startling sometimes.

"I even have some of that vegan eggnog she likes so much," I said.

This was apparently enough of an olive branch. Izzy dropped her backpack, slouched down into a seat at the table, and looked at Mark and me. "So do we have an agenda for this meeting, or what?"

We all took seats at the dining room table. Mark made a steeple with his hands, pressing his fingertips together so hard his fingers were bent. "We've got something important to talk about with you two," he announced.

"Whaisit?" Olivia asked, mouth full of cookie.

"Gross," Izzy said as she tilted back in her chair, balancing on the two back legs. "Chew and swallow first, dumbo."

"We have some news," Mark announced. He looked at me, then back at the girls, then at me again. "It's very sad news, but happy news also."

"What is it?" Olivia asked again, eyes huge.

Izzy just looked suspicious and characteristically annoyed.

Mark gazed at me expectantly, clearly waiting for me to take over.

"Well," I said, clearing my throat, "you know I went to New York to see your grandmother. She's very sick."

"Grandma Mavis?" Olivia said.

"Of course, dummy, that's the only grandmother we have," Izzy said.

"But I barely even remember her," Olivia said. "I don't know her. Not really."

I looked from her to Mark.

"Well, you're going to get the chance to know her," Mark said.

"I am?" Olivia asked.

I nodded. "She's going to come stay with us. Isn't that nice?"

"*Here?* She's going to come here?" Olivia asked.

"Yes," Mark said.

"But I thought you didn't even like her," Olivia said, snapping the head off her gingerbread mouse.

My stomach twisted into a knot. "Of course I do. I love her. She's my mother," I said.

Olivia frowned at me. "Then how come we never see her?"

"She's very busy," I said. "And she travels a lot."

"I thought it was because she's a total bitch," Izzy said.

"Language, Isabelle!" Mark warned again, voice raised and face stern.

"Well, it's the truth, isn't it? Isn't that why we, like, barely ever see her even though we only live four hours away?" Izzy looked right at me. "Haven't you been trying to spare us?"

"Spare us from what?" Olivia asked, eyes wide.

"Yeah, Mom," Izzy said, raising an eyebrow. "From what?"

"What's she going to do to us?" Olivia asked worriedly.

My heart banged out a warning in my chest. This was not going well. I took a deep breath and smiled. "Nothing, little mouse," I said. "She's not going to do anything at all. Your grandmother and I . . . we've had our differences. But she's sick and she needs us now." I looked at Mark before using his words. "She's family. And we take care of each other. No matter what."

"How long is she going to stay?" Izzy asked suspiciously.

"Well, she's very sick, so she may not be with us much longer," I explained. "But whatever time we have with her, we're going to make it count." I smiled.

"Wait," Izzy said. "Let me get this straight. This dying lady we hardly know, who you guys have both said doesn't even like children, is going to come live with us?"

"That's right," Mark said, staring Izzy down.

"You're kidding, right?" Izzy looked from her father to me.

"Not kidding," I said.

"She doesn't like children?" Olivia asked.

"Of course she does," Mark said. "And you're her grandchildren, so she loves you very much."

Izzy gave a snarky, disbelieving laugh. "Right."

"Where will she sleep?" Olivia wanted to know.

"She'll stay in the guest room," I said, eager to have the practicalities to focus on. "We're going to get it all fixed up for her."

"Does she like toast with jam?" Olivia asked. "Because I can make her toast with jam. Like you do for me when I'm sick."

"I'm sure that would make her feel much better," Mark said.

"What's wrong with her?" Izzy asked.

"She has cancer," I said.

Olivia nodded. "Sophie's dog Django got cancer and died. They had to give him special medicine that made him go to sleep and not wake up because he was so sick." She looked at me. "Do they have that medicine for people too?"

"No," I said.

"Euthanasia is illegal in this country," Izzy informed her. "You have to go to Switzerland or the Netherlands or Canada."

"Eutha-what?" Olivia said.

"Putting people to sleep like your friend's little cocker spaniel."

"He was a dachshund," Olivia said.

"Whatever."

"We're going to keep your grandmother as comfortable as we can," Mark explained. "There will be nurses coming in to help us take care of her. We're even having a special hospital bed delivered."

"The kind that goes up and down?" Olivia asked.

"Yes," I said.

Olivia frowned. "But what about Christmas?"

"We'll have it just like always," Mark said.

"Will Santa leave presents for her too? Will he even know she's here?"

"Old people don't get presents from Santa, dumbo," Izzy said.

"Maybe sick ones do," Olivia retorted. "They should, anyway. Shouldn't they?"

"I'm sure Santa will find her if he needs to," Mark said.

Olivia nodded approvingly.

Izzy rolled her eyes. I was grateful she didn't make any sarcastic comments about Santa, or even float the suggestion that he might not be real in front of Olivia, who was only six. I wanted my younger daughter to hold on to the magic for as long as possible. Olivia loved Christmas as much as Mark did. Watching her light up around this time of year was almost enough to instill a trace of the Christmas spirit in me.

Almost.

We were all quiet for a minute.

"I know this is big news," Mark went on. "It's a lot. And things are going to feel very different in our house for a while. Do you feel like you understand?"

The girls nodded.

"Do you have any questions?" Mark asked.

Olivia raised her hand, like she was at school.

"Yes, Liv?" Mark said.

"When's the last time I even saw her?"

"Mmm . . ." I thought for a second. "I think nearly two years ago. We went to visit just before Christmas. We went on that horse-drawn wagon ride, remember?"

Olivia smiled and nodded. "Grandma Mavis bought us all hot chocolate afterward."

"Yes, she did," I said, remembering how Mark and I had said no to hot chocolate, but my mother had ignored us and bought it anyway, with extra whipped cream, handing Olivia a cup.

"So she must be nice, right?" Olivia asked. "I mean, if she bought us hot chocolate."

"Of *course* she's nice," Mark said.

"But Izzy said—"

"Never mind what your sister said," Mark said, glaring at Izzy.

Izzy scowled and crossed her arms over her chest.

"But what's she really like?" Olivia asked. "What's her favorite color? Does she like ballet? Does she have a favorite Christmas song?"

I smiled at her. "You can ask her all that when you see her."

"When will that be?" Olivia asked.

"Oh, in a few days," I said. "We have some things to do to get ready. But she'll be here soon." I tried to look happy but felt my unease seeping through. Izzy seemed to catch it, looking from me to her father. Mark took my hand, gave it a squeeze, flashed me a comforting smile.

Olivia, oblivious, leapt up and started spinning around the room. "I can show her my mouse dance! And I'm going to make a sign saying 'Welcome Grandma Mavis!'"

"That all sounds lovely," I told her.

Mark let go of my hand and stood up, grabbed Olivia midspin. "Come on, little mouse. We've got cookies to decorate and a tree to trim. And I'm depending on you to put the star on top." He carried her off into the living room. Moxie trotted after them, tail waving.

Izzy was still seated at the table, studying me.

"You all right?" I asked.

"I'm just wondering."

"Wondering what?"

"What you're not telling us."

God, this kid knew me too well.

I stood up, shook my head, gave a dismissive little laugh. "You should text Theo, see if she wants to come join us. I'm roasting a chicken, but we'll have plenty of vegetarian sides."

"Are you two going to come help, or do the little mouse and I have to do the whole tree by ourselves?" called Mark.

"Be right there!" I said, ready to escape Izzy's questioning gaze. I turned back to her and said, "Come on, your father and sister are waiting."

FIVE

I CARRIED MY PHONE AND a supersized glass of wine out onto the side porch and shut the door on the Christmas music being pumped out of the TV in the living room. I'd always loved the view from here, gazing east over our property to the mountains beyond. If I looked to the left, I could see the lights from Penny and Louise's place through the bare trees. In the daytime, I could see the smoke from their chimney, hear their sheep bleating and the chickens squawking. I longed to see Penny, to tell her everything that had happened with my mother.

Next to the wreath-decorated porch door was the antique Santa door-stop, inherited from Mark's grandparents. It was cast iron and worn, a particularly terrifying version of Santa with a pockmarked painted face and rusted eyes.

I took a breath of cold, woodsmoke-scented air and stared off through the dark evening at the mountains to the west, glowing purple under the moon and stars. There was no snow yet, but I knew there would be soon. It was December in Vermont, after all.

I'd dropped Olivia off at the dance studio and said polite hellos to the other dance moms. Mark was planning to pick her up soon, but Theo and Izzy were at the dining room table with him, turning gingerbread men into zombies and ghouls with x's for eyes and bleeding wounds. When he'd started to protest, I'd shot him a look: *Be grateful they're here decorating at all.*

Walking away, I smiled as I heard Mark say, "That's a wonderful leaking-brain thing you're doing there, Theo. Very creative."

"Thank you, Mr. O'Conner," she said.

Theo seemed like a good kid. I didn't know her well—she and Izzy had only been dating a few months, but Izzy was clearly crazy about her.

Back in early October, Izzy came to me while I was cooking dinner and announced, "I broke up with Noah."

"Oh?" I'd said, knowing to keep my questions to a minimum if I didn't want to risk her shutting down.

"I'm seeing someone new," she'd said.

I'd nodded, though I was thrown off by the news. Izzy and Noah had been dating for almost two years. He was her first real boyfriend, and Mark and I had grown quite fond of him. We'd done dinners and cookouts and even a camping trip with his family.

"Her name's Theo. She's in film club with me."

"Okay," I said. Izzy looked at me like she was waiting for me to say more. I wasn't sure if she wanted validation, or if she was bracing herself for uncomfortable questions.

I went for the simple response: "Well, I can't wait to meet her." This got me a smile.

"You'll like her," Izzy said, and it turned out she was right.

Theo was friendly and polite. Some of the kids Izzy brought home barely made eye contact with Mark and me, but Theo always smiled, greeting us and asking how we were. She thanked us for having her over for meals and was especially effusive when I served her anything vegan. I knew she liked chai with almond milk and black bean burgers, so I always had some on hand—little things that went a long way with both her and Izzy.

Zipping up my fleece against the chill on the side porch, I sat down on the bench next to a very large and unsettling stuffed snowman Mark had put out—a new addition to the Christmas menagerie.

Behind me, the big living room window cast a warm glow over the porch. I could hear Mark laugh at something one of the girls had said.

I pulled out my phone, swiped and tapped to dial my brother's number. He picked up on the second ring.

"Well, did you survive the fa-la-la-ing yesterday?" Ben said in a teasing tone.

"Actually, we had to push it back to today," I said, inhaling the cold winter air and giving the snowman a suspicious sideways glare. I had the unreasonable sense that the damn thing was listening to me, daring me to outwardly bash his favorite holiday, his whole reason for existence. I thought of Frosty coming to life in the song when the children put the hat on his head—not magical at all, but downright terrifying. I scooted a little farther away from my stuffed snowman friend, took a fortifying gulp of wine.

"Ah, I see," he said with a chuckle. "So you decided to call me for a little anti-Christmas camaraderie? Our own private grinch support group?"

I laughed, felt my body relax in that way it did when I was talking with someone who genuinely got me. My brother was even more anti-Christmas than I was and fully understood the irony of the Moxie book. Hearing his voice now made me miss him fiercely. He rarely came east. The last time he'd been back in the Northeast was for our wedding nearly twenty years ago—it was also the last time he and my mother were in the same room together. He made excuses, said he was too busy with work—managing a restaurant our cousin owned in La Jolla—to take time off. I was grateful Ben had finally settled into a happy life he seemed content with. I'd escaped to boarding school as a teenager, while Ben had left our childhood home right after high school and never looked back. He'd been married twice, but neither marriage had lasted long. For many years he'd floated from odd job to odd job up and down the West Coast, with a seeming aversion to anything that resembled a normal, stationary life. But two years ago, our cousin Duane had roped him into managing an upscale seafood restaurant he owned. Ben worked close to sixty hours a week but said he loved it. Duane had recently made Ben a co-owner, and they were talking about opening a second restaurant together.

Ben and I talked once a week and texted often, but if I wanted to see my brother, I had to go to him. Not that I complained about February trips to La Jolla—walks with him along the craggy coastline, looking at all the seals and sea lions, eating amazing seafood. But now, as I did often, I wished he were closer. That I could fill him in in person rather than over the phone.

I thought of my mother asking me if I'd told him yet.

Ding-dong, the witch is almost dead.

I took another sip of wine and made myself continue. "I have news."

Ben paused. "Oh? Let me guess. You finished the next Moxie book?" He sounded genuinely excited.

I cringed. I wasn't even close. In fact, I hadn't even started. Not really. Just a few lousy sketches.

But that was my secret.

Whenever anyone asked—Mark, my agent Sarah, a well-meaning fan—I told them the book was coming along fabulously. I told myself that if I lived inside the lie long enough, it would become the truth, and the pages would start to pour out of me. It wasn't working so far.

"No," I said, then paused. "It's Mother."

He was silent. I took another sip of wine and continued. "She's ill."

He laughed. "Bullshit. She's never been sick a day in her life."

"Well, she's sick now. Really sick. I flew to New York to see her in the hospital yesterday. She's got pancreatic cancer. It's bad, Ben. They're saying she's only got weeks to live."

More silence. Was he even still there?

"Ben?"

"I'm not sure what it is you want me to say," he said, voice wooden.

"I'm not sure either. I just . . ."

I didn't want to tell him the rest. I knew what his reaction would be. I looked out at the moonlit landscape as I took in a breath to channel the strength of the familiar hills and mountains and pressed on. "She's asked to come here. To our house. To be with us while she dies."

He made a strangled gasp, or was it a laugh? "I hope you said, 'Not on your fucking life.'"

There went that warm, fuzzy, relaxed feeling I'd had. I sat up ramrod-straight on the bench, ready to defend myself against the tirade I felt coming. "Actually, Ben, we said yes. She'll be here on Monday." I delivered the words with staccato precision.

I could hear my brother breathing through clenched teeth on the other end of the line. When he spoke, his words were as sharp as a blade. "Have you lost your mind?"

"I—no, I—" I stammered as self-doubt sank in.

Was this a mistake?

No, I told myself. It wasn't. I was doing the right thing.

"I need you to respect my decision," I said to Ben, trying to sound sure of myself.

"*Respect your decision?* You're kidding, right? Do I need to remind you—"

"No," I cut him off. "You don't."

I didn't need to be reminded of any of it. While I'd managed to put the horrible memories of our mother in a box and lock that away, Ben believed that I was in denial and that the best way to deal with our past traumas was to talk about them in detail. He sometimes called me to ask questions like: "Was I in fifth grade when Mom broke my arm or was I older?" or "Remember that Thanksgiving when Mom put rat poison in the apple pie?" And he had an excellent memory—a proverbial steel trap.

I was quick to cut these conversations short by saying, "I don't know, Ben. I don't remember."

But it worked both ways, didn't it? Because when I countered with the good times, fried shrimp on the beach and dance parties in the kitchen and learning to draw, my brother claimed I embellished most of them.

"Are you still there, Ali?" he asked me now.

It was pointless to argue. Our mother was, and always would be, a monster to him.

"Rubin's vase," I said.

"Huh?"

"Do you remember when Mom taught us about negative space? She showed us that illustration, Rubin's vase. You know, you look at it and some people see a vase, some people see two faces."

"Yeah, but I don't see what's that got to do with—"

"And she asked us what it was a picture of, and we argued because I saw one thing and you saw another, but they were both there all along."

"I still don't—"

"I choose to see and remember one version of Mom and you choose another. Who's right and who's wrong?"

"Your denial is dangerous," Ben said. "Not just to you. But to your girls too, if you let that woman in your home."

I clenched my jaw. "I'm not in denial," I said. "I haven't forgotten how horrible she can be. But that was a long time ago. She was struggling, Ben."

"You need to stop making excuses for her."

"I'm not making excuses. You should've seen her in the hospital. She's changed—"

Ben barked out a venomous laugh. "People don't change, Alison. Not like that."

"Look, I've gotta go, Ben."

"You can't just—"

"We'll talk soon," I promised, then hung up.

I looked over at the puffy white snowman beside me. "Well, that went exceptionally well," I told him. He just stared at me over the top of his stuffed-carrot nose, his head lolling slightly to the left, his coal eyes cruelly mocking.

SIX

I STOOD UP, HEADED DOWN the porch steps and across the lawn to the little outbuilding I used as my printmaking studio. I'd just pop in for a minute to get my head on straight before going back to the cookie decorating. Surely Mark would understand.

We called it the barn. It was painted red, with a big sliding door on the front. The previous owners had used it for horses, and sometimes when it rained I was sure I could still smell the horse shit. We'd replaced the flooring, had the walls insulated and electricity and windows installed, along with a woodstove and a chimney. We'd even added skylights. I'd painted the walls white to make the space feel bright and open, like a blank page.

I pulled the door closed behind me, flipped on the lights, felt my body relax. I wished I could lock myself away in there for the rest of the night. But I knew I couldn't stay long—gingerbread men were calling—so I just sat on the rolling stool at my big worktable, sipping my wine while I looked at my recent drawings and prints. There were none of Moxie or her Halloween adventures. Nothing of what I was *supposed* to be working on, what I was under contract for.

What I'd been most captured (okay, maybe a little obsessed) by lately were insects, primarily honeybees. I'd done a whole series of prints of bees where they didn't belong: in bathtubs and teacups, on eyeglasses, perched on a stuffed bear. I thought these prints were some of the best work I'd done, with their very fine detailing showing each tiny hair, each gorgeous cell of the wing. But when I brought them around to the galleries and shops where I sold my work, no one was interested. The bees did not sell. Moxie did. That's what buyers and store owners wanted. More Moxie.

"Fucking Moxie," I mumbled, taking another long swig of wine.

I was tired and, lightweight drinker that I was, already a little tipsy.

I didn't drink often. It was something I'd been very careful about, knowing alcoholism runs in families. But a glass of wine now and then couldn't hurt, I told myself. And I'd promised myself long ago that I'd never let my girls see me drunk. If it ever happened, I swore, the drinking would be over forever. Not another drop.

I looked around the studio. The few sketches I'd done for *Moxie Saves Halloween* sat buried in a corner. How *was* Moxie going to save Halloween? Izzy had been throwing ideas at me for months, the most enthusiastic I'd seen her. Some of her suggestions weren't half bad, but nothing had quite clicked for me. I sighed as I pulled out one of the drawings—Moxie sitting beside a carved grinning jack-o'-lantern.

"Knock-knock!" a voice called, and I jumped. Penny opened the sliding door and stepped into the studio. "I saw the light on and thought I'd pop over." She had her thick hair pulled up into a messy bun and was in her usual paint-stained and battered overalls—what she slipped on each day when she got home from work. She reached into the front pocket and pulled out a bag of her own homegrown pot—a strain she'd lovingly named Electric Sheep. "I thought you could use this," Penny said. "Having survived Decorating Day and all." She gave me a smile, her warm hazel eyes locked onto mine.

"You have no idea," I said, giving her a hug. She smelled faintly of pot and sandalwood oil.

I'd met Penny the week Mark and I moved into the farmhouse. She and Louise had dropped by with a coffee cake and a bottle of wine to welcome us to the hill. When Penny and I started to talk, it was as if we'd known each other for years, were old friends already. We talked about what color I should paint each room, about the ways colors can evoke feelings and memories. Right from the start, part of me thought, *Here she is at last, the best friend I've always been hoping for.*

Penny and Louise had what they called a hobby farm. In addition to the carefully cultivated marijuana they grew and sold to a select group of friends, they raised sheep and chickens and kept bees. Penny was a therapist and fiber artist. Louise had been a massage therapist before her stroke, but had given it up, devoting herself instead to the farm.

While Penny was definitely the driver behind my pot habit, I blamed Louise for my bee obsession. She had learned how to infuse her own honey (my favorite was the habanero) and invited me out to the hives with her. I had spent countless hours with her this past spring, summer, and early fall studying the bees, photographing and sketching them. Louise had been very patient with me. She'd put me in a white beekeeper's suit and taken me out to the hives again and again.

I released Penny from my tight hug and she looked at me with concern—I swore this woman knew me better than I knew myself. "Tell me everything," she said, hoisting herself up to take a seat on the worktable beside me. She reached for my half-empty glass of wine and took a sip.

And I told her. I could sometimes be even more open with Penny than with Mark, because she never judged. And she was no stranger to tragedy and pain. Years ago, before I met her, she and Louise had had a son, Daniel, who died of leukemia when he was five. Many would have been destroyed by the death of their only child, but Penny let it shape her life in a positive way. She went back to school and became a therapist who specialized in treatment for grief and trauma.

Once I started telling her about the events of the past two days, the story poured out. She just sat listening, giving me her full and complete attention. At last I finished with Ben telling me it was all a mistake.

"Wow," Penny said. "That's an emotional tsunami." This was one of the things I loved about Penny—she never responded with vague therapist nonsense like, *How did that make you feel?*

"And on top of it all, it's Decorating Day!" I said. "It was supposed to be yesterday, but Mark waited until I was home. He didn't want to do it without me."

Penny smiled. "I bet the tree looks pretty."

I rolled my eyes. "Yeah, the whole house is a winter wonderland. And I'm supposed to be inside right now, putting happy little faces on gingerbread men."

"I don't suppose you have to make them all happy, do you?" She gave me a mischievous look. "Can't you do one having an existential crisis?"

I smiled. "Izzy and Theo are in there turning them into zombies with bleeding wounds and leaking brains."

"Poor Mark." Penny laughed. "No wonder you sought refuge out here."

"It's the only place I can think. But I know I should be out here working on Moxie, and I don't know how I'll get the new book done now that I've agreed to let my mother move in with us."

Penny turned to scan the drawings of bee after bee. "So no progress with Moxie, huh?"

"Nope." Penny was the only one who knew. "Sarah's begging me to send her something, anything to show them, just to prove that I'm working on it."

Penny nodded. "Can't you just whip up some sketches? Something to keep them happy for now?"

I sighed. "My heart's just not in it."

"I know," she said, setting down the drawing she held on a pile of the others and looking at me again, smiling. "Your heart is with the bees."

I smiled back at her. "But the bees don't pay the bills."

Penny nodded sagely. "Moxie's your bread and butter. The bees are your habanero honey."

I laughed. "Couldn't have put it better myself." I reached for the glass of wine, took a sip.

"I should go," Penny said, giving my arm a pat and jumping down from the table. "Let you get back to Decorating Day." She gave me a mischievous grin.

I sighed. I knew Mark was waiting for me inside.

I looked at her. "Do you think I'm making a mistake? Letting my mother come stay with us."

Penny looked at me in silence for so long that I was beginning to wonder if she was even going to answer.

"I think it'll be hard. Maybe the hardest thing you've ever done."

I felt all the air being sucked out of my lungs.

"Your mother had her share of difficulties too—a dependence on alcohol, your dad's death. It may not justify her behavior, but it could explain it. Besides, the most difficult things are what shape and define us," Penny said.

She gave me a sandalwood-and-marijuana-scented hug, kissed my cheek, and slipped out the door. I drained my wineglass before turning the lights out and leaving the bees in darkness.

SEVEN

"HOW MUCH LONGER?" OLIVIA asked, her nose smashed against the glass of the dining room window overlooking the driveway.

"I don't know."

"They said four, right?"

"Right."

"Well, what time is it?" she asked.

I smiled. "Two minutes later than the last time you asked."

"Which is?"

I showed her my watch. "Four-oh-five."

Olivia was dressed in her ballet clothes—pink tights, leotard, pink slippers, and a little frilly pink tutu. She didn't have class until six, but she had insisted on putting on her ballet things as soon as she got home from school. She wanted to be wearing them when she met her grandmother.

"So she'll know I'm a dancer," she'd explained, then had asked me to do her hair, putting it in a ballet bun and pinning it in place.

"When will she be here?" Olivia asked for the hundredth time.

I sighed. It was like waiting for Santa on Christmas Eve.

We'd spent the last few days in a mad fit of preparations: the guest room was cleaned, the bed moved out and replaced by a hospital bed. The medical supply company had also delivered a bedpan, commode, shower chair, wheelchair, and walker. A contractor came and installed grab bars and a retractable showerhead in the downstairs bathroom. I'd been on the phone with Paul several times a day. Keeping to his word, he had arranged everything—up to and including having groceries delivered so we'd be stocked up on all the things my mother ate these days: creamed soups, ice cream, pudding, ginger ale, Ensure. He even sent me a recipe for custard he'd been making for her.

He sent all her medical records to a local hospice agency he'd contacted. He had her prescriptions transferred to a pharmacy in town. We were ready. Or as ready as we could be.

And to be honest, all these preparations had given me something to focus on so I wouldn't have time to spiral out of control and ask myself: *What in God's name have I done?* There was comfort in making lists and checking items off them.

Mark and I had stood together in the guest room last night. We'd replaced its beautiful old iron bed with the rented hospital bed. There were fresh flowers on the table. Olivia's WELCOME GRANDMA MAVIS sign was taped right over the bed. The closet and dresser were emptied out, waiting to be filled with my mother's things.

"I guess this is really happening, huh?" Mark said, putting his arm around me.

"Yup," I said, the reality of it starting to sink in. My mother was actually coming. We would see her get sicker and sicker; she would be here when she died.

"Nervous?" Mark asked.

"A little," I said. I leaned against him. "Okay, maybe slightly terrified," I'd admitted, switching off the light.

"Maybe they got lost," Olivia said now.

"I doubt that, honey. I'm sure they'll be here any minute."

Izzy was upstairs in her room doing homework with her headphones on. Mark was still at work. He'd offered to leave school early, to get a substitute for his last class of the day, but I'd told him it was fine. "I've got this," I'd said, smiling as reassuringly as I could. "Besides, Paul will be here. He can babysit us, make sure neither of us kills the other or anything." Even though I'd said it with a wink, Mark did not seem amused.

Olivia backed away from the window, did three twirls across the hard-wood floor, carefully avoiding the table and chairs.

"Nice twirls," I said.

"They're not twirls, Mom," she said as she stopped spinning. "They're *piqués*." She stomped back over to the window, pressing her nose against the cold glass.

"Do you want to read a book or something?" I suggested. "Maybe do the math worksheet Mrs. Fletcher sent home with you?"

She scrunched her face into a scowl. "No! Because then we might miss her!"

I chuckled. "I don't think that's very likely, little mouse."

"I want to see her as soon as she gets here," Olivia said in her most stubborn voice. She was a kid who didn't let go of a thing once she'd set her mind to it. "I want to see her before she sees me."

"Why?" I asked.

"So I can decide if I like her or not," Olivia said.

I smiled, stroked her smooth, pinned-back hair. "Of course you'll like her. She's your grandmother." My jaw tightened as I said the words.

Olivia kept her face pressed against the glass. Her breath was fogging it. "But I barely know her at all."

I tensed. That was my fault.

I tried to put on a smile. "Well, now you're going to have a chance to get to know her. And I know she can't wait to get to know you."

She ran a finger through the fogged patch on the glass, drawing a heart, then piercing it with an arrow.

The dining room opened up into the living room on the right, where the tree was lit up, its decorations hung. There was a new glass angel watching us from the corner, even gaudier than the first: decked out in a painted pink dress with metallic gold accents, gold wings, and an oversized gold trumpet. I couldn't help but imagine another accident resulting in her demise.

There's no doubt about it: I'm a terrible person.

Olivia drew a second heart next to the first. "What's her name? My grandma?"

"Mavis." The name felt sharp on my tongue.

"I know that, Mom," Olivia said in her *well, duh* voice. "Mavis *what*?"

"Mavis Eldeen Holland."

Olivia turned and looked up at me, confused. "But that's not your last name before you married Daddy. What's that called?"

"My maiden name. And you're right, it's not. My maiden name is Russo."

"So if she's your real mom, why don't you have her last name?"

I was caught off guard by her words: *your real mom*. As if I had another secret mother somewhere. A different mother. A better mother.

"She is my real mother." I smiled at Olivia. "My last name was my father's last name. His name was David Russo."

Saying his name actually hurt, left my chest aching, even after all these years. I was only seven when he died, but his death had broken me, broken us all, in a way we'd never recover from, especially Ben. It was Ben who'd found him that day out in our father's studio in the old carriage house. Ben had come running back across the front lawn and into the house, screaming the whole way, so hysterical he couldn't get the words out when Mother and I met him in the front hall. His screams and howls filled the house, made me cover my ears. At last Mother slapped him, and he managed to get the words out: "He's dead."

They wouldn't let me out to my father's studio to see what it was Ben had found. I'd spent countless hours watching my father work in the old carriage house, painting abstract colorful designs on canvases so large he needed a stepladder to reach the top. I loved watching him work, listening to the titles he gave his paintings—*Three Horses and One Rider, The Tiger's Escape*—and desperately searched the paintings for some sign of the things he said were in there, things I could never seem to find hidden in the bright splashes of color.

Mom had gone into the studio while Ben howled and moaned, and she'd come back out ashen-faced and called the police.

"It's your fault!" Ben had screamed at her that night, after the police and the ambulance had come and gone, after they'd taken our father's body away. Ben then went back into the studio and began knocking things over, toppling canvases, throwing tubes of paint onto the floor. "You killed him!" he screamed.

My mother just stood in the corner watching, not stopping him, not speaking a word. It seemed to me that she got smaller and smaller the more he screamed, and I worried that by the time he was done, she'd be doll-sized, maybe even disappear.

I blinked the memory away before it could sink its claws in.

"What did your dad do?" Olivia asked.

"He was a painter, like my mother."

"Was he famous?"

"No."

"Do you have any of his paintings?"

"Sadly, no," I said.

My mother had cleaned out his studio after his death, throwing every single one of his paintings into a bonfire in the yard. I remember her face, soot-stained and grimly determined in the firelight. For weeks, until the snow came, there was a burned circle of earth and a pile of coals and ashes in our front yard.

"But they were married, right? Your parents?" Olivia stepped back from the window, did another twirl.

"Yes." Then I added, "Nice piqué, little mouse."

She looked thoroughly unimpressed with my newly acquired ballet terminology. "So why isn't she Mavis Russo?"

"She was. But she changed her name back to her maiden name, Holland, after my father died."

Olivia stopped her twirls and looked at me, her face scrunched up. "Why?"

"I don't know, sweetie." I rubbed my temples. I was getting a head-ache.

Olivia peered out the window again. The driveway still had only our Volvo sitting in it.

"Well, can I ask her?"

"Maybe not when you first meet her, okay? It might make her sad to think about when her husband died."

She frowned, considering this. "Daddy said she's a famous artist."

"Yes," I said.

"And she's very busy, which is why we never see her."

"Yes, that's right."

"Is that why you're an artist too? Because she is?"

I felt my body stiffen. "Maybe," I said.

The truth was, I rarely thought about it. This one thing, other than blood, that connected me to my mother.

"Maybe Izzy will be an artist when she grows up too," Olivia said, pulling me away from my memories. "Just like you and Grandma!"

I smiled, thought of Izzy's forays into art: she'd done assemblage pieces with broken dolls mixed together with mechanical parts, a stint with photography, mixed-media collages that contained broken mirrors. Lately she was making short videos. Her latest was a series called *Things That Piss Me Off*: dog shit on her boots, overly friendly cashiers, people making assumptions about her sexual orientation or even imagining it might be any of their goddamn business.

"Would you change your name?" Olivia asked me. "If Daddy died?"

The question startled me. I couldn't imagine my life without Mark. He was the one person who made me believe that I deserved the perfect life I'd somehow stumbled into, when all along I felt like an unworthy imposter.

"Well, I certainly hope he's not going to die for a very long time, but no, I would keep calling myself Alison O'Conner."

"Why?"

"Because that's who I am. And because you and your sister are

O'Conners, and I want to have the same last name as you. Our name connects us; it means we're family."

She furrowed her brow. "But your mom didn't have the same last name as you. Didn't she want to? Didn't she want to be connected to you?"

My headache intensified. I massaged my temples, trying to ease the steady throbbing. "I can't say what she was thinking. But I know that I would keep my last name."

"I like you being Alison O'Conner," Olivia said.

"I like it too," I said, as though the name were a hat I was trying on to see if it suited me. A hat I'd gotten used to, one that had kept me warm and dry and happy for years.

Was it a hat I was worthy of?

Would it blow off in a good strong wind, or would it hold?

I needed some ibuprofen. "Be right back, little mouse," I said, going to the downstairs bathroom and getting the bottle from the medicine cabinet. I downed three pills with water slurped directly from the tap. I stood up, looked at myself in the mirror, saw my mother's face looking back. The mother from my childhood.

My eyes were brown and hers an icy pale blue, but our faces had the same shape, the same nose and chin and slope of the forehead. It startled me sometimes, to see a trace of my mother in myself, to wonder just who I was looking at.

I stood squinting at my reflection, focusing on the edges.

Who do you think you are?

No one.

That's exactly right. You're no one.

For a second, I was sure I'd seen a flicker, as if I wasn't really solid.

Wasn't really there at all.

EIGHT

I RETURNED TO THE DINING room as Olivia came away from the window, did three pirouettes and a plié. Then she started practicing her mouse dance, crouching down low, creeping across the floor on tiptoes, her hands held up like little paws.

Focused on her, I hadn't seen the car pulling into the driveway, but Olivia, who'd been keeping her eye on the window even while dancing, didn't miss it.

"She's here! She's here!" Olivia ran to the window, pressing her face against it.

My hands felt cold and sweaty, every muscle in my body painfully tight. My temples still throbbed.

Run, my body was telling me. *Run and hide.*

But this was silly. I'd invited her here. She was my mother.

I swallowed down the panic, rested a hand on Olivia's back. She was thrumming with excitement.

"That's Paul?" Olivia asked as Paul got out of the driver's side door of the big black SUV.

"Yes," I said. He was wearing a long black coat and dark sunglasses.

Paul went around to the passenger side and opened the door. I held my breath as I watched him help my mother out. She moved slowly, stiffly, and clung to his arm as he gently guided her, helped lift her from the seat. She stood in the driveway swaying slightly, still holding tight to him as he supported her. He said something that made her smile, and I felt a pang of jealousy as I watched the way she leaned into him.

Her face was gaunt. Her cheekbones, always prominent, jutted out, giving her the appearance of a woman chiseled from stone. She was wearing tailored black slacks, a white sweater, an unbuttoned black coat. She had a long white scarf wrapped around her neck and a white hat to match it. Elegant to the last. And a huge change from her appearance in the hospital, with the white-and-blue johnny hanging on her bony frame.

Still, she looked small and shrunken beneath her clothes, giving her an almost mummy-like appearance. While her body might be worn down by age and illness, her eyes were the same. Even from here, I could feel their icy glare as they scanned the yard, then the house, searching for me.

"Oh, she's so tiny," Olivia said. "And what a pretty hat! And she's wearing a fancy coat! I like her already."

"I knew you would," I said. "Now, let's go out and say hello."

I took my daughter's hand, held my breath, and led her out the front door.

"You found us!" I said, as if our family had been lost, then discovered at last, shipwrecked on our own private island.

"Alison," Paul said, coming over and giving me a polite hug, kissing the air beside my cheek.

"Hello, Alison," my mother said. "It's good to see you again. Good to be here."

Paul gave me a gentle nudge in her direction. She didn't open up her arms for a hug, and neither did I. Instead, I reached forward, careful to keep my distance, the way you might with a venomous snake. But surely a handshake was safe. We shook hands as if it were our first time meeting.

How do you do? Very pleased to make your acquaintance. I've heard so much about you.

My mother surprised me by gripping my hand tightly, clawing into me with a strength I didn't expect and pulling me toward her. She enveloped me in a hug and I hugged her back, feeling her bony, hunched figure beneath the layers of clothing.

It shocked me, to feel how frail she was, how breakable she seemed.

At last she released me, looking to my left at Olivia.

"And who might you be?" my mother asked, squinting down at her.

I held my breath.

My mother smiled and continued, "A member of the Boston Ballet?"

"No, silly!" Olivia giggled.

I let out the breath I'd been holding.

"The New York City Ballet, then?"

"I'm your granddaughter! I'm Olivia. I'm six. And I'm a dancer." Olivia did a little curtsy.

"So I see," my mother said. "And a very pretty one at that."

Olivia beamed. "I can show you my mouse dance if you'd like."

"A mouse dance?" My mother grinned down at Olivia. "I don't believe I've ever had the pleasure of seeing a mouse dance. It sounds perfectly lovely."

I took in a deep breath and felt my whole body relax. Maybe this was all going to be okay after all. We'd done the right thing. It was one thing to think it, but another to feel it now that she was actually here.

Needing no more encouragement, Olivia got into position on the edge of the driveway. "You start like this," she said, crouching down.

"Not yet, little mouse," I told her. "Let's get your grandmother inside and settled a bit first."

"Yes," Paul agreed. "It was a long trip. And Mavis refused her pain meds. She didn't want to be groggy when she arrived." He looked at my mother, face full of concern. "I'm sure you're ready for a pill and a lie-down, aren't you?"

My mother winced a bit in response but didn't answer.

I looked from my mother to Paul. "Should I go get the wheelchair?"

"No need," my mother said. "We can manage just fine." She took a shuffling step forward. "I can't wait to see this house of yours. It looked very cozy in the photo spread they did in the *Globe*."

"You saw that?" I asked.

"Of course I did." She winked at me, then quoted from the article: "'With *Moxie Saves Christmas*, Alison O'Conner has created an instant holiday classic. Between the book and the old farmhouse she's turned into an enchanted winter wonderland, it's clear she's the reigning Queen of all things Christmas.'"

I sputtered out an embarrassed laugh.

"Your mother's followed your career very closely," Paul said.

"So it seems," I said. I was stunned. She'd never said anything to me about it. We always talked about the kids and Mark and the weather and her travels. We never discussed her life in the art world, and she never asked me about the Moxie book business, or any of my art projects. And I'd only brought up my publishing deal once, but she hadn't seemed very impressed or wanted to know more details, so I didn't raise the subject again.

It was strange to think she'd read the article, seen the photos of me standing in front of our trimmed tree with Moxie, pulling a tray of cookies out of the oven, and opening our heavy oak front door adorned with a large holly wreath.

"There's not much I miss, Alison," Mother said.

She took my arm, held tight, and swayed slightly. I grabbed hold of her to help her stay upright. Clearly walking wasn't easy for her, though she was doing her best to prove otherwise. She couldn't have weighed more than ninety pounds; a mere wisp of the woman she'd once been. I wondered if maybe I should have brought the wheelchair out after all.

This was the woman who'd watched me take my first steps, I told myself, who'd no doubt held my hand to steady me, to keep me upright.

"Except somehow I missed that my younger granddaughter is a prima ballerina." She winked at Olivia. "Now I wonder what other secrets you've all been keeping from me."

Olivia chuckled. "We don't have any secrets."

Now it was my mother who chuckled. "Everyone's got secrets, my love."

"Families don't keep secrets from each other," Olivia said, parroting back what Mark and I always told her, "except at Christmastime. And on birthdays too!"

"Christmas secrets are the best sort of secrets, aren't they, Olivia?" my mother said.

Olivia practically squealed with delight. "Christmas is my very favorite holiday."

"Mine too," my mother told her.

My jaw clenched. Since when? My father had always been the one to celebrate; there were years after he died when our mother didn't even bother getting us a tree. Christmas was a thing other families did. Families like Mark's who were happy to be together.

Paul went around to the back of the SUV and opened it up, grabbing a large wheeled suitcase and my mother's leather purse.

"Would you like to take this in for me, Olivia?" he asked, handing her the purse. She nodded enthusiastically and reached for it, then led us inside.

"It's this way, Grandma! And wait till you see the sign I made for you."

As my mother let go of my arm and followed, hiding my daughter from view, I couldn't help but wonder if this was a fresh start or a terrible mistake.

NINE

PAUL GOT MY MOTHER settled in her bed and gave her a dose of pain meds while Olivia and I unpacked her things. She'd brought a few nice outfits, but mostly pajamas and nightgowns, comfortable loungewear, and two pairs of slippers. There were a couple of paperback mysteries, her cell phone and charger, a sketchpad and art supplies.

"Ooh, a tiny watercolor set," Olivia said as she pulled it out of the tote bag.

"Do you like to paint, Olivia?" my mother asked.

"I like it but I'm not good at it." She frowned. "Not like Mom and Izzy are."

"Maybe I could give you some lessons," my mother said. "I used to give your mother lessons when she was your age."

Olivia beamed. She reached back into the tote bag, pulled out some pastels, colored pencils, then a wooden box. She opened the box and looked inside. "Pretty!" she said. She drew out what was tucked into the box and held it up to the light, and my first thought was: *Oh, hell no. She didn't actually bring that stone, did she?*

But of course she had. Of course she'd brought it into my house, to keep right next to her as she lay dying. She and the stone shared a complicated history; they were inextricably linked.

It was a piece of clear quartz crystal streaked through with little needlelike bands of black tourmaline. It was jagged and roughly the size and shape of a heart—not a silly cartoon Valentine's Day heart, but an actual human heart shaped like a fist.

It was impossible to think about my mother without thinking of the stone; impossible to separate the two of them. When I was a child, I was fascinated by it, but I also hated it with a vengeance I didn't realize it was possible to feel for an inanimate object.

I connected it, consciously or not, with my mother's cruelty. The stone appeared around the time she really started drinking.

And maybe, just maybe, I was envious of its ability to capture her attention at a time when I could not. The stone came, and we, her family, were pushed aside, viewed as an annoyance, a target for her fury when she chose to acknowledge us at all. She kept the stone beside her in her bedroom, fawned over it, even spoke to it with love and admiration as if it were a living thing, perfect in its beauty. And me, I was just a nuisance, a useless ugly duckling of a girl; how could I compare?

When I was a child, I'd look at the stone and think that the black strands running through it were like the black strands inside my mother, the little bits of darkness hidden deep within.

She kept it on a wooden stand on the dresser in her bedroom, amid her perfume bottles and jewelry boxes, her jar of cold cream, the beige cake of face powder she used, the waxy lipstick the color of overripe plums. Next to it was a framed photograph of her and her best friend, Bobbi, both of them looking impossibly young and happy.

I wasn't allowed near the stone. (In fact, my mother's entire bedroom was deemed off-limits.) The tourmalinated quartz was too precious, my mother always said. She didn't want the grungy fingers of children marring it in any way or carrying it off for show-and-tell, stuffed at the bottom of a crumb-filled backpack. I'd made the mistake of asking if I could bring it to school once, and my mother had howled with spiteful laughter, then sent me to my room for being so idiotic.

But sometimes I'd sneak into her bedroom just to touch it, run my fingers over its rough surface. And I'd think about its history, about where it had come from and all the reasons it was so sacred to my mother.

The stone had been Bobbi's once; that was the first compelling thing about it.

The second, and more important, was that it had made my mother famous.

Not the stone itself, but my mother's painting of it. The painting that began the stratospheric rise of her career.

Her painting of Bobbi.

Bobbi Vanderhoof had been my mother's best friend since early childhood. They'd grown up together, attended high school together, then gone off to college at Vassar together. After college, they'd traveled for several months, and when they returned from their round-the-world trip, Bobbi had the stone. I never learned where it had come from, or how she had acquired it. I only knew that when they got back, Bobbi had it with her, and they went up to my mother's studio, which was then in the attic of her parents' house, and Bobbi posed for the painting.

Then Bobbi went off to California, taking the stone with her for luck. She got a few jobs doing commercials, then a small part in a soap opera. She got married to a producer named Gene and they had a son, Carter. Eventually Bobbi landed a role on the TV show *Wishville*, about a family of witches in a small New England town. She played the mother and Witch Queen, Tamsen. It attracted enough attention to help Bobbi get the role that was going to change her career: the lead in a feature film about a psychic detective. But she was killed before filming even began.

I was six when Bobbi died, so my memories of her alive were fuzzy. I remembered watching her on TV with my mother, videotapes of *Wishville* that we viewed so often we could recite the dialogue. And when she came to visit, I felt like I knew her from her show, like she was actually a witch named Tamsen and not my mother's childhood friend. Fact and fiction blurred. This I was sure of: when Bobbi came to visit, my mother was happy. My father too. The three of them would stay up late drinking and talking and laughing. They'd sit out on the back patio, mixing pitchers of gin and tonics, playing cards, telling stories that made them laugh so hard my mother once actually fell out of her chair. Bobbi and Gene had separated, then divorced, so he never accompanied her on these visits—it was just her and sometimes her son. Bobbi would try to talk my parents into moving to California. She promised that with her connections, she could get them both work in the industry—they could be stylists or set designers.

"You belong in Hollywood," Bobbi would coo, wrapping her hand around my mother's arm. And my father would laugh, shake his head, tell her Woodstock suited them better.

My father, who wasn't a drinker, would often pass out long before my mother and Bobbi, leaving the two women to stay up until dawn sometimes, whispering to each other, finishing the last of the gin and sharing cigarettes (which my mother only smoked when Bobbi was visiting).

Bobbi's son, Carter, was older than Ben and me. He was a lanky kid with pale blond hair and dark circles under his eyes like he never slept. He was always daring us to do stuff we shouldn't—he came to visit with his pockets full of dangerous things: cigarettes, firecrackers, butterfly knives. He spun crazy tales of his life in California: the parties, the famous people, all the girlfriends he had. "You ever even kissed a girl, Benji?" he'd asked my brother once when he was only in third or fourth grade. Ben just shrugged, which made Carter laugh and tease him, promise that if he got his sorry little scrawny ass to California, he'd find him a girlfriend of his own, and if he was lucky maybe she'd even go all the way with him.

Carter said his dad had a house in the hills where there were parties every weekend, and he went on to list the celebrities who'd come, swum in his pool, done coke in his dad's kitchen. I never recognized the names of the people he mentioned, but my brother did (or pretended to) and said, "No way!" over and over.

"Way, dude," Carter would say, grinning at him, then grab him in a friendly headlock and give him a noogie.

Bobbi and my mother spoke on the phone at least once a week, often more. I'd try to eavesdrop sometimes, but my mother always took the calls in her bedroom, sitting on her antique four-poster bed. Sometimes the calls were loud and celebratory with lots of laughter. Sometimes I'd press my ear against the door and hear my mother speaking quietly to her friend, whispering even. Sometimes I was sure I heard her cry.

And then came the accident. I remember (or think I remember) my mother getting the call. How Bobbi had been in an awful car crash. How my mother said, "Oh my God," over and over, then rushed to the airport to get on the next flight to LA. She was by Bobbi's side in the hospital when she died a day later. My mother stayed out there for a week, helping Bobbi's family go through her things, plan the funeral. When she flew back to New York, she had a box of photographs and the tourmalinated quartz: Bobbi's good-luck stone.

The stone went on my mother's dresser, and I'd hear her talking to it sometimes. Sobbing as she spoke. Sometimes she'd argue with it, or beg it to give her Bobbi back, as if Bobbi were somehow trapped inside and would emerge in a puff of dust or smoke, like a genie in a bottle.

My mother's old painting of Bobbi had hung in her studio throughout my childhood, but after Bobbi's death it was moved to our living room, where it hung on the wall just to the left of the television. Bobbi as Tamsen the Witch Queen would flit across the television screen as my mother played and replayed the videos, and Bobbi as a young woman just out of college would gaze at us from the living room wall, her whole future before her and a stone for a heart.

The painting was done on a large canvas: two feet by four feet. In it, Bobbi was wearing blue jeans and a white shirt, opened to reveal a cavity, a little box in her chest where her heart should be. But in place of a heart was the heart-shaped stone—clear and streaked with black. It seemed to shimmer and glow, and the image of Bobbi herself glowed too; she wore a halo of light that radiated out from her chest. Her eyes seemed to follow me wherever I went, to watch everything I did.

When my mother returned from California after Bobbi's funeral, she took a photo of the painting and shared it with Bobbi's agent and some of her actor friends from *Wishville*, whom she'd met at the funeral. A copy of it ended up being published in a newsletter for fans of *Wishville*. Bobbi's devotees loved it. My mother had prints made. Then T-shirts. Offers to buy the original painting began pouring in, as did bids to show her work in galleries.

Over the years, my mother did many paintings featuring the stone—a few more of Bobbi holding it or sitting next to it, some of it alone, and the most unsettling: my mother and Bobbi sitting side by side, both of their chests opened up, the stone between them attached with arteries and veins, a single heart they shared, keeping them both alive.

OLIVIA HELD THE stone up, running her fingers over it, and I braced myself, expecting my mother to reprimand her. I was ready to jump in, to protect and defend my daughter.

But my mother only smiled at her.

"It's very pretty," Olivia said.

"It is, isn't it?" my mother said.

"Where would you like it to go?" Olivia asked.

"Oh, I think right here on the bedside table. So I can see it all the time."

Olivia set it down beside the lamp, in front of the fresh flowers in the vase. It seemed to glow when the sunlight streaming in the window caught it, to pulsate and throb like something alive.

"Where did it come from?" Olivia asked.

"It belonged to my very best friend. Having it close makes me feel like she's right here, close to me. Do you have a best friend, Olivia?"

"Yes! Her name is Sophie. She dances with me. Well, she used to. She moved up to level two, so we're not in the same classes anymore, but we have rehearsal together. She's the best dancer in level two. She has a lot of roles in *The Nutcracker*! She plays Fritz, Clara's little brother. She has to wear boys' clothes, but she doesn't mind because it's a good role. She's also a soldier and a snowflake and a tea dancer."

"And what about you? What are you playing?"

"Me?" Olivia shrugged her shoulders, looked down at the ground. "I'm just a mouse."

"Well, I think it's good to have one role to concentrate on. Then you can work hard and be the very best mouse."

Olivia nodded.

"When I was a girl, I took ballet."

"Really?" Olivia's eyes grew wide.

"You did?" I jumped in. "I had no idea."

"Neither did I," Paul said. "Somehow I can't quite picture it."

I couldn't either. The idea of my mother in a crowd of other little girls, following a teacher's directions, taking corrections—it seemed absurd.

"Oh yes," Mother said. "It was a lot of hard work. And in the end, I didn't practice as much as I should have, so I wasn't very good. But you"—she looked at Olivia—"I can see that you take practicing very seriously."

"I do!" said Olivia.

"That's the only way to get better at a thing. To practice and practice."

Taking the advice to heart, Olivia did a spin across the room.

My mother applauded.

Olivia sat on the edge of my mother's bed and told her all about *The Nutcracker* and dance classes and her teacher, Ms. Perez.

"I've got some paperwork to go over with you," Paul said to me while my mother and my daughter bonded over ballet. "Should we go into the dining room where we can spread out?"

I nodded, trying to quell my anxiety about leaving Olivia alone with my mother, but surely it would be all right. I was only steps away, and Paul was here, and my mother seemed so charmed by my younger daughter.

We went out to the dining room, where he pulled some files from his leather messenger bag. I kept listening to Olivia chattering away in the guest room, her voice bubbly and bright.

"Do you want some coffee? Tea?" I asked, trying to act like a normal host, to not give away my unease.

"No thanks," he said, pulling out a printed list of my mother's medications and their dosages—he'd even made a color-coded chart to help me keep track of when to give each of them. Another folder contained all the paperwork I was supposed to hand over to the nurse from Kingdom Hospice, who was coming first thing in the morning—plus all my mother's medical records. "I've already sent electronic copies of all of this, but it'll be good to have backups," he said. I nodded, once again amazed by Paul's organizational abilities—the folders he handed me even had little printed labels.

A third folder held legal documents, including a living will saying that there would be no heroic measures to keep her alive—no intubation, no CPR. He flipped through the papers, showing me everything quickly. I nodded as if I were taking it all in, but my head spun. I wished Mark were here. He was good at paying attention, at remembering details. Paul must have seen the glazed-over look in my eyes. He shut the folder and put a hand on my arm. "I know it's a lot, but you've got everything you need. And I'm just a phone call away."

Back in the guest room, Olivia giggled at something my mother said.

"Shall we go see what's so funny?" he asked, and I agreed, eager to be away from the piles of paperwork, the records that proved my mother was dying—and the certainty that I was going to be responsible for her as she did so. Besides, the curl of worry in my stomach about leaving Olivia alone with my mother hadn't quite abated.

Olivia was listing all the girls in level five who'd gotten pointe shoes. "Ms. Perez has to choose you and tell when you're ready. She says if you start too early, it can hurt your feet and body. Someday I'll have pointe shoes. You have to go all the way to Boston or New York to get fitted, that's what the level five girls do."

My mother nodded, but her head was back against the pillows. I could tell she was worn out and the pain medicine was kicking in.

Paul seemed edgy, keyed up. He pinballed around the guest room, adjusting things, and then went out to the car for the third time to make sure everything had been brought in. He declined yet again my offer of coffee or food. "At least take a seat for a little while," I said. He sat in a chair in the corner of the guest room, fidgeting like a little boy.

"Shouldn't you be getting back soon, Paul?" my mother said.

"Yeah," Paul said, standing. "It's a long trip."

Was it my imagination, or had he been avoiding eye contact with my mother all afternoon?

Was he upset with her? Upset that she'd chosen to be here and not stay with him?

Or was it something else?

And now it seemed almost as if she was dismissing him, sending him away.

"So soon?" I said. "Are you sure you can't stay? Have dinner with us? Say hi to Mark? He should be home in a bit."

He shook his head and said he had a long list of things to do, including packing up some artwork at the house for an upcoming gallery show. My mother sat up, began barking orders at him: "*Don't forget this*," and "*Tell Cheri that*"—and he diligently jotted them all down on his phone.

He turned to me. "The show is a retrospective—a look back at your mother's development as an artist. They're including early paintings and sketches, notes."

"Don't forget the sketchbooks I've got tucked away in the big black file cabinet in my studio," she said.

"I've got it, Mavis," he promised. "I know where everything is—the sketchbooks, the journals." I imagined him back at the house, unlocking the heavy black front door, stepping into the hall—did my mother still have the dark-red runner? Did the house still smell of lemon furniture polish and grief? Did she still keep all the curtains drawn tight, refusing to let in a hint of light? It made my throat feel tight to think of it, to realize that Paul knew the house better than I did now; that he belonged there, knew where my mother kept all her things.

"Don't you worry about a thing," Paul said to her. "I'll be back at the end of the week. If you think of anything you need from home, you call or text and I'll make sure to bring it."

He leaned down over the bed, gave her a quick, gentle hug, and whispered something to her. She whispered something back and he jerked away as if her words had burned him. He straightened up, then seemed to remember that Olivia and I were there in the room. He turned toward us with a lopsided, forced smile. "It was lovely to meet you, Olivia. And to see you again, Alison."

"I'll walk you out," I said.

When we got to the driveway, I said, "Are you sure you have to hurry off? Can't you stay a little longer? Please?" There it was. The hint of desperation I was unable to keep in check. I wasn't sure I was ready to be alone with my mother. Not just yet. I wanted a little more time with him here, as a buffer—he knew her so well. He knew when she was in pain, when she was tired and thirsty; he knew everything she needed, and got it for her before she even had a chance to ask.

"I'm sorry, I really can't." He looked determined. But there was something else. He looked shaken. Scared, even.

Was my mother's illness taking its toll on him? Or her increasing demands? Or was it something I couldn't discern?

He must have seen the worry and apprehension on my own face, how I was fighting the urge to grab him by the lapels and demand that he not leave me with her like this. He gave me a sympathetic look and touched my shoulder.

"You'll be fine," he promised, smiling a *you've got this* smile as he climbed into the driver's seat of his black SUV. "Call me anytime if you need anything. I'll be back at the end of the week."

He shut the car door and backed away with a quick wave that was more like a salute.

———

A COUPLE OF hours later, we'd all finished dinner. My mother hadn't been hungry but had managed to have a little soup I'd brought in on a tray.

I was in the kitchen cleaning up when someone grabbed me from behind, and I jumped.

"Sorry," Mark said as he wrapped his arms around me, whispering to the back of my head. "I didn't mean to startle you."

"I'm a little on edge, I guess," I said. "And I thought you and Olivia had already left for dance rehearsal."

"We're on our way in a minute. Olivia had to run back upstairs for her sweater."

Mark's arms around me, usually comforting, felt too tight. I didn't like being constricted, trapped, not able to move. I fought the urge to claw at his arms and pull him off me.

"Olivia's quite taken with your mother," he said.

"Mmm." I remembered how worried I'd been to leave the two of them alone. But it had been fine, of course. Better than fine. My mother had been so sweet with her, so tender and kind.

"And maybe it's all the medication she's on, but she seems . . . almost nice. Funny, even. I don't think I've ever seen this side of her." He kissed the back of my head. "This is going to be okay. We did the right thing."

I tried to relax my body and mind, to tell myself that he was right. But I couldn't shake this sense that something was off. That there was something I was missing.

"Dad?" Olivia called from the front hall. "Come on! We're gonna be late!"

"Back soon," he said, squeezing me tighter before finally letting me go.

Izzy was at Theo's. She'd gone in and greeted her grandmother before dinner, been polite, but couldn't seem to wait to get out of the house.

It was just my mother and me at home. I finished up in the kitchen, then headed for the guest room to check on her.

I took a deep breath, like a diver getting ready to go under, and stepped into her room.

"Can I get you anything else?" I asked, making my way over to tidy her bedside table. I gathered up a teacup and water glass, carefully avoiding the stone, which sat right in the center. It seemed to radiate cold, to be pushing me away from it with icy fingers. But surely that was my imagination. It was just a rock. A silly rock that I'd invested with too much power and meaning when I was a kid.

"I want to thank you, Alison. I know it can't be easy," my mother said, her words blurry, slurred. The day had been too much and her pain had caught up with her. At her request, I'd given her an extra dose of morphine just after dinner. Her eyelids seemed heavy, her eyes glazed and narrow. She sank back against the pillows, her face pale and skeletal. "Having me here."

I smiled at her. "Don't be silly. I'm so happy you're here. It's all going to work out wonderfully." I forced the words out, as if reciting a magical incantation, as if just by speaking them out loud I could make it so.

She smiled vaguely at me, closed her eyes.

I stepped back toward the door. Moxie was waiting for me on the other side, watching carefully. She seemed hesitant to come into the room. She usually loved having new people in the house, but didn't they say some dogs could smell cancer? Maybe my mother's frailty and illness was making my normally happy-go-lucky pup uneasy.

My mother popped her eyes open, lifted her head. Something about her movements was all wrong—jerky, like she was being pulled by invisible strings. "You can tell yourself that all you want," she said, her voice mocking and cruel. "But we both know the truth, don't we?"

I froze, clenched my jaw so hard I was afraid it might lock in place. "What truth is that?"

Behind me, Moxie gave a nervous whine.

My mother laughed a tired, dry laugh, then closed her eyes, drifted off without answering.

EVERYONE ALWAYS WANTS TO know about the stone. People ask, but I've never told the story to anyone but you.

The story of the stone is really the story of Bobbi.

We were together that day, but it was Bobbi who found it. She went looking for a ghost and came out with this beautiful stone.

We'd never even planned on going to Mexico. We were supposed to have gone home the week before, but neither of us wanted the trip to end, to return to the real world with all its expectations and realities. I wanted to keep traveling forever; the only time I felt truly at home was when Bobbi was by my side.

So when she suggested the Yucatán Peninsula—where we could lie in the sand, smoke some Acapulco Gold, drink tequila—I was in. It was 1972, and everyone smoked a little grass back then, even Vassar girls.

We met a young man in a little beachside bar down in the Yucatán—Miguel. He was good-looking, I suppose. My Spanish was complete shit. (Still is.) So I only understood a few words of what Bobbi and Miguel were saying, but she kept turning to me to fill me in as she and Miguel spoke.

He was telling her all about a haunted cenote not far from there. A deep pool in limestone—like a cave, but not a cave, she explained as he explained to her. I could tell she was having a hard time understanding the details; she kept having him repeat himself.

"Mal," Miguel said several times. I had no trouble understanding that word. It meant bad.

I also knew the building excitement on Bobbi's face.

I loved watching Bobbi when she talked to people. She was the most expressive person I'd ever known; she'd been the lead in every school play. But it was more than that: she had a natural charisma that stopped people in their tracks. Everyone wanted to be around her, to bask in her glow.

Men fell in love with her on the spot, and strangers just struck up conversations and told her things. Even this trip, locals happily offered her tips for the best beaches, the hole-in-the-wall restaurants and cafés that weren't in any guidebook, the safe and comfortable yet absurdly cheap lodgings. And, of course, the haunted places.

My God, was Bobbi a sucker for ghost stories, for the creepy and macabre. She absolutely loved the Tower of London, all the terrible torture devices. Manacles, the rack, that awful thing called the Scavenger's Daughter.

Bobbi had dragged me to haunted castles, the streets where Jack the Ripper had stalked his victims, the catacombs in Paris, their walls lined with the ornately stacked bones of millions of people.

Anyway, as Bobbi talked to Miguel, she got that look, the one that said soon she'd be dragging me off to a haunted swimming cave.

Miguel told her a whole complicated story about the cenote. He said that back in the early 1900s, there was a European man, filthy rich. He came down and started to build a huge estate there in the village near the water—paid lots of people lots of money to help with the construction. But he went crazy. Started talking to himself. Arguing with himself.

"Loco," Miguel said. I understood that too.

One night, the story went, this rich European got so tired of arguing with the voices in his own head that he drank a bottle of tequila, stuffed his pockets full of heavy rocks, and threw himself into the cenote, sinking straight to the bottom.

Miguel swore that if we went there and swam down deep enough, put our heads under, we'd hear him talking to us. Telling us things only the dead could know.

Bobbi and I drank more tequila and smoked some grass with Miguel— don't tell your mother I told you that part, but you're old enough for the truth—and then he picked up a cocktail napkin and drew a map with directions to the cenote.

An hour later, I was following Bobbi down a trail in the jungle with a flashlight the desk clerk at the hostel had found for us. I was afraid we'd get caught, get thrown into a Mexican jail—like I said, my Spanish was bad, but I understood what NO TRESPASAR *meant, and the signs were all over the place. Also, I was terrified of snakes, of spiders and scorpions. I kept my eyes on the little funnel of light from Bobbi's borrowed flashlight, kept begging her to turn around.*

My head was spinning from the tequila and the grass. I was sure there'd been something else in it—it wasn't a normal high. I didn't feel mellow and at one with the world; I felt like everything around me was jagged and out of place, like a puzzle with sharp edges that didn't want to go back together.

Sorry. Where was I? Following Bobbi, right. I'm sorry, I'm tired. But there's not much more to tell. And I can't stop now. This is the best part.

We got to a chain-link fence with more no-trespassing signs. Someone had cut a hole out of the chain link at the bottom, just big enough for a person to squeeze through. Bobbi checked the map, said this was the place, exactly where Miguel drew it. I protested, said she had to be kidding, could you imagine what kind of creepy-crawlies would be on the ground, and we were going to get lockjaw from that rusty fence . . . but I knew it was no good. Bobbi crawled right through that hole. And I followed her, of course.

We wound our way down a stone-lined path—then we came to a set of steps carved into the pale stone, descending into a narrow passage between two boulders. We squeezed through. The stairs were slippery, uneven. Bobbi told me to be careful and took my hand. Down we walked, the damp limestone walls rising up around us. The temperature dropped as we went down. I felt like we were walking into the center of the earth. Finally we reached the last step. There was a pool of dark water before us, perfectly still. When Bobbi shone the light into it, it reflected back up at us like a great dark mirror.

Bobbi handed me the flashlight and started to undress.

"You're not actually going in there, are you?" I said. I thought she was crazy—the whole thing, the fact that we were even there all, it was just nuts.

You know what she said? "Of course I am. I want to hear what secrets the dead guy has to tell me."

She stood for a few seconds, facing the water, her back to me, her skin pale as alabaster. She looked so perfect, like a goddess carved from stone.

She dove gracefully, barely making a splash.

I waited, scanning the surface of the water with the flashlight beam. The pool wasn't very large—maybe ten feet across.

Bubbles surfaced. But Bobbi stayed down.

I swear my heart was banging so hard in my chest that I was sure I could hear it echoing off the dripping limestone walls in the little chamber.

I called her name.

She'd been under a long time.

Too long.

I kicked off my shoes, set down the flashlight. I'm not the strongest swimmer, and that dark water terrified me, but this was Bobbi down there. My Bobbi.

Then, just as I was about to dive in, Bobbi surfaced, gasping at the air.

"Shine the light over here," she said. "I've got something."

And you know what I thought?

I thought Bobbi had found the bones of that long-dead madman. That she'd come up from that water holding his skull in her hands. I could see it so clearly—the eye sockets leaking dark water like tears.

I bent down for the light and shone it on Bobbi, who was treading water and holding a piece of rock in her hand. But it didn't look like limestone. This rock was clear, with stripes of a darker mineral streaked through it.

Bobbi blinked at the stone, turned it in her hand like it wasn't what she'd expected to see, like she was surprised. She started to say something.

"What?" I asked her.

"Never mind," she said. She swam to the edge of the pool and pulled herself out, still holding the stone.

"Well, did the dead guy speak to you?" I asked.

Bobbi didn't answer. She just kept looking at the stone like it was a puzzle she was trying to solve.

"It's pretty, isn't it?" Bobbi said.

"Sure," I told her. Then I said she should hurry up and get dressed. That place gave me the creeps. I couldn't wait to get out.

But she was right. It is a pretty rock, don't you think?

Can I tell you a secret?

Sometimes when I look at it, I can still see Bobbi in that pool—young, just-out-of-college Bobbi—holding this very stone, treading water. The look on her face. The look of absolute wonder.

Sometimes I think . . . well, it's not important.

Do me a favor, would you?

Move the stone a little nearer to me.

I like to keep it close.

TEN

MOXIE WAS GROWLING.

I opened my eyes. She was at the foot of our bed, hackles raised.

I'd been dreaming about our old house in Woodstock; my mother's house. I was a child again, walking through the dim rooms like a ghost. Nothing was where I remembered. There were doors where there shouldn't be, and I couldn't find my bedroom. I was looking for a place to hide. A good place where she wouldn't find me.

Who do you think you are? she was saying, as she hunted me from room to room.

Only it wasn't my mother. Not really.

She floated rather than walked, and her voice, it was like the sizzle of sparklers on the Fourth of July, the buzzing of insects.

She was wearing a horrible pink dress trimmed with gold.

The same dress worn by the new glass angel hanging in our living room.

But she was no angel.

The dress had turned to a shiny, hardened carapace.

Her abdomen was stretched out, bulbous, and she had six legs that skittered along the floor and wall as she moved toward me.

She was speaking to me, but I couldn't understand her words anymore. They came out in a low droning buzz.

I opened my eyes and looked at the clock: 3:03.

I sat up and gulped in a breath of air, told myself I was safe. I was an adult, safe in my bedroom with my husband snoring softly beside me.

Moxie was still on alert at the foot of our bed, growling deep and low, as if to say, *You really thought you could be safe?*

I shook Mark awake. "Moxie hears something."

"Must be a deer outside," Mark said, rolling over. "Shh, Moxie. Good girl." He sat up, reached down to give her a reassuring pat, then lay back down and plopped a pillow over his head.

Moxie sprang off the bed and started out the bedroom door, still growling. She stepped tentatively as if she was very much afraid of whatever was out there.

The giant insect-woman-angel thing in the pink dress.

Did I hear buzzing from downstairs? Or was that just Moxie's growl?

The floor, the whole house, seemed to vibrate with the droning buzz.

"Mark?" I said, shaking him again.

"Just a deer," he mumbled. "You know that dog and deer."

But when there was a deer in the yard, Moxie would bark and jump at the window.

This was different.

This was something *in the house.*

"Mark?" I said.

"Dogs . . . 'better than human beings because they know, but do not tell,'" he mumbled.

Another Emily Dickinson quote.

Dickinson had had a Newfoundland named Carlo. Mark was full of Dickinson facts and quotes, even in his sleep. But did the poet's dog wake her in the night, growling like this?

"Mark, I don't think it's a deer. She hears something *in the house.*"

No response. Just more gentle snoring.

I loved my husband, but he was useless in the middle of the night. Even when the girls were babies, it was me who always woke when they cried, me who did middle-of-the-night changings and feedings. It was me who got up to soothe bad dreams, to take temperatures, to search for monsters under the bed. It had always been easier for me to just do these things on my own than wake Mark up and hope to get him coherent enough to be actually useful.

I got up now and followed Moxie into the hall. She crept along the carpeted corridor slowly, cautiously. This was very un-Moxie-like behavior. She was one of the most chill dogs I'd ever known. Not reactive or territorial in the slightest. And I'd never known her to be afraid of anything.

I followed, pausing to open Olivia's bedroom door. It stuck, as most of the old doors in our house did, and let out a little creak as I pushed it open. Olivia was there, sound asleep, surrounded by the piles of stuffed animals that she insisted we tuck her in with each night, her ladybug night-light glowing softly.

I pulled her door closed gently, then opened the next door on the right, looked in to see Izzy asleep in her bed, with her headphones on. She looked so young, asleep in Mark's old oversized UVM T-shirt, face bare of makeup, relaxed. Vulnerable. Her room was a mess, clothes and books strewn everywhere, brightly colored empty energy drink cans on every surface. Her desk was covered with things she used for her artwork: old gears, doll parts, cut-up magazines, bits of broken mirror. I spotted a copy of the *I Ching* and a deck of tarot cards. When had my daughter become interested in divination?

There were other kids, I knew, who shared things with their mothers. Who told them about trying pot, who confessed who was hooking up with whom at parties, the little heartbreaks and dramas of teenage life. Izzy used to be like that with me. Just last year she would come home from school or a party to tell me some silly thing Noah had done, or that Chloe wasn't talking to Ella anymore, or that Sasha had been caught vaping in the school bathroom. These days she didn't hang out with the same crowd. She hung out with new kids, kids from the drama club and film club, kids in the LGBTQ Alliance. And suddenly, my daughter was a closed book. A secret keeper. Just like I had been at her age; like I was still.

Four feet in front of me, the dog stood at the top of the stairs, growling so low and deep that the walls seemed to reverberate.

"Shh, Moxie. It's okay," I told her unconvincingly. She started down the stairs, ridge-backed, head down, teeth bared. I didn't think I'd ever seen my goofy, lovable Lab quite this ferocious.

There was a definite hiss from downstairs.

And flickering lights.

I froze, holding tight to the banister, not wanting to follow her. Not wanting to see whatever was down there waiting for me.

I swallowed hard, forced my feet to move forward, as I trailed Moxie down the stairs into the living room.

The television was on, the screen showing only static, the whole room flickering from its white buzzing fire.

My mother was sitting on the couch, staring at the static on the TV, entranced, the remote in her hand.

"Mother?" I said. "What are you doing?"

She was in her white nightgown. Her feet were bare, pale, looking like alabaster against the hardwood floor.

She looked up at me in surprise. "Alison?"

"Yes?"

"What on earth are you doing here?".

I looked around the room. Saw the unlit tree looming in the corner, the new angel swaying slightly, watching us with a cold curiosity. Outside, the moonlight illuminated freshly fallen snow. I could make out the vague shape of the stuffed snowman on the bench, his back to us.

Moxie's demeanor changed completely. She yawned nervously and made her way to her bed in the corner, where she curled in a tight ball, eyes on us.

"It's my house." I swallowed, took a step toward my mother.

"Is it really you?" she asked.

"Of course."

Was this the effect of her medication? Or was it the illness itself? The stress and exhaustion of the day? I made a mental note to talk to the nurse about it in the morning. If this nighttime wandering and confusion was going to be a regular thing, we needed to be ready.

My mother smiled at me. "I'm glad it's you, Ali Alligator. Sometimes they're not who they say they are. Sometimes they put on different faces."

My mouth went dry, my heart jackhammering in my chest. "Who does, Mother?"

"Don't you remember?" she asked.

I shook my head.

My mother looked down at the remote in her hand.

"I've been trying to make a call," she said, pushing buttons. "But I can't get through."

She looked so small, so lost and pitiful. My heart ached a little to see her like this.

"That's the television remote, Mother," I explained, my voice low and soothing.

She put it to her ear like a phone. "I can't get through." She sounded frantic as she waved the remote around, then stabbed at the buttons with her pointer finger.

"Who are you trying to call?"

"Bobbi," my mother said. "I need to talk to Bobbi."

Great. A telephone call to the dead. Just what we needed to be dealing with at three in the morning.

"I need to ask her what to do. If there's a way to stop it."

"Stop what, Mother?"

She clung tightly to the remote, kept pushing the buttons. "Don't pretend you don't know, Ali. That's not going to do either one of us any good."

I walked over, gently took the TV remote from my mother's hands, pressed the power button. The screen went from crackling static to black, and the room dimmed.

"Let's get back to bed, okay?"

I took her gently by the arm, helped her to her feet. She was so light, hardly there. A whisper of a woman.

"Where are we?" she asked, looking around, panic rising.

"My house," I said again, leading her across the living room floor, into the dining room, toward the guest room, which was on the other side of the kitchen.

"We shouldn't be here," my mother said. She whipped her head around, searching the shadows.

"Of course we should. This is where I live. Me and Mark and the girls. And you're staying here with us. Don't you remember? Paul brought you this afternoon."

"It isn't safe," she said, eyes frantic. I thought of the med list Paul had left me—the instructions to give her an Ativan if she seemed agitated. This definitely qualified. One Ativan coming right up.

We got to the guest room door and I guided her through. I helped my mother back into bed, tucked her in the way I'd tucked Olivia in only hours ago.

"Of course it's safe. You're safe here. We're going to take good care of you." I spoke as soothingly as I could. It was my mommy voice, the one I used to chase away bad dreams and fevers.

She laughed. It was a crackling, dry-leaves-brushing-together sort of laugh. "You're the one who isn't safe, Alison. You're the one in danger."

My heart went cold and still inside the cage of my chest.

She looked up at me, grasped my hand with her own, which was bony, clawlike. "It's always been you."

ELEVEN

"Y OU OKAY, LITTLE MOUSE?" I asked, poking my head into Olivia's bedroom. I'd called her down to breakfast three times, and she hadn't come. She was usually the first one downstairs, putting in a complicated breakfast order: cereal with six banana slices and three strawberries, cinnamon toast with cinnamon sugar on both sides of the bread.

But there she was, still in her bed, a lump buried under her pink-and-white quilt, a barricade of stuffed animals around her.

She wriggled under the covers but did not speak.

"Olivia?" I called, staring at the lump, suddenly filled with the totally irrational fear that it wasn't my daughter under there. "What's going on, Liv?"

The lump held still.

Not Olivia. Not Olivia. Not Olivia.

I told my brain to shut up. I was feeling raw and used up. I hadn't really been able to get back to sleep after finding my mother in the living room. I kept replaying what she'd said

You're the one in danger.

It's always been you.

I stepped into Olivia's room now and paused beside the bed. I could see the slight rise and fall of covers—Olivia breathing.

But what if it wasn't her?

I shook my head, told myself I was being silly, that my nightmare and my mother's nighttime wanderings had spooked me. Just the fact of her being here in my house, the way it made my childhood world and my adult world collide, had put me on edge. The world was off-kilter. Frightening.

I wasn't normally a person who spooked easily.

I ate up horror movies, got a little thrill from the jump scares, but rarely actually jumped. I'd always found horror movies cathartic: you went into the theater and faced the terrors and blood and gore there on the big screen and came out feeling this rush because you'd confronted your fears and survived. Watching and reading horror made me feel brave in a way I don't in real life. Mark hated thrillers and horror. He preferred grand historical epics and feel-good romances. And of course he was a sucker for Hallmark Christmas movies, which he admitted were sappy and formulaic. "But that's what's comforting and satisfying about them," he'd explained. "You know exactly what you're getting; you know the couple will end up together in the end, the business will be saved, they'll learn the true meaning of Christmas." I teased him about them all the time: the towns with the stupid holiday names and fake snow, the predictable romances, the cookies and hot cocoa, the accident-prone characters who were always falling down or literally bumping into each other all the time, and the occasional appearance of the real Santa Claus. Ridiculous.

Olivia shifted under the heavy quilt, let out a little puppylike whimper.

"Knock-knock," I said as I counted to three in my head, then held my breath and yanked back the covers to reveal my younger daughter curled up, clutching her favorite stuffed animal, Big Dog.

Of course it was only Olivia. I exhaled in a rush.

She'd had Big Dog since she was a baby. He'd once been white, but was now a sickly gray, his fur matted, his big brown plastic eyes scratched and dull. Olivia looked pale and frightened there in her favorite pajamas with little ballerinas all over them.

I pushed aside some of the animals on the bed and perched next to her, put a hand on her forehead. "You feel okay?" Some of the kids at ballet had been out with the flu. Not what we needed right now. Thank goodness, her forehead was cool.

"I had a bad dream," Olivia said. She pulled Big Dog tighter against her chest.

Me too, I nearly said. *Me too.*

But it was my job to chase away the nightmares. Not to tell her about my own.

I stroked her hair. "You want to tell me about it, little mouse?"

Her chin quivered a little. "I thought . . . I thought maybe it followed me. That he was here hiding under the bed or in the closet maybe, so I didn't want to get out of bed. I thought if I stayed here and hid, he couldn't get me."

All the muscles in my body tightened.

I thought of my mother last night: *I'm glad it's you. Sometimes they're not who they say they are. Sometimes they put on different faces.*

My mother didn't seem to remember any of it this morning. When I'd brought coffee in to her first thing, she'd smiled and greeted me and said she'd slept very well. I'd asked if she'd like a TV in her room so she wouldn't have to go out to the living room, and she said she had no interest in watching television. "But you had the TV on last night," I reminded her.

"I most certainly did not," she said. "I was in here sleeping all night."

"You were in the living room," I said. "With the television on."

She shook her head and looked at me like I'd lost my mind. "I don't even like television, Alison. It's for people with empty inner lives."

Now, keeping my voice calm and level, I asked Olivia, "He who? What are you afraid of, Liv?"

Olivia scrunched up her face, lowered her voice, and looked around the room to make sure we were alone. "The Rat King," she whispered. "I dreamed I was Clara and I had the most beautiful blue dress. And I had pointe shoes, Mom, real pointe shoes like a real ballerina, and I could dance in them, all the way up on my toes—it was like flying!" She looked giddy, then her face darkened. "But *he* was there. He was watching from the shadows, from the wings at the edge of the stage. Then he was onstage, trying to get me. I kept jumping away and spinning, but he just got closer and closer, dancing toward me." Her voice got squeakier, more agitated as she spoke.

I stroked her hair. "Well, it was only a dream, little mouse. There's no Rat King or rat of any sort here."

"Are you sure?" She looked around worriedly.

"Of course I'm sure."

"Will you check?"

I got down on my knees, looked under the bed. "Nothing here," I said. "Unless you count a small dust bunny or two."

I did a dramatic fake sneeze—*aaaa-choo!*—which made Olivia smile.

I opened her closet door, saw the sea of pink and purple clothes, everything bright and sparkly and cheerful. No evil Rat King would dare try to hide in there.

"All clear," I told her. I went over to the window, opened the pink curtains and blinds to let the sun in, filling the room with light.

"Can Moxie come check too?"

I crossed my arms over my chest. "What, you don't trust me?"

"It's just . . ."

"Just what?"

"She can see things we can't."

I thought of the Dickinson line Mark had mumbled last night: how dogs were *better than human beings because they know, but do not tell.*

"Sure," I said, my voice shaky. "Let's get Moxie to come take a look." I went to the door, called the dog. She came running, tail swinging, wondering if maybe she was going to get a cookie.

"Good dog," I said, giving her soft black head a scratch. She sniffed around the room and looked at me, no doubt disappointed that there was no treat. I patted the foot of Olivia's bed and Moxie jumped up, thrilled to be invited. She crawled onto Olivia, licked her face, making her giggle. "See," I said. "She's telling you everything's all right. Now, I think the two of you should hurry downstairs and grab some breakfast. Moxie hasn't eaten yet either."

"Poor Moxie," Olivia cooed, scratching the dog behind the ears.

"We're behind schedule this morning," I said. "Moxie's tummy must be grumbling."

"Can I have gingerbread pancakes?" Olivia asked. "With whipped cream?"

"I'm not sure there's time for that this morning," I said, checking my watch. "I don't want you to miss the bus."

She made a dramatic pouty face.

"How about this: you can have cereal this morning, then we can do breakfast for dinner. I'll make gingerbread pancakes."

"And fruit salad? And bacon?"

I nodded. "All of that." I pulled back the covers fully and took her hand. "Come on, little mouse, hurry up and get ready. I'll go down and get a bowl of cereal for you and make you a lunch."

"Can I eat my cereal with Grandma in her room?" she asked, her face brightening even more.

I smiled. "I'm sure she'd love that."

Olivia frowned.

"What is it?" I asked.

"I think she was in my dream too. Grandma."

"Oh?"

"Only she wasn't Grandma. Not really. She was someone who wasn't nice."

My hand trembled as I reached for her, stroked her hair. "Well, that's how you know it was just a silly nightmare. Because your real grandma is downstairs waiting for you and she's very, very nice, isn't she?"

Olivia smiled and nodded.

I swallowed down the hard lump in my throat.

OLIVIA GOT READY in record time and came racing down the old wooden staircase, the antique maple banister hung with festive pine garland and tied with red bows. Moxie was beside her, nails clicking down the wide stair treads and across the living room and dining room as she went for her food bowl in the corner of the kitchen. It stood right beside the back door that led out to the little herb and salad garden, now dusted with a thin layer of snow. Beside the garden stood a pear tree, branches now bare, the summer's crop of pears canned and frozen and turned into jams and tarts. Olivia grabbed her bowl of cereal off the breakfast bar. Izzy was there with her own bowl of cereal and cup of coffee, headphones on, music thumping out of them as she stared down at her phone.

"Whoa, there, speedy," Izzy said, slipping off her headphones. "Where're you going?"

"I'm gonna eat with Grandma! Wanna come?"

Izzy shook her head, hunched down over her own bowl. "Nah, I'm good here." She slipped the headphones back on, the thumping now turned to an angry wail.

I was in the kitchen making Olivia's lunch. Izzy bought lunch every day, preferring the salad bar in the cafeteria to whatever we had at home. Mark had already left for work. He was out the door every day at six thirty to be at school on time. Sometimes, when he had a lot of prep work to do or an early meeting, he left before six.

Olivia ran into the guest room, carrying her bowl.

"Careful," I called just as she stumbled, then caught herself, milk sloshing.

She was not the most graceful kid.

I went over and wiped up the spilled milk.

"Well, good morning, Olivia," I heard my mother chirp. "How's my favorite ballerina?"

"I had a bad dream."

"Well, hop right up and you can tell me about it. And I'll tell you my trick for keeping bad dreams away."

I thought of last night, of my mother's warning—*You're the one in danger*—and how now, in the light of day, amid the normalcy of our morning routine, that felt like a bad dream. Still, I felt a little knot of apprehension at the idea of Olivia in there with her alone.

They would be fine together, I told myself. Nothing bad was going to happen.

This was what we'd wanted, wasn't it? A chance for the girls to bond with their grandmother.

I went back to the kitchen to finish Olivia's lunch. She liked the same thing every day: a peanut butter sandwich with blackberry jelly, applesauce, Goldfish crackers, and a juice box. If I changed anything, like switched out the applesauce for carrot sticks, or grape jelly instead of blackberry, or crunchy peanut butter instead of smooth, she wouldn't eat it.

The radio in the kitchen was tuned to Vermont Public Radio. I liked the background of people talking, filling me in on everything I needed to know about the world while I got ready for my day. They were doing the weather, talking about a cold front, the possibility of snow overnight.

"It's weird," Izzy said. The headphones were off again, her music paused.

"What is?" I asked, looking up from the peanut butter sandwich I was making. Was she talking about the weather report? Snow in December was hardly weird. In fact, there was a fresh coating outside now: an inch or so had fallen overnight. At this stage, the beginning of winter, the fresh snow always felt magical. By March and April, we'd all groan when we'd wake up to see it coating everything.

Izzy was looking toward the guest room. "Having her here. She's like . . . a stranger. But she's here in our house."

"She's not a stranger. She's your grandmother," I said, keeping my voice light and cheerful.

Izzy took a sip of coffee. She'd started drinking coffee this year but she took it with so much cream and sugar that it was more like melted coffee ice cream.

"She's creepy as hell," Izzy said.

I set down the knife I was using. "Izzy!"

"Well, it's true."

"It isn't true at all." The words came out too defensive, reminding me of all the times I'd been on Team Mom during my arguments with Ben. "She's been incredibly nice since she got here. Your sister loves her."

Izzy set down her coffee cup and stared at me with her big brown eyes lined with heavy black makeup. "That's what's so creepy," she said. "It's like . . . like she's trying too hard. She's saying and doing all the right things. But it just seems . . . I dunno . . . fake. I think I liked her better when she was a grumpy old lady who hated kids."

I opened my mouth to argue, but the words didn't come. They didn't come, I realized, because part of me believed Izzy was right. It did seem almost like my mother was putting on a show for all of us, and Olivia and Mark had totally fallen for it. And hadn't I fallen for it too, there in the hospital when she first asked to come? When she said she had no right to ask, but what she wanted most was a chance to mend things between us before she died. Wasn't it exactly what part of me had always longed to hear?

Was she manipulating us all?

But what a terrible thing to even think about an old woman who was at death's door, and trying her hardest to be grateful to her daughter's family for taking her in. I remembered how pitiful she'd seemed last night in the living room, how sorry I'd felt for her.

"I know this isn't easy," I said at last. "It's not easy for us and it's not easy for her. She's sick and in a new place. She's doing her best. That's what we all need to do."

Izzy shook her head, gave a disgusted, dismissive laugh. "Whatever, Mom."

She grabbed her headphones and slipped them back on, stared down at her phone, her thumbs flying as she started texting or Snapchatting or whatever she was doing. No doubt complaining to Theo about me. I could almost see the words:

My mom is full of shit.

I yanked her headphones off.

"What?" she asked angrily.

"Your grandmother is trying," I said. "Maybe she's trying too hard, and that shows, but at least she's trying. And I'm trying. We're all trying. And I need you to try too."

"Right," she said, narrowing her eyes to slits. "And what is it you'd like me to do, Mom?"

"I don't know, Iz. Just try to make an effort with all of this. With your grandmother being here. Be more engaged."

"More engaged. Got it," she said coolly. She slipped her headphones back on.

I turned away, finished packing Olivia's lunch, checked my watch. "Five minutes till the bus gets here," I said.

Izzy slid off her stool. "Believe it or not, I can tell time, Mom."

Ignoring her, I went into the guest room with Moxie at my heels.

The dog stopped in the doorway, watching.

Olivia was up on the bed next to my mother, who was whispering something to her.

"Olivia, it's almost time for the bus," I said, forcing an *everything's perfectly normal here* smile. "Come on out and grab your things and get your coat on. Your sister's waiting."

"Okay, Mom," she said, slipping off the bed. Then she stopped, turned back, and kissed my mother on the cheek. "I'll see you later."

"Not if I see you first," my mother said.

Olivia laughed.

Since when had my mother become the snappy comeback queen?

"Come on, Liv," I said, taking her hand. "Let's get your things together."

I led Olivia into the living room, helped her get her lunch bag into her backpack.

"Let's go, slowpoke!" Izzy said.

"I'm not a slowpoke!" Olivia stamped her feet. I shot Izzy a look. Calling Olivia slow or telling her to hurry only slowed her down more.

"Whatever. I'm heading out. I don't want to miss the bus."

"I don't want to miss it either!" Olivia shrieked, suddenly panic-stricken. She raced for her jacket and then dropped it, realizing her hat was still in the closet.

"No one's missing the bus," I said, helping Olivia into her jacket while Izzy went out the front door and started down the driveway, her black boots leaving footprints in the fresh snow. "Have a good day, Iz," I called after her. She didn't respond. So I responded for her: "Thanks! You too, Mom!"

I grabbed Olivia's panda hat and stuck it on her head, pulling the ear flaps down. "Hey, Liv?"

"Yeah?"

"What was your grandma saying to you when I came in? When she was whispering to you?"

Olivia grinned. "I can't tell you, Mom," she said, pulling on her mittens and grabbing her backpack.

Goose bumps ran up and down my arms, each little hair standing up like a soldier at attention. My jaw clenched, but I forced myself to smile. "Oh yeah? Why not?"

"It's a secret," she said with a giggle, tearing out the door to follow her sister.

TWELVE

I F SHE HADN'T HAD a hospice name badge hanging from a lanyard around her neck, I would never have guessed that the woman who showed up at our front door was the nurse Paul had hired. Teresa was wearing faded leggings, Birkenstocks over thick socks, and a Grateful Dead T-shirt. Her wild, curly gray hair was in a loose braid that hung down between her shoulder blades. She carried a battered leather satchel and wore an amethyst crystal on a silver chain around her neck.

My first thought when I opened the door and shook her hand was *Oh, shit, my mother's going to hate you.*

Moxie came and greeted her.

"Aren't you a beauty," Teresa said, giving Moxie's ears a good scratch. Moxie reciprocated by giving her hand a few good licks.

"That's Moxie," I said. "If you're not careful, she'll cover you in dog kisses."

"There are far worse fates," Teresa said.

She would know, wouldn't she—this woman who shepherded people from the land of the living to the realm of the dead.

"Come on in, my mother's room is right through here."

I led the poor unsuspecting nurse into my mother's room and steeled myself for whatever snarky comment was to come.

Teresa dropped her bag on the floor, walked right up to the side of the bed, and took my mother's hand.

I bit my lip. This well-intentioned woman definitely didn't stand a chance. My mother was not a touchy-feely person.

"Mavis, it's so nice to meet you," the nurse said, her voice soothing and genuine. "I'm Teresa from Kingdom Hospice. I'll be your primary nurse. You'll see others, but it'll mostly be me. You and I are going to be spending a lot of time together." She gave my mother a smile that seemed to warm the whole room. "And I'm going to give you and your daughter my cell number. I'm available anytime, night or day. If you have a question, if you need anything at all, you call me. If I can't help you, I promise I'll find someone who can."

Mother smiled, patted the nurse's hand. "Saint Teresa," she said. "I like your shirt."

I blew out the breath I didn't realize I'd been holding.

"Thank you," Teresa said.

"I used to love the Grateful Dead," Mother said.

I looked at her, squinting like I was trying to bring her into focus, to recognize just who this person in the rented hospital bed was. "What? You did?" There was no hiding my shock.

My mother nodded and grinned. "Oh yes. Bobbi and I used to go to their shows."

I barked out a laugh. "You're kidding!" I couldn't picture it at all: my mother noodle dancing with the Deadheads to "Fire on the Mountain" in a cloud of pot smoke.

"No, dear," my mother said. Now I was *sure* the sickness and meds were messing with her—she'd never called me *dear* in her life. I looked from her to Teresa, suspecting my mother was putting on a show for the nurse. Playing the role of a tender and thoughtful parent, dying peacefully and gratefully surrounded with love in her daughter's home.

My mother went on, "During college we followed them all over New England, up and down the East Coast, in fact. Bobbi was a huge fan—and it wasn't just the music, it was the whole experience. It was quite a scene, really, the camps that would form around the arenas—a sea of tie-dyed T-shirts, tapestries, blankets, and tents in parking lots and parks. We sold jewelry at the shows."

How had I never heard this before? "Really?" I said.

Sure, I knew my mom had graduated from Vassar in 1972 and must have lived through the whole hippie thing, but I'd never imagined her being a part of it in that way. I knew she was a fan of classic rock, that she sometimes sang along with old songs on the radio. But somehow I'd missed hearing about this entire chapter of her life.

She nodded. "Crystals and beads wrapped in wire. We camped in the back of Bobbi's old Ford station wagon and made enough money for a little food and gas to get to the next show."

I shook my head, still unable to picture any of it.

What else didn't I know about my mother and her life before me?

Teresa smiled. "It's entirely possible our paths crossed back then. I went to quite a few shows myself."

"Maybe I sold you a crystal necklace," my mother said.

"Maybe you did," Teresa said with a smile as she touched her own necklace.

"That's a beautiful amethyst," my mother said. She turned, looked at her piece of quartz on the bedside table. "It's been years since I've listened to the Grateful Dead," she said wistfully.

"I could play some later if you'd like," I suggested.

Mother smiled. "'Box of Rain.' That was always one of my favorites."

"Mine too," Teresa said. She opened her bag and pulled out some paperwork. "Okay, so today we'll get the not-so-fun stuff out of the way before the music and dancing can commence. We're going to do the intake paperwork, then we'll go over all your meds and talk about the game plan."

"The game plan," my mother said, smiling darkly, "is for me to die in the end."

My breath hitched. It's not that I didn't know and accept the truth: she was going to die, and it would be sooner rather than later. But it didn't feel fair. I wanted more time. Time to mend things, as my mother had promised. Time for us to try to get to know each other again. Hearing the anecdote about the Grateful Dead shows made me realize how much I longed to learn all the things I didn't know about her.

The truth was, I wanted more good stories, good memories to help drive away the bad ones. After my mother was gone, I wanted to be able to remember her as having once danced to the Grateful Dead and sold crystal necklaces at their shows, as an amazing artist who taught me to paint and draw, leaving behind her own legacy—a love of art passed down to me, then to my own daughter.

Teresa nodded, took my mother's hand again. To my surprise, my mother clutched at Teresa's hand and squeezed right back. "That's the plan for all of us one day, isn't it?" the nurse said. "But we're here to support you in the journey in the way you wish to go, surrounded by your loved ones and being as comfortable as possible. We're going to make sure you have everything you need."

"Sounds like we're planning a cruise," my mother said. There was a little glimpse of the mother I recognized, snarky comment and all. I had to smile, laugh out loud even. And my mother laughed with me.

We got the paperwork done and the meds sorted. Teresa set up a chart, even more detailed than the one Paul had left, to help me keep track of them. My mother had been prescribed long-acting morphine every twelve hours but could get an extra dose of short-acting morphine every four hours if she needed it. There were minimum and maximum doses to be followed based on her level of pain. We reviewed a ridiculous pain chart with a smiling green face at one end (for zero/no pain) and a red frowning face with tears (ten) at the other. She also had Ativan available for anxiety. Teresa said this was a common med—anxiety was a perfectly natural part of the end-of-life process. Then there were the pills for the side effects of the other pills—laxatives, antinausea meds—each with their own instructions for when and how much to give, and what to do if they didn't work.

My mother seemed exhausted and in considerable discomfort by the end of the visit. Teresa asked her to rate her pain from zero to ten—"You both need to practice," she told us—and gave her a dose of short-acting morphine when my mother told her she was at seven. Soon afterward, my mother drifted off to sleep.

"Is it really okay to give her so much morphine?" I asked as I walked Teresa out.

"It's our job to keep her as pain-free as possible. Am I worried about opiate addiction in a patient who's in her last weeks of life? No. If she's in pain, give her the as-needed dose. Just document it—depending on how much of the short-acting she's requiring, we may up her long-acting. But never give her more than the maximum amount listed on the bottle, unless you talk to me first. Too much could slow her breathing, even stop her heart."

I nodded.

"Last night my mother was up wandering around the house at three in the morning. She seemed . . . out of it. She didn't remember where she was or how she'd gotten here. Do you think that could be the medication?"

Teresa frowned. "Could be. Could be her illness. Probably a combination of the two. But being up and wandering in her condition is dangerous, especially in an unfamiliar space. She's too frail and unsteady on her feet. The very last thing we want is for her to fall and break a hip. We want her to spend her last days here, with her family, rather than in pain in a hospital." She paused, thinking. "Definitely put up the rails on the sides of the bed at night. And let's up her Ativan before bed. Give her two pills tonight instead of one and see if that helps. If you're both up in the night, give her more morphine and Ativan if it's after one a.m."

"Okay."

"Do you have an old baby monitor by any chance?"

"Um . . . maybe in the basement. I can check."

"It might be useful. You could put it in her room, and if she gets up, hopefully you'll hear her. Also, if she wakes up and needs anything, all she has to do is call for you."

I nodded. "If I can't find our old one I'll get a new one."

"There are bed alarms we could get too, but I don't think we want to go to that route. Not yet. We don't want to agitate her or frighten her."

"No," I said. "Definitely not."

"We just need to do all we can to keep her safe."

I nodded, thought again of last night.

You're the one who isn't safe, Alison. You're the one in danger.

TERESA WAS GONE, my mother was conked out from her meds, and I wandered the house like a ghost. I felt keyed up, restless. Moxie followed me, looking nervous, feeding off my energy.

I grabbed my phone and called Penny.

"How's it going?" she asked.

"Better than I expected, but . . ."

"What?"

"My mother kind of freaked me out last night."

"Oh?"

"She was up wandering and she seemed . . . confused. She told me I was in danger."

"Yeah, I guess that would freak me out too. Do you think the night wandering will be a regular thing?"

"I hope not. We're going to up her meds and see if that helps. During the day she seems fine. Better than fine, actually. She's funny and charming. Mark and Olivia love her."

Penny could hear the hesitancy in my voice. "But?" she said.

"I just can't let go of this worry I have. And every time I leave Olivia alone with her, I'm just waiting for something awful to happen. For her to do or say something frightening."

"And has she?"

"No. She's actually very sweet with Liv."

"Ali, this is all really hard. It's going to be a huge adjustment. Go easy on yourself, okay? Try not to let that hamster wheel of worry spin out of control."

I laughed. "I'll try."

"Stay focused on the moment. Remember to breathe. To take time for yourself. And trust that things are going to be okay. You're all going to find your way through this."

I thanked Penny and hung up, deciding to focus my energy on household chores.

I washed the breakfast dishes.

I gathered up laundry from hampers and started a load. I swept the laundry room, which was beside the kitchen in what had once been the pantry. We had kept the original deep porcelain sink in there, and some of the shelves. We stored all our cleaning supplies there, and on the right wall some extra pantry items like the glass jars of pears Mark and I canned each summer from the tree in the yard, a few bottles of wine, overflow canned goods, and supplies we used when the power went out: bottled water, candles, flashlights, a radio, extra batteries, and a little camping stove. I'd always found comfort in knowing these things were there, that we were prepared.

Mark texted at noon to check in, and I wrote back telling him all was well and that Teresa the nurse had been a hit with my mother. And apparently, my mother is a secret Grateful Dead fan, I wrote.

He sent me a series of laughing-until-you-cry emojis.

I went down into the basement, found a box of old baby things, things I'd been meaning to go through for years, and pulled out the monitors we'd used with Olivia. They were buried beneath her baby blanket, the little hat she'd worn home from the hospital, a soft rattle shaped like an elephant, and a few tiny outfits I hadn't been able to part with.

Seeing it all hit me with a pang of nostalgia, a sense of time moving too fast—how was the little baby who'd worn that pink onesie six years old already? I lifted the clothing and blanket to my face, hoping to catch a scent of her baby self, but all I smelled was the musty staleness of the basement.

Mark and I had not planned to have a second child. Izzy was going to be our one and only. It was something we discussed, something we were both comfortable with. The truth was, I'd been so stressed during my first pregnancy and Isabelle's infancy that I wasn't sure I could do it again. Izzy had been a difficult baby—she was colicky, cranky, and only seemed to settle when she was in motion. The kid did not like to be put down. Mark and I wore her strapped to our chests and danced and bounced her to sleep. And Mark believed having one child was the right thing to do, ethically, in an overpopulated world.

I was thirty-seven when I got pregnant with Olivia. Izzy was in fourth grade. I was on the pill. I wasn't supposed to get pregnant—it was the very last thing Mark or I expected. I remember showing him the drugstore test I'd taken—the two of us blinking down in disbelief at the plus sign.

I'd cried while he held me, promised me it would be okay. "We can do this," he'd said. "We can have this baby. But if you don't want to—"

From the moment I saw that plus sign, there was never a question in my mind. I knew I wanted this child. I was scared, yes. Felt like I was too old, like it might test me in every possible way. But yes, I wanted her. I wanted her desperately. I told Mark all of this, asked if he was sure it was what he wanted too. He agreed without hesitation, both of us crying as he kissed me, kissed my face, my belly, started talking to the baby, who was only the size of a sesame seed. He went out and got pickles and ice cream to celebrate (a truly disgusting combination) and we stayed up all night after putting Izzy to bed, talking about what they might be like, this new child who'd come into our lives.

"Our little accident," I called her jokingly, and he corrected me.

"There are no accidents," he'd said. "Not really. Everything happens for a reason."

Then my worrying started. "But I'm thirty-seven. There are risks. What if something's wrong? What if we can't afford it? What if I—"

"It's a leap of faith," he said, wrapping his arms around me, kissing me. "A leap of faith we're taking together, side by side, just like always. Forever and ever. "

I BROUGHT THE monitors upstairs to the kitchen and loaded them with fresh batteries. They seemed to work fine.

I went into Olivia's room, made the bed, and piled it with all the stuffed animals that were on her floor. I grabbed a book and a few toys to stage a play session with them: Big Dog was reading a book on Labrador retrievers; Samuel the skunk was playing Go Fish with Hedgie the hedgehog; Trixie the rabbit was hanging upside down from the bedpost—she was always getting into mischief. Olivia got a kick out of seeing what her menagerie had been up to while she was away at school.

Then I went into Izzy's room, stepping tentatively, as if there might be a bear trap or trip wire waiting. A secret camera stashed somewhere maybe, ready to capture proof that I'd trespassed, had been nosing around, searching for . . . what? Drugs? A stash of unexplained money? Some tiny thing that might give me some insight into my older daughter's world and what secrets she might be keeping?

It felt all wrong, violating her privacy like this.

I froze, took a step back, telling myself this wasn't the right thing to do. Mark wouldn't approve. He was all about everyone in our family respecting one another's personal space.

"Teens need autonomy," he was always saying. "We need to give Izzy permission to make her own decisions, her own mistakes."

Izzy, who tended to rebel against anything she deemed normal and conventional, sometimes even rebelling just for the sake of rebelling, was a straight-A student. One of those kids who excelled at whatever she threw herself into. And she'd thrown herself into a whole variety of things over the years: ballet, field hockey, gymnastics, chess club, drama club, and, these days, the high school film club and her art projects.

"She's exceptionally talented," her art teacher, Ms. Paresky, had said at our last parent-teacher conference night while showing us a series of collages and small sculptures Izzy had made from trash collected from the river behind the high school. Hiding in each sculpture was a monster with red light-up LED eyes. A symbol representing the scourge of pollution, Izzy had explained.

She had one of the trash collages hanging on the wall above her bed now: an old bicycle wheel transformed into a strange mandala, the spokes woven with ribbon, candy bar wrappers, rope, hair. Peeking out from behind the spokes was a dark face with glowing red eyes: the monster of things abandoned and discarded. It spooked me—my daughter's ability to bring life to trash, to make it feel like a sinister creature watching me from her wall.

I turned away from the wheel monster and took in the rest of Izzy's room, which was in its usual state of disarray. There were clothes scattered on the floor—impossible to tell what was dirty and what was clean. The desk was cluttered with her computer, books, drawings, a strange assortment of objects she used for her collage and assemblage pieces: cut-up magazines and newspapers, broken clock parts, blue jay feathers, nuts and bolts. There was a soldering iron and a hot glue gun. The *I Ching* and the tarot deck I'd noticed last night.

I stepped forward, studying the bedside table: a coffee cup, an empty energy drink can, chargers for her phone and headphones. I opened the drawer. More chargers, pens, a single earring, a safety pin, hand cream, the butt of an old black eyeliner pencil, a couple of AA batteries. Nothing shocking or nefarious. No weed or vape pens or strange pills. I shut the drawer, and held very still, listening.

There was a faint buzzing.

I thought of last night. Of my dream. Of my mother chasing me, my mother the wicked insect angel. I was sure I could feel her behind me, watching, reaching for me with quivering little feelers, grotesque wings outstretched.

I swallowed hard. My mouth tasted like tin. I turned around.

Nothing.

Of course not.

My mother—my actual mother, not the nightmare insect-angel version—was sleeping downstairs. And the girls were at school. Mark was at work. Moxie was curled up on her dog bed in the living room.

It was only the first full day of my mother being here, and I was already losing it.

Not good. Not good at all.

I needed to get a grip. Take a nap to help clear my head, maybe. I thought of Penny's advice and took a deep breath.

Then held still, listening again.

There was something there in the silence; something that didn't belong. Not the hiss and thump of the old radiators or the click and hum of the refrigerator coming on downstairs. Not the sighing creak of the house settling.

This was a small buzz. The tiniest taps, like fingertips against glass.

Thump, thump, thump.

It was coming from behind the heavy blackout curtains hung over Izzy's window. The girl didn't like sunlight.

I stepped forward on rubbery legs.

My fingers brushed the surface of the heavy dark curtains, grabbed an edge.

I don't want to see, I don't want to see, I don't want to see, a voice in the back of my head screamed.

There it was again, louder this time.

Buzzing. A soft *thump, thump, thump.*

Something outside, tapping on the glass, wanting in.

My body rigid, I jerked open the curtain. Winter sunlight blinded me for a second, made me squint my eyes nearly closed. Then I saw it.

There was a large black fly banging hopelessly against the double-paned glass of the window.

No.

Not just one fly.

I looked down and saw that below that one there were dozens of them. Thick, fat flies all huddled together in the bottom corner, buzzing, banging against the window, trying to get out. They formed a grotesque mass that seemed to move as one, roughly shaped like a human hand, pressing against the glass, thudding and tapping.

Wincing, I unlatched the lock on the window and yanked the sash up, cold air streaming in. The flies readjusted, crawling over each other, the fingers on the hand stretching out. I grabbed a video equipment catalog from Izzy's desk and used it to shoo the horrid little intruders outside. I shoved at them with the catalog, corralled them, whacked at them once they were in the air. They were slow, sleepy almost, as they flew drunkenly away once forced outside. A few of them remained in the room, buzzing heavily around, thumping into the walls and ceiling. I swatted at the ones I couldn't force out the window, their not-so-tiny bodies making a sickening mess on the rolled-up glossy catalog. When I was sure I had every last one of them, I yanked the window closed and latched it, let myself catch my breath.

I wiped the fly guts off the walls, threw away the catalog. I searched Izzy's room for food left out, some reason for them being there: a rotting apple core, a plate of crumbs. There was nothing but the coffee cup and a few empty energy drink cans. I grabbed the cup and cans and left the room, my skin feeling twitchy, my eyes searching the shadows for movement, my ears listening for the buzz and thump of any little intruders I might have missed.

THIRTEEN

I'VE BEEN WAITING FOR you," my mother said.

She'd been asleep for nearly three hours.

She was leaning back against the pillows, her hair going in strange directions, her skin a pale and sickly yellow against the white pillowcases. The dark circles under her eyes looked like sockets. She was sinking into herself, becoming more skeletal by the hour.

"I didn't know where you were," she said, sounding as distressed as a little girl who'd gotten lost in the grocery store, separated from her mother. "I woke up and there were bars on my bed and I couldn't get them down." She reached for the side rails and rattled them.

"I'm sorry," I said. "They're not bars, they're rails so you won't fall out of bed. You should have called out to me. I was just in the kitchen, I would have heard you. I've been making homemade chicken noodle soup," I added with a smile. "Paul said it's one of your favorites."

I stepped into her room, carrying the baby monitor, the Bluetooth speaker, and my iPad.

"What's all this?" my mother asked, frowning.

"The monitor is so I can hear you if you call for me, no matter where I am in the house. Or if I go out to my studio." I showed her the little battery-operated receiver I'd carry with me.

"So no more waking up wondering where you are? Wondering if anyone's going to come at all?" She stared at me accusingly. "Feeling like a prisoner."

I felt terrible.

"I'm sorry," I said again. "With the monitor set up, all you have to do is call and I'll be right in," I promised. "I'll be able to hear you from anywhere in the house."

"And what's that?" she asked, looking suspiciously at the Bluetooth speaker I was setting up.

"A little surprise," I said.

I cued up a playlist on my iPad.

"Just wait," I said. "You're going to like this."

"Box of Rain" started to play. I smiled at my mother.

"What the hell is this?" Mother hissed, eyes narrowed into slits, snake-like, cold and silver.

"The song you asked for," I stumbled. "The Grateful Dead. Remember you said—"

"Turn it off!" Mother ordered. "Now!"

"But you—"

"I don't listen to music like that! It's noise. Dirty white noise." Spittle flew from her mouth as she spoke. She'd bolted up to a sitting position, her hand gripping the safety bar on the side of the bed, rattling it, trying to push it down like she was going to either run away or come at me.

What had happened to the wistful Deadhead from this morning? The one who'd called me *dear*?

Was this the medication? The pain?

Had she just totally forgotten requesting the song?

I stopped the music. "Okay," I said, doing my best to keep my voice calm and cheerful. "I'm sorry. I thought—"

"You didn't think. You never think," she said.

Her words were like hooks that dug into me, dragging me back to my childhood, to the way she'd get mean after a few drinks.

She's sick, I told myself. *She woke up alone and she was scared.*

I took a deep breath, determined to turn this around. "Is there something you'd rather hear?"

She grinned up at me. But it was a twisted, maniacal grin. A smile I recognized from when I was a little girl. A rictus grin tightening every muscle in her face, showing her little yellow teeth.

The scars on my back twinged.

I wanted to run. To get the hell out of there.

"A bird with a broken wing at the bottom of a well," she said, her voice a low hiss.

My heart banged hard in my chest. "I beg your pardon?"

"A pitiful scream no one can hear."

My mouth went dry. I started to back out of the room. "I . . . I'm going to check on the . . . on the soup," I stammered.

"*Eee-eee-eee*," Mother squeaked. "Poor little blue jay dying all alone down there."

"I'll be back with a bowl of soup and some crackers," I told her, forcing the words out as I fought not to run screaming from the room.

My mother smiled. "*Eee-eee-eee*," she sang. "You remember, don't you, Alison?"

I ducked out of the room, shaking my head. *No, no, no, no!*

I hurried to the kitchen, leaned my back against the wall and made myself take deep breaths. My legs felt weak and rubbery. I slid down so that I was crouched, all tucked up like a little girl, hiding there in the corner of my kitchen. Tears burned my eyes.

Moxie came to check on me, nosing at my face.

"I'm okay, girl," I told her.

But I wasn't okay. Not really.

It was impossible.

There was no way for my mother to know about the bird in the well. No one knew. No one had ever known. Not Ben. Not even Mark or Penny. No one. Ever.

I closed my eyes and saw it, heard it: the broken blue jay at the bottom of the well, its screeches echoing through time and space, finding their way back to me.

IT HAD HAPPENED about a year or so after my father died. His suicide had left me wrecked and angry all the time. I didn't want to process or try to make sense of things. I was eight years old, and my world had been turned upside down and inside out. I wanted to hurt everything around me.

In addition to the constant anger, I felt alone in a way I never had before. My mother's drinking escalated without my dad there anymore to run interference, to keep her in check. She took to day drinking, and when I got home from school in the afternoon, I never knew who'd I find there. A kind mother who'd baked cookies and wanted to go to town so we could visit the bookstore or get new art supplies, or a drunk mother, angry as a hornet and looking for someone to sink her stinger into.

I was always exhausted when I got home from school: it was mentally and physically draining to pretend all day, to play at being a good and happy girl, a straight-A student whose mother didn't drink, whose father hadn't killed himself, whose back wasn't covered in scars.

Ben had changed too. He was around less and didn't have much time for his little sister anymore. He had either soccer or basketball practice every day after school and wouldn't come home until dinnertime, and usually not even then, choosing to go eat at a friend's house and play video games, maybe even spend the night. When he was home, he locked himself in his room after dinner to do homework and play video games and wouldn't open the door when I knocked and called out to him.

But I didn't have sports or friends to keep me after school, so on the days my mother greeted me in the front hall, reeking of gin, saying, "I'm afraid I'm not quite myself today," I took that as a warning to get out and stay out. I went out into the woods, no matter the weather.

I'd drop off my school bag, put on sturdy boots, and grab Ben's BB gun.

It was stored in the back of the hall closet along with my dad's old red-and-black-checked wool hunting jacket—one of the few pieces of his clothing my mother hadn't thrown into Hefty bags and hauled off to the Salvation Army. I'd put on the huge jacket that I was lost inside, grab the gun, and slink out the back door in the kitchen, crossing the backyard. Our house, a large two-story colonial painted slate gray, felt like a prison I was escaping from. Even with the lights on, the house always felt dark and cold, as if it were made of damp stone and not hundred-year-old wood. The curtains were always closed and the windows never opened: the house was stuffy and airless, like being in a tomb.

My mother's studio was at the rear of the house in what had once been the old enclosed porch. You got to it through a door at the back of the dining room. The back door in the kitchen led out to the patio—this was the door I'd sneak out of carrying the gun, quietly easing the door closed and running across the patio, then the lawn and toward the woods that lined the rear of the property.

I never let myself turn and look back as I walked away. To catch my mother's attention as I made my escape was bad luck. I kept my eyes on the trees and my hands wrapped tightly around the gun as I moved, feeling both her and the house itself watching me.

The woods behind our house went on for miles. There were old logging roads where people rode dirt bikes and four-wheelers in warmer weather and snowmobiles in the winter. But I stayed off the roads, making my own path through the dense forest, exploring.

I'd walk for hours, shooting at anything that moved. Or anything that didn't. I shot up NO TRESPASSING signs. Old beer bottles. Aimed at squirrels, chipmunks, birds, although I never got one. My aim was terrible.

About a mile behind our house, off a long-forgotten trail, I'd discovered an abandoned cellar hole where a house once stood. I never told my mother or brother about it. I never took either of them back there to show it to them. It was my secret discovery, a place that was mine and mine alone.

The crumbling stone foundation was shot through with saplings and layered with decades of leaf litter. I'd found things in and around where the old house had stood: a rusted pot, an old glass bottle, a silver spoon, a metal button. I used to imagine the family who might have lived there once, and in my mind, they were the mirror version of our family: a mother and father, son and daughter. I told myself they'd been happy. They'd had a good life. They'd stayed together and loved each other very much. Then, when the unfairness of their imagined happiness felt like it was too much to bear, I conjured terrible things to have happened to them: a flu, a fire, a murder-suicide. I took away their happily-ever-after ending and made it gruesome. And now I was standing, literally, in the ruins of their lives, feeling very pleased with myself.

Behind the cellar hole was an old well, a circle of stone that went down about forty feet. It was dried up—no water at the bottom, only a carpet of rotten leaves. I'd drop acorns and pebbles down just to watch them plunge to the bottom without a sound. I made little figures out of twigs, forming arms and legs, small bodies bound together with grass. I'd line them up along the edge and push them in just to watch them fall.

Sometimes I'd talk to the well, shout down into it, my own words echoing back out at me. I talked to my father, mostly, raging at him. "WHY, WHY, WHY?" I shouted. "HOW COULD YOU LEAVE US?" I'd yell and cry and think about how his arms around me had felt solid and safe, about the huge paintings he did that he saw whole worlds inside, about how he'd called me his Moppet. "I HATE YOU!" I'd yell down as if he now resided there like a magic toad living at the bottom of the well.

Then I'd wipe the tears from my eyes with the sleeve of his scratchy wool jacket, pick up the gun, and go back to shooting.

I never expected to hit anything.

I dreamed of it, though.

I wanted to hit a wild creature. To make it suffer.

I felt something sick and poisonous inside me, and I thought that if I could just hurt something else, it might make my own pain less severe. That it might somehow make things better.

But when I actually hit the blue jay, saw it fall from the spindly aspen tree, hop around trying desperately to fly, its wing badly damaged, it didn't feel cleansing or cathartic. It felt like I'd become a monster.

I stood over it, watching it flutter and hop in circles, screeching.

My heart banged in my chest, a frantic bird of its own. My hands on the gun were slippery with sweat and ached from gripping it so tightly.

I tried to kill the blue jay. To put the poor squeaking creature out of its misery. I found a big rock, held it over the bird, but couldn't bring myself to drop it.

Eee-eee-eee went the bird, frenzied, flapping in circles.

But it turned out that I was not a killer. Only a maimer of innocent creatures.

I took off my father's coat, then my sweatshirt, which I used to wrap up the frantic bird, thinking I should run home, try to find a vet or a bird rescue center. Call some adult who could help me.

But that's not what I did.

Because if I brought it home, I'd have to tell everyone what I'd done.

Have them see me for what and who I truly was.

Admit that my mother was right after all: I was a kid not worth loving. I was a terrible, worse-than-useless child with something dark and poisonous inside me. Maybe she really should have drowned me at birth.

I carried the bird, wrapped in my sweatshirt, to the well.

I held it there a second, over the opening that looked like a great dark mouth.

I felt the blue jay fluttering desperately in my hands, its tiny bird heart racing.

I dropped it down.

Watched it fall.

I turned away, hurried off, thinking that maybe I'd be able to forget about it. To not hear its pitiful, desperate cries. But the rounded walls of the well just amplified it.

Eee-eee-eee, it cried after me as I ran through the woods, away from that old well, tripping on roots, branches scratching my face.

Eee-eee-eee.

It was the most terrible thing I'd ever done.

Even now, all these years later, I found myself back at that well in my nightmares, listening to the bird screech.

I knew it was long gone, its bones turned to dust, but I could hear it still.

And now the sound was coming from my mother's room.

"*Eee-eee-eee,*" she cried, a perfect imitation.

But how could she have possibly known?

FOURTEEN

W HO'S GOING TO BRING me to rehearsal at the opera house this weekend?" Olivia asked.

"I don't know yet, sweetie. It's only Tuesday. The weekend feels like a long way off right now." My head ached. I was feeling raw and tired, completely used up, and it was only six p.m.

"But it's *not*," she said. "Not really. And whoever goes can sit and watch the dress rehearsal. Don't you want to see me in my mouse costume?"

"I think I'd rather be surprised when we're there on opening night," I said.

Olivia made a pouty face, shoved a bite of pancake into her mouth.

"The mouse costumes are the same every year anyway," Izzy said. "The same ones I wore way back when I was a level one."

Olivia's eyes got huge. "You were a mouse?"

"Of course. All level ones start out as mice."

Olivia stared at her sister, mystified, unable to believe that way back before Olivia was even born, Izzy had been a mouse.

We were sitting around the table having breakfast for dinner, as I'd promised Olivia this morning: gingerbread pancakes, bacon, and fruit salad. This morning felt like a million years ago. I stabbed a grape and it jumped away from my fork.

"Are you all going to be able to come on opening night?" Olivia asked.

"Of course we'll all be there," Mark said.

"But who's going to stay with Needle?" Olivia asked, suddenly worried.

"Needle?" I said. Had I heard her right?

I glanced over at Mark and he gave me a *that kid says the darndest things* shrug. He was right, of course. Olivia had quite an active imagination, and on top of that, sometimes her thoughts seemed to come so fast that she couldn't get them out quickly enough and the words got mixed up.

"Grandma," she corrected. "She can't be alone, right?"

I nodded. "Right. I don't know. I honestly hadn't thought about it until just now, but we've got plenty of time to figure it out. Maybe we can get Teresa or one of the nurses from hospice. Or maybe Penny could come sit with her? I'm sure she'd be happy to help out and I think she and your grandmother would get along well."

"I wish Grandma could come see the ballet," Olivia said.

"I know, sweetie," I said. "Me too. But she's just too sick to sit up for that long."

"Gina's dad, Will, is shooting a video on opening night," Mark said. Will worked for the local cable access station and was always in charge of making a professional-quality video of *The Nutcracker*. "I'll talk to him, see if we can get a copy right away. Then we can have our own private showing with her at home."

"In Grandma's room?" Olivia asked eagerly.

"Sure," Mark said. "We can wheel the TV in and all watch together."

"With popcorn? Like on movie night?" she wanted to know.

"Popcorn, Twizzlers, Butterfingers. All the good stuff," Mark said.

Olivia wriggled in her seat with excitement. "Will you watch it with us too, Izzy? In Grandma's room?"

"Sure," Izzy said. "Can someone pass the syrup?"

I'd invited my mother to join us at the table, but she was too tired, and asked to have dinner on a tray. I'd been tiptoeing around her all afternoon, both wanting and dreading to bring up the subject of the blue jay. How could she possibly have known about it? She hadn't mentioned it again, though. No more terrible *eee-eee-eee*s. She'd been downright pleasant when I went back in with her soup, which she claimed was the best she'd ever tasted. She was equally effusive about the pancakes—"I don't believe I've ever had a gingerbread pancake before, and certainly never for dinner, but I can see why they're Olivia's favorite food—they're delicious, Ali." Despite her compliments, she didn't eat much of anything. A few bites here and there.

Olivia had been chattering excitedly about rehearsal since she got home from school: how next weekend she'd be at the old opera house with her ballet company all day Saturday, blocking the scenes, trying on costumes, and doing a full dress rehearsal. The show was the following weekend.

Izzy seemed in good spirits and keyed up too. Bouncing her leg, talking more than usual, being uncharacteristically patient and friendly with her sister. She'd even gone in and had tea with my mother when she got home from school—her idea. Listening from the hall, I'd heard them laughing together, felt a little pang as I realized it had been a while since Izzy and I had laughed like that.

"So how was your day, Iz?" Mark asked her.

"Awesome," she said. "Really awesome." She grabbed another pancake and doused it in syrup, then looked up, eyes shining. "I have a new idea for a project. I think it's gonna be great."

"Oh?" I said. "Tell us."

"I'm going to do a video diary. And eventually, when I've got enough footage, I'll edit it into a documentary," she said. She was talking fast, the way she did when she was really jazzed about something.

"Cool!" Olivia said. "You're gonna make a movie?"

Izzy nodded.

"Can I be in it?" Olivia asked.

"Of course, dumbo."

"Can I wear my ballet things?"

"You can wear whatever you want," Izzy said. "Ballet things, your goofy fairy wings, your pink cowboy boots . . . all the stuff you normally wear."

"A documentary about what?" I asked.

"About our family. About Grandma being here and how totally fu—"

She looked at her sister and stopped herself. "How *interesting* it's making everything. And things around here are only going to get more intense and interesting, right?"

I frowned at her, bit my lip. "I don't know, Iz, we'll have to ask your grandmother how she feels about being filmed."

She'd never been a fan of being photographed. I didn't imagine she'd like having a video camera stuck in her face, especially now. I remembered Ben chasing her around with his Polaroid for a while when we were kids, trying to get a photo of her. She'd always duck out of the way, turn around, cover her face. In the end, she got so annoyed with his constant attempts that she broke the camera by throwing it across the room.

"I already talked to her," Izzy said. "When I went in and brought her tea after school? She loves the idea!"

"Really?" I said.

Izzy nodded. "She said I could interview her and she could, you know, like, tell me the story of her life. She said she thinks it'll be good to have a record of her time with us here, something we can look back on later."

My mother was notorious for hating interviews. In an article in the *New York Times* a couple of years ago, she was referred to as "the reclusive American painter Mavis Holland." She often sent Paul in her place to gallery openings and museum events.

"I just . . ." The words dried up. Wasn't this what I wanted? For my daughter—for both my daughters—to get to know my mother? What was I so afraid of? Why did the very idea of it make my skin crawl?

"You said I should make an effort," Izzy said, exasperated. "That you wanted me to be more involved."

"Yes, that's true. But I didn't—"

"Well, this is what I came up with, Mom. It's my way to be more involved. If you don't approve, then—"

"I think it's a great idea," Mark said. He looked from Izzy to me, said, "I'm sure your mother approves. She just wants to make sure we're respecting your grandmother's wishes and privacy."

"Of course," Izzy said. "I'm not going to shoot stuff that would embarrass her or anything. I'm not a total idiot. I'm not gonna show her on the commode or all wasted and drooling from her meds or whatever. Really, she seems excited about being interviewed. You can ask her yourself! And I think it would be kinda cool, you know? It's a way for me to get to know her, and her to get to know me, which is what you want, right, Mom?" She looked right at me, challenging me to tell the truth.

I swallowed, couldn't make any words come out, so I gave a weak nod.

"Well, I can't wait to see the result," Mark said. "I love that you're taking on such a big project. Your documentary will be amazing, Iz, I just know it."

Izzy smiled, her face coloring a little.

We ate in silence for a minute, until Olivia animatedly returned to the subject of her ballet rehearsals.

I looked down at my plate, catching movement. There was a fly there, perched on the edge, tasting the maple syrup with its terrible little proboscis. I flicked it away, and it took off in a zigzagging flight path like a little drunkard.

"You okay, Mom?" Izzy asked.

"Just a fly," I said.

"Where?" asked Olivia, putting her hands protectively over her own plate.

"It flew away," I said, looking around, not sure where it went, whose plate it might dive-bomb next. "But it just reminded me . . . you haven't been keeping food in your room, have you, Izzy?"

She looked at me like I'd just asked if she had a secret pet shark in her closet. "Um, no, Mom." She stabbed a raspberry with her fork like it might try to run away.

When Izzy was little, there had been an incident with red Jell-O that ended with the hallway carpet being permanently stained. After that the no-food-upstairs rule had been instated.

"Well, I went in there this morning and there were flies," I said. "A bunch of them."

"Eww!" Olivia said. "Izzy's got flies!"

"Shut up, rodent face!" So much for Izzy turning a new leaf and being nice to her sister.

"Izzy," Mark said, a warning tone in his voice.

"Maybe you can put them in your movie," Olivia said. "The flies. Maybe you could train them or something. Like a fly circus." She giggled.

Izzy gave her sister a disgusted look, then turned to me and Mark. "There weren't any flies in my room when I left for school this morning," she said.

"Are you sure they were flies?" Mark asked me as he helped himself to more pancakes.

"They were definitely flies," I said. "There was just one of them down here on my plate. Didn't you see it?" I looked around the room, up to the ceiling, wondering where it had gone.

Izzy was looking at me like I'd lost my mind, like maybe I'd hallucinated the flies.

"It's the wrong time of year for flies," Mark said.

"Well, that may be true, but they clearly haven't gotten the message," I said.

Mark frowned at me, then turned his gaze to Izzy.

"No food in your room," he told her.

"But, Dad, I—"

"No buts," he said.

"No buts, no buts, no buts," Olivia sang, which quickly morphed into an entirely inappropriate rendition of *I like big butts and I cannot lie*. She didn't know any of the other words, so she kept repeating that line over and over, ad-libbing a few extra lyrics. Then somehow it turned into Queen's "Fat Bottomed Girls"—a song Mark had played for both the girls on numerous occasions—and Mark and I looked at each other, knowing we should stop her, but laughing too hard to try. Then Izzy chimed in, joining Olivia in the chorus, banging out a rhythm on the table with her hands. And just for those few hysterical moments, flies forgotten and my mother quietly napping in her room, Mark and I looking at each other across the table, laughing so hard we were tearing up, everything felt right in the world.

FIFTEEN

"HOW DOES A PERSON know something that it's impossible for them to know?" I asked.

Penny looked at me quizzically. We were out in my studio. It was nearly ten thirty. The kids and Mark and my mother were all tucked in and sleeping soundly (well, probably not Izzy, who was usually up until eleven or midnight reading, working on art and videos, and texting with Theo). I held Olivia's old baby monitor in my hand. The volume was turned up all the way, and I could hear my mother's jagged breathing, harsh and uneven—not at all like the soft breath of a baby the receiver had once transmitted.

I'd given my mother the increased dose of Ativan on top of the morphine right before bed, and she was sound asleep. She'd seemed weaker and more withdrawn this afternoon and evening. Just as she was drifting off, she'd asked where Paul was. I told her he'd be back on Friday. "And Benji?" she asked.

I was surprised to hear her bring up my brother. As far as I knew they hadn't spoken in years. And she hadn't called him Benji since he was a little boy.

"He's in California," I said. "Where he lives."

Did she know anything about his life there? Did she ever think about him? Ever wonder what he might be like, this adult version of her only son?

My mother had nodded. "Bobbi lives there too," she'd said. "Laurel Canyon. She says I should come visit again soon."

She'd closed her eyes and drifted off.

It was cozy in the studio. I'd started a fire in the woodstove and all the lights were on. Through the windows I could see snow falling: fat, fluffy flakes that didn't look real—more like the fake snow in one of Mark's Hallmark Christmas movies.

Penny and I were sharing a joint.

This was the only time I smoked: late at night when I knew the kids and Mark were in bed. Mark knew I indulged and was fine with it, though he had no interest in joining me. He was happy with a beer now and then, a splash of rum in his eggnog at Christmastime.

I repeated my question to Penny, rewording it a bit. "Can you explain it? How a person could know something that there's just no way for them to know?"

I'd been driving myself crazy with this all day, going around and around, trying to come up with a logical explanation for my mother knowing about the bird in the well.

"Like, for instance, how I'm supposed to know what exactly you're talking about right now?" Penny said, cocking one eyebrow.

"Yeah, like that," I said, laughing. She laughed with me. Just being there with her made me feel relaxed, like all was well with the world.

We'd been looking over the few sketches I had for *Moxie Saves Halloween*. I'd hoped going over them with Penny might get the wheels turning, give me a flash of inspiration, so I could make some sort of progress. But my mind was elsewhere. It was back with my eight-year-old self out in the woods, holding a BB gun and looking down into that old well.

Penny picked up a new sketch I'd been working on before she came: a close-up of a thick-bodied fly. She frowned at it. I did too. Why had I even drawn it?

"Do you want to tell me what you're actually asking me?" She set down the drawing and fixed her hazel eyes on mine.

I took another hit off the joint, let the smoke seep into my lungs, then exhaled, watching it drift up.

"I did something awful when I was a kid. Something I never told anyone about."

Penny nodded, waiting, keeping her eyes on mine.

So I told her. I began with my father's suicide, how I was furious all the time after, mad at him for leaving us, mad at my mother for drinking more once he was gone, mad at the whole world. I told her about taking Ben's BB gun and shooting the blue jay, not having the guts to actually kill it and put the poor thing out of its misery.

"I dumped it into an old well. I just left it there and walked away. It was screeching. Just hopping around in circles, flapping its shattered wing along with the good one, desperately trying to fly. I swear I could hear that bird the whole way home, even once I got back inside the house."

I hear it still, I almost told her. *I've never stopped hearing it.*

Penny was looking at me through the haze of pot smoke, not saying anything. I couldn't read her expression at all, and it made me nervous.

"Do you think I'm a terrible person?" I asked.

"No, Ali. Of course not." She took my hand and gave it a squeeze. "I think you were an eight-year-old kid in a lot of pain. A kid who'd been through an unspeakable loss, a kid suffering abuse and keeping it all a secret."

I nodded at her, swallowed the lump in my throat.

"Did you ever kill anything else? More animals?"

"God, no!"

"Then not only are you not a terrible person, but we can rule out possible psychopath too." She smiled.

I didn't feel very comforted.

"But I haven't told you the weirdest part yet," I said.

"Okay," Penny said, nodding. "You know I love weird."

"This afternoon, my mother brought it up. The bird in the well. She knew all about it—right down to what kind of bird it was. But that's impossible. Because I was alone that day. And I never told a soul about it. Until now."

Penny exhaled, watched the smoke drift up, then looked at me. "Are you sure you never told her? Or mentioned it to your brother?"

"Positive. It's one of those secrets you never tell anyone, you know? That you spend your whole life knowing is yours and yours alone." I bit my lip. "My mother knowing about the bird . . . it just feels . . . impossible. I've been going over it again and again. How could she know?"

Penny tucked a curl that had come out of her ponytail back behind her ear. "Well, maybe she was there in the woods, watching. Maybe she followed you."

"That's what I've been trying to tell myself, because there really isn't any other explanation, but I don't really believe it. I mean, why would she do that?"

I remembered how thick the woods were, dark and full of shadows. My mother was not an outdoorsy, nature-loving sort of person. Her idea of an adventure was a trip into town, or taking the train into the city. Except for outings like those, she rarely ventured beyond the house, or even out into the yard. And the paths I followed to get to the old cellar hole were unmarked and rough, hard to navigate. It was difficult to imagine her creeping along drunkenly, staggering her way through the woods without my noticing.

That old abandoned house site in the woods was mine and mine alone. I'd never taken Ben there or told him about it. It was my secret place. Where I went to escape my mother on the days she was drinking; the afternoons I arrived home from school and she warned me that she was not herself. The idea that she might have followed me into those woods, might have been there, watching like a shadow, felt all wrong, like the worst sort of trespassing.

"Maybe she was worried about you?" Penny suggested.

I laughed. "Not very likely."

"Well, her following you seems more likely than her being psychic," Penny said.

"True." I looked down at my drawings: the bees, the fly with its thick hairy body and compound eyes staring back up at me. "Do you think there are people like that? People who just know things. Psychics?"

I thought of Izzy. Of the book and tarot cards in her room. Of the wishful thinking that it might be possible to have some sense of what the future held, to know things it was impossible to know.

Penny smiled. "I'm open to the possibility. But do I think your mother is one? Probably not. No more so than any other mother. Wouldn't you say you pick up on things about your own kids? You can tell when something's off? Sense things without them telling you?"

"Sure," I said. I knew when my girls were lying. Knew when something was troubling them. But did I get clear visions of things that happened to them when they were away from me? Certainly not.

I looked at Penny. "You should come meet my mother."

She quirked a brow. "So I can tell you if I think she's got otherworldly gifts?"

I rolled my eyes. "No. Just so you can meet her. You should stop in for coffee. What about tomorrow morning?"

She nodded. "Sure. My first appointment isn't until eleven."

"Perfect," I said. "Stop by after the girls leave for school. The nurse comes at ten, so we'll have a little time."

"I'd like that. I have to admit, I'm very curious about this person."

"You know what they say about curiosity," I warned.

She frowned, took my hand again. "Ali, can I give you some advice?"

"Of course."

She gave me that deep, penetrating Penny look I knew so well. "Don't give her any more power than she already has."

"What do you—"

"I mean, don't go thinking she's got supernatural abilities. She can't see into your head."

"I know that."

"You're not a defenseless little girl anymore. She can't hurt you."

I nodded, told myself that what Penny said was completely true.

So why didn't I believe her?

SIXTEEN

THE BIRD WAS SCREECHING again.

I was there, standing in front of the old circular well, afraid to look down into it. I heard the bird cry out, *eee-eee-eee*, but it was louder, more ragged, almost like a human voice.

A voice calling *Ali, Ali, Ali* . . .

Slowly I moved forward, put my hand on the rough cemented stone, willed myself to look down, but I kept my eyes clamped shut, not wanting to see.

Whatever was waiting for me down there was terrible. Too terrible. I couldn't look. But I had to. I had to see. I heard Penny's voice: *You're not a defenseless little girl anymore.*

I counted to three and opened my eyes wide.

I was in my own bed, Mark beside me.

No well.

No bird.

It was only a dream.

I turned, put an arm around my husband, felt the comforting rise and fall of his chest, the warmth of his body. I looked past him at the clock on his side of the bed: 4:43 a.m.

The baby monitor crackled and hummed, but it wasn't just static . . . there was a voice, soft and low: *"Eee-eee-eee."*

"Your mother's calling you," Mark mumbled, rolling over.

I held still, listening.

"Ali, Ali, Ali," my mother whispered.

Holding the monitor in my hand, I got up, shuffled across our carpeted bedroom, out into the hall. The monitor hummed. My mother was whispering now, soft and low, saying words I couldn't make out. It sounded like she was speaking to someone.

"Are you sure?" my mother said, voice clear. "Does it have to be this way?"

I heard the metallic clunk of the side rail of the bed being lowered.

I raced down the stairs, ran smack into the growling dog in the center of the living room.

"It's okay, girl," I said. "It's just Mother."

There was a low droning hum coming from my mother's room.

Moxie backed away, went over to her bed, and whimpered.

I crossed the living room and dining room, went down the hall toward the guest room.

As I drew near, I heard her singing: *"Don't sit under the apple tree with anyone else but me, anyone else but me . . ."* her voice crackly as an old vinyl record.

"Mother?" I said, stepping into the room.

She laughed. "Is that what you think?"

The room smelled rank, like she'd soiled the bed.

"Did you have an accident?" I asked, moving closer. But the sheets looked clean.

She laughed again. "Life is one big accident, don't you think? The very fact that human beings are here at all is nothing but a series of accidents. Right place at the right time, wrong place at the wrong time. Stars colliding. Primordial muck holding just the right elements to support life."

She was sitting at the edge of the bed with the railing down. It was cold. Too cold. I looked and saw that the window was open.

"It's freezing in here," I said, hurrying to close and latch it. "Why did you open the window?" I was horrified by the idea that she'd gotten out of bed on her own. She was so weak and frail, so unsteady on her feet.

She didn't answer. Just sat, rocking slightly.

"Mother?"

She lifted her face, looked at me. Her hair hung down into her eyes, which looked almost black, like the eyes of a doll. "I am not your mother."

"Of course you are."

"No. I most certainly am not."

Even though I'd closed the window, I still felt a blast of cold air. It seemed to be coming directly from her. Like she was a woman made of ice.

I took a step back, swallowed. I made myself say the words, ask the question. "Who are you, then?"

She grinned. "Have you truly forgotten?"

She reached for me, her hand long and bony. Were her fingers stretching, arms unfurling like terrible wings? I jumped back and flipped on the light switch.

She was just my mother, breathing a little too hard, hunched over at the edge of the mattress, looking like she might go tumbling off at any minute.

I put a hand on her shoulder. "Let's get you back into bed. And get you something to take the edge off. How's your pain?"

"Terrible," she said, voice shaking. "Unspeakably terrible."

I guided her back into bed, tucked the covers around her, and slid the bed rails up. Then I gave her both the short-acting morphine and the little Ativan tablet that dissolved under her tongue. I wrote down the doses and the time on the chart beside her bed.

She looked up at me, blinking, like she was trying to recognize me. "Why are you doing this to me? Why are you freezing me like this?"

"You had your window open," I said. "I'll grab you another blanket. Make you a nice hot cup of tea."

"Where are we?" she demanded, looking around.

"At my house," I explained.

"Why are we here?"

"Because you're staying with us. Remember?"

"It's a mistake," she said. "I don't want to be here. I need to go home."

"Let me just make you a cup of tea. You'll feel better."

"Call Paul," she insisted.

"Okay. We can call him. But it's so early. It's not even five in the morning. Let's have some tea. Are you hungry? Maybe we can have a little breakfast? A poached egg? Then we'll call him, okay?"

I turned, opened the closet, got another quilt down from the top shelf. I brought it over, laid it on top of the bedcovers. "That's better isn't it?"

She leaned back with her head against the pillow. "Be right back," I said. "One cup of mint tea coming up."

"I don't like mint tea," she said.

"You liked it yesterday. You said it was your favorite."

"Chamomile," she said.

"Chamomile it is." I went into the kitchen and made the tea, being careful not to make it too hot. I wanted to warm her up, not have her scald herself. I carried it back in and set it on the bed tray.

"This is all wrong," she said, gazing around the room, then down at the cup I'd brought in.

"The tea?" If she told me she wanted mint, I might lose it.

"No. The tea is fine. But how did I get here?"

"Paul brought you."

"He needs to bring me back home, then. It isn't safe. Please. Let's call him. Right now."

I took a deep breath and let it out slowly. "Mother, I—"

From upstairs came a scream. A loud, frantic scream that seemed to split the air apart, make the walls vibrate. It went on and on, getting higher, louder.

This was the sound of Olivia in pain. Terrible, terrible pain. The only time I'd ever heard her scream like this was when she broke her arm last year.

"I told you," my mother blurted out, eyes wide and terrified. "It's not safe."

I turned away from her, bolting out of the guest room and for the stairs.

SEVENTEEN

OLIVIA WAS SCREAMING, HIGH-PITCHED and desperate, as I raced through the dining room and living room, took the stairs two at a time, Moxie right behind me.

How could Olivia still be breathing, screaming this hard, this loud without a break?

Mark was in the upstairs hall nearly to her door. He'd turned the lights on, and they seemed impossibly bright. His eyes met mine and we exchanged a look of pure panic.

My heart was racing, jacked on adrenaline. The door to Izzy's room opened across from us. "Mom? Dad?" she asked, blinking at us.

Mark slammed open Olivia's door and we both rushed in expecting . . . what? Something terrible. Because that's the kind of screaming it was.

But Olivia was unharmed and in one piece.

I let myself breathe. Mark flipped on the lights.

Olivia was standing in the center of her bed, clutching Big Dog to her chest, her little face red and contorted as she screamed. She was so hysterical, she didn't even seem to see us. And for half a second, I barely recognized her. It was as if a wild, feral child had slipped into my daughter's bed, put on her *Nutcracker* pajamas. Her eyes looked huge, glazed with tears. Her covers and stuffed animals were off the bed on the floor.

"Olivia? What is it?" Mark asked. "What's wrong?"

She continued to scream. It was as if she were in some other place, the land of fear, and couldn't hear us.

A bad nightmare? A sleep terror?

What were you supposed to do for a sleep terror? Wake the child? Not wake her? I tried to remember and couldn't.

"Look at me, Liv," Mark said, his voice firm and calm. He walked toward her. She turned to him. "Tell me what's wrong."

Olivia pointed to the floor, where some of the stuffed animals we so carefully tucked in around her each night had fallen off the bed and lay in a pile. There was Freddy the pink teddy bear, Trixie the brown rabbit, Hedgie the hedgehog, Samuel the skunk, and others beneath.

But something was wrong.

One of them was moving.

"Mark!" I yelled, jumping back and pointing.

"The Rat King!" Olivia sobbed.

It was not (as far as I could tell anyway) the King of the Rats, but an actual common gray rat with a long naked tail and glistening coal-black eyes. It emerged from under the pile of cute plush animals, then turned and crawled back into the heap. It looked so grotesque there, slithering over the face of Olivia's beloved pink bear.

I'd caught glimpses of rats before but had never seen one this close. I was surprised by its size. The head and body must have been about ten inches, and its tail added another good six inches. It was so much larger than the mice we sometimes caught in the kitchen or the pantry, chewing holes in boxes of saltine crackers and bags of maple granola.

Olivia had forbidden us to harm the mice (and Mark was a firm believer in not killing any living thing), so we had a little metal catch-and-release trap. We'd capture a mouse, bring it out to the field behind the barn, and let it go. I was convinced it was the same mouse showing up again and again. That once it had tasted the organic Vermont maple granola we kept in our pantry, there was no keeping it away.

The creature that was now slinking over Olivia's stuffed animals would not have fit in the little metal mousetrap.

Its fur was a dark gray, nearly black, and shiny as an oil slick. It moved like oil too—viscous and flowing, its body seemingly more liquid than solid.

"Get me something to catch it with!" Mark ordered, staring down at the rat. "Stay up on the bed, Liv." Olivia had stopped her ungodly screaming, although she was still crying, her whole body heaving with sobs.

Looking desperately around the room, I spotted the pink plastic wastepaper basket under Olivia's desk, dumped the crumpled papers it contained out on the floor, and passed the solid plastic bin to Mark. I noticed Izzy was standing in the doorway with her camera in front of her, recording. How long had she been there?

Mark held the pink bin over the rat, moving it as the rat moved. Then, in one quick motion, he flung it down, trapping the rat beneath it.

"Nice, Dad!" Izzy cheered.

"I need something to cover the top," he said. "A board or thick cardboard or something."

Catching sight of the oversized hardcover picture book of *The Nutcracker* on Olivia's desk, I grabbed it and brought it over. The image on the cover showed Clara watching while the Nutcracker and the Rat King had swords drawn on each other. The Rat King had glowing red eyes, a red cape, and a spiky gold crown.

"I'm going to gently lift the edge, you slide the book under," he said. I got down and followed his instructions, keeping my fingers away from the edge as he lifted and I carefully slid the book beneath, imagining a vicious creature with long yellow teeth that probably carried rabies or some terrible plague.

"Excellent," he said. "We got him." He reached down and held the book in place while he gently turned the pink wastepaper basket right side up. We could hear the rat scrabbling frantically inside, flinging its heavy body at the slick sides of the trash can.

Olivia let out a little sob. I went to her, knelt on the unmade bed, and wrapped my arms around her. She sank down and clung tightly to me, her little body finally starting to relax.

"It's okay," I whispered to her. "Daddy got him."

"I've gotta ask the obvious question here: How did a rat get into Olivia's room?" Izzy asked, still holding the camera, filming.

"I don't know," I said. "Rats are good at fitting through little spaces. It's cold outside and our house is nice and warm."

"We've never had rats before, though," Mark said, frowning at the wastebasket and the creature thrashing around inside it as he carried it gingerly toward the door, as if he were holding a bomb.

"He wasn't small when he came in," Olivia said.

I released her from the hug, but stayed close beside her on the bed, keeping one arm around her. Her body was still shuddering.

By now Izzy had stepped into the room and had the camera pointed at her little sister. "What do you mean, Liv?" she asked.

"I mean, he was the Rat King. When he came into the room, he was up on his hind legs, and he was bigger than Daddy."

"You were dreaming, sweetie," I told her, rubbing comforting circles on her back.

"I was not dreaming," Olivia insisted. "I was wide-awake."

"There's no such thing as the Rat King," Izzy said from behind her camera. "Not really."

"Is so, and there he goes," Olivia said as Mark carried it out, the huge *Nutcracker* book clamped over the open top of the wastebasket so the enormous rat would not escape.

Scrabble. Thump. Scrabble. Thump.

Izzy panned the camera, following her father.

I let go of Olivia and slid off the bed, kicked at the pile of stuffed animals on the floor, making sure the rat hadn't been accompanied by a friend. My foot hit something hard. I bent down, pushed aside Freddy and Trixie, and let out a funny little strangled-sounding gasp when I saw what was beneath them.

"What's your grandmother's stone doing in here?" I asked.

"I don't know," Olivia said. Her face was splotchy, and she was still choking back sobs.

I looked Olivia in the eye. "Did you take it?"

"No!"

"Well, how did it get in here, then?" I asked.

Izzy stepped back to frame both me and Olivia in her shot.

"I don't know," Olivia said again, tears in her eyes. "Maybe he brought it?"

"He who?" I asked.

"The Rat King."

"There is no Rat King," I said, my voice high and shrill.

"Is so," Olivia said. "Didn't you see? Daddy just carried him outside."

I made myself take a breath. "That was a rat, Liv. Just a regular old rat."

"He changed back. Before you came in."

"Olivia—"

"Grandma Needle will believe me," she said.

I clenched my jaw. "Why do you call her that?"

"Because that's what she told me to call her. Needle Sivam. I think it's kind of a silly name, but she said it's one of her names and I can know it because I'm special."

My skin prickled. "One of her names?"

"Mm-hmm. She said in time, she'll teach me the others too. Then, once I know them all, we'll really know each other. She says I'm her special girl. Her trouper."

I heard footsteps moving toward me and turned, startled, to see Izzy pointing the camera at me. I'd forgotten she was there, had been filming the whole time.

She moved in for a close-up. I put up my hand. "Would you get that fucking camera out of my face, please!"

Izzy backed out of the room, keeping the camera on me. "Sure, Mom," she said. "Whatever you say." I heard her pad down the hall, no doubt chasing after her father and the rat, hoping to get a shot of its release; the thick, shiny body slithering off into the snow-covered field behind our house.

I WAS PICKING up the stuffed animals, tucking them back in around Olivia, smoothing her damp hair and asking if she wanted waffles or pancakes for breakfast, when Mark came back in, carrying the now-empty pink wastepaper basket and the book. Izzy was at his heels.

"Where's the rat?" Olivia asked, clearly terrified.

"He's gone, Liv," Mark promised.

"But he might come back."

"No. He won't."

"The mice we bring outside come back sometimes."

"Well, the rat isn't going to," Mark said. He looked pale, shaken.

"How do you know?" she demanded.

"Because he's dead, Liv. I killed him."

"I can vouch for that," Izzy said, pointing the camera at us all. "I can show you the video if you want. It was kind of awesome. He got it with that old cast-iron Santa on the back porch. Rat guts everywhere! Who knew a rat could bleed that much?"

My body stiffened.

"Enough, Isabelle," Mark reprimanded.

"What happened to catch and release?" I said.

"It was a rat, Ali. Not a little field mouse."

I nodded. Point taken. But still, the image of my sweet, animal-loving husband smashing a creature to death with the cast-iron Santa made me feel queasy.

"Daddy killed the Rat King," Olivia said.

"I did indeed," he said. He set down the basket and went over to give Olivia a hug and kiss the top of her head.

"You're like the Nutcracker Prince!" Olivia said.

"Yeah, but it was way cooler than in the ballet," Izzy said. "The Nutcracker Prince doesn't use a metal Santa Claus to bludgeon the rat to death."

"Unnecessary details, Iz," I said.

"Well, that's what happened," she said. "I'm just reporting the facts. Recording them. Isn't that what a documentary filmmaker is supposed to do?"

I rolled my eyes at her.

"Daddy, guess what? Mommy said the f-word," Olivia tattled.

"Did she now?" Mark asked, looking over and giving me a weak smile. "Well, I think in moments of stress we all slip up. To tell you the truth, I may have said a few bad words myself this morning."

"You definitely did when you were out in the yard swinging that Santa," Izzy said, patting her camera. "It's all documented right here."

"Alison!" my mother's voice squawked over the baby monitor.

"What now?" I said out loud, dreading whatever else the morning might hold.

"Where's my stone?" my mother hollered, her voice tinny through the old monitor. "What have you done with my stone?"

EIGHTEEN

I HURRIED DOWNSTAIRS TO MY mother, feedback from the baby monitor screeching as I carried it into her room, making my mother scream with it. She covered her ears and howled along with the monitor's staticky squawk.

"Sorry!" I said as I shut the machine off, stopping the noise. "Everything's all right." To prove it, I held up the stone to show her. "Look. See, I've got it. It's okay."

"What have you done?" she asked, eyes icy, accusing.

She stretched out her hands for the stone, scrabbling at the air desperately as I passed it to her. She snatched it away from me, scratching my finger, then held it close, studying it, as if searching for cracks or damage. Or maybe she thought I was trying to pass off a fake. Like I'd sold off the real one and was giving her a chunk of striated glass in its place.

"I just found it in Olivia's room," I explained. "She must have taken it. I'm sorry."

I expected her to ask if Olivia was okay. She'd heard the screaming coming from upstairs, watched as I'd gone tearing out of her room to see what had happened to my daughter. To the little girl she claimed to love. To the little girl she said was so special that she'd shared her secret name with her.

She says I'm her special girl. Her trouper.

My mother frowned, her eyes darkening. "She *stole* from me?"

My body stiffened as I bit back the words: *She's fine, by the way, thanks for asking.*

I forced a smile. "She didn't mean any harm. I'm sure she just wanted to look at it. She's so drawn to it, and I—"

"This is not acceptable, Alison. I don't want anyone touching my things."

"I know. I'll talk to her. Make sure it doesn't happen again."

"*No one* is to touch this stone," my mother warned, and as she spoke, I was transported back to my childhood, to a time when she caught *me* in her room, looking at the stone, studying it.

"Out!" she'd screamed then. "Out, before you ruin everything."

Eight-year-old me had scrambled backward out of the room, apologizing, saying, "Sorry," over and over.

"You don't know what sorry is," she'd said. "I'll make you sorry."

As if reading my thoughts, my mother now said, "If she does it again, she'll be sorry."

Enough was enough. I squared my shoulders, let out an angry hiss of air through flared nostrils. I couldn't step back in time and protect my younger self, but I sure as hell could protect my daughter. "She's a six-year-old child, Mother. A child who happens to adore you. She's drawn to the rock because it's yours, because it means so much to you. If I were you, I'd be *honored* that she borrowed it. See it for what it was: her looking for a way to be closer to you." My words flew out, fueled by a simmering rage.

My mother only stared.

"And if you ever, *ever* threaten either of my children again, I'm sending you to a nursing home."

My mother cackled. "It seems someone has grown a pair of balls."

I clenched my jaw, trying to restrain my building fury. "And I won't put up with crudeness either. Not in my house."

"You don't know what crude is, little girl."

"Shall I go get my phone and call Paul now? Ask him to start making arrangements to have you moved into a facility? Tell him I need you out of here by the beginning of next week?"

"You wouldn't dare," my mother said.

"Try me," I said.

"So this is what it's come to," Mother said, trying out a pitiful tone. "You threatening a dying old woman." She pouted cartoonishly.

"You're the one who brought us here," I said. "And you're the one who can turn it around. I don't need you to be the perfect grandmother or the perfect guest in my home. I just need you to be decent. Grateful. And to never threaten my children again."

We stared each other down like two gunfighters in an old western.

At last she nodded, which was the closest I'd get to an agreement, a truce.

I felt a strange satisfaction, having stood up to my mother for once.

"Like I said," I told her, "I'll talk to Olivia about the stone and make sure she doesn't borrow it again. I don't want you to say a word to her about it. Do you understand? Not a word."

My mother nodded. "I'll be quiet as a mouse," she said. "Or should I say . . . a rat?" She smiled mischievously.

She must have heard us upstairs. Or heard Izzy and Mark leaving the house with the creature. She giggled like the rat was part of some practical joke she'd played.

The uneasy feeling in my chest grew.

AFTER A CUP of my extra-special candy cane hot cocoa and a bowl of chocolate chip oatmeal, Olivia seemed back to her normal self. I told her that her grandmother was too tired for a morning visit, so she sat at the breakfast bar chattering away until it was time to get dressed for school. Mark went to work and the girls headed off on the bus. At eight thirty, there was a knock on the door. Then it opened, and Penny called out, "Hello?"

I'd forgotten I'd invited her for coffee with my mother. I cringed a little, hoping my mother would behave. But then again, maybe it was better if she didn't, if Penny got to see the not-so-nice version of her. It seemed my mother had everyone else fooled. And surely my sensitive, perceptive best friend would be able to see the real her.

"Come on in," I called from the kitchen. "I was putting more coffee on for us."

Penny came in, taking off her coat and boots and joining me in the kitchen, carrying a dish. "Louise made us a blueberry sour cream coffee cake," she said, smiling proudly. She set down the cake and gave me a hug and a kiss on the cheek. She was dressed in her therapist clothes: wool tights and a long blue skirt, a purple shirt with one of her chunky hand-knit sweaters over it. Her hair was braided and held back by a leather barrette with a polished stick running through it.

"Wonderful! Hey, you should have brought her along."

Penny picked off some of the crumbled topping from the coffee cake and had a nibble. "She was caught up in stuff at home. There's some sort of drama with one of the chickens getting broody and she wants to put a stop to it before any of our other girls get the same idea. She's got some tricks she's trying—one of them involves sticking a bag of frozen peas under the poor hen to get her off her eggs." She shook her head in a *can you even believe it* way.

I laughed. "Sounds like Louise has got her hands full."

"I'll say! Also, we didn't want to overwhelm your mom. Louise can drop by another time to meet her. It'll give her an excuse to bake another coffee cake."

"Sounds perfect." The coffee was perking and I was getting down cups.

"Anything I can do to help?" Penny asked.

"Sure. You can slice that and put it on plates for us."

Penny knew my kitchen just as well as her own and grabbed the plates, a knife, and forks.

"How's your morning going?" she asked as she sliced the cake.

I laughed. "Well, it began with my mother screaming for me at four thirty—somehow she'd gotten out of bed and opened the window."

"Well, that's definitely not a great start to the day," Penny said, putting the first generously sized piece of coffee cake onto a plate.

I nodded in agreement. "And then Olivia was hysterical because she woke up around five and—you aren't going to believe this—there was a *rat* in her room."

"A rat?" Penny set down the knife and looked at me, eyebrows raised. "An actual rat? Not a mouse?"

"Oh no. This was definitely not a mouse. This was a legitimate, full-sized rat. And it didn't help that poor Olivia keeps having nightmares about the Rat King from *The Nutcracker*. Then an actual rat shows up in her room—so of course, now she thinks it *was* the Rat King."

"Poor thing," Penny said. "We do get rats in the barn sometimes. We have to keep all the grain and food for the sheep and chickens in metal trash cans. One year, they were so bad we put out poison. We haven't had to for a while, though. I think having so many cats helps keep them away."

"Well, Mark killed ours with a cast-iron Santa."

"No way!" Penny laughed. "Mark? *Your* Mark? Emily Dickinson scholar, lover of all things Christmas? The guy who catches mice, gives them cute little names, and then lets them go?"

"None other."

"Wow! Now, that I'd love to see."

"You may be in luck. Apparently Izzy filmed the whole thing."

Penny laughed again and shook her head. "Never a dull moment in your household."

As if on cue, my mother called out. "Alison? Alison! Where are you?"

"Okay," I said, turning to Penny. "I guess we can't put it off any longer. Come on and meet my mother."

Penny nodded, her warm look helping to melt away my misgivings.

I led her into the guest room carrying a cup of tea for my mother. Penny had the plates of coffee cake.

"Mother," I said, "I'd like you to meet my friend Penny. Penny, this is my mother, Mavis."

"It's wonderful to meet you, Mavis," Penny said with a warm smile.

"Are you one of the nurses?" my mother asked.

"No. I'm Alison's next-door neighbor."

"And best friend," I added.

"And I brought a blueberry sour cream cake my wife made," Penny said, holding out a plate for my mother.

I held my breath, wondering what judgment my mother might pass or uncomfortable comment she might make at Penny's mention of a wife.

"Lovely," my mother said, smiling, accepting the slice of coffee cake. "Come sit beside me. I want to hear all about you and your wife who made this delightful-looking treat."

My mother was full of surprises.

She took a bite of the cake as Penny pulled a chair close to her bed. "Delicious!" she proclaimed. "Is that cardamom I taste?"

Penny smiled. "That's the secret ingredient. Just a touch. And freshly grated lemon zest."

"Amazing," my mother said, closing her eyes for the next bite. Then she opened them, looked at Penny, and asked, "So tell me, how long have you known my Ali Alligator?"

Penny smiled at the old nickname. I wanted to smile too—but somehow, after the events of the morning, I couldn't bring myself to do so. She was definitely putting on the charm. Maybe, I was starting to think, the key to keeping her on her best behavior was to have a constant stream of visitors. The trouble only seemed to happen when the two of us were alone.

"We met when she and Mark moved here. Gosh, it must have been nearly ten years ago now, right, Ali?"

I nodded. "Yeah, Izzy was in first grade. The same age as Olivia is now. That doesn't seem possible."

"Time is a funny thing," my mother said. "It goes so fast, doesn't it? One minute, your children are the sweetest little toddlers; the next, they're gone, out of the house with lives of their own." My mother spoke ruefully, making it sound as though she actually missed my brother and me.

Penny stayed for nearly an hour. My mother was sweet and charming. This was my Grateful Dead–loving mother. The mother who called me *dear* and told funny stories about what I was like when I was little, how I was a nervous child, afraid of sidewalk cracks and eggs that were too runny. "She used to overthink every little thing, find something to fret about and worry herself sick over," my mother told Penny. Then she turned to me, said, "I hope you've outgrown that now, Ali. All that worrying over things you can't control. Inventing trouble."

I nodded at her. She looked to Penny. "What do you think, Penny? Is my Ali Alligator still inventing trouble?"

Penny caught my eye, smiled. "No more so than any of the rest of us," she said. "Now, speaking of trouble, let me tell you what poor Louise is up to at home with our laying hens."

My mother cackled at the story, admired Louise's dedication to the birds and their egg production.

By the end of the visit, Penny had promised to come back soon with Louise and to bring my mother some of her marijuana-infused honey. My mother had surprised us both by admitting that she'd once loved to indulge in the occasional joint or batch of pot brownies, although she hadn't done so in years. "Back in college, Bobbi and I smoked all the time," she said. "Everyone did back then."

She clutched Penny's hand as they said good-bye, added, "You must be a wonderful therapist—so insightful and such a good listener. I'm so glad Ali has you in her life."

Penny smiled, not even bothering to ask how my mother had known she was a therapist. It hadn't come up in our visit at all. Penny had told my mother all about the farm, the animals, Louise and her honeybees, her Electric Sheep strain of homegrown weed. But she hadn't once mentioned anything about her professional life. And I certainly hadn't said anything. My mind worked at the problem, probing at it the way you poked at a sore tooth, tentatively and carefully, until I came up with a plausible explanation.

Olivia must have mentioned it. I could picture it: my chatterbox of a girl telling her grandmother all about her friends, then ours, including her aunties next door, Penny and Louise.

NINETEEN

PAUL ARRIVED AT NOON on Friday, just as promised. He looked thinner, paler than he had at the beginning of the week. There were blue-black circles under his eyes.

I went out to the driveway to meet him.

He hugged me, one of those weak hugs people give because they feel they should. Then he pulled away, saw my face, and looked worried. "Everything okay?" he asked. "Is Mavis . . . ?"

"She's doing okay," I said. "Things are going well for the most part."

His shoulders relaxed. "Good." His eyes darted from the house to me and back again.

"Mother seems to be settling in fine. We have our ups and downs." I paused, thinking that was quite an understatement. "But overall, I'd say it's going okay."

I looked at Paul. His expression made it clear he suspected I wasn't being a hundred percent truthful.

"The hospice nurse is working out?"

"Yeah. Teresa's great. She's really down-to-earth. At first I was a little worried that she wasn't Mother's type, but it turns out they really like each other. Teresa comes every morning. In fact, you just missed her."

"I'm glad it's going well. Is Mavis up now?"

"Oh yes, she's been eagerly awaiting your appearance."

He nodded, though I thought I caught a hint of disappointment on his face. But that was silly—surely he hadn't come all this way hoping to find her asleep. "Good, good. I've got some paperwork to go over with her.

And I brought some more of her possessions from the house in Woodstock. Some books and personal things to help her feel more at home." He reached into the backseat where a couple of bags and a box were piled.

"Paul?"

"Yeah?"

"You know my mother well. Probably better than anyone else. Better than me, certainly."

He opened his mouth, then snapped it shut, lips pressed together. He nodded.

"The thing is, I was wondering, before she got sick, was she . . . I don't know, showing any signs of confusion?"

"Confusion?"

"It's just . . . well, it's little things. She's been wandering; getting up in the middle of the night and leaving her bed. And there are times she seems genuinely addled. She doesn't seem to know where she is. She even got the bedroom window open one night."

He looked worried.

"It hasn't happened since. Most of the time, she's really clear. But now and then . . . well, it's almost like her whole personality changes. She's even told me she's not really Mavis."

"Not Mavis?" Paul's jaw tightened, and he squinted his eyes like I was going out of focus. Like maybe I wasn't really Alison.

"And a couple of times she's gotten agitated, told me she shouldn't be here. That it's dangerous."

"Dangerous?" He raised his eyebrows.

"I was talking about it with Teresa, and she wonders if there might be a dementia component to some of this behavior."

He shook his head. "No. Not that I'm aware of, anyway. I've never seen any signs of it. Mavis . . . well, she's always been sharp, perfectly clear."

"Probably just her illness and the medicine, then."

The lines in his forehead deepened as he gave me a seriously worried look. "Are you really doing okay with this, Alison?" he asked. "I know it's a lot, having her here. If you need more support, we can get more nursing care, have someone here round the clock if necessary."

"No," I said. "Really. I'm fine. I've got this."

"You look tired," he said.

I bit my lip to keep from saying, *You do too, Paul.*

And honestly, I was tired. I hadn't been sleeping well. All night I tossed and turned, listening to the static on the old baby monitor, imagining I heard things in it: whispers, buzzing, the far-off cry of a bird.

"It's been . . . a difficult adjustment," I admitted. "But we're in a routine now. And really, we're doing fine. You'll see."

"And Mark, the girls, are they okay with all of this?"

"Yeah, they're fine. Better than fine, actually. Mark finds Mother quite charming. Olivia's in love with her. Even Izzy's warmed up to her. She's been interviewing Mother, making a video diary."

"A video diary?"

"Mother seems to be enjoying it, being interviewed and filmed."

His face twitched into a smile. "Your daughter will have to tell me her secrets. I've been trying to get Mavis to do interviews for years."

He looked from me to the house.

"We should go in," I said. "She's been waiting for you. She'll be so happy to see you."

His eyes were fixed on the front door, and for half a second, I was sure he wasn't going to come in. That he was just going to hand me the papers and take off. His expression told me that going into the house to see her was the very last thing he wanted to do.

And again I found myself wondering, was it the grief and horror of her illness and impending death that scared him, or was it something more?

"PAUL," SHE SAID when he walked in.

"None other," he told her. He went to her bedside, leaned down, and kissed her cheek, the skin pale and delicate as tissue paper. "It's good to see you, Mavis," he said.

"If it's so good, why didn't you come sooner?" she asked.

I couldn't tell if she was teasing or genuinely upset. Maybe a little of both?

"Because we agreed on Friday." There was a sheen of sweat on his forehead.

"Did we?"

He nodded. "I was at home tending to the enormously long list we'd made. I got all of the paintings, sketches, and journals off for the Toronto retrospective. And sent the new pieces to Ravenwood in New York. I started going through the things you asked me to, closing up the house. I've been quite busy." His voice faltered. Paul, who was normally so sure of himself, so in charge, seemed to be struggling. He opened his mouth as if he was going to say something more, but no words came.

"Good," my mother said. "Nice to hear you're earning your keep."

Paul seemed to wince a little, then forced a smile. "I've got a small pile of things that need your signature and a few questions. Are you up for it?"

"Of course." My mother sat up, looking suddenly very alert.

"I'll leave you two to it, then," I said. "I'll go make a pot of coffee. And I've got some fresh cinnamon rolls."

"Sounds perfect," Paul said, rummaging through his bag and pulling out a file folder.

In the kitchen, I put the coffee on and popped the cinnamon rolls in the oven to warm them. Then I loaded a plate with the warm pastries and approached the room.

"Please," I heard Paul saying. "It can't be true."

I stopped short, then stepped off to the side in the hallway, listening.

"Don't pretend you didn't know all along," my mother said. "You're one of the cleverest people I know, Paul. The truth has been staring you in the face and you've just refused to look at it."

Were they talking about her illness? Her approaching death and his denial of it?

"But it's not possible," Paul said.

She laughed. "You have no idea what is and isn't possible."

He said something in a low, breathy tone, something I couldn't make out, and my mother laughed again, but it was a wicked, cruel laugh. Then she whispered something that came out sounding like an extended, sinister hiss.

There was silence for a few long seconds.

"No," Paul said firmly. "I won't. I can't."

"Oh yes, you will. After all I've done for you, Paul? You have no right to deny me."

More silence, then a whisper, followed by footsteps coming my way. I scrambled back out of the hall, toward the kitchen, still clutching the plate of cinnamon rolls.

Paul nearly ran into me.

"Paul?" my mother called from her room. "Come back!"

He looked at me—frantic, helpless—shook his head, and hurried for the front door.

"Paul!" my mother called from her room. "Don't you dare leave!"

I set down the rolls on the dining table and followed him through the front door, not even bothering to close it behind me as I hurried out to the driveway, where he was unlocking his SUV. I shivered in the cold without a coat.

"Paul? What's going on?"

He turned from the open car to me. "I don't—I can't—"

"Talk to me, Paul."

"I'm sorry," he said, his eyes teary. "I'm so, so sorry. It's my fault. I should never . . ." He trailed off. "But I didn't know. I swear."

"I don't understand. Please, come back in, have a cup of coffee, we can talk."

He got into the car.

"Paul!" I could hear my mother yell from inside the house.

Paul looked from the house to me, his face full of anguish as he turned the key in the ignition. The engine roared to life.

Inside, my mother bellowed Paul's name, then other words I couldn't make out—was she yelling at him in another language?—followed by a low moan and a crash.

Paul looked at me, eyes wide with fear, as he shifted into reverse. He rolled down the window. "That's not Mavis," he said as he pulled away.

TWENTY

"H OW ARE YOU FEELING?" I asked. My mother had been asleep for most of the afternoon. Now that she was up, I'd brought in some tea and one of the cinnamon rolls I had warmed earlier.

I'd found her on the floor when I ran back inside after Paul left. She'd gotten the railing down and stepped out of bed, losing her balance, grabbing for the bedside table and knocking everything on it to the ground: her cell phone, a glass of water, her stone. She'd banged her arm in the fall. It didn't look broken, and she said she hadn't hit her head, but I'd called Teresa and she'd come right away. Together we'd managed to get my mother settled, bandaged the scrape on her arm, and given her a heavy dose of Ativan. Teresa said we'd been fortunate—she was bruised but had no serious injuries—and suggested that it might be time to rethink the bed alarm. "If she falls again, we might not be so lucky next time." I'd promised to be more vigilant, more careful. I didn't want to do anything to make my mother feel like more of a prisoner than she did already.

"I thought you might be hungry," I said to my mother now, setting my offerings down on the bedside table.

She didn't look at me. She was staring instead at her arm, which was wrapped in gauze. Mummy arm.

"Mother?"

That's not Mavis.

"I know what you've come to ask me," she said.

"Oh?"

Were her eyes darker? Her lips thinner as they stretched into a wicked little smile?

Not Mavis.

"Go ahead and ask," she dared. "Or are you too much of a coward?"

My throat felt dry and tight. "What is it you think I've come to ask?"

Not Mavis.

She remained silent. Watching with a grin, waiting.

"Okay," I said. "Do you want to tell me what happened with Paul today? Why he left so abruptly?"

Her grin widened. "Poor Paul. He's gone off and lost his head."

"What do you mean? Did something happen between you two?"

"Wrong question."

"But that's—"

"That's a weak question, Alison. Have some balls and ask a good one."

Not Mavis.

"Okay." My mind scrambled. What did I want to know? I blurted out the first question that popped into my head. "Why did you tell Olivia to call you Needle Sivam?"

My mother smiled up at me, such a wide smile that it looked as if it might hurt her, as if her face might actually split and her jaw come unhinged like the jaw of a snake about to swallow its prey.

"There was a little girl who had a little curl, right in the middle of her forehead," my mother sang out.

"Your name is Mavis," I said.

"What if it's not?" she said. "What if I'm not really Mavis? Not anymore."

I blew out a breath. The room seemed to get smaller, darker.

Or was my mother getting larger? Her limbs lengthening?

I blinked. Impossible.

"Okay then. If you're not Mavis, who are you?" My voice came out small and high, my scared little girl voice.

The words Paul spoke as he drove away drummed inside my skull, a terrible cacophony:

That's not Mavis.

That's not Mavis.

That's not Mavis.

"I wear Mavis like a skin," she said. "I'm her and I'm not her. I'm so much more."

There was a crackling laugh, like fire overtaking dry grass.

"So is Needle your real name?"

"I have many names, most of which you could not speak even if you tried."

The hairs at the back of my neck stood up. There was something strangely familiar about this speech.

I looked at her there on her rented hospital bed, and swore I saw her face change. Instead of a shrunken old woman, she became my younger mother—the mother from my childhood. The wrinkles disappeared, her cheeks filled out, her hair darkened. And then, for a split second, she became something else entirely. A creature with beady coal-black eyes, a pointed snout, large yellow incisors.

Olivia's Rat King.

I jumped back, turned away.

When I made myself look again, she was my dying mother, wrapped in blankets, her scraped arm bandaged in gauze.

Of course she was.

The lack of sleep was getting to me. The nightmares. The stress of having her here. And the stupid rodent and Olivia's story about the Rat King.

And Paul's bizarre, frantic departure.

His crazy words: *That's not Mavis.*

Get a grip, I told myself, closing my eyes tight.

This is what my mother does, I reminded myself. *She tells lies. She fucks with my head.* This was just my mother up to her old, cruel tricks.

"Needle Sivam," I said, picturing the letters in my head. Years of writing backward for printmaking helped me see it right away, even in my mind. I opened my eyes and looked right at her. "Is Mavis Eldeen backward."

She cackled. "Clever girl."

"But why? Why have Olivia call you by your name spelled backward?"

Was it a game? A riddle? A test to see if Olivia could figure it out?

"Maybe because I'm what Mavis sees in the mirror," she said.

I looked at her, this sick old woman, realizing that the very last thing I should be doing right now was going down the rabbit hole with her.

"What do you see when you look in the mirror, Alison?" she asked.

I brushed her question aside and asked her another. "You said you have other names?"

Were they riddles too? Puzzles to be solved?

She nodded. "Olivia calls me Needle," my mother said, her voice a low hiss. "But you . . . you, Alison, may call me Azha."

It was the voice I recognized from long-ago childhood nights when she'd crawl into my bed and whisper terrible things.

And didn't I recognize the name?

Hadn't I heard it before?

"I'm sorry . . . what?"

She clucked her tongue, shook her head. "Honestly, Alison. Do I have to spell everything out for you? Hold your hand? Walk you through every fucking step? It's A-Z-H-A!"

I staggered back away from her, heart hammering, my jaw clenched, grinding my teeth together.

Her eyes were so dark they were nearly black.

"Don't you remember?"

I shook my head, backed my way out of the room.

TWENTY-ONE

SO HE REALLY JUST took off?" Mark asked. It was a little before ten and we were in bed under our heavy down comforter. It was usually my favorite time of day: these last moments in the evening when Mark and I were snuggled together, sharing little details from our day, retelling each other the best parts, or sometimes processing difficult things together. Mark had turned off his reading light, and I had my laptop open. The blue glow of the screen lit the room: the antique dresser with the framed wedding photo we kept on top of it, the oval mirror above it. We had matching bedside tables: Mark's was stacked with books of poetry, papers to grade. Mine had a couple of sketchbooks and drawing pencils, a book on the history of Halloween that Mark had bought for me, hoping it would provide inspiration for the new Moxie book.

I'd been filling Mark in on Paul's departure, telling him all the things I couldn't say in front of the girls earlier.

"He couldn't get out of here fast enough. I overheard them arguing—they were both so upset. She asked him to do something but he said no. The next thing I knew, he was practically running out the door."

"Wow. Well, you said he's been taking her illness really hard."

"That's true, but—"

"Which makes sense. He's kind of been like a son to her."

I don't know why this bothered me, but it did. Maybe it was jealousy—Paul had been close to her over the years, had been part of her day-to-day life in a way that I hadn't.

"I know," I said.

Paul knew my mother in a way I never would.

Just as I knew her in a way he never would.

It was strange to think about, as if we knew two very different people.

I'd often wondered if he had any real idea of what my and Ben's childhood in that house with her had been like. Surely he must have suspected. The fact that Ben refused to even talk to her had definitely made Paul curious. He'd asked me once, long ago, "What happened between Mavis and Ben? What did she do?" I knew how loaded the question was, felt him searching my face, wondering what she'd done to me as well but knowing better than to ask. I never answered Paul, just shook my head, changed the subject. He never asked about it again.

"He's been with her for years," Mark said now. "Not just working for her, but living there in the carriage house."

I'd wondered about that too. What made him stay? What was his life like there? Did he have friends of his own? A lover who came to spend the night once in a while? He'd told me he had no family and I'd never heard him or my mother mention anyone he was close to. I knew nothing about his personal life. I doubted he had much time for one.

And what about the hold my mother had over him?

Evidently it wasn't complete, because this afternoon he'd refused her.

What on earth had she asked of him? I couldn't imagine Paul ever saying no to my mother.

"He obviously cares very deeply about her," Mark said beside me. "And she for him."

"They definitely have a strong bond," I agreed. "She was in such a rage when he walked out on her—it was terrifying."

"Have you talked to Paul since he left?" Mark asked.

"No. I tried calling. Left a bunch of messages. I sent him a couple of emails too."

He nodded. "Let's give him some time. I'm sure you'll hear from him before too long. He's probably feeling awful for leaving so suddenly."

That's not Mavis.

I'd kept myself busy throughout the afternoon, trying not to think about what had happened or the bizarre things my mother had told me. Trying to tell myself that she was sick, upset about Paul, heavily medicated. I'd cleaned the kitchen, done laundry, made the girls quesadillas when they got home from school. Olivia had gone tearing into my mother's room to show her a funny little chicken pillow she'd made in art class. I'd stood in the doorway watching them, terrified that my mother might start spewing frightening nonsense about not being herself to my little girl. But my mother was sweet and charming, cooing with delight over the pillow. "I made it for you, Grandma Needle," Olivia had said. "I love it," my mother had responded. "It's the nicest gift anyone's ever given me."

Mark snuggled up next to me and peered at the screen on my laptop.

"Learning the constellations?" he asked, then read: "'Azha, a star in the constellation Eridanus.'" He frowned. "I don't know that one."

"Eridanus is a river. At the feet of Orion."

He nodded, looked down at the screen again. "'The name Azha translates to *the hatching place*.'" He looked at me. "So why are we learning about this particular star?"

"Something my mother told me."

"Oh? I didn't realize she was interested in astronomy."

"She isn't." I said it like I had some idea about my mother's interests. Like I knew her at all. "At least, not that I know of," I added.

He watched me, waiting.

I shut my laptop, decided to try a new tactic: the truth. "She told me that Azha was her real name."

Mark smiled. "She's named herself after a star? I think that's sort of lovely, don't you?"

"I don't think I'd call it lovely."

"So what would you call it?"

"I don't know, Mark. Weird? A little creepy, maybe?"

That's not Mavis.

"She told Olivia to call her Needle Sivam, which is Mavis Eldeen backward. When I asked her about it today, she told me she had many names but I could call her Azha. And Paul, before he left—" I paused, wondering if I dared go on. If I should tell him everything.

Mark gently closed my laptop. "Ali, your mother is very sick and on a lot of meds. She's going to say some pretty screwy stuff. You can't go looking for the sinister in every little thing she says or does."

"I feel like . . . like she's playing with me. Only I don't understand the game."

"Alison—"

"I know, I know. She's sick. And I have a wild imagination."

"I'm just saying, take things in context."

I nodded.

"And my best advice right now?" Mark said. "Put away the laptop. Get some sleep. You look exhausted." He kissed my cheek, my forehead.

"I will. I'm just going to check my email again. See if Paul got back to me. Also, I'm waiting to hear from Sarah. She was meeting with Kit and John today, asking for another six months' extension for me, for the new book."

"You can't keep putting them off," he said, lying back on his pillows, closing his eyes.

"I know," I said. "And I'm making progress. Really." The lie felt like a cannonball sitting in my gut. "It's just . . . with my mother here, with Christmas coming and everything, it's gonna be slow going."

"I'm sure they'll understand. Good night, my love," he said, rolling over, his back to me. Within two minutes, he was snoring softly. I'd always envied his ability to fall asleep so easily, so quickly, no matter the circumstances.

I flipped open my laptop and looked down at the screen, scrolling to the next page of search results for Azha.

My fingers grew tingly and I heard a strange buzzing as I clicked on one of the links.

The world grew smaller, darker, as if I was looking at everything through a tunnel.

Surely I wasn't understanding what I was reading. Surely this was impossible. The words seemed fuzzy and strange, as if they were written in another language, impossible to comprehend.

The buzzing got louder, seemed to be coming from everywhere: the walls, the ceiling, the floor.

It surrounded me, got closer, closer still, until I could feel it, the vibration of it.

The source of the buzz was there in bed with me, just beneath the covers, between me and Mark.

I held my breath, jerked back the blanket.

The glowing screen of my phone shone up at me.

It was only my phone.

I was getting a call from a New York number I didn't recognize. Maybe Paul was calling me back from someone else's phone?

"Hello?" I spoke quietly as I answered, not wanting to wake up Mark.

"Good evening. This is Sergeant Herrera from the New York State Police. I'm trying to reach the family of Paul Deegan."

My heart hammered. Had something happened?

"I—I'm a family friend. As far as I know, Paul doesn't have family he's in regular contact with."

"I'm at his residence now, 278 Spring Hill Road. He has a Mavis Holland listed as his emergency contact but she doesn't appear to be at home. Is that his wife?"

"No, no," I stammered. "She's his employer."

"But he lives at the residence with her?"

"He lives in the carriage house—he's her assistant."

"Do you know where I can reach Ms. Holland?"

"She's actually here, staying in my house."

"May I speak with her?"

"No, I'm sorry," I said. "She's quite ill and heavily medicated at the moment. I'm her daughter, Alison. Please, what's this about?"

Mark shifted beside me.

"We got your phone number from Mr. Deegan's phone—nearly all of his recent calls had been to you. I'm sorry to have to deliver this news over the phone. . . ." He paused and I waited, my heart slamming up into my throat. I knew what he was going to say and I didn't want to hear it. I wanted to hang up before he had a chance. "Mr. Deegan was in an accident this evening on Route 212."

"Oh God," I said. "Is he—"

Tell me he's all right. He's in the hospital but should be fine. Thank God for airbags.

But that wasn't what he was going to say, and I knew it. "He was killed instantly," Sergeant Herrera said, his voice faltering a little. He sounded young, like he didn't have a lot of experience delivering horrible news over the phone.

"No," I whimpered. "How? What happened?"

"We believe he hit a patch of ice and lost control coming into a turn. He flipped, went down an embankment. The top of his vehicle was sheared off and Mr. Deegan was . . ."

"What?" I asked, suddenly needing to know the details. Had he been thrown from the car?

"Well, he was, um . . ." He cleared his throat. "I don't know how much detail you want. And I'm really not supposed to—"

"Please tell me," I said.

"Well, he was—" Sergeant Herrera's voice trembled as he spoke. I understood that whatever had happened to Paul had been bad—had shaken this man. He seemed hesitant to tell me, but it almost felt like part of him longed to tell me—to share with another person the horror of whatever he'd seen. "Like I said, he was killed instantly. He was . . . decapitated."

I let out a whimper, unable to find words.

I tried to focus on what the trooper was saying, details about where they'd taken the remains of the car (which was registered to my mother), how he was passing my contact information on to the coroner, how I should try to find any relatives Paul might have had, his next of kin.

Mark rolled over, opened his eyes, and looked at me. "Who is it? What's happening?" he asked.

My mind spun. I saw Paul tearing out of the driveway after uttering the words that had stunned me: *That's not Mavis.*

I heard my mother telling me about her many names.

And about Paul. How he'd run off.

He's gone off and lost his head.

I felt bile rise into my throat, burning.

This wasn't real. This couldn't be happening.

"What was that?" Mark mumbled as I ended the call. "Is everything okay?"

But I couldn't answer.

Things weren't okay.

Not at all.

I stared down at my computer, still open on my lap.

I reread the first paragraph on the page I'd clicked on just before my phone began to buzz:

Azha, an ancient female demon, often depicted with the body of a serpent and the head of a bird. Greedy, cruel, and spiteful, she is said to offer great wealth, fame, whatever your deepest desire—in exchange for your soul.

"Hon?" Mark said, sitting up.

I slammed my laptop closed and let out a sob.

TWENTY-TWO

MY MOTHER WAS IN the house with the nursing assistant, getting a sponge bath. Mark had taken Olivia to dress rehearsal at the opera house. Izzy was out with Theo—they went to a matinee every Saturday with a group of friends from film club. I was in the barn, reading an article online entitled "Signs Someone You Love May Be Possessed by a Demon." They included personality changes, violent behavior, strange speech, and unusual movements.

> The person's physical form may appear to change: they can appear older, younger, their eye color may shift, the entire structure of their face and body may appear different. The demon has the ability to greatly manipulate its host, as if the human were a puppet made of malleable clay.

I looked down at the notes I'd been taking, adding: *The ability to change form.* In caps, I wrote: *PERSONALITY CHANGES. VIOLENT BEHAVIOR*, underlining the words. On the bottom of the page was a drawing I didn't remember doing; something I must have sketched while my mind was full of jumbled thoughts. It was Azha, a creature with the head of a bird (I'd drawn a black bird with a crest, like a shadowy blue jay) and the body of a thick black snake. In my version, a part of the creature was familiar to me: I'd given it my mother's icy blue eyes.

My own eyes burned. I hadn't slept much last night after the call from the state trooper. And when I did start to drift off, I dreamed of Paul's accident. In my dreamscape rendering, Paul came around a corner and Azha was in the road, waiting, snake body writhing, blue jay head screeching *eee-eee-eee.*

I rubbed at my eyes. The back of my neck and my shoulders ached. I needed more caffeine.

I looked at my watch. It was a little after three in the afternoon. I'd been at this for nearly two hours: scouring websites and taking notes, ordering books on demons and demonic possession. They were books I'd be far too embarrassed to purchase at our local independent shop, where the booksellers all knew me by name, greeted me when I came in the door, recommended titles to me—and, of course, stressed me out no end by asking how the next Moxie book was coming along.

The deeper I delved into this demon research, the more twisted and tangled up I felt. On the one hand, everything suddenly made sense. It was almost a relief to have an explanation for my mother's personality and behavior. On the other hand, the logical part of my brain told me this couldn't possibly be real. Demons didn't exist except in the pages of horror novels and the flickering glow of late-night movies.

Impossible, I told myself.

But what if it wasn't?

"Knock-knock!" a voice called, muffled, outside the barn door.

I jumped, nearly falling off my stool.

I tried to croak out, "Who's there?" but the words dried up in my throat.

Azha, she would hiss.

Azha who? I would ask, reciting a silly knock-knock joke, a riddle.

But what would the punch line be?

Az-ha-ungry and I'm going to open my mouth and swallow you whole.

The barn door slid open, and I turned and saw Penny sticking her head through.

Relief flooded through me.

"Hey," she said, coming in. "You okay?" She took a long look at me. I could read her concern already.

I closed the laptop before she could see what was on the screen. "Not really," I admitted. I wanted to run to her, bury myself in one of her comforting sandalwood-scented hugs.

"Mark texted me. He asked me to come check on you." Her eyes went from the closed laptop to my notebook, and I closed that too. But I was sure she'd seen the creature I'd drawn.

"He did?"

My husband had texted me a couple of pictures of Olivia in her mouse costume and had checked in to see how I was doing. I told him I was busy working on the new Moxie book. The nursing assistant, Janice, was scheduled to spend the afternoon with my mom, so I was taking a break out in my studio.

I hadn't shown Mark what I'd found online about Azha. I could only imagine what he'd say, the concerned but derisive look he'd give me while explaining that it simply wasn't possible.

Penny nodded. "He told me about Paul. Said you were badly shaken by the news. That you didn't get much sleep last night." She hugged me. "It's terrible, Ali. I'm so sorry." She released me from the tight embrace and studied my face, eyes boring into mine, trying to see all I wasn't telling her.

I nodded, rubbed my neck. "I still can't believe it. It's like something from a bad dream. Paul was just here yesterday. He had the accident driving back to Woodstock. He and my mother had a fight. He was so upset when he left. I keep thinking that if I had just found a way to get him to stay, to work things out, or at least calm down, then maybe—"

"You can't play the what-if game, Ali. You have no idea if his being upset led to the accident—and even if it did, that's not your fault."

"I know."

"An accident is just that," Penny said, taking my hand and giving it a squeeze. "An accident. Sometimes terrible things happen and no one's to blame."

I nodded. I thought about the loss of Penny and Louise's son. Not an accident, exactly, but a tragic fate no one could have predicted. The world was filled with terrible things.

Mark had told me the same thing again and again: that nothing I could have done would have changed what happened to Paul. And the logical part of my brain understood that I couldn't have prevented it.

But still, I kept replaying the strange visit, wondering what I might have done differently. I glanced down at my messy worktable. My drawings, the notes I'd made, my laptop with email confirmation of the books I'd ordered.

That's not Mavis, Paul had said.

"How's your mother taking it? They're very close, right? I can't imagine what she must be going through."

I bit my lip. "She doesn't know."

Her eyes got big. "Ali, I get trying to protect her, but—"

"I know, I know. I need to tell her. I need to discuss arrangements with her. See if Paul had any family I should notify. And it was her car he was driving, so we'll have to deal with all of that. The coroner called this morning asking what funeral home we wanted to use—he had a local place he recommended. Just when I think this nightmare can't get any worse, it does."

"Sounds like the sooner you tell her, the better," Penny said, tucking an unruly curl behind her left ear.

"I know. It's just—I need to find a good time. She was in a lot of pain when she got up, and asked for extra meds. Then she was drifting in and out. Then her nurse, Teresa, came for a bit. And now Janice, the LNA, is in there with her. She's giving her a bath, changing the sheets. Sitting with her for a bit to give me a break."

Penny looked at me, waiting. Normally I found these intense looks from her comforting, but now I felt caught.

"I'm going to tell her later this afternoon," I reassured her, "after Janice leaves. As long as she's awake and lucid."

"Promise?" she asked.

"Promise," I said.

She gave me a warm smile. "I can be there with you if you want. You know, for moral support."

I shook my head. "Thanks, but I can do it."

"I'm sure it'll be a terrible shock," Penny said.

I nodded.

"I'll text you later to check in. See how she took the news." I understood that this was my best friend's way of holding me to my word that I'd actually tell my mother this afternoon. "Maybe Louise and I can come by tomorrow and bring her a treat. More coffee cake? Scones?"

"Sure," I said. "She'd like that, I'm sure."

"We'll come tomorrow then," she said.

She looked down at my closed laptop and notebook. "So what are you working on out here?" She stared right at me as if daring me not to tell the truth.

"I—" I tried to lie. To make up something about doing research for the next Moxie book. Trying to figure out how Moxie was going to save Halloween, if Halloween even needed saving. But she was my very best friend, and I couldn't lie to her. And I knew that even if I tried, she'd see right through me. I sighed, wondering how to begin.

"Remember a long time ago when you told me your theory about guardian angels? Good spirits watching over us, protecting us, helping to guide us?" At the time, I'd thought it was kind of a flaky idea, but Penny was into all that new-age spiritual stuff.

She nodded. "Yes."

"Do you still believe that?"

"Absolutely."

I ran my hand over my notebook, fingers worrying their way over the metal spiral on its spine. "Well," I said, "if there are good spirits, doesn't it make sense that there might be bad ones too?"

She frowned at me. "What is it you're asking me, Alison?"

"Paul, before he left yesterday, he said the strangest thing. I was asking him what was going on with my mother, what had happened between the two of them, and he said to me, 'That's not Mavis.'"

"I don't understand." Penny looked perplexed. "Not Mavis?"

"Do you believe in demons?" I asked.

"Demons?" she repeated slowly.

I'd come this far. There was no point going back now. "Yesterday my mother, after Paul left—she was upset too. In a rage, really. She'd gotten herself out of bed to try to get to him, I think, and ended up falling, hurting herself. Later she was talking all kinds of crazy shit, and then she said . . . she told me her true name was Azha."

"Azha? A-Z-H-A?"

"Yeah. And I looked it up. It's the name of a star. But it's also the name of an ancient demon." I watched Penny. She said nothing, her face unreadable. But she kept her eyes locked on mine, just like always. "I even found a picture. It has the head of a bird and the body of a snake, terrible claws." I opened my notebook, flipped to my drawing of the creature. "Azha offers wealth and fame and whatever a person most desires. It grants wishes in exchange for your soul."

Penny gazed at me, face blank, totally calm. There was no judgment in her eyes. But there was also none of the love, the sense of connection I usually felt when she looked at me. This was her therapist look. Was this how she regarded her totally delusional clients, so ripped open by trauma and grief they weren't sure what was real and what wasn't?

"So you're saying you believe your mother is what, exactly? Possessed?" She seemed to choke out the last word.

"I know it sounds crazy, that's what I thought too at first, but then

I started looking into it, and the stuff I've learned about Azha, about possession . . . it makes sense."

I looked down at my notebook, ready to share the research I'd done, offer her my proof.

Penny believed in guardian angels, and in the healing power of crystals, and in the insight a tarot reading could give. So she was the perfect person to have an open mind about all of this, to accept that it might be possible. And she was my best friend, the person who got me no matter what. She'd believe me. If I showed her, told her everything I knew, she'd have to believe me.

But I was wrong.

She shook her head. "A demon, Alison? You're saying you actually believe your mother is possessed by a demon?"

My stomach twisted into a tight knot when I saw the way she looked at me: her eyes tinged with confusion, worry, and complete disbelief.

"There are records of Azha going all the way back to the—"

"Alison," she said, putting a hand on my arm. "There is no Azha." She was speaking to me slowly, calmly. The same way I'd told Olivia there is no Rat King.

I pulled my arm away. "So, what? You think I'm crazy?" My tone came out snappish, defensive.

She sighed. "No, Ali. I don't think you're crazy at all. I think this is your mind's way of making sense of things. Of giving a reason for the things your mother did to you. It's easier to believe she has a demon inside who made her do the horrible things she did; easier than accepting that she abused you."

I snapped the notebook closed, felt my defenses rising. Penny was my best friend. The one who always took my side, had my back. If she didn't believe me, no one would. "So you don't believe in demons? In evil?"

She rubbed her hands together like she was cold. "Oh, I definitely believe in evil. People do all kinds of fucked-up, evil things. But because of trauma and mental illness, lack of coping skills or support—or maybe just because they are mean assholes. Not because they have the devil inside them. Over the history of humanity people have mistaken mental illness for possession. But we know better now." She looked at me pointedly.

I nodded to show her that I knew better too, of course.

She was right. Hadn't some part of me always longed for an excuse and an explanation for the things my mother had done? Something beyond *she was just sick*. Something to truly prove that I hadn't deserved any of it.

"There's darkness in the world," Penny said, "and I have no doubt that your mother's got darkness in her. But darkness doesn't always equal the devil or any of the lesser demons."

I nodded again. Of course it didn't. My hand was on my notebook, pressing the cover down, keeping it closed, as if the ideas it contained might just come leaping out.

Penny reached into her shirt, pulled out a little purple pouch on a string around her neck.

"What's that?" I asked.

She took it off, handed it to me. "My friend Carmen made it for me," she said. I'd met Carmen a couple of times at Penny and Louise's parties. She ran a little bookstore and crystal shop in Burlington and did tarot readings. "It's a charm of protection. I'm supposed to wear it when I see my clients so I don't absorb their negative energy and carry it home with me. But I think maybe you need it more now than I do." She smiled. "Go ahead, put it on."

I put the string around my neck. "What's in it?"

"Oh, I'm not sure. Herbs, roots, a crystal, I think."

"Thanks," I said.

"You're more than welcome." She stood up to go. "Ali?"

"Yeah?"

She frowned, picked at a bit of fluff on her sweater. "I wouldn't mention any of the demon stuff to Mark. He's worried enough already."

"No! Of course not." I was sorry I'd mentioned it to her. I certainly wasn't going to bring it up with Mark. "Forget I said anything, okay? I know it's a crazy idea. You're right. It's just me trying to make sense of something awful and impossible. To give a reason, however irrational, for the things my mother did. Thank you for not judging."

Penny nodded. "Do yourself a favor," she said, looking at my notebook and laptop. "No more demon research. If you're going to come out here, do some work on Moxie."

"Moxie it is," I said, tucking the purple charm under my sweater. I flashed Penny the most reassuring smile I could muster. "She's got a holiday to save and I've got a deadline."

TWENTY-THREE

MOTHER?"

My mother's eyes were closed. But she was smiling. Playing possum.

The room was cold. Too cold. I looked to make sure the window was closed, and it was. The walls, painted a light cream color, looked dingy and dark, as if a shadow had fallen over them. Olivia's WELCOME GRANDMA MAVIS sign hung above my mother's bed; the chicken pillow Olivia had made for her was beside her on the bed. The stone sat on the bedside table, and I thought, for one terrible instant, that it was the stone that had sucked all the light and color from the room.

Janice had just left. I heard her car pulling out of the driveway and then down our road. As I'd walked her out, she was cooing about what a sweetheart my mother was. "Smart as a whip," Janice had said. "You know, she told me she could predict the winning Pick Four lottery numbers for tonight. She made me promise to stop at the store on the way home and buy myself a ticket. Says she's got a way of knowing things."

I smiled an *isn't that funny* sort of smile but felt chilled to the core.

"She's a spunky one," Janice went on. "But such a dear."

It was a little after four. Mark and Olivia would be home soon. I needed to go get the breakfast and lunch dishes washed, clean up the kitchen, and start dinner. I'd promised Olivia spaghetti and turkey meatballs.

"Are you awake, Mother?" I stepped closer. The overhead light was on, as was the light on her bedside table. It still seemed dark and cold in the room. "I have something to tell you."

I knew I needed to explain what had happened to Paul. There was no more putting it off.

It didn't help that I was expecting a text from Penny at any moment asking how my mother had taken the news.

My mother's smile seemed to broaden, but her eyes stayed closed. Her arms were at her sides, her hands clenched into fists, as if she was getting ready for a fight.

Resisting the urge to retreat, I leaned down close to her, so close that I could smell the apple shampoo, the baby powder Janice had dusted her with. But beneath it, a foul odor. Rot. A body deteriorating.

She smelled like a corpse.

"Azha?" I whispered.

Her eyes flew open and her smile widened, showing yellow teeth clenched together. "Isn't it nice to know at last? To have the truth out in the open?" she asked. "No more hiding. No more pussyfooting around it. Now we both see each other for what and who we truly are."

I nodded, trying to gauge what she was up to. Was this really a delusion brought on by her illness or the meds—a way for her psyche to justify a lifetime of cruelty to those who loved her? Was it just a game she was playing? One final mind-fuck to leave me reeling?

And when she looked at me, what and who did she see? Part of me wanted to ask her, but another part really didn't want to know.

"What's that?" she said, sitting up, pointing to the bundle around my neck with a crooked finger, knuckles swollen from arthritis.

"Something Penny gave me." I held it up, smiling. "A good-luck charm."

"It stinks," she said, her face contorting to show her disgust as she turned away.

"Do you really think so?" I put it to my nose. I thought it smelled lovely. I caught a hint of sage, of lavender, and something deep and earthy underneath it.

"Take it off," she ordered. "It smells vile. Like shit."

I tucked it back under my shirt, took a step back. "It's just a silly charm."

"What is it you want, shit girl?" she snapped. Then she tutted, shook her head, bangs of silver-white hair falling across dark eyes. "Oh, that's right. You've come to tell us about Paul, haven't you?" She made an exaggerated pouty face, bottom lip out, eyes wide and sad. She looked like an absurd cartoon, a caricature.

Did she know already? How could she?

"He's dead, poor thing. He went off half-cocked and lost his head." She giggled, sounding strangely little-girlish.

"How did you know?" I asked, breathless, startled.

"*Who killed Cock Robin? I, said the Sparrow, with my bow and arrow,*" she sang. "*I killed Cock Robin.*"

"How did you know Paul was dead?" I asked again, my voice stronger and louder this time; my *answer me, damn it* voice that was full of a strength and confidence I did not feel.

"*Who saw him die? I, said the Fly, with my little teeny eye, I saw him die.*"

I remembered the flies in Izzy's room, their thick bodies as they huddled in a mass against her window. The soft thudding sound they made.

I looked around the room, half expecting to see more of them, sure I heard a faint buzzing.

"Answer me," I demanded. "How did you know about Paul?"

Her smile faded. "I know everything. I am the sparrow and the fly."

"No one can know everything."

She laughed again, a terrible grackle-like laugh. She lay back, rested her head on the pillows piled up behind her. "True enough. You caught me in my lie. Aren't you the clever one? The cat who swallowed the canary and is all proud and pleased, chest puffed out, head held high." She stared at me. "Meow, meow, meow."

I looked at her, the way her face contorted as she made cat sounds—and I was sure, for a few seconds, that this wasn't truly my mother but some grotesque facsimile of her.

She fiddled with the edge of her quilt. "The truth is," she said, "I know many things. Not all things."

"What else do you know?" I asked, testing her. What was I hoping for? That she'd tell me something it was impossible for her to know, something that would prove that she was actually a demon?

That's what I wanted: proof that this was real. Or a way to catch her in a lie, to prove that it was only a game she was playing. Surely it had to be a game.

The sane, rational part of my brain knew I should end this now. Just walk out, leave the room, start dinner. Not engage in conversation. Not encourage this insanity. What did it say about my own mental health that I was even playing this game with her?

I thought of Penny's expression of concern and disbelief. If she could see me now, I knew she'd ask me what the hell I was thinking.

"It would be easier to list the things that I don't know," my mother (or the thing that was posing as my mother) said.

I crossed my arms over my chest. "Such as?"

She narrowed her eyes, which seemed all black as if her pupils had blown up, erased everything else. "Why did you say yes to having us here?"

"Us?"

"Your mother and I. Host and symbiont. Why did you say yes?"

"Because it was the right thing to do."

"*No, no, no!* Wrong answer." She sprang up into a sitting position again, reminding me of an absurd jack-in-the-box. "You had a reason. *An agenda.* Were you hoping for closure? Reconciliation? A happy ending?"

I shook my head, took a step back. "There are no happy endings."

There was the wicked smile I recognized from my childhood. "Maybe there's hope for you yet, Alison. Maybe you're not half as dim-witted as I've always believed."

I clenched my jaw. "You said *us*. Host and symbiont. Does that mean my mother is still in there?"

"Pieces of her."

"Only pieces?"

"She's a broken puzzle. I'm the glue holding it all together."

I nodded, took a long, slow breath to try to displace the unease I felt spreading through me. "Can I talk to her now?"

"No, she's not home." She gripped the quilt again, wringing it in her gnarled hands.

"I want to speak to her."

"*Ding-dong, ding-dong,* ring the bell all you want, shit-for-brains, worthless girl, she's not going to answer. You're stuck with me tonight."

"How long have you been there?"

She took in a long, rattling breath, coughed, then leaned back against the pillows. "Oh, longer than you could conceive, with your tiny little mind, your pathetic sense of time and space. I have been here for eons. I am older than the oldest stone."

I was shaking inwardly. "I mean, how long have you been there inside my mother?"

There it was again, the scornful shake of the head, the disapproving *tsk-tsk*. "You're asking the wrong questions." Her voice seemed to be losing its edge. She sounded tired. Or maybe she was disappointed in me, just like always.

"What questions am I supposed to be asking?" My voice was squeaky, a little too loud, betraying my fear and frustration.

"Honestly, Alison. Do I have to spell it out for you? Lead you down the crooked path to the questions that should be oh-so-fucking obvious?"

I said nothing. Again I questioned my own sanity for even staying in the room, listening to her, playing along.

It wasn't real. It couldn't be.

That's what I told myself, but deep down, I felt something shift inside me: a terrible truth beginning to settle in my chest, making it harder to breathe.

She gave a huffing sigh of disgust. Her breath smelled like old meat left in the sun. "Your mother's body is dying."

I stood up straighter, my own body tensing. "I'm well aware of that."

"So you might ask yourself what happens to me when she dies."

A chill swept over me as she stared me down, her black eyes locked on mine. For a terrible moment I had the sense that she was moving closer to me, that her body was floating up, stretching out into a snakelike shape, writhing its way toward me.

"You know, don't you?" she said at last, a grin turning up the corners of her pale lips, her tongue flicking out, lizard-like, to moisten them.

"You need to go elsewhere?" I guessed. "Into another . . . host?"

Wasn't that the way it happened in movies? A demon moving like a parasite from one innocent victim to the next?

"That's right." She nodded weakly. "Keep going, follow the thread."

I closed my eyes. And just like that, I was back in my childhood bed, my mother beside me, whispering in my ear. *I should have spared you. Drowned you at birth, maybe, not let you suffer the things that are to come.*

The heavy truth I felt in my chest blossomed into something huge and dark, taking my breath away.

Even then, she knew.

She knew I would be next.

I understood then, why she'd asked to come here. To be with me at the end of her life. She didn't want reconciliation or forgiveness.

She wanted *me*.

My body.

My soul.

"It's me," I said, opening my eyes, looking right at her.

She nodded, a sickly smile spreading across her face. "It's been you all along."

I grabbed the railing on the side of her bed to help me keep my balance.

"Do you have any idea what I can do for you? What I can give you? The places we can go together?" There was a terrible gleam in her eyes:

excitement, hope. Color seemed to rush into her pale cheeks. She sat up again, leaning forward, reaching for me.

"N-no," I stammered, stepping away.

"You think you've had success with your silly little puppy book? You don't know the meaning of success. Imagine it, Alison: your name at the top of best-seller lists, people lining up for hours to get your autograph, more money than you could ever spend."

I shook my head.

It wasn't real. This was a sick old woman trying to spread her sickness to me.

"It's your mother's dying wish," she said.

"And if I say no? If I refuse?"

She barked out a laugh.

"There is no refusal. It's not a *choice*. It's not like picking out your outfit for the day. It's not like saying you don't care for steak and would rather have chicken."

"No," I said, voice shaky. I thought of my girls, of what would happen to them if I wasn't me anymore, if I became someone—something—else. I stopped the thought because it was absurd. I was playing right into my mother's hands. For surely she was not truly a demon named Azha but my mother, playing the cleverest and cruelest trick, one final terrible game to leave me reeling while she died. I remembered what she used to say to me when I was little: *You need to be less gullible. You can't believe everything you hear, Alison.*

"There's nothing to refuse, *Mother*. None of this is real," I said, my mind spinning as I fought desperately to stay in the land of the sane. A land without demons. A land where my mother was just a sick old woman in a rented hospital bed hoping to pull off one final mind-bending trick on her only daughter. "You're making it all up. Admit it."

There was no demon. No possession. There couldn't be.

She raised one eyebrow in a dramatic, mocking *Am I?* expression.

"Admit it!" I snapped. "You're just fucking with me. Fucking with me like you always used to fuck with me."

I remembered the time she'd told me we'd lost the house and would have to live in our car, the horrible time she'd told me my brother was dead. It was all just a game to her.

Now she smiled, lay back, closed her eyes, and resumed singing, more weakly this time: *"All the birds of the air fell a-sighing and a-sobbing when they heard the bell toll for poor Cock Robin."*

I stepped forward again, put my hands on her frail, bony upper arms. "Would you stop with the fucking singing?" I shouted at her.

"Alison?"

I turned. Mark was in the doorway, his face stricken.

"Ouch," my mother said in a small, weak voice. "You're hurting me, Ali. Please stop," she whimpered. "Don't hurt me again. Please."

I let go, stepped back, raised my hands like a criminal caught in the act. Mark came into the room and, with his hands planted firmly on my shoulders, pulled me away from my mother, rescuing her.

TWENTY-FOUR

THE LITTLE GIRL SITTING on the mall Santa's lap was screaming, and who could blame her? He was obviously an imposter in his shiny polyester suit, fake beard, vinyl boots. The helper elf was trying to soothe the poor kid, offering her a tiny cellophane-wrapped candy cane. The little girl's frazzled mother was begging her to stop crying, just for a minute, so they could take the picture.

"It's Santa," her mother kept saying. "You love Santa, don't you?"

The girl, who couldn't have been more than four, thrashed and struggled on Santa's lap in her good red dress as her mother held her there. "Please," her mother begged. "Just be still for one minute."

"No!" the girl screamed, red-faced, hysterical. "No! No! Nooooo!"

I flashed the mother the evilest look I could muster, then walked away from the torture session toward the food court.

Mark had insisted I get out of the house, do some shopping, maybe even meet a friend for lunch. Something to take my mind off the terrible news about Paul. Get some space from my mother.

"What was going on with you in there?" he'd asked me yesterday after extricating me from her room, saving my poor feeble mother from her abusive daughter. He watched me worriedly, like he was no longer sure what I might be capable of.

"Nothing," I said.

"Well, your *nothing* might just leave ugly bruises on your mother's arms." There was a terrible edge to his voice.

"I was barely touching her! If you'd heard what she was saying—"

I stopped myself, knowing any explanation would sound like a stupid—and possibly crazy—excuse.

He let out a long breath. It sounded like a hiss, or a balloon deflating. "Alison, I understand that things are complicated and difficult right now, for you, for all of us, but if we're even starting to slip into anything that could be considered elder abuse, we need to find another place for your mother to go. Right away. I'm sure there are some lovely private institutions that do end-of-life care."

"No," I said firmly. "I'm fine—it's fine. She's staying." No way was I sending her somewhere else. We had unfinished business. I needed to find out if what she'd told me could possibly be true. Confront her if it wasn't. And if it was (I knew I was crazy for even considering the possibility), it was up to me to find a way to stop it.

"Well, you clearly need a break," Mark had insisted. He said it with a smile, as if exiling me from the house was a miracle cure-all. As if spending the day shopping was something I might actually enjoy. Did my husband know me at all?

"I'll make some calls. Get some extra help. A few more hours a day of care from the hospice agency. You said your mother likes that LNA, Janice, right? We'll see if we can get her in a little more often. And there's Penny—when I talked with her this afternoon, she offered to help however she could. And she seems to really like your mom." I'd grimaced a little here and tried to make it look like a smile. "We don't need much," Mark went on. "Just someone to sit with her. Make her meals. Give you some time off. You can get more time in your studio. You can take Moxie for a walk—get out of the house for a bit every day."

I wasn't an idiot. I understood Mark wanted a babysitter for me as much as for my mother.

"Sounds great," I had said with a smile. "Thanks. You're right. I've been really stressed. It's . . . a lot."

He massaged my shoulders. "You don't have to be Superwoman here, Ali."

"I know," I'd said.

"You need to take care of yourself. Maybe you should think about seeing that therapist again . . . the one you liked up in Burlington? Cara? Was that her name?"

I nodded, glanced down at the ground, then caught myself and forced myself to make eye contact. "Carla," I said. "And yeah, maybe I'll give her a call."

The truth was, there had been no therapist. Carla was a work of fiction. Therapy was something Mark had pushed hard for a couple of years ago when I wasn't sleeping well, when I felt the whole world was looking at me and my life and seeing a cheerful, Christmas-loving woman who baked cookies and was the art lady at her daughter's preschool. "I am a hoax," I'd said to Mark back then.

"You are a successful artist and children's book author, and an amazing wife and mother," he'd countered.

"It's all a carefully constructed lie," I'd said. "I'm an imposter."

That was when he'd insisted I see someone professionally. I had no intention of baring my soul to a stranger. I'd been there and done that years ago, and it hadn't gone well.

But I needed to appease my worried husband, so I made up Carla and drove to Burlington every week and sat in a café having coffee. I came home from my supposed therapy appointments refreshed, with tales about how much progress I was making and how very helpful Carla was.

Give people what they want to see, I'd told myself.

Another survival skill learned from childhood. Show up at school in nice clothes, get good grades, don't make friends or enemies with the other kids, raise your hand in class and smile at the teachers. No one will ever suspect that the reason you won't change in front of the other girls in the locker room for gym class is because you have deep scars on your back made with the tip of a knife, that your arms and legs are covered in bruises. The other girls and the gym teacher will watch you go into the bathroom stall to change and think you're a modest girl, a good girl. A bit shy, but is that really so terrible?

THE MALL SMELLED like floor wax, artificial balsam, pretzels, burnt sugar from the fudge shop. Every store, every kiosk, every column was dripping with bright lights and tinsel. I felt like I needed sunglasses to protect me from all the shine and glitter.

15 DAYS TO CHRISTMAS blinked a big red digital sign in front of a card and stationery shop: a warning.

I hated malls and shopping almost as much as I hated Christmas. Put them together and it was my own private idea of hell on earth. Leave the seasonal merriment to Mark, and to Penny too, who had bonded with my husband over their shared enthusiasm for this festive time of year.

But Mark had instructed me to shop. Said it would be therapeutic. So I would shop. I would not think about demons or possession or my mother or what had happened to Paul. I would not think about the email I'd just gotten from my agent, Sarah, begging for sample artwork for the next Moxie book because the publisher refused to push back the deadline again.

I would lose myself in the crowd of shoppers, in the bright lights and festive music, in the *ho-ho-ho* of the jolly mall Santa in his polyester suit.

And lose myself I did. It was all too much. Overwhelming. I felt panicked. My shoulders and neck were tense. A headache was beginning to pulsate at my temples. I had to keep looking at my list to remind myself what I was even doing there.

Christmas shopping. Buying items and checking them off after purchase. People did it all the time. Many people claimed to enjoy it. I looked down at what I'd written:

A quirky tie and book of poetry for Mark
An iPad Pro for Izzy
Something Nutcracker-themed for Olivia

A nice journal and fountain pen for Penny
A tart pan for Louise
Mother—?

No idea there. But I was hoping something would jump out at me.

First, before doing any actual shopping, I needed some coffee. Maybe a little caffeine would help with my quickly blossoming headache. And my eyes felt tired and gritty—I'd had another lousy night of sleep.

I made my way to the food court, ordered a latte with an extra shot of espresso at the coffee kiosk (the barista was dressed as a sexy elf in a low-cut green velour dress), and took a seat near the thirty-foot-tall artificial Christmas tree complete with absurdly oversized presents wrapped in colored foil and piled onto a blanket of rolled-up white fluffy cotton. The fake layer of snow was littered with empty soda cups, receipts, a crushed pack of cigarettes. One of its edges looked singed, like someone had tried to set it on fire.

Tinny Christmas music was being piped through the mall sound system: "Walking in a Winter Wonderland." The coffee tasted like scorched sugar and melted plastic. I sipped it, desperate for the caffeine as I watched shoppers come and go, laden with bags, carrying trays of greasy mall food: pizza, General Tso's chicken, corn dogs, and curly fries. I saw a few people smiling and laughing, but most of them looked distinctly lacking in holiday cheer. A winter wonderland it was not.

I opened my purse, took three ibuprofen with a big gulp of coffee, then grabbed a pen and started doodling on my list, sketching a little Christmas tree, of all things.

MY CRAPPY LATTE had gone cold. And I was still sitting and had made no progress with my list. I blinked at my watch, disbelieving—an hour had passed since I'd arrived at the mall.

I looked down at my drawing. The Christmas tree—which had grown (magically, I thought, like the tree in *The Nutcracker*) and now ran the entire length of the page along the right side—was covered in strange ornaments that weren't really ornaments at all: bees, flies, and wasps seemed to crawl over it. I could almost hear them buzzing. And there, at the top, where the star should go, rested a macabre version of Mark's glass angel: half-human, half-insect, its compound eyes staring out at me.

I picked up my list with the tree drawing and stood up, determined to get this shopping done, when my phone rang in my purse. Maybe Mark was calling to check on me. Had he texted while I was drawing and I hadn't heard the familiar ping, and now he was worried?

I pulled my phone out.

"Hello, I'm looking for Alison O'Conner?"

"Yes, that's me."

"My name is Francis Lefler. I'm the director of Lefler Funeral Home in Woodstock, New York. I understand you wanted to speak with me about making final arrangements for Paul Deegan?"

"Yes," I said. "Thanks for getting back to me."

I'd called the funeral home this morning and spoken to a nice young woman who asked questions I didn't know how to answer; clearly sensing it wasn't going well, she'd offered to have the director call me back to make arrangements.

"If you have a few minutes, we could go over some things."

"Of course," I said, sitting back down at the table in the food court.

"Do you know what Mr. Deegan's wishes were? Burial or cremation?"

"Um . . . I'm afraid I don't know."

"Okay. We'll come back to that. What sort of service are you thinking of? Did he have a religious affiliation?"

"I—I have no idea. I'm sorry. I can ask my mother, but she's not always in a clear state these days."

There was silence on the other end. At last he said, "There isn't any family?"

"I don't think so. Not that he was in contact with, anyway." I repeated the words I'd heard, but the truth was, I didn't know. What if he did have family somewhere, someone who would want to know he was gone?

"Have you found a will? Sometimes people keep a final-arrangements document with their will and advance directive."

"I—" I didn't want to admit that I hadn't looked. "I haven't yet, no." He was quiet again.

I knew what I had to do. It filled me with absolute dread, but I knew I had no choice. There was no one else to do it.

"Mr. Lefler, I apologize for not having answers for you. But I'll get them. Give me a couple days and I'll do my best to track down any family, look through Paul's papers." I promised to call him by Tuesday with answers to his questions.

The idea of going back to Woodstock, to the house I grew up in, hit me like jumping into a pool of ice water. My jaw clenched and I shivered.

When was the last time I had been there?

I'd gone home briefly the summer between boarding school and college, packed up a few things, then driven up to Vermont, where I'd gotten a summer job at an art camp for little kids.

That was the last time I'd set foot in the house. The place had felt more unfamiliar and cold than ever, and wherever I went, I felt like the house was watching me warily, breathing me in. It was as if the house and my mother had become one all-encompassing entity. My mother and I had avoided each other, creeping around the dark, shadowy rooms like two strangers. I remembered that I'd carried pepper spray and my cell phone with me everywhere I went, and slept with the door locked and my desk chair jammed under the knob. I was supposed to stay for a week. I lasted only one night. I spent every college break after that working, staying at first with friends and their normal families, and later in my own apartment. I had no intention of ever going back to that gray colonial and the pieces of my past it held.

When Mark and the kids and I visited, we stayed at a nice inn in Woodstock and never set foot near the house.

But I could do this.

I was a rational adult. And it was only a house, not a monster looming. Surely I'd get there and find nothing scary: just dusty memories hiding in the corners.

Strangely, I felt the house pulling me now, almost daring me to come back. Part of me wanted to see it again, sure that once I set foot inside, I would see it was just a house and had no power over me, not anymore.

I started taking a mental inventory of things I would need to do. I was good at lists, thanks to lessons gleaned from my husband, who was a master of organization. I did them well. I needed to arrange for someone to be with my mother for the day, maybe Teresa or Janice or even Penny. If none of them could make it, Mark could take a day off and stay home. I'd get the keys to the Woodstock house from my mother. I'd drive there and check on the state of things. Was there still a housekeeper who came once a week? Paul had said he'd been cleaning it out, closing it up. How far had he gotten? Were there things that needed tending? Plants that needed watering? Mail to be collected? Bills to be paid?

I'd search the carriage house Paul had lived in, looking for any information about possible family members, last wishes, a will. And while I was there, I'd look for other clues too.

Clues about my mother, about Azha, about what, if anything, Paul really knew.

TWENTY-FIVE

HOW WAS SHOPPING?" MARK asked when I got home. He'd jumped up from the couch to greet me. The Hallmark Channel was on, playing one of his much-loved Christmas movies. A man and a woman were sipping hot cocoa in a park full of fake snow. I was sure I recognized the woman from some long-ago, nearly forgotten TV show.

I thought of Bobbi. If she had lived, would she now be playing a family matriarch in one of these sappy holiday movies?

"Great," I lied. "I got everything on my list."

The house was warm and smelled of balsam pine. The lights on the tree glowed cheerfully in the corner of the living room. The angel glowered at me from where she hung in the corner, swaying slightly.

Mark kissed my cheek, smiled at the bags.

"I got the iPad Pro for Izzy and a cool 3D *Nutcracker* puzzle for Olivia. Also a ballet book she doesn't have—*The Encyclopedia of Ballet*. It's beautifully illustrated."

"Sounds perfect," he said. He started poking through the bags.

"No snooping," I chided.

He backed off, hands up. He was so like a little kid when it came to all things Christmas.

I set the bags on the dining room table.

"So, how's my mother been?" I was almost afraid to ask.

"Fantastic," he said.

I bit my tongue to keep from asking if she'd said or done anything odd while I was gone.

"Penny and Louise came for a bit and brought some amazing tarts and one of those little crocheted blankets Penny makes."

I nodded. "That was sweet," I said.

"Yeah, your mom loved it. She was really touched. She's got it draped over herself right now."

I could imagine the scene, my mother playing the role of a grateful but sickly grandma to a T.

"After they left, I made us toasted cheese sandwiches for lunch," Mark said. "And we played cribbage."

"No kidding?"

"She's a hell of a card player," he said. I nodded, remembering how she and my father used to play cards, how they'd play late into the night when Bobbi came to visit. "She skunked me! I think all the action tired her out, though. She's been sleeping for the last hour or so. Oh, and I called Kingdom Hospice. Janice is going to start coming every day for a couple of hours. There's also another LNA, Paige, who can help out if we need more. And Penny and Louise offered to help in any way they can."

I nodded. "Great, thanks for arranging that. Where are the girls?"

"Olivia's at Sophie's. And Izzy's at school."

I frowned. I'd lost an hour somehow in the food court, but was I losing track of days now? "On a Sunday?"

"She's with Theo and the kids from drama club. They're doing that parade thing? I think Izzy's recording it."

I nodded, remembering now that Izzy had said something about it last week. How a bunch of kids were going to dress up as Krampus and parade through town banging drums. Izzy called it "an anti-Christmas art happening" and thought it might be something I'd enjoy. "You should come check it out," she'd said, and seemed to genuinely want me there—which was unusual these days. Maybe her interest in the new Moxie book, the one I was busy avoiding, had softened our sometimes-fractious relationship. Izzy was a big fan of ghouls and costumes of all kinds, and she loved Halloween. My latest project, stalled though it was, seemed to have increased her respect for me somehow. But with all the stress of taking care of my mother, I'd forgotten about Izzy's Krampus parade. "Do you know what time the parade is?" I asked.

"Six," he said. "And she was hoping you could pick her up after. They're going through the downtown to the high school. She needs to be picked up there around seven."

I checked my watch. It was only five. "No problem. I'll go early and watch the parade."

"Should be pretty cool," Mark said. "One of the kids is going to be on stilts. And they were trying to get permission to carry actual torches. I don't know if that was ever okayed, though."

"Maybe just as well," I said, smiling. I took off my coat. "Listen, there's something else we need to talk about."

"Okay." Mark sat down at the dining table and I joined him.

"I need to go to Woodstock. I'd like to go tomorrow if we can arrange care for my mother."

I tried to sound as matter-of-fact as possible—like heading to my mother's house in Woodstock was something I did all the time.

"Oh?" Mark looked truly perplexed.

"The funeral home director called me wanting to make plans for Paul's service. I didn't have a clue what to tell him. I need to go to the carriage house, look through his things. Maybe I can find information about any family he may have? Or a will? The man is kind of a mystery to me and the only way I'm going to learn anything is to search through his stuff. And I need to check on my mother's house. Grab whatever mail is there and do whatever I need to start having it forwarded here. See if there are bills that need to be paid, trash that needs to go out, plants that need to be watered, a housekeeper who needs to be paid. All the stuff Paul did."

Mark frowned, rubbed his chin. "Makes sense. It's just . . ."

"What?"

He took my hand. "You've got so much on your plate. I just wish there was someone else to do all of that."

"Me too," I said. "But I'm it."

"I'll go with you," Mark said. "We can have Penny come stay with your mother and the girls."

"No need," I told him. "I'll be fine on my own. But if you could take the day off and hang out here with my mom, be on dad duty when the girls get home from school, that would be great."

"No problem," he said.

"Are you sure?"

He nodded. "Absolutely. I talked with Gregory, told him what was going on here with your mother, and he says I should take off all the time I need. We've got a couple of great subs who are more than capable and always looking for more hours."

I nodded. Gregory, the head of school, was a good friend of Mark's— not only did they work together, but they played racquetball twice a week after classes ended. I wondered how much Mark had really told him—if he'd shared details about my past with my mother, his worries over what having her here might be doing to my mental health.

"I'd love to spend the day with Mavis," Mark said. "It'll give me a chance to redeem myself in cribbage." He smiled, but it was soon overtaken by a look of concern. "Are you sure you'll be okay going to Woodstock on your own?"

"Of course. I'll be in and out as fast as I can. Paul was a super organized guy, so I have to believe all his paperwork will be easy to access. And I'm sure there isn't much to do in my mom's case—it shouldn't be that difficult."

I gave him a reassuring smile, then stood and gathered up my shopping bags. "Now I'm going to go hide these gifts before the girls get home."

"Good plan," he said. "I'll get dinner started. I'm making burritos. But first, I'm going to see what happens with my heroine and her two men.

Does she stay with the arrogant, ridiculously wealthy guy she's engaged to back in the big city, or end up with the ruggedly handsome one from a small town who owns a Christmas tree farm?"

"Gee, I wonder," I said sarcastically.

"Don't be a hater," he said.

I shook my head as I carried my bags up the stairs. How had I ended up marrying such a sentimental sap?

I hid the gifts for the girls in our closet. And I slipped the box with Mark's tie and a poetry anthology he didn't have yet into my underwear drawer.

HEADING DOWN THE hall, I passed the open door to Izzy's room. The screen on her laptop was glowing as if someone had just been using it. Odd.

I went in, looked around. Nothing. No one.

I listened for flies, even pulled back the heavy blackout curtains. No bugs this time. Only the view of our backyard through her window. I looked out at our little vegetable plot, now covered in snow, at my studio. To the right, around the corner, I knew the pear tree stood, its branches bare.

Feeling as if the computer was beckoning me somehow, I sat down at the desk and checked the laptop screen.

It was open to editing software. Izzy had been editing clips of interviews with my mother.

Curious, I clicked on the first one, keeping my ears pricked for Mark—I knew he wouldn't approve of me snooping like this without her permission. And he was right, of course—the need for privacy is a normal part of adolescent development. I knew that; I knew that teenagers needed to individuate from their parents. But still, I was dying to see what sorts of things Izzy had been filming, what persona my mother might have shown her.

I pushed play.

There was my mother lying in bed, grinning.

The camera was focused on her face. There was a ring of light in both her eyes—Izzy must have set up special lighting.

"So tell me, do you have a boyfriend, dear?"

I felt myself stiffen, afraid of the tirade Izzy might go on, invoking words like *assumption, patriarchy, gender identity.*

But she didn't.

"No," she said, a disembodied voice behind the camera. "Actually, I have a girlfriend. Her name is Theo."

My mother didn't pause or show any sign of trying to suppress a look of shock or dismay. She only nodded, smiled. "And do you love this girl? This Theo?"

Izzy chuffed out a little laugh, the camera moving.

"Was that a funny question?" my mother asked.

"No. It's just . . . no one's ever asked me that. Not even Theo." She paused. My mother stared at her, clearly still waiting for an answer. "But yes, I do love her."

A piece of my heart broke just then, listening to my daughter's voice, listening to her confess her truest feelings to my mother. I knew they were words she'd never dream of speaking to me. Was it being behind the camera that made it easier for her to open herself up? Or was it knowing that she was talking to a dying woman?

"You should tell her," my mother said.

Izzy said nothing.

"I was in love once," my mother said.

"With our grandfather? The man you were married to?" I could hear Izzy's voice catch. "I don't even know his name."

"His name was David. David Russo, and I loved him, yes. But I wasn't madly *in love with him.* Not that deep and desperate love they write songs and poems about. I've felt that true love only once." My mother looked away from the camera. Were those tears in her eyes?

I hovered my finger over the trackpad, knowing I should hit pause. I ought to shut the computer down, stand up, and walk out of my daughter's room. But I couldn't make myself. I had to know what she was going to say next.

"Who was it?" Izzy asked.

My mother turned back to Izzy. "Her name was Bobbi."

HER NAME WAS BOBBI.

I've told you about her, Isabelle. The one who found the stone back in Mexico, remember?

God, she was beautiful. Not just pretty in the traditional sense, but charismatic. She turned heads. When she walked into a room, she had this . . . this radiance, this aura, that made people turn and look, and once she caught your eye, it was hard to look away. She was mesmerizing. That's the word I would use.

I remember that last day I painted her. The painting that everyone talks about, the one that would one day jump-start my entire professional career. Do you know the painting I mean? Has your mother ever told you about it? Shown you? No, I didn't think so. Well, it's not hard to find. Just jump on your computer and type my name in. It's one of the first things to come up. The piece I'm most famous for. Like Warhol's Marilyns.

But we had no way of knowing the places that painting would take me back then. We were just kids, really. Two kids in love, wanting so badly to hold on to what we had.

It was after we got back from our trip. Bobbi had the stone, of course. We were up in my bedroom, up in the converted attic at my parents' house that I'd turned into an art studio. I really wanted to paint her that day—she complained she wasn't in the mood, but I talked her into it. It was our last day together. Bobbi was flying out to a family wedding in Colorado the next morning, and after that, she was heading for California. It was always her dream—Hollywood. For as long as I'd known her, ever since we were little girls, she said she was going to go off and get famous, be an actress.

We'd been talking about this forever, how Bobbi would leave. But it hadn't felt real. Not until that moment.

I'd felt her pulling away from me the last few days of our trip. She seemed strangely distant, withdrawn. Even when she curled up next to me, ran her fingers down my throat to my chest and left them resting there just above my heart, even when she whispered, "I love you," I could feel something, a shadow there. I understood that it was just Bobbi starting to pull away, a little at a time so it wouldn't hurt as much when she left. Bobbi, imagining her life without me. The life she'd always dreamed of in California.

I had to keep reminding her to hold still. Bobbi had never been good at holding still, at posing.

She asked why I couldn't just take a bunch of photos and do the painting from those, why we had to spend our last day together doing this.

But that was exactly how I wanted to spend it. I wanted to capture that moment forever: Bobbi just as she was right then, the sun coming in the attic window behind her making her seem to glow, the way she stared so intensely at me. It was this look. This look that I told myself meant you will always be mine.

It was Bobbi's idea, to put the stone in the painting.

I was just going to paint her standing there near the window, but then she grabbed the stone, held it up just over her chest where her shirt was unbuttoned. "Make the stone my heart," she said.

We'd taken it to a jeweler in Mexico after she found it. He told her it hadn't come from that area. He couldn't explain how she'd found it at the bottom of a cenote.

Bobbi kept it with her wherever she went, slept with it beside her, couldn't seem to stop looking at it. Sometimes I even caught her talking to it.

It was silly, really, but I felt a little jealous. Jealous of a rock.

Do you think that's foolish? No? I did. But I couldn't help it. We feel what we feel, don't we, Isabelle?

We talked while I was painting. I asked her to tell me what really happened down in the cenote. If she'd actually heard the voice of the dead man.

She nodded.

"Well, what did he say?" I asked.

Bobbi smiled. Said I wouldn't believe her if she told me.

"Try me," I said.

Bobbi looked at me then, really looked at me, her eyes pulling me in. "I really love you, you know," she said.

I knew she did. And I loved her too. But I told her it didn't matter.

None of it mattered. Because she was leaving.

I was being petty, I know. And I didn't want to ruin it, our last day together, by blaming her. But the words were out and I felt rotten as soon as I'd said them.

Bobbi was silent for a minute, holding perfectly still. Then she said, "What do you expect me to do?"

"Nothing," I told her, keeping my eyes on the painting, not on her. "I don't expect anything."

And I didn't. I wasn't a fool. I knew how the world worked. I knew we weren't going to ride off into the sunset together, live happily ever after in our own little house with a white picket fence.

I looked at her around the edge of the canvas. Bobbi, still clinging to the stone, holding it tight against her chest, gave me a bittersweet smile. "Here's what's going to happen," she said. "What the voice told me down there in the water."

At the time, I didn't believe some ghost voice in the water had actually talked to her. Bobbi had a flair for the dramatic. She liked to make things up—to take little bits of truth and embellish them.

"I'm going to California. I'm going to get a small acting role that will lead to a bigger role. I'm going to be famous."

I asked her about me, wondering what, if any, role I might have in this vision of Bobbi's future. "What am I supposed to do while you're off getting famous?" I demanded.

"You're going to stay here and marry David," Bobbi said.

I threw down my paintbrush. It was a ridiculous suggestion and I was furious with her.

David was a well-meaning, shy boy I'd dated on and off for years. He lived in Woodstock and had studied art at Yale. I'd relied on him when I needed a date for a party or function, when it was expected that I wouldn't just show up with Bobbi. Like I said—times were different. People expected a well-rounded young Vassar girl to have a boyfriend. I had David.

Bobbi started going on and on about how perfect David was for me, listing all these reasons. "He's sweet, his family has money, he's an artist, and he's over the moon about you. Just read his letters if you need any reminding."

David wrote me a letter every week, professing his love, telling me I was all he thought about, making plans for what we'd do when we were next together: a new restaurant he couldn't wait to take me to, a tour of art galleries in the city. Bobbi and I had read all his letters together, giggling. "Poor David," we'd said.

We pitied him. We felt sorry for him and made fun of him. And now here was Bobbi telling me I was supposed to marry him?

"But I don't love him," I told her.

"You will," Bobbi said. "And remember, just because you marry David and decide to love him doesn't mean you have to stop loving me. Whatever we do, wherever we go, whoever we marry, we'll always have each other. No one can take that away."

Then she held up the stone, looked at it, then at me. "You'll always have my heart," she said. "And I, yours. And knowing that—it'll just have to be enough."

TWENTY-SIX

I SAT IN THE CHAIR, looking at the laptop screen, reeling.

Here it was: the truth.

And didn't it make sense? Hadn't part of me always suspected but been hesitant to think too hard about it, to actually admit it?

I found it heartbreaking that my mother had this whole secret life, and unnerving that everything I thought I knew about her growing up was wrong. I hadn't known my mother at all. But the things I did know now clicked into place.

I knew my parents hadn't had the best relationship; even as a small child I understood that my father felt inadequate and was always trying so hard to win her love and attention.

I remembered how happy my mother had been whenever Bobbi came to visit, the glow she got even just talking with her on the phone.

And I knew that my mother had been ripped apart by Bobbi's death, that she was never the same after.

And now I fully understood why.

And why that damn rock meant so much to her: it was her connection to Bobbi. She'd lost her true love. All she had left of Bobbi was her stone heart, so my mother clung to it, slept beside it, argued with it, begged to have Bobbi back. Even now, as she lay dying, my mother kept the stone within reach, always in sight.

Again, I found myself pitying my mother.

There were tears in my own eyes as I watched my mother on Izzy's computer screen.

"She was my best friend," my mother confessed to Izzy. "And my lover. And my whole world. Until she wasn't."

The camera moved, jerked a little, as if Izzy herself had been so shocked by this revelation that she let the camera slip.

"So you guys were, like . . . together?"

"Yes, very much so."

"Did anyone know?"

"A few people. Our closest friends. And others guessed at it. I think my mother suspected, but she never asked, and I would have denied it if she had. It wasn't like now. People weren't as open and accepting. There were . . . repercussions for things like that. It was a long time ago, Isabelle."

"So . . . what happened?"

"Like I said, things were different. There were expectations." Her face tightened, and she looked away from the camera. "Bobbi went to California and starting acting, just like she always said she would. I stayed back east and married David, like she told me to. She got married too. We had children. Went on with our lives. Saw each other for a week each summer."

"But you still loved each other?"

My mother nodded.

"You were both living these lies?" Izzy's voice came out like a gasp, like she couldn't believe it.

"Isn't everyone, in one way or another?" my mother asked.

"I—did your husband know?"

"He suspected—no, he more than suspected—I'm sure he knew. But he never asked, and I never told him. Simpler that way."

"But you stayed with him? Even though you loved her?" Izzy asked, incredulous.

"We talked about it all the time. Leaving our husbands. One day being together. But the time was never right. And when we did talk about it . . . well, it was like telling each other a story we both wanted to hear, something we both knew couldn't ever come true. And then . . . then she was killed." My mother looked down at her quilt, twisting the edge of it in her fingers. "A car accident."

"Oh my God," Izzy said, the shock and sorrow in her voice palpable. "I'm so sorry."

"Well. It was a long time ago," my mother said again, her face hardening. She turned and looked at the stone on her bedside table before reaching for it, running her fingers over its craggy surface. Then she turned back and faced the camera and Izzy behind it. "Lifetimes ago."

The video clip ended. I sat staring at the now-still image of my mother looking at me from the screen.

Checking to make sure I wouldn't be seen sneaking out of my daughter's room—Mark would be apoplectic if he discovered what I'd done—I crept out into the hall and back into our bedroom and shut the door.

Then I pulled my phone out of my pocket and dialed Ben's number.

"Heading into work, Ali, I can't talk long."

"Did you know about Mom and Bobbi?" I sat down on our neatly made bed.

"Huh?"

"That they were more than friends? That Mom was . . . was in love with her?" I kept my voice low, not wanting Mark to come up and hear.

"Umm, no. It never exactly came up. She told you this?"

"Well, no. Actually, she told Izzy."

There was a long pause. "And why, exactly, would she tell Izzy?"

"Izzy was interviewing her—she's doing a video project. About Mother being here. She's doing a video diary that she's hoping to turn into a documentary."

"So Izzy's spending time alone with Mother?"

"Well . . . yeah."

"Jesus, Ali! You should be supervising. Who knows what she might say or do."

"Ben, honestly, she's not in any shape to do much of anything but lie in bed." I bit my lip, wanting to snap: *Not that you would know*. I felt a little curl of resentment—he was off in California, choosing to have nothing to do with this, while my mother was here, in my home, dying. But it had all been my choice, hadn't it?

"And the girls are both really bonding with her," I told my brother, defending myself and my decisions. "Mark loves her too. They played cards all afternoon."

Oh, and she told me her real name is Azha and she's actually a demon. I decided to hold back on this particular bit of news for now.

"Great. That's just great. It really warms the cockles of my heart to hear it." His voice dripped with sarcasm.

"About Mother and Bobbi? Do you think it's true?"

"It's a strange thing to lie about if it's not," Ben said.

I thought of what Izzy had said when my mother first arrived, how Mother was trying too hard, that she was saying and doing all the right things, but they seemed fake.

"Unless . . ."

"What?" Ben asked.

"Unless it's a way to get to Izzy. To gain her trust. Izzy told Mother about her girlfriend, Theo. And that's when Mother told her about Bobbi."

Maybe my mother was showing everyone exactly what they wanted to see, doing whatever it took to win them over.

Except that, in my heart, my mother's confession didn't surprise me in the least.

"But it all makes sense, doesn't it? I mean, part of me feels like I kind of knew it all along."

"Does it matter?" my brother asked.

"What do you mean?"

"I mean, does it matter if it's true or not? It doesn't change anything. It doesn't give her an excuse for who she is, or was, or the things she did. Having some secret lesbian affair changes nothing, Ali. Maybe she did love Bobbi. Maybe she was miserable about having to live this double life, devastated when her true love died. But honestly, this whole *The Price of*

Salt kind of secret history doesn't excuse her. What about all the closeted gay people from back then who *didn't* become abusive narcissists? If anything, if it is true—it makes it worse."

"Worse how?"

There was another long pause. The phone line buzzed and crackled.

"Because if she was really so in love with Bobbi, then we know she was capable of love. And frankly, that just hurts."

I wasn't sure what to say. I fought the urge to tell him that of course she was capable of love, that she'd loved us.

But had she?

I wasn't sure what to believe. But Ben was right. It did hurt.

"I've really gotta go," Ben said. "Ali?"

"Yeah?"

"Be careful."

TWENTY-SEVEN

I STOOD ON THE SIDEWALK of Main Street, waiting for the parade to begin. I was right in front of the Book Cellar: a clever tree-shaped stack of what must have been hundreds of books was strung with lights in the front window. Snow was falling hard. White lights and green wreaths were wrapped around all the lampposts in town. And the other store windows held similarly festive holiday displays: the kitchen shop was full of red and green cooking accessories and wreaths made from decorated red Bundt cake pans; the hardware store had a lit tree in the window and signs saying WE HAVE CHRISTMAS LIGHTS AND BULBS, SNOW SHOVELS, ICE MELT, STOCKING STUFFERS. A large stocking was displayed with tools sticking out of it: a crescent wrench, a screwdriver, a hammer, and a pair of new work gloves. The bagel shop had both a menorah and a Christmas tree in the window—and the tree was decorated with small bagels. Get Roasted advertised their peppermint lattes as "Santa's Favorite." I'd just gone in for a black coffee, which I held in my hands, feeling it warm me through my thin gloves. I had my hood up, but large flakes of snow fell down onto my face, collecting on my eyelashes. I shuffled from foot to foot to stay warm. There was a small crowd waiting along the sidewalks of our picturesque Main Street, mostly families of the drama club kids, and other high school students. It was like living inside a Christmas village snow globe, or even, God forbid, like the set from a Hallmark Christmas movie.

"Hey, Alison, I thought that was you!"

I turned to see Marie, one of the owners of the Book Cellar. "I've actually been meaning to call or email. I was hoping you could come sign some stock for us."

"Absolutely," I said. "Love to."

" 'Tis the season. Got a pub date for the next Moxie book?" she asked.

"Not yet," I said. "It's not quite finished. Close, though. Very close."

"Can't wait," she said.

Neither can I, I thought.

"I'll come by in the next couple days to sign stock," I promised.

She thanked me and headed across the street to join her husband, who had his camera out.

It was ten after six. At last the police arrived, lights flashing as they parked cars at either end of Main Street, closing it to traffic.

I heard the parade crowd before I saw them—the raucous cacophony of a banging drum, the clattering of bells, howling and screaming.

I don't know what I'd expected—but surely not this.

They came from the north end of Main Street, out of the darkness and swirling snow like creatures from a nightmare or fever dream. There were about twelve of them, all in elaborate and terrifying costumes. They wore grotesque papier-mâché devil masks with horns: large curled horns, small straight ones. One was dressed in layers of burlap. Another sported a torn and ragged Santa suit. One was up on stilts, towering over the others, a long tattered robe flowing behind. Still another wore white robes splattered with blood and carried a small, child-sized human arm, waving it menacingly at the crowd.

The snow fell hard around them as they moved through the downtown, banging the drum, rattling cowbells, shrieking and growling like creatures let loose from the underworld.

Mothers pulled their children closer to them on the sidewalk. Shopkeepers stepped out to look on, eyes wide, like this clearly was not the parade they'd been expecting. Just last week, Santa and Mrs. Claus had led a parade along the same route, ringing bells, passing out candy canes, shouting, "Merry Christmas"—this spectacle couldn't be further from that.

And then I spotted the figure who had to be my daughter.

She was all in black. A black cape, and a terrifying black mask with long curled horns, an open mouth full of pointed teeth. Her eyes glowed red from LED lights. I only knew it was her from her familiar battered Doc Martens and the video camera she held as she circled the others, running to the front to get a shot of all of them taking over the street, moving to get a close-up as one of the demons left the group and approached a small child, growling at him, making him jump back and cling to his mother.

"It's too scary," one of the mothers lining the sidewalk complained.

"Fucking brilliant," a teenage boy said to his friends.

I stood frozen, watching, holding my breath as the Christmas demons shambled by, clanging, clattering, banging, howling, and hissing like the wild things they were.

I felt disoriented—dizzy with the sense that my Hallmark movie-worthy small-town landscape had been turned inside out.

I thought of the video clip I'd seen in Izzy's room: how it made me realize that everything I thought I knew about my mother growing up had been wrong. The world was not as it seemed. She'd kept secrets, big secrets from me—worn a mask of her own. And hadn't I done the same? Keeping secrets from my own girls? Pretending to be something I wasn't?

Izzy spotted me, trained her camera on me for just a few seconds, no doubt capturing the unsettled look on my face. I did my best to smile at her, but I'm sure it looked more like a grimace.

"WHAT DID YOU think?" she asked a little later, when she hopped into the car at the high school parking lot. She was still wearing the cloak and the black horned mask. Her voice came out slightly muffled.

Snow was falling hard, but the car was warm, the heater cranking away.

"You guys were terrifying," I said. "I loved it."

She nodded, the mask slipping a little. She reached up to adjust it.

"So what, exactly, were you all supposed to be?" I looked at her sideways, telling myself it was just Izzy in there. The red eyes glowed back at me. The horns looked sharp enough to draw blood.

Around us, other kids in masks were being picked up by their families. The door of the gym opened and boys on the basketball team came running out into the snowy parking lot in shorts and team jerseys.

"Krampus," she said. "He's a creepy figure from an old European legend that originated in Germany, I think. The Germans have all the great dark stuff. Anyway, Krampus came along with Saint Nicholas at Christmastime. Saint Nicholas gave gifts to the good little boys and girls and Krampus punished the ones who were naughty. He beat them with sticks. In some stories, he steals the children, even eats them."

"You're right," I said. "That's certainly dark."

She nodded and continued talking excitedly from behind the mask. "It's like the antithesis of how bright and cheery and commercial our Christmas has become. It's this whole other dark side of Christmas, which is just perfect, right? I mean, here it is the darkest, coldest time of the year. What better time for a demon?"

She looked at me from behind the horned mask, its red eyes still turned on and glowing, watching me.

My heart seemed to skip a beat, then speed up. My fingers were trembling. I wished I hadn't had so much coffee today. I swallowed down the tight feeling in my throat.

I heard my mother's voice in my head: *You, Alison, may call me Azha.*

Izzy took off the mask, set it on her lap, and I felt myself relax. She was just my daughter again and it was a relief. I smiled at her gratefully.

"So are we going home or what?" she asked, running a hand through her hair.

I sat frozen, suddenly not wanting to go back home.

Home where my mother waited.

What better time for a demon?

"Sorry, of course," I said as I turned the wipers on, put the car in drive, and pulled out of the high school parking lot.

The roads were covered with a thin layer of snow.

"Your mask is amazing, by the way," I told her, glancing over at her. "Are those LED lights?"

She laughed, rolled her eyes. "No, Mom. They're little pieces of legit hell coal."

I laughed back, shook my head. "Well, can you do me a favor and try not to scare your sister with it when we get home? And no Krampus stories either, okay? She's got enough nightmare material with the Rat King."

She nodded, reached into the mask, and turned off the glowing lights.

We were quiet for a while. Izzy turned on the radio, then changed her mind and turned it off.

"Did you like Theo's costume?" she asked, looking down at the mask, not me.

"Which one was she?" I turned left from Granite Street to Farm Hill Drive, which would take us all the way home. There were no streetlights out here, and the trees on either side of the road seemed to form a dark tunnel. The snow fell hard, limiting my visibility. I slowed, letting the snow tires and all-wheel drive do their work as we crept up the hill. The pavement ended and we hit the dirt road.

"The one in white."

"The one carrying the bloody arm?"

"Yup, that's her."

I turned, smiled at her. "You two really are perfect for each other," I said.

She sank back into her seat, grinning.

"Though I think you may have scarred a few small children for life," I added.

She laughed. "That's kind of the point, Mom." She looked down at her mask, fiddled with the horns. They looked so sharp at the tips—

I wanted to warn her to be careful. "To remind people, even little kids, that there's evil in the world. We can try to pretend there isn't, that the only thing sneaking around in the night is Santa with his bag of toys, but that's just bullshit, right? And the sooner we see the truth, the better off we'll be."

TWENTY-EIGHT

THE THREE-AND-A-HALF-HOUR DRIVE TO Woodstock Monday morning passed in a blur. One minute I was leaving home; the next I'd reached the driveway of my mother's house, listening to the robotic voice on the GPS that had guided me the whole way: *You have arrived at your destination.*

I stopped at the mailbox, grabbing the hefty stack of mail inside and skimming through it: catalogs, junk mail, a few bills, all addressed to my mother. The only thing with Paul's name was a magazine, *Art in America.*

I put the car in drive and continued down the long driveway.

As I approached the house, I thought, *Oh, hell no,* and considered turning around. I slowly crept forward, eyes on the house, which seemed to be waiting for me. *Expecting me.*

It was smaller than I remembered, though no less foreboding. In my mind, it had always been huge and looming, a monster covered in weathered cedar shakes the color of smoke. I navigated the Volvo down the crushed-stone driveway and parked. There was a detached garage to the right and a carriage house off to the left, where Paul had lived for the past fifteen years. The building that had originally been my father's art studio, but I hadn't been inside since I was a kid. It was where my father had died, and even though my mother cleared it out and got rid of all his things shortly after his death, I'd still avoided the carriage house. I knew if I entered, I'd look up, wonder which rafter he'd used, what had happened to the rope, imagine what he might have looked like when Ben found him. I also didn't want to see it all cleared out, my father's paintings and personal effects thrown onto the bonfire my mother had built in the yard, as if she could destroy all traces of him, make him drift away in the smoke. I wanted to remember the carriage house the way it had been when I'd go in and sit watching him work, standing on a ladder to cover huge canvases in bright splashes of color, turning to me and saying, "Do you see the giraffes, Moppet? I put another one hiding behind the tree. You're the only one who'll ever know she's there."

So I'd stayed away from the carriage house. Years later—when Ben and I were long gone—my mother had it refurbished, turning it into an apartment for Paul. Over the years, I'd wondered from time to time if Paul believed in ghosts. If he ever felt my father's presence.

I pulled up to the front of the house, turned off the car, and sat staring at this place where my mother lived, where I'd grown up and hadn't returned since I was a teenager.

I remembered the idea I'd had during that last visit, that my mother and the house were connected, that the house itself was an extension of her somehow.

It hadn't always been such a foreboding place. Back when my father was alive, before my mother started drinking, the house had felt bright and cheerful. Then, as my mother changed, the house changed with her. The windows were locked, the heavy curtains drawn tight year-round. Family photos were taken down, as were my father's paintings, even drawings Ben and I had done. My mother had most of the interior walls painted a dull gray—oystershell—that made the whole house feel like it was covered in a dense fog.

I grabbed my mother's keys from my purse and my phone from the console, got out of the car, pulled my coat tight against the chill. I was standing under the shadow of the house, feeling it watch me, dare me to enter, the dark windows looking back at me like soulless eyes.

I stepped away, out of its shadow, then lifted my phone and dialed Mark's cell, thinking that hearing his voice might make me feel better, give me the courage I needed to get through this.

"Hey, you," he said when he answered. "Everything okay?"

I closed my eyes, imagined him there in our bright home full of holiday decorations, the girls' artwork, our well-loved furniture—the antithesis of the cold and cheerless place standing before me.

"Yeah, just wanted to let you know I made it."

"Early too."

"Yeah, traffic was light."

"Is it weird?" Mark asked. "Being there again?"

"Weird is kind of an understatement," I said, looking up at the house. Behind me, wind rustled through the trees, seeming to whisper a warning.

"If it's too much—"

"It's totally fine," I said. "I'm a big girl. I can handle this. I'll do what I need to do and then get out of here. I'll text when I'm on my way back. I'll definitely be home by dinner."

"Sounds good," he said. Then, "Oh, a package came for you. Did you order books or something?"

My demon books.

"Christmas presents," I said without missing a beat. "No snooping!"

Mark laughed. "Okay, I won't open the box. Gotta go. Teresa just got here."

"Okay. Hey, thanks again for staying home with Mother."

"No problem. I enjoy her company," he said.

We said good-bye, and I hung up, keeping my eyes on the house.

"Let's do this," I said out loud, my own private pep talk as I approached the stone front steps, the steps I'd climbed thousands of times going back and forth between home and school, or out to play in the yard and the woods behind the house.

As I walked in, I felt like a little kid again, tiptoeing so my mother wouldn't hear me, wouldn't caw out, "Who's there?"

I never knew who I would meet up with when I stepped off the bus and crossed the threshold. Would it be Fun Mom, who had brownies waiting for me and wanted to hear all about my day at school, or Drunk Mom, squinting at me like I was an intruder in her life, someone who didn't belong? "You again?" she'd say, a mix of surprise and profound disappointment in her voice, maybe with a not-so-hidden trace of loathing, like I was something she'd scraped off the bottom of her shoe.

"Where have you been?" Drunk Mom would ask accusingly, eyeing me over the rim of her martini glass even though it was only three thirty in the afternoon.

"School," I'd tell her, adjusting my backpack.

"Is that so?" she'd ask, as though there were other options, other places for a kid to go each day from seven thirty to three thirty, picked up and dropped off by a yellow bus.

"I'm not myself today," my mother would sometimes say. "So it's best if you don't bother me."

"Of course," I'd answer, ever obedient.

Then I'd watch her stagger off to her art studio, the large room at the end of the house that had once been an enclosed porch, which she'd had converted to a year-round work space. I remembered it as being the only room in the house where the curtains were always open. Yet even with sunlight streaming in, my mother's studio had often felt oppressive and terrifying—a place so full of her that even when I'd been invited in, I felt I didn't belong, like the room itself wanted to spit me back out.

As I stood now in the front hall, I could almost hear the ghosts of both versions of my mother calling me simultaneously: *Is that you, Ali Alligator?* and *Where have you been, useless girl?*

I could feel her presence all around me, as if some part of her was still here, in the walls, the floor, the old plaster ceiling.

Something in the house shifted. There was a low creak.

"Hello?" I called.

But there was nothing. No one.

I reminded myself that my actual mother was back at my house in Vermont, sick in bed, dying. There was no one here to jump out of the shadows, drag me off while hissing, "Where have you been?" in my ear.

Where have you been?

"Away. I went away to save myself from you." I said the words out loud, talking to the ghost version of my mother, the mother of my childhood. But she only laughed mockingly, whispered:

And yet here you are.

I flipped on the lights, did a quick circuit of the living room, the kitchen and pantry. It was all just as I remembered it. The same simple Shaker furniture. The same plain pale-gray walls. The same blue pottery dishes in the cupboards. I opened the refrigerator. Not much except a jar of olives, some fancy mustard, and curry paste. The tiled floor in the kitchen was polished, the granite countertops shimmered. It looked and felt like a place no one actually lived in—as if everything was there just for show. Even with the lights on, the room felt dark, cave-like, and air-less. The back door in the kitchen was locked, and I went and looked out the window at the flagstone patio, remembering how it was this door I'd escape through wearing my father's coat, carrying my brother's BB gun. For an instant, I was sure I caught a glimpse of her—the ghost of my little girl self—a shadow slipping into the woods.

I turned and walked away.

There were no plants downstairs that needed watering. Nothing alive that needed to be cared for.

The house looked and smelled clean; no doubt the housekeepers were still coming once a week to mop, dust, and vacuum. There was a service that had been coming for years. Did they have their own key? I'd have to find a way to get in touch with them.

I left the kitchen and moved to the dining room, where the polished cherry table stood surrounded by six chairs, awaiting one last dinner that would never happen—not in this house, anyway. It was the table at which Ben and I had sat as we suffered through countless meals.

At the end of the dining room stood the door that led to my mother's studio. I put my hand on the knob, hesitating. Growing up, it and my mother's bedroom were the two places deemed off-limits. We weren't to enter unless invited, and if we dared break the rules, there were terrible consequences.

I pushed open the door and stepped inside.

Because it had once been the sun porch, there were large windows on three sides and a door leading out to the backyard. The room should have been filled with natural light, but heavy blackout curtains now kept it entombed in darkness. I went to the far wall and drew open the curtains, letting in the winter light.

No materials littered any surfaces: no tubes of paint, no brushes, no palette with freshly mixed colors. The smells of oil and turpentine hung faintly in the air like ghosts.

It was strange, being here. There was a long worktable set up along one wall, with tools hung on a pegboard. I had set up my own studio in much the same way, I realized with a start. Had I copied this from her? I must have without realizing it. She didn't have the large antique printing press I did, and our tools were different, but so much was the same, including sketches tacked up on the walls, just as I did. I moved in for a closer look. They were anatomical drawings: close-ups of hands with the skin pulled back, tendons and bones carefully rendered and labeled. There were several sketches of birds. I looked more closely. Blue jays, all of them.

Eee-eee-eee, cried my mother's voice in my mind, a near perfect rendition of the screech of the bird itself.

I turned away from the drawings.

A wooden easel was set up in the center of the room with a canvas on it. Someone—my mother? Paul maybe?—had covered it with a sheet. I stepped over to it, gently lifted the sheet to take a peek at whatever painting my mother had last been working on.

It was me.

A younger version of me. Me at eight years old, uncombed hair pinned back with plastic barrettes shaped like butterflies, my face utterly devoid of expression. And cupped gently in my hands was a blue jay with a broken wing that hung at an unnatural angle.

Eee-eee-eee.

TWENTY-NINE

DROPPED THE SHEET BACK down, covering my child-self like I was putting a ghost costume back on.

I backed out of the studio on shaky legs and shut the door a little too tightly. If only I could have locked it closed forever.

Where have you been, Ali Alligator? What took you so long to come home? Eee-eee-eee.

I turned, sure that I wasn't alone. That I was being watched.

But of course it was just me in the empty house.

Who's there?

Just me, Mother, I answered wordlessly. *Still just me.*

Being in this house was messing with my head big-time. I needed to leave. Get the hell out before something in me cracked that I wouldn't be able to fix.

Do a quick walk-through and get out, I told myself. *Make sure there are no leaks, no open windows, no plants to water upstairs.*

I headed up the wide oak steps that led to the bedrooms on the second floor. The house seemed to hold its breath, waiting to see what I was going to do next.

I opened the closed door to Ben's old bedroom. The shades were drawn, the bed made with a neat blue bedspread. One of Ben's model airplanes was on the desk, alongside a stack of his books. No plants. No leaks. Nothing that needed fixing or tending to. I closed the door and headed down the hall.

I paused at the entrance to my own childhood bedroom.

One look, I told myself.

Surely there was nothing there.

She'd probably gotten rid of everything (maybe even burned it in a fire in the yard), turned the room into a guest room, or storage.

But when I pushed open the door, my heart nearly stopped. I blinked. And just like that, I was twelve years old again, about to leave home for boarding school in Connecticut.

The room was just as I'd left it.

A strange museum to my past self.

The single bed was covered with the old red-and-white-checkered quilt I'd slept under throughout my childhood—something made by my grandmother, a woman I'd never met. On the simple pine desk was a jar of pencils I'd sharpened a lifetime ago, a desk lamp coated in a thin layer of dust, a dictionary lying open beside it. I walked over and looked down at the two open pages, scanning the words there, wondering what the young me might have been looking for: *pennyweight, pensive, pentacle, penumbra*.

On the shelves were the books on drawing and art that my mother bought me for each birthday and Christmas, a plastic Breyer horse and rider. Chestnut, I had named the horse.

There was my old bedside table with a lamp on it. The wind-up alarm clock with the glowing hands, silent now. And on the shelf below the lamp and clock was the illustrated children's Bible that Aunt Frances had given me.

Aunt Frances, who had never really approved of my mother, had rarely visited after my father's death, sending Ben and me cards on our birthdays with quotes from Scripture and five-dollar bills tucked inside.

Aunt Frances, whose funeral I had attended just last April.

I backed out of the room, having the strangest sense that if I stayed a moment longer, I'd be trapped there, sucked back through time to my childhood self, and I'd have to live through it all again.

I closed the door, heart lurching in my chest.

I thought I heard something: a faint scuttling in the walls. Mice? Rats?

"Check all the rooms and go," I told myself aloud as I made my way down to my mother's room at the end of the hall.

I opened the door and squinted into the darkness, but I sensed immediately that I was not alone. The shades were drawn, not letting any light sneak through. I groped along the wall until my fingers found a light switch.

I'd been right—I wasn't alone.

There were eyes watching me.

Bobbi's eyes.

My mother's painting of Bobbi.

I hadn't even realized that it wasn't where I remembered it last being, hanging on the living room wall beside the television. Now it hung above my mother's bed, so Bobbi could watch over her each night as she slept.

Bobbi and her cut-open chest, revealing the stone heart.

What did my mother see when she looked at the painting? What did it make her think of? That Bobbi had hardened her heart to her, that she'd left her, gone off to California, gotten married, chosen some other life? Or did she look at Bobbi, then at the stone on her nightstand, and think she'd gotten her lover's heart at last?

Bobbi stared at me, the stone in her chest seeming to pulsate, to beat itself back to life. I realized the truth of the painting that I'd somehow missed as a child: the look on Bobbi's face, the quiet hunger, the intimacy. The look that said: *We share a secret, you and I. I am yours and you are mine.*

Had my father truly known about their relationship?

And once Bobbi died, how was he supposed to measure up to the ghost of my mother's true love? Did he watch the way she stared at the stone she kept beside their bed? Did he hear her talking to it, begging to have Bobbi back?

I turned away from the painting, from Bobbi, immortalized forever at twenty-one years old, her chest opened up to reveal her clear stone heart pierced with needlelike strands of black tourmaline.

I went to my mother's closet, opened the door, and breathed in the smell of her clothing, her perfume. I looked at the row of shiny dress shoes she'd never again put on for an opening at a gallery, and my chest ached. I imagined one day soon coming back to this closet, packing up all the shoes, the dresses and blouses still smelling of her perfume, boxing them up and sending them off to a charity shop.

There was a quilt folded on the top shelf. I remembered it from my childhood—snuggling with my mother under the zigzag pattern of curved blue and white fabric pieces. Her own mother had made the quilt; my mother explained that the pattern was called the Drunkard's Path. We'd trace the weaving steps of the drunkard with our fingers, laughing while my mother told me about her own mother—how she was an artist too, but she worked with fabric instead of paint.

Now I took the quilt down, thinking I'd bring it home, surprise my mother with it.

That's when I noticed that tucked behind it were two boxes, about the size and shape of shoeboxes.

I blinked stupidly at them.

They had been labeled neatly in black Sharpie. One said BEN, the other ALISON.

I reached for the box with my name on it, my fingers hesitating, not sure that I really wanted to see.

But I needed to know.

I took down the ALISON box and set it on the bed. I lifted the lid. A musty smell drifted up.

"What the hell?" I muttered as I peered down into it.

Inside was a strange nest woven together from what appeared to be hair and scraps of cloth. I reached in, felt something hard inside. I pulled back the hair and fabric, sure I recognized the pattern—I'd had a favorite dress with those same yellow and white stripes. And was that my hair? Tucked inside were three baby teeth, a dried flower, and a little round piece of wax with a simple design carved into it: a box with an X in it and four dots in each triangle made by the X.

I recognized the symbol right away.

I had the same thing carved into the middle of my back, right between my shoulder blades.

THIRTY

M Y HANDS WERE TREMBLING as I tucked the boxes—mine and Ben's—into the backseat beside the quilt. I'd opened Ben's box and discovered it nearly identical to mine: a nest of hair and fabric, baby teeth, a carved bit of wax with the X and four dots.

What the hell were they, and why did my mother have them hidden on her closet shelf?

The scars on my back tingled.

I checked my watch. I'd only been in the house for half an hour but it had felt like forever. I looked at the carriage house, deciding that the sooner I got it over with, the sooner I could get in my car and get out of there.

The air in the carriage house smelled sweet, floral, and I soon saw why: there was a pot of flowering hyacinths on the table. It was a uniquely painful sight—a pot of purple flowers, surely bought by Paul himself, that had now outlived him. They made the air too sweet, almost cloying. They were nearly dried out, wilted from lack of water. I wasn't sure whether to try to revive them or throw them away.

The place looked nothing like my memories of my father's chaotic studio. Back then, it was dark and jumbled and felt claustrophobic with his giant paintings leaning against the walls, the stepladder he worked from opened up in the center of the room, the large pieces of wood he used as palettes lying around the floor. He worked on the lower floor and kept his supplies—large canvases, stretchers, extra tubes of paint—upstairs. His once-upon-a-time art studio was now a tidy little apartment with a high cathedral ceiling that followed the roofline. I glanced up at the exposed heavy wooden rafters and couldn't stop myself from wondering which one my father had looped his rope around.

Don't think about that, I told myself. *Be here in the present. This is Paul's house.*

But Paul was dead now too.

He went off half-cocked and lost his head.

I closed my eyes, focused on my breath as Penny had taught me to do, then opened them again.

I had work to do. I needed to focus.

Downstairs was one large space. The kitchen with a breakfast bar stood along one wall next to a small living area. There was a bathroom in the back corner. Steps led up to a bedroom loft. It was a bright and cheerful place with the low winter sun streaming through the south-facing windows. I glanced out and had a perfect view of the main house. More importantly, I realized, my mother must have had a great view of Paul— *easy to keep an eye on you.*

I examined the shelves, found books of poetry, books on art and art history, objects from nature: the skull of a bird, a piece of quartz, a paper wasp nest. There was an old manual typewriter and a pair of opera glasses. It was all very aesthetically pleasing. I saw no photographs, though, nothing that felt personal or gave me any sense of who Paul might have been outside my mother's orbit.

Maybe, I thought, he truly didn't have a life outside my mother's orbit. Maybe she was the sun he revolved around. Maybe that was enough: dedicating his own life to making sure hers ran smoothly, this woman who had seen something in him no one else had, who had believed in him and encouraged him to be more, to live larger. And he'd clearly cared for her. Spoke of her with admiration, gratitude, even reverence.

I closed my eyes, heard his last words to me: *That's not Mavis.*

There was a desk along one wall and it was heaped with chaotic stacks of paperwork—mostly sketchbooks and notebooks but a few art books and stray papers as well. I stepped up for a closer look and saw it was mostly my mother's papers and old sketchbooks and diaries. He'd been going through them, marking pages with colored sticky notes—no doubt this was while he'd been deciding what to include in the shipment to the Toronto gallery for my mother's retrospective. There was a legal pad covered in Paul's neat writing that listed some of the things he'd sent them so far: a watercolor she'd painted back in college, sketches of Bobbi made around the time she'd painted the stone-heart portrait, a self-portrait my mother had done just after my father's suicide, assorted notes and photocopied journal entries.

At the bottom of the page was one word, circled: *Pyxis*.

Odd.

Was it an art piece of my mother's?

At the front of the jumbled piles, just to the left of Paul's legal pad, was a red hardcover sketchbook. Paul had inserted sticky notes to bookmark certain pages. There were papers and sketchbooks on the floor as if they'd fallen or even been thrown there.

I looked at the mess on and around the desk and thought that such chaos was uncharacteristic of Paul, whom I'd always known to be neat and organized. This looked like he'd been rifling through things in a frenzy and throwing them around. There was no order at all. Leaving a mess like this seemed very un-Paul-like.

I turned away from the disarray of the desk and went up the little steps to the sleeping loft. It was an open space with a wrought-iron railing that looked down on the rest of the apartment. There was a bed, a nightstand, a low dresser against one wall. Against the other wall stood a rack made from what looked like antique copper pipes, which Paul used as a closet. His dress shirts and pants hung there. A couple of suits. A denim shirt and a black leather jacket. At the bottom was a neat row of shoes and boots. There was something terrible about it, all the expensive shoes lined up, their polished leather formed perfectly to Paul's feet, the carefully selected and cared-for clothes hanging like strange ghosts.

The bedside table held a lamp but nothing else. I opened the drawer. There was a blank notepad, a pen, and a printout from an online travel company confirming Paul's one-way flight to Belize. I looked at the date. It was booked for the day before yesterday.

"Belize?" I said out loud.

He hadn't mentioned anything about an upcoming trip.

I looked at it again, saw that he'd booked the flight the night before he'd come to see us. He'd made the reservation Thursday evening and had planned to catch a plane out of JFK Saturday morning.

Had he told my mother he was leaving? Was that what had upset her?

I closed the drawer and went over to the dresser. Now I was really invading Paul's privacy. But what choice did I have? I opened the top drawer and peeked in: boxers and socks, all black and all neatly folded. The middle drawer held T-shirts on one side and pajamas and workout clothes on the other. The bottom drawer was filled with neatly folded jeans on one side. And on the other, a metal file box.

Something creaked behind me.

A rafter with a rope tied around it, a body swinging.

I turned, heart hammering. There was nothing. No one. Only bright winter sunlight streaming through the windows, chasing the ghosts away.

I hurriedly pulled out the file box, set it on the bed, and popped it open. Inside were neatly labeled files: TAXES, WILL AND ADVANCE CARE DIRECTIVE, FINANCIAL, MEDICAL.

I pulled out Paul's will and advance care directive.

I skimmed the will, and saw the executor listed: *I hereby appoint my nephew, Jack Coppage of Keeseville, Essex County, New York, as Executor.*

Now we were getting somewhere. So much for not having any family.

I'd do some research on my computer back at home—with any luck, I'd be able to quickly locate this nephew. Telling him about Paul's death was not something I looked forward to, but the idea of being able to pass on all of these responsibilities and decisions to an actual family member filled me with a sense of relief.

Scanning through the will and financial paperwork, I confirmed what I'd already suspected: Paul was quite wealthy. He owned an impressive portfolio of taxable stocks and bonds, and a hefty retirement account. It seemed he'd made a lot of money in cryptocurrency as well.

My mother had taken good care of him, paid him incredibly well, and he'd socked most of it away.

I put the important papers, including Paul's will, into a folder and went back downstairs. I had what I'd come for. Time to go.

Back in the main room, I shoved the folder into my bag, dug out my keys. But something bothered me, reached for me with tendrils like fingers and wouldn't let go.

I turned back to the desk. It resembled the scene of a robbery more than a coherent attempt to get things ready for an exhibition. It looked like Paul had been sifting through things in desperation. Searching. But for what?

I went back over to the desk and started sorting through the mess. I picked up a sketchbook and found my mother's drawings of flowers and trees. Another had notes and drawings for a series of large paintings she'd done ten years ago called *The Forest of Bones and Teeth*.

All I found were old sketches of my mother's. Copies of reviews of her work, interviews she'd done over the years. A syllabus left over from her brief stint teaching.

Then I picked up the red sketchbook at the front, next to Paul's notepad.

Only when I opened it, I saw it wasn't a sketchbook, but a journal.

My mother's journal.

I turned to the first entry: October 4, 1984. It was not long after Bobbi had died. The entry was short:

> *It's been almost three weeks and it still doesn't feel real. I don't think it ever will. I keep replaying our last conversation when she called the day before her accident. She sounded so upset.*

She wasn't making any sense. Is there something I could have said or done? Something that might have stopped her from getting into her car the next day and driving over 100 miles an hour on that curvy little road? Something that might have kept her alive?

I suppressed a little shiver—these were the same questions I was asking myself now about Paul. It seemed a strange and terrible coincidence.

I flipped forward to the first page Paul had bookmarked with a sticky note. He'd written on it: *First realization that she's not herself.* I swallowed down the hard knot in my throat and read the entry.

November 17, 1984

I have been experiencing moments of missing time. I wake up in strange places and find it's hours, even days after the last thing I remember. I tried to talk to David about it, but he seems frightened of me. He's always taking the children out, leaving me here alone. Maybe he's trying to give me space to grieve.

This morning I woke up and found a brand-new painting in my studio. Another of Bobbi and the stone.

There was also a note in my writing that I didn't remember making: Amanda Gould, Hydra Gallery, and a number in California. I called the number and spoke to Amanda, who was delighted I'd called back and said she'd been given the okay to double her offer for a new painting of Bobbi and the stone. The amount was enough to pay off the rest of our mortgage.

What is happening to me?

Some kind of shock?

Memory loss from trauma?

Or is it something more?

The next bookmarked page made my mouth go dry:

November 29, 1984

*I feel it inside me. Sometimes I can hear it speaking, telling me
I can't hang on forever. That I'm not strong enough to win.*

*"If you give in, if you work with me and stop fighting me,
the world can be ours. I can give you anything you desire."*

Last night, it told me its name: Azha.

Every hair on my body stood on end.

Fingers shaking, I moved to the next bookmarked page:

February 21, 1985

*I am running out of time. Losing more of myself day by day.
The children are frightened of me. When Azha is in control,
I say and do terrible things. David looks at me like I'm a
stranger. I have been frantically trying to learn all I can. I spent
yesterday in the city at the New York Public Library. A very
kind reference librarian helped me; then after, I went to an
antiquarian bookstore.*

*I have been trying to find a way to beat it. To send it away.
To keep David and the children safe.*

But it gets stronger each day.

On an undated page was a messily scribbled note, only half-legible: *Spell for Binding*, then something about a full moon, a string, salt water, a sacred seal.

At the bottom of the page, two words scrawled in huge letters:

TOO LATE

I jumped ahead to the next marked page—the ones in between were mostly full of strange scribbles, incomprehensible words and shapes.

May 4, 1985

> *David is dead.*
> *Suicide.*
> *But not really.*
> *Azha made him do it.*

I slammed the book closed, heart clenching like a tight fist in my chest. *Breathe*, I told myself.

She knew. She knew what was happening and was powerless to stop it.

I looked at the journal, at the mess on the desk, and began putting things together. I imagined a scenario: Paul, finding these notes while going through my mother's things for the retrospective. Paul, who must have always sensed there was something not quite right about my mother. But even when he saw the truth laid out in her own words, he didn't want to believe it. So he'd come to my house and asked her himself.

I remembered the conversation I'd overheard:

Don't pretend you didn't know all along, my mother had said. *You're one of the cleverest people I know, Paul. The truth has been staring you in the face and you've just refused to look at it.*

Even then, he hadn't wanted to believe, insisting it wasn't possible, but knowing the truth, feeling it in his gut and understanding the terror of it. Running from the house, hurrying to get back to Woodstock, pack his things, get on that plane, and get as far away from Azha as he could.

That's not Mavis.

THIRTY-ONE

W HEN DID MOM START going crazy?" I asked, keeping my voice low.

"Huh?" Ben said. "It's, like, six thirty in the morning here, Ali."

I was in the living room. The girls were at school and Mark was at work. My mother was in her room with a cup of tea and a bowl of oatmeal. I was waiting for Janice to arrive for her morning shift.

When I'd gotten home yesterday, I'd done an online search and easily found contact information for Paul's nephew, Jack: his Facebook page, his LinkedIn profile, and his physical address and phone number. It never ceased to amaze me how easy it was to find anyone these days. I'd called, explained who I was and what had happened. He'd seemed shocked, but stated that he and his uncle were not close. He was surprised to learn he was the executor of the will. Paul had had little contact with anyone in his family in years. Jack said he would tell the rest of the family and get in touch with the funeral home and make arrangements. He'd let me know when the service would be, and he and I would arrange a time for him to come and go through the carriage house. In the meantime, I gave him the name and number of the lawyer Paul had used to draw up his will—surely he'd have a copy on file. I also told him I'd overnight the copy I had along with Paul's other paperwork.

After dealing with Jack, having dinner with my family, and getting the girls up to bed, I'd gone out to my studio and stayed up late looking through the demon books I'd ordered; learning about dark entities, cursed objects, possession, exorcism, talismans, sigils.

I'd looked through my mother's journal, studying each passage, re-reading her chronicle of losing herself to the demon.

There was a photocopied page glued into the diary—something from a book on Mesopotamian art she'd found at the library.

The caption she'd cut out and underlined read: *Azha, a demonic goddess with the head of a bird and the body of a snake, was said to have a tremendous hunger for human souls.*

Beside it was a photo of an image of Azha carved into a small cylindrical stone vessel.

She was said to be able not only to easily change form but to store her essence within a vessel or object, such as this pyxis circa 1500 BC.

Pyxis. The word Paul had written down on his notepad.

I felt like I had all the dots in front of me, I just needed to figure out how they connected.

"She wasn't always that way," I said to my brother now. "Don't you remember? Back before Dad died?"

"I don't know, Alison."

I blew out an exasperated breath. I wasn't in the mood for his selective amnesia.

"She was happy. I know you remember. She'd play games with us. Do those scavenger hunts. Sing silly songs. All the adventures she'd take us on—going to the aquarium in Boston, the drive-in in our pajamas. The time we went to Cape Cod just so we could have the best fried shrimp on the planet."

"I don't remember," Ben said, but I knew he was lying.

I shook my head, disgusted, which was silly; my brother couldn't see me.

"I went to Woodstock yesterday," I told Ben. "To the house."

"No shit?"

"No shit."

"Was it the same?"

"Eerily so." I remembered the feeling I'd gotten walking through the house like a ghost of my own childhood self, expecting my mother to pop out at any minute and demand to know what I was doing there. "It was like I stepped back in time. All of our things were still there. Like in our bedrooms and stuff. It was very strange." I paused. "I found other stuff too. Weird shit."

"Like what?" he asked.

"She had these boxes with our names on them."

"Like keepsake boxes?"

"Kind of. But full of freaky shit. Bits of our hair, baby teeth, scraps of clothes."

"Don't lots of parents save that kind of stuff?"

"Yeah," I admitted. "But not like that."

He was quiet.

"Now, please," I said to Ben. "Think. When would you say Mother started to change?"

"I'm not in the mood for this, Ali. She was a worse-than-shitty mother. Does it really matter when it started?"

"I just thought—"

"What?" he snapped. "That if you could pinpoint the exact moment, you'd be able to give her an excuse, put a 'poor tormented artist' spin on things? 'Oh, her husband killed himself and something broke inside her and she was never the same, poor thing, so she started locking her children in closets and cutting them up with kitchen knives.'"

"Ben, I—"

"She was fucked-up well before Dad died," Ben said. "That was what killed him. Her."

"He killed himself," I said. "It was his decision. He put the rope around his neck. He jumped from the chair."

My jaw clenched. I thought of the words in my mother's journal: *Azha made him do it.*

The room seemed to waver around me.

"She left him no choice," Ben said. "She was always pestering him. Berating him. Making him feel smaller and smaller until he was hardly there, a speck of a man, then, *poof*, one day he disappeared altogether."

"That's not fair, Benji."

"No one calls me that, not anymore." I could hear him breathing hard and fast, as if he'd just run a race. "I've gotta go, Ali."

"Wait," I said. "What if . . . what if she wasn't really our mom when she did those things to us, to Dad."

"What are you saying, Alison?"

"What if she was someone else . . . *something* else?"

"Like who? What? Are we talking aliens here? *Invasion of the Body Snatchers*? Or robots, maybe—*The Stepford Wives*?"

"A demon," I said. And just like that, the word was out. There was no going back now, so I forged ahead. My words tumbled out quickly, frantically. "She told me she's a demon named Azha, and at first I thought it was impossible, that she was just messing with me, but then I found out that Paul knew—he'd discovered the truth and I think he actually tried to warn me the day he died. And wouldn't it make sense, explain so much? The change in her personality, all the terrible things she did? I've been doing all this research, and I found this old journal of hers—"

"Have you lost your fucking mind, Alison?"

"No, I—"

"Because that's how you sound. Like a genuinely crazy person. Not just what you're saying, but the way you're talking, all wound up, spinning out of control, out of touch with reality. You sound just like *her*."

"I—I—" I stammered.

"I'm not going to do this with you, Alison. I just can't," he said. And then he ended the call.

I paced around the kitchen, brewed another pot of coffee.

I ranted at my brother inside my head.

I was not crazy. I was not like her.

But Ben was right about one thing: my mother's descent into illness happened before our father died. Well before. Her drinking, her cruelty, began right after Bobbi died.

That's when she changed.

When she came back from California.

That's when she started having the periods of missing time. When she felt herself starting to change.

I went up into our bedroom, dug through the closet, and pulled out the box that held my father's suicide note.

I had kept it all these years, tucked away with other mementos from my childhood: a broken locket, a certificate for winning the fifth-grade spelling bee.

I pulled it out now, still in its envelope addressed to my mother. She'd crumpled it up and thrown it away after his death. But I'd taken it out of the trash, smoothed it, hidden it inside my dictionary.

I opened it now, the paper worn and brittle.

> *Mavis,*
>
> *I cannot go on with this any longer. I don't know who you are anymore or who I am when I am with you. We've badly lost our way and I am sorry for my part in it.*
>
> *David*

It was Ben who'd found him.

Our father had been out in his studio in the carriage house—the transistor radio playing classic rock, the tiny fridge full of beer.

I looked at the note once more before carefully folding it up.

I don't know who you are anymore.

Did he write those words because she truly wasn't herself anymore?

What if it wasn't just the grief over Bobbi's death that had changed her?

I thought of her coming back from California with her suitcase full of old photographs and Bobbi's good-luck stone.

The stone I'd catch her talking to, arguing with, begging it to bring Bobbi back.

I remembered the text from the art book my mother had copied and saved: *She was said to be able not only to easily change form but to store her essence within a vessel or object, such as this pyxis circa 1500 BC.*

I thought of the section in the demon book I'd read, about cursed and possessed objects, the ability of evil spirits to reside within them.

"Holy shit," I said aloud.

It was the stone.

Azha had attached itself to the stone. Maybe before Bobbi had it, maybe after.

The stone was like the pyxis in the book.

I didn't know the details, but I was suddenly sure that when my mother came back from California, it wasn't just the stone she'd brought back. It was something else. Something that had taken up residence inside her, growing, festering, casting its dark shadow over everything. That's why she couldn't be far from it. Maybe Azha still needed it.

I heard knocking and jumped.

Janice. It had to be Janice.

I raced downstairs to find her waving at me frantically through the front window. Moxie was there waiting to greet her. I opened the door. "Come on in."

"She was right!" Janice said as she flew into the room, patting Moxie on the head.

"Huh?"

"Your mother. Those Pick Four numbers she gave me. Wait until I tell her!"

She hurriedly shrugged off her coat and headed toward my mother's room.

"The Pick Four numbers were right!" she announced. "I won! By all rights, I should give the winnings to you. Or at least split it with you."

My mother smiled. "No need," she said.

"Twenty-five hundred dollars!" Janice said. "Can you believe it! That was a hell of a guess, Mavis!"

"It wasn't a guess," my mother said with a sly smile.

I looked at the stone on her bedside table, a strange glass heart streaked with black.

Was the stone a vessel, a beautiful hiding place for something dark and terrifying?

Something that watched me right now, out of my mother's eyes?

Janice patted her on the shoulder. "Oh, that's right," she said with a wink. "You know things, don't you, Miss Mavis?"

My mother nodded. She looked from Janice to me. "A great many things," she said, her eyes locked on mine.

THIRTY-TWO

SAT IN THE STUDIO, the books on demons and demonic possession I'd ordered stacked in front of me, my notes spread out on the table.

I reread the beginning of a chapter titled "How to Rid Yourself or a Loved One of a Demon or Dark Spirit":

> *The first step is to understand all you can about what it is and where it came from. Is it a true demon? A poltergeist? A vengeful spirit? Do not simply ask this being to tell you about itself—dark spirits are tricksters and are not to be believed. The more you know about the entity you are about to do battle with, the greater your chances of finding a way to banish it.*

Understand all you can about what it is and where it came from.

If my theory was correct and the demon was connected to the stone, there was only one person alive, other than my mother, who might be able to help me learn more about it. It was a long shot, but it was all I had. I spent a few minutes searching the internet, and soon had a phone number. Once again I was amazed—it was ridiculous, how easy it was to track someone down these days.

Bobbi's son, Carter, was in real estate now. An agent in LA.

He picked up on the second ring. "Carter Dixon here."

I thought of the lanky boy who'd come to visit each summer; the boy who carried a knife, who dared my brother and me to share cigarettes with him, who spun wild, fabulous stories about his life back in California.

"Hi, Carter? This is going to seem out of the blue, but it's Alison, Mavis Holland's daughter."

There was a long pause. I heard traffic noises behind him, realized he was talking to me from his car.

"Your mother's friend, Mavis. From New York. They grew up together."

"Yeah, yeah, I know who Mavis is. I'm just surprised to hear from you. The last time I saw Mavis was at my mom's funeral. She sends a card every year at Christmas, though."

It was probably Paul who sent the cards, I thought. I imagined him sitting down with my mother's address book, mailing holiday greetings to all the people in it, signing them himself: *Love, Mavis.*

"But I remember you. Ali Alligator, right? And your brother, Benji. How's he doing?"

"Good. He's actually in California."

"Oh yeah? Where?"

"La Jolla. He and our cousin own a restaurant there."

"Nice. La Jolla's beautiful. I'm still in LA. I keep trying to leave but I guess the city's got its hooks in me. What about you? Where are you living?"

"Vermont. I'm married. We've got two girls."

"Nice," he said. He didn't mention a family of his own, and I didn't ask.

There was a pause filled with the sound of traffic buzzing by, a truck blowing its air horn. He must have been on the highway.

He was clearly waiting to see why I'd called. At last, he spoke again. "So, I'm guessing you're not calling because you're interested in buying a place in LA? Although if you are, I'm your man."

"The thing is," I began, "my mother's quite ill."

"Oh, hell, I'm sorry to hear that."

"Thanks. She's staying here at my house with my family and me. And her being here, well, it's got me going down memory lane. And my older daughter—she's sixteen—is doing this video diary, asking my mother all about her life. And Mother's talked a lot about Bobbi. They were so close growing up."

I didn't know what I was hoping to find out, but my heart beat fast with excitement. Carter might know something, be able to give me some clue about the stone and where it had come from—something that might help.

"Yeah, they were," he said. He was quiet for a beat, and I wondered, in that silence, if he'd ever suspected that his mother and mine had been more than friends.

"My mother, she's got that stone of Bobbi's. You know, the one from the painting?"

There was a long pause. "Yeah, I know the stone you mean."

Behind him, I heard the faint wailing of a siren.

"She's got it beside her right now. She keeps it close."

I could hear him clear his throat. "Good," he said. "Better her than me."

My skin prickled.

"Oh?"

The siren was getting closer to Carter, louder.

"I always hated that stupid rock."

"How come?" I asked, trying to sound completely naïve. And trying to keep the excited rush I felt under wraps. I was right about the stone. I knew it.

"I just . . ." He paused. "I know this is going to sound ridiculous, but I always believed it was evil. I was totally scared of it when I was a kid. I blamed it for all the bad things in my life."

There it was. So obvious even a kid picked up on it.

"Bad things? Like what?" In my mind, he'd had a picture-perfect life, with a TV star mom living in the Hollywood Hills.

The siren went by along with a blaring horn, loud enough to startle me.

"My mother wasn't exactly the good witch she played on TV."

"Oh?"

"She struggled. My dad always said she had an 'artist's temperament.' That was what drove him away. He left us when I was just four. Can't blame him. She was moody as hell. She'd be loving and doting one minute and cruel and abusive the next."

My skin crawled. This story was a little too familiar. "I'm sorry," I said. "I had no idea."

"She was probably bipolar or something, I don't know. I don't think she was ever diagnosed or anything. She drank a lot—that much I know. And she used to talk to herself. And she talked to that damn stone. Begged it for stuff. Argued with it. It was like this living, breathing thing to her. After my dad left, there were three of us in that house: her, me, and the stone."

I swallowed hard. I knew the feeling too well.

"One time she got all mad and crazy and threw it away. Then she got up in the middle of the night, went out to the street and tipped over the trash cans, ripped open the bags, talking to herself, calling herself all kinds of terrible names. The neighbors came out to see what the hell was going on. But once she found the stone, she calmed right down, went back inside, left me out there to clean up the mess." He was quiet for a few seconds. "I swear, sometimes I thought that stone was alive. You know how you have those crazy ideas when you're a kid?"

"Yeah," I said. "I had a lot of crazy ideas myself back then."

I sucked in a long breath of air, thought that my ideas back then were nothing compared to the crazy ideas I had now: demons living in stones and possessing people, turning them into cruel, abusive mothers.

"Anyway, after she died, when your mom asked if she could take it, of course my aunts and I said hell, yes. I never wanted to see that damn thing again."

"Do you know the story of where it came from? My mom mentioned that Bobbi found it in Mexico. You know, when they were traveling around after college?"

"My mother never told me about it," he said. "It was a regular round-the-world tour they did, though, I think. My mom had a lot of pictures from that trip. Other stuff too—ticket stubs, hotel receipts, brochures."

"Did she?"

"Yeah. She had a scrapbook she used to show me when I was a kid. I don't know what happened to it, but I always thought it was so cool— seeing pictures of my mom and yours in England, Italy, Morocco, and hearing her stories. It felt like this magical time to me, a time before I existed when my mom was traveling the world. She looked so happy in all those pictures. And she got happy when she talked about the trip, about Mavis. But there was a certain sadness to it too, you know? Wistful is the right word, I guess."

"They were very close," I said, waiting to see if he would say anything more, but he remained silent. "And I think . . . I think that trip was kind of the last hurrah for them, you know? Your mom moved to California not long after they got back. They both got married, got caught up in their own lives. They saw each other and talked on the phone a lot, but they were living on opposite sides of the country, worlds apart."

He made a little murmur of agreement. The traffic noises had lessened. Had he gotten off the highway? "I remember visiting you guys sometimes in the summer," he said. "My mom and your parents would stay up half the night drinking and playing cards, and we'd sneak out to spy on them and watch movies we weren't supposed to. Remember when we camped out in the tent in your backyard?"

I laughed. "You and Ben nearly set it on fire with those bottle rockets."

"Your dad was so mad!"

"But our moms were laughing, remember?" I asked.

"They were always happy when they were together," he said.

"They were."

"I'm sorry as hell to hear about Mavis," he said again.

"Thanks. I'm sorry about your mom too. And sorry to hear that things were difficult for you growing up. I had no idea. I always thought your mom was the greatest."

"She could be." Carter was quiet for a moment. "When she wasn't telling me what a piece of shit I was, or carving designs on me with a kitchen knife."

My breath got stuck in my chest. "Designs?" I croaked the word out.

"Sorry. Forget it. I shouldn't have brought it up. She was a piece of work, my mother. Complicated isn't the half of it."

"Please," I said. "Tell me. What kinds of designs?"

"Stupid Etch A Sketch kind of shit. Shapes. Patterns."

"Circles?" I asked. "Spirals?"

"Some. Hey. Why do you ask?"

"How about a square with an X in it and dots in the triangles made by the X?"

I heard a wheezing intake of breath. "How . . ." he stammered. "How did you know that?"

"I—" My voice faltered. "It was just a lucky guess. Look, it's been great talking to you, Carter. I'm sorry, I've really gotta go."

I hung up before he could ask me any more questions that I didn't know how to begin to answer.

THIRTY-THREE

THE SCARS ON MY back tingled as I sat in my seat at the opera house, shifting in an effort to get comfortable. I thought of the scars on my brother's back. My mother had marked us both. And Bobbi had marked her son too. I tried to make sense of it. Did it mean we belonged to the demon? I wriggled again, crossed my legs, then uncrossed them.

Mark squeezed my hand. He leaned in and whispered, "You okay?"

"Fine. Excited to see our little mouse."

The vast hall felt too small, too crowded. All around us were the parents and families of other young dancers, and so many other people I knew from the community: quilters, artists, shopkeepers, the children's librarian, the man who owned the taco truck, the town clerk who collected our property tax checks four times a year. They'd all packed into the old opera house to see *The Nutcracker*.

Mark sat beside me and Izzy beside him. She'd brought her camera and was waiting to try to catch some good shots of her sister. She'd sneaked backstage before the show to get some candids of everyone in their costumes, including a great one of Olivia posing with all the other level one mice.

At last the curtain opened. There were Clara and her family, greeting party guests. The adults and children danced, Drosselmeyer arrived with his gifts, gave Clara the nutcracker. Then the strange nightmare scene where everything changed: Clara fell asleep. The clock struck twelve. The Christmas tree grew bigger and bigger, and the mice arrived, followed by the rats. There was Olivia doing her mouse dance across the stage, paws up as she twirled and skittered with the other mice. They cowered in terror as the rats arrived, led by the Rat King. He was especially terrifying in his big papier-mâché rat mask, brandishing his large silver sword. All the little mice were trembling, Olivia most of all. Even from the seventh row, I could see the terror in my daughter's eyes as she watched the Rat King cavort across the stage, dueling with the Nutcracker and his soldiers. It seemed an unfair fight: the rats were going to win. Then Clara threw a slipper at the Rat King, killing him, and he was carried off by the rats, followed by the mice.

The Nutcracker, with his big blocky headpiece, was transformed into a handsome prince in white tights, and he took Clara's hand and led her through the snow to the land of sweets.

As I watched, a realization came over me. You had to fight magic with magic. The demon wasn't going to go away on its own. It wasn't going to refrain from entering me when my mother died just because I told it not to. It was an ancient, dark, and powerful force. And I needed something magical to help me: my own band of soldiers, my own magic slipper, bravely thrown. I needed to go back into my own childhood, to find the girl I used to be, the girl who believed in magic, who performed little spells out in the woods, who had a knife that could banish evil.

When the first act ended and the curtain closed, I grinned wildly, happily, and applauded so hard my hands stung.

"I LOVE PEPPERMINT stick!" Olivia said.

"Peppermint ice cream is gross," Izzy said.

"Peppermint stick is the best because it's pink and you can only get it at Christmas."

"It looks like Pepto Bismol," Izzy said.

"Well, your rocky road looks like poop."

"Enough!" Mark ordered.

We were settled in a booth at Sugar and Spice. Mark and I were sharing a hot fudge sundae, but I wasn't having much of it. I'd ordered a coffee and Mark had frowned. He didn't think it was such a great idea when I'd been having so much trouble sleeping lately, but I'd assured him it was fine.

"Can we bring some ice cream to Grandma Needle?" Olivia asked.

"I think that's a great idea," Mark said. "We can get them to pack a pint and bring it home. What flavor?"

"Peppermint stick, of course!" Olivia said. She stood up, stepped away from the table, and did a little twirl. She still had on her stage makeup—bright pink blush and winged eyeliner. Normally we would scold her for leaving her seat and dancing in a restaurant, but it was her special night—the regular rules didn't apply. It was a night when magic was possible.

"Wasn't the Rat King scary this year?" Olivia asked.

"Yeah," Izzy said. "That new rat mask is awesome!"

"Carrie Forge played the Rat King," Mark said. "You used to dance with her, didn't you, Izzy? Isn't she a grade ahead of you at school?"

I remembered Carrie from Izzy's dance lessons. She was a shy kid and hadn't been the strongest dancer. She'd come a long way.

Izzy took a bite of her rocky road. "Yeah, she's a senior. And I've gotta say, I would never have guessed that was her up there in the mask. She's, like, really quiet and awkward and shy and stuff. But she was the perfect Rat King. It was like . . . like she was transformed."

Olivia nodded. "Ms. Perez kept telling her, 'Be the Rat King. Leave Carrie backstage.' I guess it worked. It was like her whole body changed. She seemed to get bigger, even. I think she was really scary."

The girls dug into their ice cream, talked about which costumes had changed since Izzy performed in *The Nutcracker* and which were the exact same. "I remember my rat mask smelled really gross," Izzy said. "Like whoever had worn it the year before ate garlic every night and it, like, permeated the mask." Olivia laughed. Said the mouse costumes smelled like mothballs, and one girl had an allergic reaction to the detergent or something and broke out in hives.

I watched them talking, laughing—happy.

I imagined what might happen if Azha got inside me, turned me into a monster; transformed me the way putting on the Rat King costume had turned meek little Carrie Forge into a menacing villain. Would I take up day drinking? Lock Izzy in a closet? Tell my darling little Olivia that I should have drowned her at birth?

My chest grew heavy and tears pricked my eyes.

"You okay, Mom?" Izzy asked.

Olivia gave me a worried look. "Mommy?"

I smiled, wiped at my eyes. "I'm fine. Just thinking how happy I am. How lucky we all are. And how proud I am of you, little mouse," I said, leaning over the table to wipe a dab of ice cream off her chin.

"Then why are you crying?" she asked.

"Because I'm so happy," I said.

Olivia laughed. "That's silly! Crying when you're happy."

"I guess it is," I agreed, laughing with her.

That's when I knew: I would not, could not put my girls and Mark through it. If I couldn't find a way to stop the demon, I'd go away. Kill myself, even. I thought of that scene in *The Exorcist*, when Father Karras tells the devil to take him, then jumps out the window. Would I be able to be that strong and brave? I had to be, I thought, as I looked at my girls. I had to do whatever it took to save them.

PENNY WAS WAITING in the living room when we got home. She'd readily agreed to stay with my mother while we attended the ballet at the opera house, but she seemed pretty stricken to me now.

"Everything all right?" Mark asked her.

"Of course. Fine," she said, with a grim, forced smile.

Olivia was bouncing off the walls.

"I'm gonna go tell Grandma we got her ice cream! Will you put some in a dish for her, Daddy?"

"Of course," Mark said. He turned to Penny. "Would you like some peppermint stick ice cream, Penny?"

"No, thanks," she said.

He headed to the kitchen with the pint we'd bought, humming the "Dance of the Sugar Plum Fairy." Olivia thumped down the hall. I could hear my mother calling out to her, "There's my favorite ballerina! How was the show? Tell me everything!"

"Okay if I go to Theo's?" Izzy asked.

"Sure," I said, and gave her the keys to the Volvo. "Back by eleven, okay?"

She headed out, leaving Penny and me alone. Penny was pulling her coat on. She wouldn't make eye contact with me. Something was wrong.

"Penny," I said, putting a hand on her arm, tried to get her to look at me. She stiffened, pulled away from me. "What happened?" I asked.

"Your mother—" Penny began, voice hushed as she looked around to make sure no one would hear.

"What?"

"Nothing. I just got spooked, is all."

My throat felt dry and tight. "Spooked by what?"

What had my mother done?

"Penny?"

She said nothing, just zipped up her coat.

"I've got to run, Ali. I've got to get home." She went out the door without another word. I watched her head down the driveway and disappear into the darkness.

THIRTY-FOUR

OLIVIA WAS CURLED UP on my mother's bed, listening to her sing a song.

I held still in the doorway looking in at them, a forgotten shadow, a spy who didn't belong. I thought of the glass angel hanging in the living room, always watching.

A deep unease settled in my chest and stomach as I watched my daughter cuddling with my mother. It took every bit of resolve I had not to run into the room and rip Olivia away, carry her off to safety. I told myself my daughter was safe. The demon wouldn't dare harm her. It was me it wanted.

My whole body ached from exhaustion, and my eyes stung and felt gritty.

I'd been up late last night in my studio searching the demon books for something that might help me. I read chapters on the history of demonic possession, famous cases, exorcisms, sigils and charms to keep people safe from demons, the language of demons.

I'd texted Penny:

Are you okay? I'm out in the studio if you want to share some Electric Sheep and talk. If my mom did something that freaked you out, you can tell me.

She didn't respond.

I'd stayed in the studio and looked through the books until my eyes were bleary, then closed them, put my head down.

My mother sang out, her voice low and hypnotic:

"I have seen you, little mouse,
Running all about the house,
Through the hole your little eye
In the wainscot peeping sly,
Hoping soon some crumbs to steal,
To make quite a hearty meal.
Look before you venture out,
See if pussy is about."

"I don't want the kitty to eat me, Grandma Needle!" Olivia squealed.

"Oh, no kitty will get you, my love. You're my clever little mouse, aren't you?"

Our whole family had been in my mother's room earlier. Mark had dragged the large-screen TV in and attached it to his laptop so he could share the video of *The Nutcracker* one of the other fathers had taken. Olivia was wearing her ballet outfit. We'd made popcorn, and Mark had bought candy and soda. And when the show was over, Olivia had stayed in with my mother, snuggled up next to her in bed, telling her stories about the silly antics backstage, how her friend Sophie had snorted grape juice, which she wasn't supposed to be drinking, and gotten it all over her costume and they had to rinse it out and she'd danced with it still damp. She told my mother about how scary the Rat King was, and how you'd never know it was Carrie in that costume—she was so nice, but once she put on that mask, she became terrifying.

I'd carried the empty popcorn bowl and soda glasses into the kitchen; now I hovered in the doorway, watching and listening, not wanting to enter the room fully and break the spell, but hesitant to leave the two of them alone for long.

"I wish you could have seen me for real in *The Nutcracker*," Olivia mused, her head on my mother's bony shoulder. I felt a pang as I remembered how I used to snuggle my mother the very same way when I was little and she'd read me stories. It was strange to think I'd been that small once, that vulnerable, that trusting.

"Oh, I did," my mother said, smiling. "I did see you, little mouse."

"How?"

"I was there in spirit, watching."

"What do you mean?"

"Do you ever have a dream where you realize you're dreaming, and you realize you can go wherever you like, do whatever you'd like?"

"Yes!"

"It's like that. My body is sick here in bed, but with my mind, I can go flying all over the world."

"You can go all over the world and you came to the opera house to see me?"

"Of course. There's no one else I'd rather see."

Olivia threw her arms around my mother. "I love you, Grandma Needle."

"And I love you, little mouse."

I was clenching my hands so tightly that my fingernails were clawing into my own palms.

"Do you want to watch my dance again?"

"Yes, let's watch the whole thing again, from the beginning."

Olivia bounced up and pressed play on the laptop. The ballet began on the TV screen, the closed curtain opening for the party scene.

I backed slowly away from the doorway.

Mark was upstairs in his office grading papers. I took the baby monitor with me as I pulled on my coat and headed out to my studio, listening to my mother and Olivia chat as they rewatched *The Nutcracker*, its gorgeous Tchaikovsky score playing in the background.

"Don't you think Clara is pretty?"

"Oh yes, but not as pretty as you, little mouse."

I stiffened, thought of the magic mirror in "Snow White": *Who's the fairest in the land?*

As I approached the barn, I saw that the lights were blazing. I must have left them on last night.

I pulled open the barn door and blinked stupidly at what I saw there.

Mark was standing in front of my worktable, the color drained from his face. He turned, looked my way, then back at the table. "What the fuck is all of this, Alison?"

I'd heard him use what he referred to as "the f-bomb" only a handful of times since I'd known him. He always said there were plenty of colorful words in the English language and that swearing wasn't necessary if you had a good vocabulary.

I took in a breath, ready to explain the demon books.

But then I saw the drawings. Dozens of them. Maybe hundreds.

Terrifying drawings. Insects. Ants. Rats. Bees.

Intermixed with them, blended into the wings of the bees, the bodies of the rats, were symbols.

Symbols I recognized.

"I—I don't know," I stammered, puzzling over the drawings.

Mark's eyes blazed with a disturbing mixture of worry and anger. "What do you mean, you don't know? *You* did them. They're *your* drawings."

"I—"

What was worse?

Admitting I didn't remember making them?

Denying they were mine? (Except that they obviously were—I'd recognize my own work anywhere.)

Claiming that I was just working out some new ideas?

I remembered my mother's journal entry about her periods of missing time. Making a painting she didn't recall. Was the demon already practicing with me, seeing how easy I would be to enter, like a run-down roadside motel with a flashing VACANCY sign?

"I was up late last night doodling," I managed.

I scrambled through my memories of the previous evening. I'd been out here looking at the books. I'd dozed off. When I woke up, I was in our bed, with Mark beside me.

"Doodling?" He picked up a bee with angry black scribbles for eyes, strange symbols on its wings. He pointed at the wings. "These are like the marks you have on your back, Alison."

I nodded.

And the marks Ben has. And Bobbi's son.

Mark picked up one of the books. "*Demons Among Us*," he read aloud. He picked up another. "*The Dark History of Demons and Demonic Possession.* What is all this?"

I didn't dare tell him.

My husband was looking at me like he didn't know me at all. I had to do something.

"People process things in all different ways, Mark," I said. "I process things by drawing."

"And the books?"

"Research. Inspiration."

"This is all very fucked-up," he said. "You realize that, right?"

My body felt light, as if I were made of tissue paper. A see-through woman, hardly there.

I'd made the drawings.

I'd made them but didn't remember making them.

What else didn't I remember?

What else had my mind blocked out?

Mark bit his lip, looked from the books and drawings to me. "Have you called your therapist?" he asked.

"Not yet," I said.

"I need you to promise me you'll call and make an appointment."

I nodded. "I'll call tomorrow."

He started making his way to the door, but as I watched him, a question bloomed, coming to life like a poisonous mushroom pushing itself up from dark ground.

"Mark?"

He turned back.

And now it was me who eyed him accusingly.

"What were you doing out here?"

He never came out to my studio. It was an understanding we had. He didn't come in unless I invited him out to look at something. My creative process was precious and private, and he'd always respected that.

He blinked at me. "I was looking for you," he said.

But I knew he was lying. He knew damn well I had been in the house with Olivia and my mother.

He'd come out here to spy. To see what his off-in-the-head wife might be up to. And he'd gotten just what he'd been looking for. Proof that I was losing it completely.

I watched him leave, then turned back to the pile of drawings I didn't remember making.

I studied the symbols I'd worked into the bees' wings, the flies' eyes: little spirals, a circle with a cross, a square with an X and dots in each triangle the X made.

I didn't just recognize the symbols from my own back, or from my brother's, or the ones that Carter had confirmed.

I'd seen them somewhere else.

I picked up the demon books, started flipping through the pages.

There they were, tucked into the back pages of one of the more esoteric books I'd ordered, one written in strange old English.

Sigils to keep you safe from daemons.

I scanned the pages.

These were ancient marks of protection.

Apotropaic markings used to ward off evil.

And I'd seen them somewhere else, I realized. I opened my mother's red journal and found them there, scribbled on pages between entries.

"Oh my God," I said aloud, realization beginning to wash over me.

The strains of Tchaikovsky crackled out of the baby monitor.

"Rewind it so we can watch your mouse dance again," I heard my mother say to my younger daughter.

I paced, thinking.

I flipped through the books again, found a chapter on spells and charms to keep people safe from demons. It instructed a person to make a small sachet or even a doll with bits of hair and snippets of clothing and nail clippings, to mix in salt and protective herbs. To pour wax on top and carve a protective symbol into the hardened wax.

The strange nests I'd found in my mother's closet hadn't been used to curse or bind us. They'd been made to protect us.

I pulled out my phone, hit my brother's number.

"Don't tell me," Ben said. "Mom's started spewing pea soup? Or her head's spinning?"

"They're marks of protection," I told him.

"What are you talking about, Ali?"

"The scars on our backs. She wasn't trying to hurt us, Ben. She was trying to save us. She knew what she was becoming. She knew we were in danger. The part of her that was still our mother did it to save us."

I had to tell him, had to find a way to explain that we'd had it all wrong. That our mother, our true mother, was the hero in the story, not the villain.

I could hear Ben's ragged breathing getting harder and louder. "She sliced into our fucking skin, Alison. She turned our backs into her own masochistic graffiti walls, scribbling shapes into us just to watch us bleed and daring us not to scream. Do you remember that? How she'd promise it would be over fast if we'd just hold still and let her do it?"

And I did remember.

Ben muttered, "I can't do this with you, Ali," and hung up on me.

I remembered how my mother would cry as she cut me, apologize, tell me how sorry she was, that it was for my own good.

"One day you'll understand," she'd said.

And she was right.

I finally did.

She wasn't marking me to hurt me.

She was marking me to save me.

To keep the demon away.

This was my real mother being ravaged by the demon, fighting to hold on to some piece of her true self, fighting to protect her children.

It wasn't going to enter a body with sigils of protection etched into its skin. Maybe it couldn't truly harm us because of the marks.

But didn't they still work now? Had the magic worn off somehow? How was the demon going to enter me when my mother died?

The baby monitor crackled, and I heard my mother's voice cooing to Olivia. "You are by far the best mouse on that stage. And next year, you'll be better still."

"One day maybe I'll be a rat like Izzy was."

"Dream bigger than that, Olivia. One day you could be the star of the whole show. Not just this little opera house ballet, but a real ballet in a real city like New York. Wouldn't you like that?"

"More than anything," Olivia said.

"And you shall have it," my mother said.

That's when I understood. The reality of it hit me square-on like a sledgehammer to my chest. My body reeled as I let the knowledge sink in.

It wasn't me the demon wanted.

It was my little girl.

THIRTY-FIVE

H EY," I SAID TO Izzy as I knocked on her half-open door. "Okay if
I come in?"

"Sure." She was sitting at her computer, editing footage of our family
watching *The Nutcracker* video. It felt very meta: a video of people watching
a video of people performing onstage.

Izzy paused it on a framed close-up of Olivia snuggled up beside my
mother.

"You've been filming your sister and grandmother together a lot, huh?"

Izzy nodded. She picked up her phone, clicked around on it, probably
checking for texts from Theo. Definitely making a point of not giving me
her full attention—something I'd gotten used to these last few months.

The shiny black Krampus mask with its pointed horns was on her
bureau. It was watching me with its dim red eyes. It looked dangerous.

I see you.

I see everything.

I turned away from it, told myself not to look. But I could feel it
watching.

Izzy's room was in its usual state of disarray: bed unmade, clothes
and shoes on the floor, empty energy drink cans littering every surface.

"Have you ever noticed anything . . . weird with the two of them?"
I asked.

Izzy looked at me over the top of her phone. "Weird in what way,
Mom?"

"Just, anything odd. Anything that doesn't seem right."

"What, like *inappropriate?* What is it you think Grandma is doing?"

"Nothing, I just—"

"What did she do to you, Mom?"

"Huh?"

"When you were a kid? What happened between the two of you? What makes you hate her so much?"

I took a step back. "I don't hate her."

"So what is it, then?"

I sighed. Stepped deeper into the room, perched on the edge of Izzy's rumpled bed. She was so like me. And we'd been close once, not all that long ago. If there was anyone I could trust, anyone who might believe me, it was Izzy. I decided to tread gently, to feel her out as I went along before I said too much. And with all the time she'd been spending with my mother, all the footage she had, maybe she suspected something wasn't right. Maybe she even had actual clues that might help me.

"I don't think she's herself," I said. "Not all the time."

Izzy let out a high, strained laugh. "What does that even mean, Mom?"

I didn't respond.

"Okay," Izzy said, putting on a serious face. "So who is she, then? I mean, if she's not herself."

I looked over at the Krampus mask watching me. Had it shifted its gaze somehow? Impossible.

"You think she's, like, got multiple personality disorder or something? Or dementia?"

I shook my head. "Nothing like that. Though I did at first. Teresa and I discussed the possibility of memory loss."

"And what did Teresa think?"

"She's not sure. She says there could be a dementia component. It could also just be your grandmother's cancer. Or the meds she's on."

"Makes sense," Izzy said.

"Remember when she first got here?" I said. "How you said she seemed fake? Like she was trying too hard?"

Izzy nodded.

"Do you think that still?"

Izzy shrugged. "I think . . . she's a little different with each of us. But then again, aren't we all like that?"

I nodded, knowing she was right—we were all a little chameleonlike. We all had our own masks.

She frowned, looked at the computer monitor, at her sister and grandmother cuddled up together. "It is weird, though, isn't it? How close she and Olivia got so fast. All their little secrets and stuff." She looked a little pained at the idea. Was she jealous?

I swallowed the hard lump in my throat. "Has your sister shared any of them with you? The secrets?"

Go carefully, I told myself. *Don't say too much. Don't push.*

"Nah." She looked down at her phone, then back at me. "Well . . . there is something."

"What?"

She wasn't meeting my eye. "Olivia asked me about it. Grandma told her that you'd been in the hospital once, a long time ago. Back when you were in high school."

My jaw clenched so hard that my teeth clacked together.

"A mental hospital," Izzy said, looking up to study my face.

"She told your sister that?" I asked, words strained.

Izzy nodded. "So is it true?"

"No," I said, the word too sharp, too loud.

No one knew about that particular incident. Not even Mark or Penny. And I wanted it to stay that way. The idea that Olivia knew, and now Izzy—it drove a spike into my chest.

It had happened my sophomore year of boarding school. My memories of that whole period were fuzzy. I felt detached from myself and my emotions and moved through my days like a sleepwalker. I'd been experiencing more frequent periods of missing time—dissociative episodes, I knew now.

During one of them, I apparently took every pill I could find in the dorm—everything from Tylenol to muscle relaxants to my roommate's birth control pills—and woke up in the psych ward, where I'd been transferred after having my stomach pumped. I stayed for two weeks. The doctors prodded me with questions. They asked me about the scars on my back. I told them a friend had done them because I asked her to. They asked if I liked hurting myself and having others hurt me. I said yes. I did one-on-one therapy. I did group therapy and art therapy and played checkers with kids who were way more messed up than I was. Girls whose arms were thick with scars, girls who couldn't eat without puking. My mother came to see me once while I was there. I still remember the disappointment on her face. And I never forgot what she told me. *It's one thing to feel pain, Alison. It's another to flaunt it, to share it openly with the world. Have some fucking dignity and keep your brokenness to yourself.*

Izzy looked at me now, narrowing her eyes. Could she tell I was lying? "Why would Grandma tell Olivia that?"

"I don't know, Iz, to scare her? To make her scared of me?"

"But why?"

I looked over at the mask again. "What if . . ." I said. Did I dare go there? I looked at this girl of mine, so like me. Me and not me.

I remembered when she was little, how we used to play a game where we'd try to read each other's minds. I'd say, "I'm thinking of a color," and Izzy would shout, "It's orange!" and I'd laugh and take her in my arms and say she'd read my mind because she was my special girl and she knew me better than anyone.

"What, Mom?" Izzy asked.

I looked back to the mask on the dresser. The unlit red eyes watching me, daring me to go on.

"You know the stories about Krampus? Where do you think they came from?"

Izzy shrugged. "Long dark winters. A time when people weren't afraid to scare children into being good with freaky stories. Like all those fucked-up fairy tales. The original Grimm stuff is pretty dark, right?"

I nodded. "But do you think there was any truth to them? The stories about Krampus?"

Izzy barked out a nervous laugh. "Um . . . are you asking if I think Krampus is real? That's kind of like asking if Santa might be real, right?"

"There have been stories about dark spirits, demons, possession, for as long as people have been recording stories."

"Wait," Izzy said. "Are you saying . . . what . . . that you think Grandma is possessed?" She blinked at me. "By . . . Krampus?"

We both laughed nervously.

I held my breath, wondering if it was a mistake to confide in her like this. But if I could get her to believe me, or to at least be open to the possibility, then I'd have an ally. Someone to help me watch, gather clues, figure out what to do next. Someone to help me save Olivia.

I shook my head. "Not Krampus," I said. "A few days ago, she told me her true name is Azha. I dismissed it at first, but . . ."

"No fucking way." Izzy looked away from me and down at her phone, which was still clutched tightly in her hand. Maybe she was going to text Theo an SOS—My mother's gone round the fucking bend. Send help!

"I've talked to Azha, Izzy. And I've also talked to my mother. She's still there, pieces of her. But this Azha, this demon or spirit or alternate personality, whatever it is—it's stronger. It's been there a long time."

"I, I don't—" Izzy stammered. She looked at me, then at the monitor, where her grandmother and Olivia were communing with each other, then back at me. "I've been videoing her every day. I've got hours of footage. Interviews and stuff. She just seems like Grandma. She's tired sometimes. I can tell she's in pain and sick. But a demon?"

"You see what she wants you to see," I told her. "The demon in her has worked hard to gain everyone's trust, Iz."

"But why? I mean, if the demon is so evil and all-powerful, why be nice?"

"It needs us."

"Why?"

"I think Azha needs to go into another body once your grandmother dies." I looked at Izzy, waiting. Then I looked at the monitor: Olivia cuddled up next to my mother.

It didn't take Izzy long to catch on. Ten seconds, maybe. She was my clever girl.

Her eyes grew huge. "You're saying it wants Olivia?"

I nodded. "But I'm not going to let it have her."

"How are you going to stop it?" Izzy asked, her voice high-pitched, little-girlish.

"I'm going to find a way."

She looked scared. "What are you going to do, Mom?"

"I don't know yet. I have a few ideas, but nothing solid."

"Is there going to be like an exorcism or something?" she asked, sounding hopeful. "If there is, could I, like . . . film it?"

"Izzy! I'm telling you your sister is in danger and you're thinking about your movie?"

"Sorry." She bit her lip. "I don't get it. Is the demon just going to, like . . . jump into her or something? Is Olivia going to breathe it in like . . . like inhaling a germ?"

"I don't know," I admitted. "I don't know how it works. But I do know that it wants her."

Izzy nodded. "Did you tell Dad all this?"

"No," I admitted. "I didn't tell him because I know he wouldn't believe me."

I thought about Paul. Of how he'd learned the truth the day before he died; a truth that filled him with fear and made him try to run. I wished I could bring him back, wished he were still with us, wished I could ask him to help me figure it all out, help me find a way to stop Azha.

I looked at my daughter. "What do you think?" I asked. "Do you believe me?"

Please, I thought. *Please.*

She bit her lip, looked down at her phone, then back at me. "I think there's a lot of fucked-up stuff in the world. Stuff we don't always understand. So yeah, I guess I believe it's possible."

I leaned over and threw my arms around her. "Thank you," I said, relief flowing through me. "So will you help me?"

"How?" Izzy asked, sounding unsure. Like she had regrets already.

"Keep filming the two of them. Look for clues. Anything that might help. The more we learn about the demon, the better our chances of foiling its plan."

"Okay."

"And, Iz—don't let on that you know anything. Don't try to talk to the demon. Don't say the name Azha. It can't know you suspect anything."

"Mom. You know I won't."

"And in the meantime, keep a close eye on your sister when she's with Grandma. I'm doing the same, but with someone else on the lookout, we can keep her safer while we figure this out.

"And most importantly, don't tell your father or your sister or even Theo. No one else can know. Promise me."

"I promise," she said.

And I hugged her again, grateful to have at least one person on my side.

THIRTY-SIX

M OM?" OLIVIA ASKED IN a voice thick with sleep. I moved some of her stuffed animals aside to make room for myself on the bed.

"Shh, little mouse," I whispered into her hair.

She smelled like apple shampoo. Like milk and cookies. Like a warm blanket dried in the sun. Like everything good in life all rolled into one little being. Sometimes, like right now as I held her close, it was hard to believe something so perfect had come from me.

"I love you," I whispered. And I did. I loved her so much, I felt like my chest might explode.

The room was illuminated by her ladybug night-light.

Ladybug, ladybug fly away home, your house is on fire, your children alone.

I hoped the light would be enough to see by. I pulled back the covers, lifted her nightgown. My fingers trembled.

I had to do this. Had to try.

"What are you doing?" she asked.

"We're going to play the word game," I said, trying to keep my voice cheerful, light. The same game I'd played once with my own mother. The game where one person's fingertips traced letters on the back of another.

"'Kay," she said sleepily.

Usually we wrote *I love you*. Or silly things like *I want cookies*.

I uncapped the permanent marker, brought the tip to her back.

"What's that smell?" she asked, lifting her head from the pillow.

"Nothing," I said, stroking her hair, settling her back down. She laid her head on the pillow, closed her eyes. Trusting me.

I started drawing.

"It feels funny," she said.

"Do you know what I'm writing?" I asked, the way I did each time we played the game.

"Is it a *W*?" she asked.

"No," I said, "guess again." I worked quickly, drawing, hoping that writing the symbols in marker would be enough, that blood didn't have to be spilled, pain inflicted, to make the magic work. The truth was, this didn't feel magical at all. It felt desperate and silly. It felt like I was becoming everything I had always dreaded I might be—the crazy woman who went sneaking into her daughter's room in the night to scribble nonsense on her back, terrifying her.

But I had to try, didn't I? If there was even a slight chance that this might work . . .

"You're not spelling anything at all," she complained, pulling away. "You're just scribbling."

"Hold still, little mouse," I said, pulling her back.

"No!" she shouted. "I don't like it!"

"Shh, Olivia," I said in my most soothing voice, stroking her hair. "I have to finish. I'm writing a whole secret message on your back."

"Stop, Mommy! Please."

The door flew open, and the overhead light flashed on.

"What are you doing, Alison?" Mark stared down at me, at the marker in my hand, at the drawings I'd done on Olivia's back.

I blinked at him. "I'm . . ."

I'm saving our daughter.

"Get up," he snarled, looking at me like I was a total stranger, someone who'd sneaked in uninvited. He looked at me with a fury I'd never seen. And I believed, in that moment, that he was capable of hurting me. That it was taking a great effort on his part to refrain from lashing out.

Olivia was crying now. When he sat on the bed, taking my place, she sprang into his arms, sobbing.

"I'm sorry," I said. "Little mouse, I—"

"Get out, Alison," Mark ordered, eyes blazing.

I stood frozen.

"Now," he ordered.

With my legs shaking, I left the room, ran into Izzy in the hall, the camera in her hand pointed directly at me. "What's going on?" she asked.

"Nothing," I said. "I was just trying—"

"What, Mom?"

"I thought it would help."

We could both hear Olivia crying hard, taking gulping breaths.

"What did you do?" Izzy demanded, her voice snarling with accusation.

I shook my head and walked past her, down the hall to our bedroom. I went in, shut the door behind me, and crawled into bed, pulling the covers up over my head like I was the scared little girl trying to make the rest of the world go away.

Ten minutes later, Mark entered the room and yanked the covers back.

"Can you please explain what just happened in there?" he asked. His face was flushed and his eyes had darkened. "Why you were drawing those crazy little marks on our daughter?"

"I—"

"I'm not an idiot, Alison. You think I didn't notice that they're just like the scars on your own back? The ones you've been drawing out in your studio? What's this about? What were you possibly thinking?"

I shook my head. There was nothing I could say here to make things right. Any explanation I could offer would only make the situation worse.

"What do you think this is doing to her and Izzy, Alison? Seeing you like this?"

"Like what?"

"You're scaring the hell out of them," he said.

"I'm trying to protect them," I said, my voice raised, furious. Why couldn't he see that? "That's all I've ever wanted. I never should have brought my mother here. It isn't safe for them."

"Your mother is not the problem here, Alison," he said, voice shaking. He had tears in his eyes. "I agree that we never should have said yes to letting your mother come here. Because I had no idea how hard it would be on you. That it would trigger . . . whatever all this is that you're going through. And for that I'm sorry."

I looked at him, said nothing.

"You are not yourself," he went on. "And you haven't been since she got here. The kids see it. Penny sees it. We're all worried sick about you."

"But I—"

"I'm going to call Gregory and tell him I won't be back at school until after the break. I'm going to stay home with you and your mother. We'll call your therapist tomorrow. We'll get some more help from hospice."

He leaned in, wrapped his arms around me. "I'm sorry," he said, more gently now. "But we're going to get through this. We're going to do it together. It's going to be okay, I promise."

I wanted to believe him. Truly I did.

But I knew the truth. Felt it down deep.

Things were not going to be okay.

Olivia was in terrible danger.

And I was running out of time to save her.

THIRTY-SEVEN

PENNY WAS WEARING A hand-knit green sweater as she opened her front door, music flowing out along with a blast of warm air and wonderful smells. Her gray hair was in a long braid with sprigs of spruce woven into it. "Welcome!" she said, kissing my cheek. "Happy Yule!" She eyed the tray of festively decorated gingerbread men I was holding. "Ohh! Beautiful! Did Izzy sneak any zombies in?"

I shook my head. "Not this time. They're all Mark's work."

It was the first time I'd seen Penny since her evening with my mother. She hadn't responded to my calls or texts. Then, this afternoon, I got a text reminding me about their annual Yule party: Just checking in to make sure you and Mark are still able to come tonight! followed by a string of emojis: two champagne glasses raised in a toast, a Christmas tree, a candle burning. I texted back: Wouldn't miss it for the world! followed by a bunch of hearts.

We'd left Izzy in charge at home. I had reminded her once again to keep a close eye on Olivia when she was with my mother, to not let the two of them out of her sight. Theo was over, and when we left, the two older girls and Olivia were playing cards with my mother in her room. My mother had seemed tired and had asked for extra morphine. I doubted she'd even be awake for much longer. They'd ordered pizza, and Izzy had promised to call if there were any problems at all. I was still nervous, but Mark reminded me that we would be right next door. Five minutes away.

Mark had been watching me carefully all day, following me around the house like a worried shadow. True to his word, he'd called the school and arranged for a sub to cover the final days before winter break, citing a family emergency. He'd also sat with me while I pretended to call my fictional therapist to leave a message asking for an appointment as soon as possible. When I hung up, he threw in a new caveat: he would come with me to my first appointment. He wanted to talk to the therapist about his concerns, to meet her for himself and hear her thoughts on the best course of treatment.

"She's *my* therapist, Mark. I don't think people usually bring their husbands unless it's for couples counseling."

"Surely she'll understand my concern. She might think it's helpful to hear my perspective—and frankly, I need to hear hers. I wonder if we might need to consider medication, Alison," he'd said. "Or maybe some time away."

"Time away?" I'd frowned at him.

"Time to focus on you. On healing."

I couldn't believe what I was hearing. "You mean a psychiatric hospital?"

He cringed a little. "There are nice places. I was looking online and there's a private clinic in New Hampshire, in the White Mountains. It's pretty pricey and it looks like our insurance would only cover about a third or so of the cost."

I narrowed my eyes until I was squinting, making him seem smaller and smaller. "You actually looked into this. Without talking with me?"

He nodded. "It seems like a great fit. And we could find a way to manage the expense. They offer a payment plan. I think it would be really helpful. They specialize in—"

"You have to be fucking kidding me," I'd said.

He took in a long, slow breath. "Okay. Let's take things one step at a time. We'll meet with your therapist and see what she thinks."

PENNY AND LOUISE'S living room was packed with people—some I knew, others I didn't. There were members of the art guild Penny and I belonged to, women in fancy dresses, a man wearing a set of stag horns. Across the room, a woman in a green dress sported a pine wreath around her head, lit up with little LED candles. She saw me looking and waved. It was Carmen, who owned the occult store in Burlington—the one who'd given Penny the herbal protection pouch my mother hated. I waved back and continued scanning the room. There were candles burning on every surface, cheerful Celtic music thumping from an unseen speaker, a fire crackling in the fireplace. It was warm and cozy and I was very glad to be there.

"Where's Louise?" I asked Penny.

"In the kitchen, putting some finishing touches on the cake."

Each year Louise made a very elaborate Yule log: chocolate sponge cake rolled up with whipped cream, covered with sculptured chocolate-frosting bark and even marzipan mushrooms.

"There's a big pot of warm grog in there." She waved her own half-empty cup to show me. "You should go grab yourself a mug."

I knew from past solstice parties that Penny's grog was potent stuff, very heavy on the rum.

"I definitely will," I said, then added, "Thanks again for sitting with my mom the other night."

"Hm? Oh, it was no trouble," Penny said, looking away.

"I wanted to ask," I said. "You seemed . . . a little shaken when you left. Did she say something? Do something?"

Penny shook her head. Her cheeks were flushed. She took a sip of her grog. "It's just—"

"What?"

She lowered her voice. "Did you tell her about Daniel?"

I shook my head. "Of course not."

"Could Mark have mentioned it?" She looked at me, brow furrowed.

"I don't know why he would have."

While Penny and Louise talked openly about the son they'd lost, and kept beautiful photographs of him around the house, it was not a subject that Mark or I ever brought up with them. And we certainly wouldn't bring it up with anyone else.

"Well, your mother knew about Daniel. She knew things that were—" She stopped herself.

"Things that were impossible for her to know," I finished.

Penny nodded. She opened her mouth and then stopped. Her face twisted with anguish.

"What is it?"

"Nothing." Penny turned away, looked into her nearly empty cup. "I think she was just pulling my strings, trying to get a reaction."

"What did she say, Penny?"

Her hand trembled as she clenched the cup tightly.

"Ready for grog?" Mark asked as he approached, holding two steaming mugs of the stuff. "Louise filled our cups to the brim!"

"Actually, I think I'm about ready for a refill," Penny said with forced cheer. "Excuse me." She wandered off, pausing to chat with guests as she crossed the room.

"Let me set down the cookies," I said to Mark.

The solstice celebration was always a potluck, and the dining room table was covered in dishes of all sorts: casseroles, dips, platters of veggies and charcuterie, breads, a sliced ham. I added our tray of gingerbread men to the side table loaded with desserts. There was chocolate-dipped fruit, cookies of all sorts, fudge. Someone had even brought truffles. There was a tray of brownies with a little sign warning that they were cannabis-infused. At the far end of the room a little bar was set up on the buffet. There were clean glasses, bottles of wine, hard liquor and mixers of all sorts, a bucket of ice.

Mark handed me my cup of grog, then said, "I think I see Abe Young over there. I'm going to go say hi." Abe was an English teacher at the public high school, and he and Mark both volunteered at the teen center in town. They did a poetry workshop with the kids each spring.

"You want to come with me or are you okay on your own?" He gave me a concerned look.

"I'm fine, Mark," I snapped. "You don't need to babysit me all night."

I turned and walked away from him without waiting for a response, making my way toward Carmen, who was standing on the other side of the dining room, her candlelit wreath making her easy to spot. I wove through clusters of people talking, laughing, raising their glasses to toast.

"Happy Yule," I said when I reached Carmen. "I don't know if you remember me. I'm Penny's friend, Alison."

"Of course I remember you," she said as she stepped forward and gave me a tight hug. "You're the printmaker and author. *Moxie Saves Christmas*. You're the closest thing this little town has to someone famous."

I laughed. "I don't know about that."

"Are you enjoying the solstice celebration?" she asked.

I raised my cup of grog. "A holiday celebrating the lack of sunlight is much more my thing than one that celebrates a bearded fat man who brings presents."

"The winter solstice is more than the shortest day of the year. We're not focused on the darkness here," she said. She touched the glowing candles on the wreath around her head. "We're celebrating the coming of the light. The rebirth of the sun. Tonight we honor the stillness between one cycle and the next. It's a time to pause and reflect on what has been, and to make wishes and plans for what will be."

I nodded and smiled. "It makes a lot more sense to me than Christmas."

"Christmas borrowed a lot from the ancient pagan traditions," she said.

Except they left out Krampus, I thought.

"I was actually hoping I'd run into you here," I confessed.

"Oh?"

"I wanted to thank you."

"For what?"

I pulled the charm out from where it was hiding under my sweater.

"Penny passed this on to me. She thought I could use it. So I wanted to express my gratitude to you."

"Ah, the amulet of protection. I'm glad it's helping."

"I think it has been. But to tell you the truth, I could use some more help."

"All right. What is it you need?"

I looked around. There was no one close to us. Mark was still in the living room, engaged in conversation with Abe. Penny came out of the kitchen, calling, "Who needs more grog?" A woman in the corner of the living room was taking a fiddle out of its case, and the man with her was tuning a guitar.

I looked back at Carmen, lowered my voice. "What do you know about demons?"

"Demons?"

"My mother," I went on. "She's been staying with us. She's very ill."

"I'm sorry to hear that."

"But there's more to it than that. I think . . . no, I don't just think, I'm sure that she's . . . possessed."

Carmen raised her eyebrows. "Possessed?"

"By a demon named Azha." I spoke the words as quietly as I could, not wanting anyone to hear me. Conversation buzzed and crackled around us. There were occasional bright pops of laughter.

Carmen was silent for a few seconds as she studied my face.

"You realize that possession, true possession, is a very rare thing? It's not like television and the movies."

"I know. I've been reading up on it. Trying to get my head around all of this. Here's what I know: I've spoken to the demon. And I'm convinced that it's not my mother. That she truly has a demon possessing her. It's been going on for quite some time." I took a breath, then let it out. "The demon told me it needs another host when my mother dies. It wants . . . I think it's got its eyes on my little girl."

Carmen said nothing, but her shock showed in her eyes. She looked around the room. Was she making sure we wouldn't be overheard or looking for someone to come rescue her?

Louise had just brought out the cake, and people were moving in to ooh and ahh over it. The couple in the corner started to play a cheerful-sounding jig. A few people in the living room had started to dance. No one seemed to be paying attention to Carmen and me off in the corner.

"Please," I said. "Everyone thinks I've gone crazy. But this is real. I'm sure of it. And I'm running out of time to act."

Carmen shook her head. "I don't like the word *demon*, but if it's true that your mother has an evil spirit attached to her in some way, that's very serious. And very dangerous."

I nodded. "I think it's attached to an object. A stone. It needs the stone somehow. Needs it to stay close by. My mother . . . well, she was her normal self before she got this stone, back when I was a kid. Then, once it was in her possession, things started to change—*she* started to change. I didn't realize it then, but I can see it now, and I found an old journal of hers where she describes feeling the demon take over. And the woman who had the stone before that—I believe she was possessed too. Then she died, and the stone went to my mother."

A group of women stood talking in a circle just off to our left, and now they all laughed uproariously at something. Carmen looked over at them, then back at me. "Spirits can attach themselves to an object like that."

"Happy Yule!" someone shouted. Glasses clinked together.

The man with the guitar began to sing: "*'Tis the darkest night of the year . . .*"

I leaned closer to Carmen. "But it's also attached itself to her. It's living inside her. Using her."

"What you said about the demon needing the stone somehow is correct. The spirit may be inhabiting your mother now, but that's not its true home. Think of it like a visit to a hotel. Staying there may be nice—you get some perks—but it's not where you truly belong. Not where you go to be safe."

"So how can I destroy it?"

Carmen shook her head. "You can't. The best you can hope for is to bind it."

I glanced up. More people were dancing now. And some were singing along, words I was only half paying attention to, about darkness, dying light.

Mark had finished his conversation with Abe and was making his way toward us, his eyes locked on me.

"Bind it?" My mouth was dry. I took a sip of my grog, but it was too warm and sweet.

"Find a way to get it out of your mother and keep it from entering anyone else."

A woman beside us laughed uproariously.

"And how do I do that?" I asked.

Mark had nearly reached us. I could see the worry in his eyes as he watched his unstable wife talking urgently to a woman wearing a lit-up wreath on her head.

Hurry, I willed Carmen. *Tell me quickly.*

The singing in the living room reached a fevered pitch, the fiddle screaming.

"You get this rock and take it far away from your mother and your little girl. You do a binding spell. And you hide it away, bury it, drop it deep in the ocean, put it someplace where no one is ever going to find it."

I thought of the scribbled, barely legible words in my mother's journal: *Spell for Binding*.

Had she tried? Tried and been too weak? Tried and failed?

I felt Mark's hand on my shoulder. "What are we putting in a place where no one can find it?" he asked jovially, but underneath I could feel the worry radiating from him.

I forced a smile, fought the urge to give Carmen a panicked, *please don't tell him* glance. "Carmen was giving me some advice about what I should do with the false starts on the new Moxie book. I was telling her that I feel like what I began with is all wrong, but I keep going back to it and it's just bogging me down. I think she's right—it's time to start fresh."

Carmen nodded. "Sometimes we just need a symbolic act to put an end to something difficult, to help us begin again." She looked meaningfully at me before she drifted away. "Good luck with your project. Come see me in the shop if you need any more help with things."

THIRTY-EIGHT

M Y MOTHER HAD TAKEN a bad turn. We'd brought back a tray of food from Penny and Louise's solstice party, but she refused to eat any of it. We'd been giving her the maximum dose of morphine, but she said she was still in pain and begged for more. Teresa consulted with the doctor at the hospice agency, and they agreed to up her morphine dosage. Her pain was controlled, but the medication knocked her out.

I was running out of time.

JANICE WAS SITTING with my mother while she slept, working through another one of her sudoku books.

It was the first day of Christmas vacation, and Olivia was off at her friend Sophie's. Izzy was in her room, and Mark was doing God knew what—probably watching another Hallmark Christmas movie.

And I was out in my studio, learning all I could about binding spells. I was looking through the books I'd ordered and visiting page after page online, taking notes. I'd studied my mother's cryptic description in her journal and wondered if she'd actually tried it. I thought I had the gist of it down, but would it be enough? Calling on the elements, wrapping the object in string or rope, saying, "I bind you" again and again. It felt . . . futile, even silly. Like a little spell could possibly help.

Then the barn door flew open. I expected to see Penny, hear her call out, "Knock-knock!"

But it was Mark. No knock. No call. He just came walking in, his face somber.

"What's going on? Is it Mother?"

"We need to talk," Mark said.

"Okay." I shut my laptop and turned away from what I'd been doing.

Mark moved closer, surveying what I had on the desk: the demon books, the drawings and notes. There was no hiding them.

"I'm worried about you," he said. "We're *all* worried about you."

"I'm fine," I said. "I'm sorry if I've been worrying you, but really, I'm okay."

Mark crossed his arms over his chest. "I know there's no therapist in Burlington."

I froze, unsure how to respond. Did I argue? Lie? Or tell him the truth?

"There is not, nor was there ever, a Carla Slesar working as a therapist up there." He looked at me. "You made it up."

"It's been a long time," I said, feeling myself shrinking, getting smaller and smaller. "Maybe I'm remembering her last name wrong."

He shook his head. "You went week after week, came home and told me about all the progress you were making, how you were able to open up to her. But it was all lies."

"She—"

Mark shut me down, cut me off before I could continue. "Please don't lie to me anymore. It's not going to do either of us any good."

"Mark, I—"

"I'm supposed to be the one you share everything with. When did that change, Alison? When did you stop trusting me?" He looked so sad, so brokenhearted.

"Of course I trust you! I'm sorry," I said, taking his hand. "I know things have been crazy. I haven't been myself." I cringed a little at my own words. That was exactly what my mother used to say to me: *I'm not myself today*. "Having my mother here has been a lot."

"Your mother, who you believe is possessed by a demon," he said.

I dropped his hand.

How did he know? Then, to answer my question, he told me, gave me the final punch to the gut. "Izzy told me everything."

"Wha . . ." I felt all the air go out of me, scrambled for words as my daughter's betrayal reverberated through my entire body. "What did she tell you? She must have misunderstood—"

"She showed me the video she made, Alison."

"Video?" I said weakly, remembering the way Izzy had held the phone as she talked. Was the camera on me the whole time?

"She recorded it," Mark said. "When you went into her room and told her about your mother being possessed. How you believe the demon is after Olivia. Izzy recorded it because she was worried about you." He looked at me, the anger and hurt from earlier replaced by something far worse: pity. "Is this really what you think, Alison? And even if you *do* believe it—you're going to pull Izzy into this? Ask her to help you? She's a child, for God's sake."

"I thought—" *I thought I could trust her. I thought she'd understand.* "I know it sounds crazy. It sounds made-up. But if you'd look at the facts. If you'd just listen, then I think—"

"No. I'm not going to listen to this. I can't. I won't. You're not thinking clearly. You're not yourself."

"My thinking is perfectly clear."

"Is it?"

He looked again at the jumbled mess on my worktable: the drawings, books, and frantically scribbled notes on demons and binding spells.

"Alison, your mother told me about your hospitalization in high school. About your dissociative episodes. Your suicide attempt."

I forced my words out through a clenched jaw. "I bet she did."

"Your mother isn't the enemy here. She's worried about you. We're all worried about you."

"So you keep saying."

"Tell me I don't need to be worried. Tell me that these thoughts you're having make sense to you. That you haven't had any periods of missing time, that you remember each minute of each day, that you're clear and present and here with us all the time."

"Of course I am," I said.

But it was a lie, wasn't it? Did he see it in my face, the shadow of the truth?

"I don't think it's safe for you to be around your mother or the girls right now," he said.

His words knocked the breath out of me. "Wha—at? You're kidding, right?"

Not safe? What did he think I was capable of? And couldn't he see that I was the only one *protecting* the girls?

"I've made some calls. The clinic in New Hampshire I was telling you about—the Rabbit Hill Inn—they specialize in trauma, in dissociation." He spoke clearly and calmly, in his taking-control-of-things teacher voice. "I talked to the director—Dr. Hinesburg. He thinks you'll really benefit from their program and he's got an opening. It's a beautiful place in the mountains, they do art, there's even an indoor swimming pool. We'll have a nice Christmas here, then the next day, the twenty-sixth, they'll have a bed waiting for you."

I barked out a bitter laugh. "This isn't the turn of the century, Mark. You can't just decide I'm a madwoman and ship me off to the asylum."

He frowned. "I don't want to ship you off anywhere. I was hoping you'd see that this is a way to help you. That you need a break. Some space. Some time to deal with things. I'm hoping you'll go willingly: if not for yourself or me, then for the girls."

His words pierced me, twisted their way in like a corkscrew.

"You know I would do anything for our girls," I said.

He nodded at me curtly. "It's decided, then. I'll drive you over the day after Christmas. Penny and Louise will come stay with the girls and your mother. I've already spoken to them."

It was all planned, decided. Even Penny and Louise were in on it.

I was backed into a corner with no way out. If I refused, it would only be more evidence that I "needed a break"—and I suspected that between Izzy's recording, my drawings and notes, and the invented therapist, it wouldn't be difficult to convince a doctor that I was a danger to myself or others, and I'd end up admitted to a psych hospital with or without my consent.

I took a deep breath and blew it out.

"Okay," I said. I even managed a smile, though I felt my eyes filling with tears.

The clock was ticking.

I had only two more days to stop Azha, to free my mother and save my little girl.

THIRTY-NINE

I WOKE UP JUST BEFORE five a.m., crawled out of bed, and dressed in the dark while I listened to Mark snoring softly.

Moxie greeted me in the hall and followed me down the stairs, padding softly behind me, wondering what I was up to and if by any chance it might involve early breakfast or treats.

It was Christmas Eve. We'd planned to spend the day baking and decorating yet another batch of cookies—even though it felt like I had just barely scraped the last of the colorful, cement-like icing out of the crevices of the dining room table—and watching movies, and maybe going sledding on the hill behind the house if there was enough snow. In the evening, we'd leave a note and a plate of cookies out for Santa, and a carrot for the reindeer, and hang up the stockings.

I left a note on the breakfast bar:

Had some last-minute Christmas errands to do. Back later.

I even drew a happy little sketch of presents under the tree.

I knew Mark would freak out, panic, think the worst when he discovered I'd sneaked out under the cover of darkness. But what choice had he left me?

I paused, sure I heard movement upstairs. But when I listened, there was nothing. The whole house seemed to be holding its breath, waiting to see what might happen next.

Then I crept into my mother's room, moving as silently as I could.

Her breathing was ragged, raspy. Her mouth was open. Her face looked more gaunt, even skeletal, and her skin was as pale as the white pillowcase behind her.

I moved stealthily to the other side of the bed, carefully watching the rise and fall of her chest. When I reached for the stone, I expected her eyes to snap open, for her to let out an alarmed scream. But she slept on.

The stone was heavy in my hand and seemed to grow colder the longer I held it.

I grabbed my coat and purse and slipped out of the house like a ghost. I crossed the yard to my studio to get the tote bag I'd packed last night. In it was the Spell for Binding I'd laboriously copied by hand, along with a white cloth and white string, a box of salt, a piece of parchment and a pen, and a white candle and matches. I placed my mother's stone in the bag, relieved to no longer have it in my hands. Then I crossed the yard to the driveway, brushed the snow off the windshield of the Volvo with my mittened hand, and backed down with the headlights off, praying the engine hadn't woken anyone. Mark's Blazer and Theo's Subaru with its FUCK NORMAL PEOPLE bumper sticker were in the driveway, both covered with a thin blanket of snow. I watched the house as I pulled away, waiting for lights to come on, but none did.

Once on the main road, I turned on the headlights, cranked up the defroster, and headed for the highway.

TWO HOURS LATER, I crossed the state line into New York on Route 7. The sun was up, making the fresh crystals of snow on the trees sparkle like they were dipped in glitter. The world around me felt like a movie set—too pretty to be real. My phone buzzed on the seat beside me. Mark again. He'd left a dozen worried texts and phone messages in the last hour. The most recent of them made it clear he was slipping from worry to anger. "Where the hell are you, Alison? Call me as soon as you get this."

I shut off my phone and stuck it in the glove compartment.

I made only one stop, to fill the tank with gas and get a large cup of coffee and a cruller that tasted like deep-fried cardboard dipped in sugar paste.

It was a little after nine when I arrived at the house in Woodstock. The sky was full of slate-gray clouds, and the house itself looked just as ominous. Its black windows seemed to watch me like all-seeing eyes. It felt like it was waiting for me. And, though I knew it was ridiculous, part of me believed I'd find my mother in there waiting for me. The mother of my childhood, gin-soaked and cruel, my demon mother, demanding to know where I'd been.

I grabbed the bag and unlocked the front door.

The air inside felt stale, and it was too quiet. I didn't even hear the hum of a refrigerator, or the plunk of an ice-maker, or the soft whoosh of hot air coming through the vents from the roaring furnace in the basement. The house felt like it was playing dead, holding its breath, waiting.

"Hello?" I called, feeling foolish.

Who was going to answer?

My mother? No, she was back at my house, too weak to get out of bed. My childhood self?

Maybe.

Maybe some trace of the little me still skulked through the shadows like a ghost.

I made my way up the stairs, knowing just where I was headed, what I was looking for.

I flung open the door to my old bedroom, and had the sense, for a moment, that someone had just been there.

I stepped into the room, breathing in its musty smell. The bed was still neatly made with the old red-and-white quilt, but was there the vague impression of a resting body there in the center? I shook my head. Surely not.

Turning, I pulled open the door of the closet: it was mostly empty, but there were some abandoned things—a red sweater that had never fit right, a pair of sneakers with the canvas worn through in places, a blue dress I didn't remember ever wearing. I closed the closet door, went over to the bed.

I sat on the edge of the mattress, remembering the knife I used to keep tucked under the pillow: Descender. Each morning when I woke, I'd tuck it under the mattress so my mother wouldn't find it.

It couldn't still be there, could it? Was it even real? Or something I'd imagined, made up? How much of memory was truth and how much an embellished fiction?

Had I really once had a magic knife that I believed would protect me from evil?

I ran my fingers under the mattress and felt the sting of something sharp. Carefully I worked my way along, grabbed the hilt of the knife, and pulled it out, my index finger cut and bleeding.

It wasn't much to look at, this great magic knife. It was an old hunting knife with a bone handle and a blade designed for gutting deer. The blade was tarnished, pitted with rust. But the knife felt good in my hands. Familiar. Safe.

As I held it, a memory flashed into my head, how I'd given it a magical charge with the power of the elements: burying it in dirt, washing it with salt water, waving it through a flame, then through the air, then giving it its name under the light of a full moon *You are Descender*, I'd said aloud, *a knife of magical protection and power, you will help me to banish the dark ones and send them back where they came from.*

Where had I learned all that? From a book?

No.

I remembered now as I held the knife, which seemed to thrum in my hands.

My mother had given me the knife. She'd brought it to me back when she still had the strength and resolve to keep the demon inside her at bay, to compartmentalize; the ability to act of her free will and teach me what I needed to do to protect myself from what she knew she would one day fully become. She'd given me the knife for the same reason she'd marked my back with magic sigils: the hope it would one day save me.

It made my chest ache now, thinking about it. About how frantic and desperate and frightened she must have been, feeling this terrible presence gaining power inside her, knowing she needed to do all she could to protect Ben and me, to prepare us for what was coming.

"This is not just a knife," she'd told me. "We're going to turn it into a magic knife, an athame, and it will be a powerful object of protection. I hope that you will never need it, but one day you may, and you need to be ready." For a whole month we charged the knife, washed it with salt water, smudged it with smoke from burning herbs, buried it in earth, let the moon shine down on its blade. When it was ready, my mother said, "Now, for the final step, you need to name your magic knife and tell it what you need it to do for you." I'd chosen the name Descender because it was a knife for banishing the darkest of creatures, sending them back where they came from. My mother told me it was a good name and that everything was going to be all right because the magic was strong inside me.

I wished now for whatever magic I'd had back then to return to me, to help me do what I had to do. Would it be enough? The adult me clumsily doing a spell of banishment I'd read on the internet and on the faded pages of my mother's journal?

I had to try.

I thought of Paul, of how loyal he'd been to my mother, how he'd subsumed his own ambitions and desires to care for her. I imagined that if he were still alive, he'd want me to do this. He'd probably help me if he could—anything to save Mavis. If I closed my eyes, I could almost feel him there standing behind me, my father and Bobbi too—all of them rooting for me, telling me to keep going, to do what needed to be done.

I threw my knife into the bag and left my childhood bedroom and all its ghosts and memories, and headed out of the house and into the woods.

FORTY

THE PATH WAS GROWN over, hardly recognizable, but my body knew the way. The sun was out now, melting what little snow was left in patches on the ground. I considered the light and the relative warmth a good omen. I walked through the birches and maples and poplars, picked my way around the brambles and roots. I remembered how I used to believe they all spoke to me; that the trees and rocks and wind whispered secrets in my ears. That they were my truest friends. I touched some of the larger trees as I walked along, the bark cold and rough beneath my fingers. *I remember you*, I told the trees silently. And I asked them to watch over me now, to help me with my task.

Each step I took felt like a step back in time. I was a kid again walking this same path wearing my father's old wool hunting coat, holding my brother's Daisy BB gun in my hands. My mother was back in the house reeking of gin and cruelty: *I'm not myself today*. The woods were my safe place, my secret place, and I would often fantasize about not going home at all: building a little fort, eating berries, drinking water from the brook, sleeping on a bed of pine boughs.

I remembered shooting at anything that moved, telling myself I was brave. That I could slay any beast.

And now, armed with my old knife, I'd come to slay the biggest beast, to put the monster that had ruled my childhood to rest; to bind the demon and free my family.

As I walked, I couldn't shake the feeling that I was being followed, watched. I kept stopping, turning around. But I saw only black-capped chickadees, a cardinal, a chattering squirrel. I had the sense that they were trying to tell me something, to warn me, perhaps.

I heard a familiar *eee-eee-eee* and looked up, saw a blue jay watching me from the low branch of a nearby tree. I moved on, and it followed, squawking at me, staying close.

Before I knew it, I had reached the clearing where the old cellar hole was. It was closer to our house than I remembered. And it was more grown over now—the clearing smaller and darker, the old foundation so obscured I almost walked right by it. Trees were growing up inside the place where the house once stood, the rock and mortar foundation more crumbled, the whole thing slowly returning to the earth. One day no one would ever know that a house had once stood here, or that a child used to come play in its ruins.

I remembered the happy family that I used to imagine had lived here once long, long ago. A mom and dad and a boy and a girl who'd loved each other very much. Then I thought of the way I'd given them all a cruel ending in my made-up stories. I had killed them all in a house fire, made them all die from the flu. I didn't believe in happy endings back then.

Did I now?

Yes, I told myself. I needed to believe.

A twig snapped somewhere behind me. I turned quickly, sure I saw a flash of movement through the trees: a shadow here and then gone. But there was nothing. Just my mind playing tricks on me. The ghosts of my childhood coming to give me one last scare.

The woods seemed to close in around me, the brambles thick, the bare branches and needled pines leaning together, blocking out the light.

The well was there, waiting for me behind the ruined house, its ring of stones sinking into the ground and camouflaged by tall weeds. My heart clenched as I moved toward it, sure I could hear the ghost of that blue jay screeching at me: *Eee-eee-eee. How could you do this to me? What kind of monster are you?*

But it was only the live blue jay scolding me.

I reached the edge of the old well and looked down into its black eye. I saw only darkness and shadows, the circular rock wall going down, down, down into nothingness. I imagined a pile of dead, forgotten leaves at the bottom, the remains of the tiny bird skeleton resting beneath them.

I listened for the terrible screech of the blue jay, but there was only silence.

Had I actually expected to hear it, after all these years? That the bird I'd consigned to such a sorry fate would still be there waiting, distraught?

Where have you been?

How could you leave me here all this time?

I turned away, reached into my tote bag, and began. I knelt on the ground, the damp leaf litter and old grass soaking my jeans. I peeled off my gloves and got to work.

I laid the white cloth out on the ground, set my mother's stone in the middle of it. I could almost hear it pleading angrily, demanding to be brought back to my mother. It looked duller, less alive already. It knew what was coming.

The sun in the east, behind me, made the shadows of the trees seem to dance in the clearing as the wind blew. They became figures: terrible angels with wings—as I watched, they turned into insects thrumming, buzzing.

I lit the candle, picked up the rock, and passed it through the flame. "With the power of fire, I bind you."

I scraped through the damp leaves, scrabbled up some cold dirt, and sprinkled it down on the stone. "With the power of earth, I bind you."

The wind picked up, making the tree-shadow insect-angels dance more frantically, reach for me with terrible pincer-like claws.

I poured the salt water from the jar I'd brought. "With the power of water, I bind you."

I heard my mother's voice in my head. My mother the demon. *Useless, know-nothing girl.*

I leaned over the rock, blew on it. "With the power of air, I bind you."
Who do you think you are?

I took the piece of parchment, drew sigils of protection—the same symbols that had been carved into my back with a knife, that I'd drawn on Olivia's back with a marker—and wrote the words as I spoke them: *"I bind you, Azha, demon of darkness. I take away your powers. I trap you in this rock for all eternity. You will not enter another soul. So mote it be."*

I was sure I heard movement—the crack of a branch, the rustle of dead leaves—in the trees near the path by which I had arrived. I looked up, saw a gray squirrel racing up a red pine tree. The insect-angel shadows in the clearing seemed to encircle me now, running long icy legs and claws over me, sending chills all the way through me.

I pulled out my knife, used it to cut my index finger, wincing as I let drops of my own blood fall on the paper.

Carefully I wrapped the stone in the paper, then in the white cloth. Chanting, "I bind you, I bind you, I bind you," in a monotone, doing my best to believe in the words, to feel their power, as I wound the bundle with white string and tied it tightly.

I held my knife against the rock, the tip still sticky with my blood. "By the power of the Descender, I bind you. I send you back where you came from."

The wind died down.

The terrible insect-angel shadows began to retreat; to become tree branches again, swaying gently in the warm winter breeze.

My knife seemed to buzz and thrum in my hand, electric and alive; it had been waiting all these years for just this moment.

Then I picked up the bundled rock, sure I could feel it pulsate, beat faintly like a living heart in my hand.

My mother's heart, Bobbi's heart, the heart of the demon Azha.

I stood, looked down into the black eye of the old well, and dropped the bundled-up stone into it, watched it fall, disappearing into the darkness.

I turned my back, half expecting to hear a cry from the well: *eee-eee-eee.*

But there was nothing.

Only silence.

Beautiful, peaceful silence.

It was done.

FORTY-ONE

I T'S OVER," I TOLD my mother. I leaned down and kissed her head. She seemed to have shrunk in the hours I'd been gone. Her face and skull strangely birdlike, her hair hanging in feathery wisps around her head. "It's gone. The rock. Azha."

Her breath came in slow rasps.

I had called Mark when I was on my way back, to tell him I was fine, my errands were done, and I'd be home by dinner.

"Where the hell have you been, Alison? We've been worried sick. I was about to call the police."

"I'm fine," I'd repeated. "There were just some things I needed to take care of before Christmas. Before I go off to Rabbit Hill."

"Well, your mother's taken a turn for the worse," he'd said. "Teresa's here now and she thinks it might only be a matter of hours. You better hurry home.

"I can't believe how fast it's happening," he added. "She was up and talking and joking with us just yesterday. Now it's like she barely has the strength to open her eyes."

I understood.

It had been Azha giving her body strength, Azha keeping her alive. She was a weak shell providing a home for the demon until it was ready to move into its next host.

But I'd sent the demon away.

I'd fixed things and freed my mother at last.

Home now, alone with her, I looked down into her face. Her eyelids fluttered open.

"I'm . . . sorry," she whispered.

"I know," I told her. "And I understand now. I understand. I know that it wasn't you. I forgive you."

"And I love you," I added.

She smiled and closed her eyes.

We stayed like that, side by side, for hours. We kept the little bedside light on but turned off the overhead light. I declined Mark's frequent offers of food or respite. I didn't want to leave her alone.

Sometimes I dozed, sitting in the chair by her bed, still holding her hand, my head resting on the side of the mattress. Mark came in at one point and tried to turn off the little lamp, but I stopped him. "No," I said. "Leave it on."

My mother had had enough darkness.

I dabbed at her lips with a little dampened sponge on a stick. I rubbed lavender lotion onto her hands and arms.

I told my mother stories: the good memories from my childhood.

"Remember when you took us all the way to Cape Cod for fried shrimp? How we sat on the beach and talked about what it might be like to be seagulls, just catching the wind and soaring?"

A little after midnight, Mark came in again, touched my shoulder, and kissed my head. "Merry Christmas," he said. "Do you want to take a break and I'll sit with her for a while?"

"I'm okay here," I said.

"I'll make some tea," he said. "I got the presents under the tree and the stockings up."

I nodded in thanks. "Tea sounds good."

Moxie came and lay down in the doorway, refusing to enter the room even when I coaxed her with treats.

"Come on, girl, it's okay," I said. "It's safe. The bad thing is gone."

Moxie eyed me warily, refused to budge.

My mother's breathing began to change. It became louder, a

mechanical-sounding hum, like a far-off engine getting closer, cutting out and starting up again.

Her eyes snapped open. They were so dark they looked black.

"Who killed Cock Robin?" she singsonged quietly.

I let go of her hand, jerked away.

Moxie stood up in the doorway, growling, hackles raised.

No. No. No.

It couldn't be.

The room seemed to get smaller around us, darker; the bedside light flickered, dimming like the bulb was about to go out.

The temperature dropped.

"Impossible," I whispered, standing.

My mother grinned up at me, a forced and hideous grin. "Think you can get rid of me that easily? Stupid girl."

"Azha?" I said, the word coming out like a gasp, a final breath.

"Maybe," she whispered, her voice weak. "Maybe there is no Azha. Maybe I've just been fucking with you all along." She stopped, catching her breath, closing her eyes. "Maybe you're just going crazy, Alison. Maybe your family is right."

My mind spun. Was it possible?

I heard a buzzing, a soft *thump, thump, thump*. I turned and saw thick-bodied, fat flies gathered on the dark pane of glass at the window. And through it, I was sure I saw a figure, a face with a long snout, dark beady eyes—Olivia's Rat King. But as I watched, it became my own reflection.

"Where's my stone?" my mother demanded, spittle flying, eyes open wide again. She reached out, grabbed hold of my arm with bony fingers, her grip viselike. "What have you done with my stone? I need it."

"It's gone," I told her. "Far, far away where no one will ever find it."

She sank back into the pillows, panting. She let out a little moan. "It hurts, Ali Alligator. Oh God, it hurts!"

I reached for the morphine. Teresa had switched her from pills to liquid, since she was having difficulty swallowing, and she opened her mouth for me like a baby bird while I trickled drops onto her tongue. I didn't count them.

The flies thumped at the window. The lamp flickered, then went out. The only light came in through the open door from the hall.

My mother licked her lips, then smiled up at me. "You've already failed."

No. I was not going to let Azha win. She didn't have the stone. She had nowhere to go. Nowhere to hide. She was weak and scared. I could feel it.

"I bind you, Azha," I said. "By the power of earth, air, water, and fire, I bind you."

"You've always been a stupid girl," she said. "A cruel girl. I know what you did to that blue jay. How you left it there in the well to die. Do you know how it suffered, Alison? In pain, starving, unable to fly?"

I reached into my bag there beside the chair and pulled out the knife, Descender. The knife my mother, my true mother, had given me, had taught me to use.

I hope that you will never need it, but one day you may, and you need to be ready.

I touched the blade to her chest. "I bind you." I said it with all the quiet intensity I could muster.

She thrashed beneath me, made a whimpering sound.

"By the power of this knife, Descender, I bind you. You will not leave this body. You will not enter another. *I bind you.*"

"Alison!" Mark yelled from behind me. "What the hell are you doing?"

I froze, with the tip of the knife pressed against my mother's chest, just over her heart.

"Put down the knife, Alison," Mark ordered, stepping slowly into the room.

My mother was slack, unconscious. I watched and listened for a breath, but there was none.

Eight months later

FORTY-TWO

'VE DECIDED WHERE I want to go to college."

"Oh?"

"UCLA. Film school."

I'd come into Izzy's room to check in and see if she might want to invite Theo for dinner. It was a warm, late August afternoon. Sunlight filtered in through the windows—both the heavy curtains and the windows themselves were open, letting in a lovely breeze. Crickets and cicadas hummed outside. I could hear the soft bleating of Penny and Louise's sheep, the occasional squawk of a chicken.

I'd been trying hard to fix things with Izzy, but ever since I got back from my six-week stint at Rabbit Hill, she'd been cold, more standoffish than ever. I was determined to keep trying, though.

Olivia was easy: as soon as I got home, she clung to me, chattered nonstop, showed me new dances she'd learned, begged me to read to her each night. We'd slipped back into our regular routine easily, as if I'd never been away. Only now our regular routine included her asking me to tell her stories about her grandma. Olivia missed her desperately and talked about her all the time. "Tell me again about the time she drove you to Cape Cod for fried shrimp," she would say.

Izzy remained distant with me. She seemed closer than ever to Mark, and I was happy about that, but I couldn't help feeling envious.

I looked around her room, saw it was a little tidier than usual. There was no sign of the Krampus mask. Her desk was still a mess of papers, notes, colorful energy drink cans.

"That's terrific," I said. "UCLA is quite competitive, but there's no reason—"

"I'll get in," she said brusquely. "I've already been emailing with one of the faculty members there. She saw my documentary. She thinks I'd be a perfect fit for their program."

Izzy's documentary, simply titled *Mavis*, had won the New England Young Filmmakers Award—she took first place, and got a $10,000 scholarship to the school of her choice. She'd entered the documentary into some other competitions and festivals and was still waiting to hear from them.

She had it open on her laptop now.

"I'm really proud of you," I said. "It's an impressive piece of filmmaking."

"Thank you," she said.

Moxie came up, looked into the room, lay down in the hallway outside.

I'd been in my studio most of the day and had finished up the final image for *Moxie Saves Halloween*—the cover print, which showed Moxie beside a cheerful jack-o'-lantern. My agent and editor were thrilled with the scan I'd sent them, and already asking about a third book—what holiday Moxie might save next.

I could smell the lasagna Mark was making for our celebration dinner. Olivia was in the kitchen helping him, insisting that she got to make the garlic bread.

I looked down at Izzy's computer screen again. The film was open in her editing software. "Are you making changes? Editing it some more?"

She gave me a wry smile. "This is the director's cut," she said.

"Oh! I didn't realize there would be a director's cut. That's cool."

"Do you want to see the new ending? The *real ending*?"

"Sure," I said. She stood up, offering me the chair at her desk. Then she set up the screen and clicked play.

I was watching myself. Even after viewing the film numerous times, I still wasn't used to seeing myself on-screen.

But this, this was different. Far more unsettling. There I was, standing in the driveway of my mother's house in Woodstock, dressed in my black down jacket, shouldering the old tote bag we'd once used to carry towels and beach toys but that I'd filled with the things I needed to bind the demon.

I blinked in disbelief.

Izzy had been there? How was that possible?

I remembered the feeling I'd had that day, of being watched. But I'd thought it was just the memories of the old house, the ghosts of my childhood.

It looked like Izzy had been filming from the edge of the property, using a telephoto lens to get a close-up from far away.

"You followed me?"

She nodded.

"How?"

"Theo drove," Izzy said.

I remembered seeing Theo's car in the driveway that morning, beside mine, covered in a thin layer of snow. They must have heard me and woken up, followed me all the way to Woodstock. I hadn't even noticed.

"I don't understand," I said.

She smiled, but there was something unsettling about the smile. It was too big, too broad. Her eyes were strangely dark.

A lump formed in my throat. I tried, unsuccessfully, to swallow it back down.

"Keep watching," she said.

She stood behind me at her desk as I watched, a strange shadow looming over me. She was humming softly, a familiar song I couldn't name.

There I was on the screen of her MacBook Pro, going into the house, then leaving through the back door, crossing the yard, walking into the woods, my tote bag slung over my shoulder.

The camera followed at a distance.

"Where's she going?" Theo whispered.

Izzy didn't respond. Her camera lens just kept following me.

There was no music, as there had been in Izzy's final version of the documentary. There was only the sound of feet crunching through the dead leaves and sticks, the patches of snow. Her shaky camera—no tripod—was focused on my back.

Izzy kept humming behind me now. The tune bothered me; I wanted to ask her to stop.

Downstairs, Olivia laughed loudly.

Outside, the insects hummed and chirped and buzzed.

On-screen, I watched myself approaching the well, taking the things I'd brought out of the bag. The camera zoomed in as I spoke the words, completely inaudible from far away, wrapped the stone in cloth, cut my finger and dripped blood onto the parchment, then dropped the stone into the well, watching it fall.

I stared at myself on Izzy's laptop. Saw a frazzled and desperate woman. A woman who would do anything to protect her family, who would have thrown herself down into that well if it would have helped.

And now there she was, turning away from the circle of stone, a glint of a smile on her face because she thought she'd won. That it was over. That it could possibly be that easy.

The camera followed me as I walked away, moving through the shadowy forest.

Then, all of a sudden, Izzy was in the frame.

"Are you sure about this?" I heard Theo say.

Izzy had a rope tied around a tree. She threw it down into the well. She looked at the camera and nodded.

"No," I said out loud now as I watched my daughter on the screen. "No."

Behind me, I recognized the song my daughter was humming: she'd added the lyrics: *"Who killed Cock Robin? I, said the Sparrow, with my bow and arrow. Who saw him die? I, said the Fly, with my little teeny eye, I saw him die."*

My throat felt tight and I sucked in a wheezing breath of air. "No," I mumbled again uselessly.

An insect bumped against the outside of the window screen. I looked and saw a large fly there. Another landed beside it. Then another. They danced and buzzed, trying to get in.

"Just be careful," Theo said to Izzy on the screen.

Izzy climbed down the rope into the well. She moved easily, all the years of dance and gymnastics giving her the strength and agility she needed to shinny down gracefully.

At last she reached the bottom.

Theo kept the camera pointed at her, the light turned on, illuminating the scene at the bottom of the well.

"No," I said again, as if I could call back through time, warn my daughter, find a way to haul her back up.

She picked up the wrapped bundle. "Got it," she yelled to the camera. Then, slowly, she unwound the wrappings, whispering.

"What's that you're saying?" I asked.

"An unbinding spell."

"Where on earth did you learn—"

"You can learn anything on the internet these days, Mom," she answered matter-of-factly.

I watched in horror as she tucked the stone inside her coat like she needed to keep it warm. Then she clambered back up, making the whole thing look ridiculously easy.

Izzy reached in front of me now to hit the pause button. Then she went over to her bedside table, opened the drawer, and pulled out a bundle of purple cloth. She unwrapped it carefully, though she didn't need to; I knew what was inside.

"Grandmother knew. She knew what you were going to do. She knew and she told me. She told me what needed to be done."

"My God."

She shook her head, laughed. "Haven't you figured it out yet? Your God has nothing to do with this."

There was now a large group of flies at the window, pressing to get in, crawling over each other, buzzing loudly.

"It was you," I said. "It was you she wanted all along."

Izzy smiled.

She spoke in a voice that was hers and not hers. A voice that took me back to my mother, to my childhood. "I chose her the day I met her. Back when she was just an infant. I knew even then what she would become. What we could become together."

"No!" I yelled. "No! It's not too late. Izzy, listen to me! We've got to do the binding spell, go see Carmen, she'll know what to do."

I reached for the stone, but she jerked it away from me. I went for her, knocking the desk chair over. "Isabelle, please," I shouted.

She laughed, triumphant, and then her expression grew serious. "You need help, Mom," she said. "It's just a rock. Just a pretty rock Grandma gave me.

"It scares me," she went on, her eyes tearing up, "seeing you get these crazy ideas."

I knew without turning that Mark was behind me.

"Alison," he said, voice level.

I turned and nearly crumpled when I saw his face: the fear, the pity.

He reached for me, wrapped his arm around me, guided me out of our daughter's room.

"Have you been taking your medicine?" he asked.

ACKNOWLEDGMENTS

A MILLION THANKS, AS ALWAYS, to my agent, Dan Lazar. To Jackie Cantor, who helped me find my way through the novel and bring these characters to life. To Amara Hoshijo, for her ongoing support and mind-blowing editing skills. To Jen Bergstrom, Jessica Roth, Bianca Ducasse, and the whole team at Scout Press: it is an absolute honor to work with each and every one of you; you are the best! To my friends and fans on Facebook who encouraged me to face my fears and write a demon possession book. To Lola, our own rescue Lab, who was the inspiration for Moxie and has taught me the importance of play and treats and long walks in new places (and that it's okay—totally understandable, in fact—to be a little afraid sometimes). And lastly, to Drea and Zella, who buoy me up and encourage me to keep going when the going gets tough—I love you both!